WHITER THAN WHITE

About the Author

Marion Field trained as a teacher and worked in Canada and Uganda as well as England. She became Head of English in a large comprehensive school in Surrey and eventually took early retirement to concentrate on writing. *Whiter than White?*, her first novel, is her tenth book and she has had many feature articles published in a variety of magazines.

She has an acting diploma from LAMDA and acts with a local Dramatic Society as well as performing her own one woman shows and giving talks about her writing experiences. She is an active member of her local Anglican church.

By the same author
Biography
Don't Call Me Sister!
Shut up Sarah
Susanna Wesley: A Radical in the Rectory
How to Books
Improving your Written English
Improving your spelling
Polishing up your Punctuation and Grammar
A Writer's Guide to Research
Working as a Nurse (in collaboration with Esther Bartlett)
Children's book
Noah's Mud and other Recipes (in collaboration with Elaine Ashmore)

About Highland Books
You are invited to visit our website www.highlandbks.com to learn more or to download our catalogue. We may also from time to time post errata. If you wish to tell us of significant mistakes you are welcome to e-mail us at errata@highlandbks.com.

To Pamela

WHITER THAN WHITE

With very best wishes
Marion Field

a novel by

MARION FIELD

First published in 2002 by Highland Books, Two High Pines, Knoll Road, Godalming, Surrey GU7 2EP.

Copyright © 2002 Marion Field. The right of Marion Field to be identified as author of this work has been asserted by her in accordance with the Copyright, Designs and Patents Act 1988.

All rights reserved. No part of this publication may be reproduced or transmitted in any form by any means, electronic or mechanical, including photocopying, recording or any information storage and retrieval system, without either prior permission in writing from the publisher or a licence permitting restricted copying. In the United Kingdom, such licences are issued by the CopyrightLicensing Agency, 90 Tottenham Court Road, London WIP 9HE.

Cover Design by Steve Carroll

ISBN: 1 897913 59 1

Printed in Finland by WS Bookwell.

ACKNOWLEDGEMENTS

I should like to thank the following people who helped me either with my research or by reading and checking the work for me.

Mrs Elaine Ashmore-Short
Mrs Esther Bartlett
Mrs Sue Chapman
Mrs Cathy Comber
Mrs Gena Dodd
Mrs Margaret Etheridge
Miss Lauren Evans
Ms Debbie Fleet
Miss Bridget Forshaw
Mrs Meriel Forshaw
Mrs Jennifer Lord
Dr Graham Lytton
Miss Kishori Macwan
Mrs Philly Morrall

DEDICATION

To my friend Elaine who helped me sort out the plot

Chapter One

"No sign of a grandchild for me yet, Jenny? You'll have to hurry up, dear. You're not getting any younger." Dorothy Bradley gazed hopefully at her eldest daughter. She ignored the razor glances being hurled at her by the second of her tribe of five daughters.

"I'm only twenty-six, Mum. Give me time." Jenny compressed her lips and moved away.

"How can you be so insensitive, Mum!" exclaimed Eleanor when her sister was out of earshot. "She and Peter have been trying for ages."

"Oh dear. Why didn't she tell me?"

"She knew how much you wanted a grandchild."

"She wouldn't have much time with this new job. Why can't she be content to stay at home and look after her husband?"

"You really are the end, Mum. You know you can't wait to get back to nursing. Why are you doing that 'Return to Nursing' course?"

"That's different. I stopped nursing when I had Jenny and I looked after you all and …"

"Well, Jenny hasn't got any kids to look after yet, has she?"

"I do hope she will soon. How's that handsome surgeon?"

"As arrogant as ever." Eleanor turned away. She had no intention of discussing Mr David Baines, Manor Hospital's latest heart-throb, with her mother. "I'd better circulate." She moved swiftly away wondering where her father was. Social gatherings did not appeal to him and he often disappeared. She frowned. Where was he? Easing her way through the crowd and past the laden buffet table, she slipped out of the room. Leaning against the wall, she took a deep breath and relaxed her facial muscles. She felt as though her smile had been fixed on with superglue. Her feet hurt too. She couldn't remember when she'd last sat down. Dare she remove her high-heeled sandals? She decided against it as she probably wouldn't be able to put them on again. She and her sisters had worked tirelessly to prepare this surprise party for her parents and it appeared to be a great success in spite of her father's disappearance.

She must find him. He was probably in the garden. Crossing the hall, she entered the kitchen which was still littered with debris from the morning's preparations. She opened the back door and skirted the house to reach the patio where a few people were scattered around, drinking wine and eating. Eleanor replaced her smile as she passed them and headed for the familiar figure she could see at the bottom of the garden.

"Dad."

He turned. "Hullo, Eleanor. I suppose you've come to chase me back to the bun fight."

She grinned. "You hate it, don't you? I'm sorry. But Mum's in her element. You know how social she is."

He sighed. "I know. I just had to get away for a few minutes." He caught her sceptical glance. "All right. It's been longer than that."

"Have you had something to eat?"

"Yes. The food's delicious. You've all worked very hard."

"Even Melanie took her head out of a book long enough to help and Kate was delighted to put off her homework."

"What about Lorna? Didn't she pull her weight?"

"Oh she helped a bit. But she's so excited about starting college next month, that she can't keep still for long."

"She never could," said her father indulgently, thinking of his bubbly eighteen-year-old daughter. He paused and then said thoughtfully, "I hope she behaves herself at college."

Eleanor glanced at him. "Oh, I'm sure she will. You mustn't worry. You've brought us all up to know right from wrong. We know how to behave."

He laughed. "You sound very mature."

"Well, I am."

"You're a great help to your sisters, you know, Ellie. They listen to you. Do you think Melanie's all right?"

"Melanie? Yes, I think so. Why?"

He frowned. "I'm not sure. She's always had her head up in the clouds but recently she doesn't even seem to be on the same planet as the rest of us."

"I expect she's thinking about her novel."

"Do you think she'll ever finish it?"

"I don't know. She hasn't been very good at sticking to things so far, has she?"

"What about you, Eleanor?"

"Me?"

"A little bird told me there's a new surgeon in your theatre."

Eleanor sighed. "Oh not you too. Mum's already tried to grill me. He's only been there a month and we've hardly spoken except at work."

"What's he like?"

"If you really want to know, I can't stand him. I admit he's very good looking but he knows it."

"Is he a good surgeon?"

"Yes," admitted Eleanor. "He's very good – and he knows that too."

Her father laughed and linked his arm in hers. "Come on. Let's go back to the party and I promise I'll talk to everyone I meet."

She laughed as they started to walk back. "I'll believe that when I see it."

Entering through the patio doors, a buzz of conversation greeted them.

"Edward, we wondered where you were."

"Steve, Joyce, how nice to see you." Edward Bradley shook hands warmly with the couple. Steven Williams had been the local Anglican parish priest for the past five years and Edward was his churchwarden. Eleanor left them to chat and headed for the buffet table. It occurred to her she was hungry. She found Jenny beside her.

"You hungry too, Ellie?"

"Mm. I've just realised I haven't eaten anything since about seven this morning and it's nearly four now."

"It looks good, doesn't it?" Jenny helped herself to a slice of the salmon which had obviously been popular with their guests. "Have some before it all disappears."

"Are you looking forward to next term?" Eleanor queried as she obeyed her sister and piled her plate high with quiche, sausage rolls, vol-au-vents and salad.

"I am, of course, but I'm nervous too. Being head of a department is quite a challenge. I do hope I don't make a mess of it."

"Of course you won't. You're a brilliant administrator."

"Thanks for the vote of confidence. I haven't had my timetable yet. I hope they've given me enough free periods."

"Leaving it a bit late, aren't they?"

"Oh that's nothing new. We're used to it. It's total chaos for the first week. How's Manor Hospital?"

"Surviving. I've had a few days off. I needed it."

Jenny shuddered. "I don't know how you do it."

"Do what?"

"The theatre. All that blood and ..."

"Oh, don't be ridiculous. It's a job like any other."

"How's the latest dishy surgeon?"

Eleanor gave an exclamation of annoyance. "If anyone else mentions him, I'll scream."

"Sorry. Let's find somewhere to sit!"

"Isn't it a lovely party? The wrinklies are really enjoying it." Lorna bounced up beside them.

"Lorna, I wish you wouldn't call them that," said Jenny disapprovingly as her younger sister grabbed a handful of sausage rolls.

"We're going to find somewhere to sit. Come and join us," suggested Eleanor.

"No thanks. It's boring sitting still. I have to be on the move." She tossed back her mane of long blond hair which flicked Eleanor's face on its journey. Eleanor blinked as she watched her sister hurtle off, snatching some vol-au-vents as she left.

"I wonder if she'll manage to sit still in lectures," mused Jenny as they left the house to sit comfortably on the patio steps.

"She'll have to. Dad's worried about her."

"Is he?"

"Well she *is* a bit wild."

"Say it. She's a flirt. The boys flock round her like bees round a honey pot."

Eleanor grinned. "That's not a very original simile for a newly appointed Head of English."

"And you can't say *very* original," swiftly retorted Jenny.

"Touché."

"It was a lovely party. Thank you so much, dear." Dorothy Bradley came in and gave her daughter a hug. Most of the guests had gone and Eleanor was clearing up in the kitchen.

"The others helped."

"I know but it was your idea, wasn't it? You're always so thoughtful."

"Want some help?" Lorna stuck her head round the door.

"Yes. Can you clear the table? We've made some space here for the leftovers to be put."

"OK." Lorna whirled out of the room.

"I'll go outside and bring in the rest of the plates and glasses." Eleanor opened the back door and was immediately intercepted by Carol. They'd been friends ever since primary school and Carol was also a nurse and worked in the same theatre as Eleanor.

Carol indicated her companion. "Ellie, I'd like you to meet Chris Davenport. He's the new tennis pro at the Health Club. Chris, this is Ellie, my oldest friend."

"Not so much of the old if you don't mind," Eleanor quipped. Her eyes travelled upwards to meet a pair of amused brown eyes which immediately locked onto hers. Her heart did a double somersault and landed in her mouth as she allowed her hand to disappear into his.

"I'm very pleased to meet you. I've heard a lot about you." His voice was low and cultured. They continued to stare at each other and he was still clasping her hand.

"It was the most amazing thing. I wanted to improve my tennis and I booked some lessons and Chris was my tutor."

Carol's voice bubbled on but Eleanor wasn't listening. Her heart had bounced back to its normal position but was pounding so hard she thought she was in danger of fainting. Her stomach was also churning and she was suddenly aware that if she didn't soon break the spell that gripped her, she would disgrace herself. Hurriedly retrieving her hand, she wrenched her eyes away.

"Lovely to meet you." She hurtled out of the door she'd just entered and blundered towards the patio at the bottom of the garden. She stopped as she heard raised voices.

"It's no good nagging, Jenny. I won't do it and that's final."

"But why not, Peter? Why are you so set against adoption?"

"I don't have to give you a reason. I just don't want to adopt." Her brother-in-law's voice grew louder.

Eleanor leant against a nearby tree and imbibed large gulps of air. Her sister and brother-in-law continued to snipe at each other but she had to recover at least some of her equilibrium before she tried to pour oil on the angry waters. She shut her eyes and saw again deep brown eyes above a smiling mouth. Had she fallen in love at first sight? Was that what it felt like? She snapped her eyes open and took some more deep breaths. She mustn't think of him. He was Carol's friend. Her thoughts needed a new direction and the sudden crash of crockery behind her galvanised her into action. She stepped towards the combatants.

"Is this a private quarrel or can anyone join in?" As soon as she'd said it, she realised how insensitive she sounded. Of course it was a private quarrel. She should have crept away. But it was too late now.

Peter stood up. "See if you can talk some sense into her, Eleanor. If we can't have our own kids, I don't want someone else's. And why she has to bring it up now when she's about to start a new job, I can't imagine." He marched back to the house.

Eleanor sat down beside her sister who was sobbing quietly. A broken plate and shattered wine glass lay in front of her. The remains of the food and wine was congealing into a gooey mess decorated with shards of broken glass and china. She carefully removed a piece of glass before it attacked her foot and put her arm round Jenny.

"He does have a point, you know."

"But why? He knows I'm desperate for kids. I feel such a failure, Ellie. I can't even do such a simple thing as get pregnant. Sometimes I feel I'm only half a woman."

"Oh Jenny, don't be so ridiculous. Lots of women take time to get pregnant."

"But we've been trying for so long now. I don't understand why Peter won't adopt."

"He never talks about his family, does he?"

"He hasn't got one. His parents are dead and he was an only child."

"I still think it's odd he never mentions them."

"I don't see why. Anyway what's that got to do with it? I'm desperate, Ellie."

"Jenny, how can you possibly think about it when you've got this new job to worry about? Perhaps if you weren't so obsessed with the idea of having children, you might relax and it would happen."

"I *am* relaxed. There's nothing wrong with me. I've had test after test and so's Peter. Anyway you're hardly an authority, are you?"

"I'm sorry. I was only trying to help."

"Well, don't. We've got to sort this out ourselves." She stood up. "Sorry, Ellie. I know you're only being kind. I'd better go. See you at church, tomorrow?"

"Yes, of course." Eleanor stood up and they kissed briefly. They had always been close but recently Jenny had been pale and withdrawn as her obsession to have children grew. She and Peter, a successful barrister, had been married for five years and Dorothy Bradley had not been the only one to wonder why they hadn't yet started a family.

"I'll go and get something to clear up this mess. You'd better go and find Peter. And do be nice to him. I'm sure he's suffering too."

Eleanor was thoughtful as she made her way back to the house. She was worried about her sister. How would she cope with a new demanding job when her head was full of babies?

"You look as though you've got the cares of the world on your shoulders."

"Oh!" Eleanor jumped and for the second time that day her heart started its gymnastic routine as she stared into the brown eyes that had been etched into her memory.

"I hoped I'd get a chance to speak to you again. Would you like to come out for dinner one evening?"

"But I thought Carol ..."

"Oh, we're just good friends. Don't worry about her."

It sounded too glib but suddenly she didn't care. She gave a radiant smile.

"I'd love to."

"Fine. I'll ring you. What's your number?" He pulled out a pen and found a piece of paper. She gave it to him as Carol joined them and took Chris's arm in a proprietary fashion.

"I wondered where you'd got to, Chris. I think we'd better be going. It was a lovely party, Ellie. I'll see you next week."

As they walked off, Chris turned back and winked at Ellie. She grinned back. It wasn't the first time she'd attracted one of Carol's boyfriends. Several years ago she'd been one of the bridesmaids at a wedding. Carol had been the chief bridesmaid and, as such, had obviously expected to pair up with the best man. But Eleanor had been attracted to him and had deliberately sabotaged her friend's chances. They had been eighteen at the time and, looking back, Eleanor was not proud of the way she had behaved. Fortunately it had been Carol's pride rather than her heart which had been damaged but there had been a barrier between the two girls for some time; eventually diplomatic relations had been resumed after the gentleman in question moved away from the area. That incident, Eleanor hoped, had been forgotten.

Chapter Two

The next day the Bradley family attended St Peter's together. It was an unusual occurrence as Eleanor was sometimes working while Lorna, Melanie and Kate, the youngest sister, often preferred to be with their friends; Peter and Jenny were still searching for their 'spiritual home' and visited a different church every week. However, the thirtieth wedding anniversary had brought them all together and they were to continue the celebrations with lunch at a local hotel.

Dorothy and Edward were taken aback when, in the notices, Steve referred to their wedding anniversary and the congregation turned to look at them as applause broke out.

"I was so embarrassed," Dorothy said later as they sat in the bar sipping pre-prandial drinks. "I didn't expect him to mention it."

"He always does," said Eleanor. "You know that. I don't know why you were surprised."

"Your table's ready." A smart waitress appeared beside them. She led them into the restaurant. The hotel had once been a stately home and the restaurant was housed in the library. Most of the valuable books had been removed but some leather-bound volumes remained while other bookcases contained mock shelves of books. Their table was in a bay window. The cutlery and glasses gleamed on a white tablecloth. Edward pulled out a chair for his wife while Peter did the same for Jenny. The waitress made a half-hearted attempt to assist Eleanor and the other girls had to fend for themselves.

"How's the gorgeous Simon, Mel?" asked Lorna as they sat down.

"Lorna, for goodness' sake!" Eleanor looked angrily at her younger sister.

Melanie looked down at her plate, blushing furiously. She looked as though she were about to cry.

"She's in love with him, aren't you, Mel?" Lorna could never resist teasing her older sister.

"That's enough, Lorna." Edward looked severely over his glasses at his wayward daughter. "It's time you learnt to think before you speak. Why do you always have to upset people? I hope university will knock some sense into you but I doubt it. You really are a very silly girl."

"Dad!" Lorna was outraged. "It's no secret Mel's in love with her boss. I can't see what she sees in him – *and* he's married. I expect she hopes he'll publish her novel."

"Oh …" Melanie could no longer deal with her sister's needling. She stood up, knocking over her chair and rushed out of the restaurant sobbing. The rest of the diners fell silent before the unfolding drama.

"You really are the limit, Lorna." Eleanor left the table to follow her sister. Someone really should take Lorna in hand, she reflected. She was completely thoughtless and totally selfish. The worst thing about her was that she never seemed to realise how hurtful she could be. Perhaps college life would help her to mature. She was obsessed with boys and apparently thought of little else.

Melanie was leaning over the washbasin in the 'Ladies', sobbing uncontrollably. Eleanor put her arms round her.

"You mustn't take any notice of her, Mel. You know what she's like." Melanie hiccuped and muttered something. "What? I didn't hear what you said."

"I … I d–do love S–Simon."

"Oh dear," said Eleanor inadequately.

Chapter Two / 17

Simon Hampton ran a small publishing company and Melanie had recently started to work as his personal assistant. She dealt with all his correspondence, arranged interviews with authors and was occasionally even asked to read a manuscript and give her opinion.

"He's so nice to me, so kind, so gentle. No man's ever looked at me before and I never thought I'd find anyone like him."

"But he's married, dear."

"Oh, I know but it doesn't make any difference. His marriage isn't working."

"Did he tell you so?" asked Eleanor cynically.

"He didn't need to. She's a bitch."

"Melanie!"

"Well she is."

"Have you met her?"

"No. I've just talked to her on the phone. She's always nagging – wanting to know where he is, telling him to pick up the kids."

"Oh, he has kids too."

"You know he has."

"I didn't actually. You've never really talked about your work, Mel. You're such a quiet little thing usually. You've obviously got hidden depths. Mum and Dad would be horrified if they knew how you felt."

"Well they know now," muttered Melanie sulkily. She scrubbed her face with a handful of tissues from the box provided. "I hate Lorna. Why is she always such a cow?"

Exasperated, Eleanor stared at her sister. She had never seen this side of her before and it worried her.

"We'd better go back. We can't spoil Mum and Dad's anniversary, can we?"

"What do you mean 'we'?" Melanie hurled the tissue ball towards the waste bin. It missed and Eleanor retrieved it and redirected it. "You mean me, don't you? It's all my fault."

"Nonsense. If it's anyone's fault, it's Lorna's. Now wash your face and we'll go back."

Melanie sniffed. "I don't want to. I want to go home."

"Well you can't," snapped her sister, who was rapidly losing patience. "A thirtieth wedding anniversary doesn't happen every day and I won't have it spoilt."

"It's all right for you. You're perfect. You never have any problems."

Eleanor sighed as she watched Melanie repair the damage. As she never wore make-up, she looked little different from normal apart from her reddened eyes.

As they returned to the table, a chastened Lorna muttered, "I'm sorry, Mel. I shouldn't have said that."

"No, you shouldn't."

"I've said I'm sorry."

"Oh all right." Melanie viciously pulled out her chair and sat down.

"What are you going to have to eat?" Her father handed her a menu. "The rest of us have ordered."

"I'm not hungry." She caught Eleanor's furious glance and muttered, "I'll have the chicken salad."

"I'll have the lamb ragout." Eleanor closed the menu and handed it to the hovering waitress.

"I'm having the vegetable lasagne," fifteen-year-old Kate announced smugly. "I think it's obscene eating animals. Just think of the poor little things running around in the field and then being killed and eaten. Ugh! It's disgusting!"

"That's enough, Kate," said Edward firmly. "Just because you've suddenly decided to become vegetarian, it doesn't mean the rest of us have to follow you."

Kate subsided sulkily and the rest of the lunch passed off without any more incidents although Melanie said little and Lorna kept throwing anxious glances at her. Eleanor hoped she might have learnt a lesson but she doubted it. Peter and Jenny appeared to have made up their differences and everyone else was making an effort to counteract the unpleasant scene. Afterwards they went back to the house for a cup of tea before separating to go to their various establishments. Peter and Jenny returned to their house and Eleanor went back to the Nurses' Residence where she had a flat. She would start work early on Monday morning.

The next day the screech of the alarm woke her at six o'clock. Struggling up from a deep sleep, she fumbled to turn it off and turned over. For some moments she lay, cocooned between a dream world and reality. Her mind was a blank page on which memories from the weekend were appearing like pictures from a Polaroid camera. The most vivid one was that of a tall handsome man with brown eyes and a melting smile. But she mustn't think of him. He was Carol's friend. But if he asked her out, she knew she would go. Light filtered through the plain curtains and she opened her eyes and stared at the stains on the ceiling which had been caused by a tenant on the next floor letting her bath water overflow into Eleanor's flat. Fortunately the damage had been minimal but so far the authorities had refused to redecorate.

She must get up. She wondered what operations were scheduled for today. If she didn't hurry, she'd be late. Swinging her legs out of bed, she rubbed her eyes and drifted into the small bathroom to run the shower. Showered and dressed, she felt ready to cope with the day. She put the radio on before plugging in the kettle and dropping some bread in the toaster.

As she munched, she thought back over the weekend. On the whole it had been a success she thought, but she was worried about Jenny and Melanie. Jenny was showing every sign of becoming obsessed with having a baby. How was she going to cope with the demands of her new job if half her mind was on her marital problems? Melanie was of even greater concern. Eleanor frowned as she absentmindedly spread some marmalade on her toast. Her younger sister had always been so quiet and studious. She had been overshadowed by her ebullient siblings, Lorna and Kate, so her obvious unhappiness had not been noticed. Why hadn't Mel talked to her before? She'd always been her sister's confidante. Her colleagues also told her their problems as she was a sympathetic listener.

The time signal for six-thirty cracked her thoughts and hurriedly she washed up her crockery, leaving it to dry as she went to collect her belongings and pin up her thick dark hair so that it would not escape from the hat she had to wear. As a theatre sister, she had to make sure the theatre was ready for the day's operations. The apartment block was only a short walk from the theatre complex and as Eleanor stepped outside, she took a deep breath of the clear air. There was no cloud in the sky and not a breath of wind. It was obviously going to be a glorious day. What a shame she would have to spend it cooped up in the operating theatre. She went into the building and made her way to the theatre where gynaecological operations were performed. Looking at the list pinned up on the notice board, she saw that David Baines was the surgeon on duty. She hoped he wouldn't upset any of the nurses. Most of the younger ones were frightened of him because he was so professional and expected perfection from those around him.

Going into the locker room, she discarded her own clothes and replaced them with the 'scrub suit' of dark blue trousers and white top. Her hair she completely covered by a linen hat. She kicked off her shoes and put on the ones she kept for the operating theatre. Slamming her locker door shut, she went to inspect the theatre. The nurses on duty over the weekend had left it ready for her. She adjusted a light and laid out the instruments that would be needed for the first operation, a hysterectomy.

"Morning Sister." Anne, one of the registered nurses on her team, bounced in. "Lovely day, isn't it?"

"It certainly is. Did you have a good weekend?"

"Yes thanks. How did the anniversary party go?"

"It went well. It was nice to have all the family together again."

"I don't know how you managed to keep it quiet."

Eleanor laughed. "Nor do I! Especially with Lorna and Kate knowing about it. It must be the first secret they've ever kept."

"Morning." Carol and David Baines arrived together. For the rest of the day Eleanor was busy handing instruments, clearing up after one operation and preparing for the next. Occasionally she was aware of the very blue eyes above the surgical mask. When they glanced fleetingly at her, she was annoyed to feel a slight pull of attraction but most of the time they were intent upon the intricate work his hands were performing.

It was late when they finished and there had not even been time to snatch a quick cup of coffee. Eleanor felt like a zombie as she headed for the sluice room to clear up after the day's operations. Like all National Health hospitals, they were understaffed. Her feet hurt and she couldn't wait to kick off the shoes she'd worn all day and change back into her own clothes.

"You've done a good job today. You must be tired." She hadn't heard the surgeon come in and, startled, she turned quickly, dropping the instruments she was about to put in the autoclave for sterilisation. Stooping to pick them up, she was irritated to find herself blushing. Unfortunately, David Baines stooped to help her and stars exploded as their heads collided.

"Sorry."

"My fault."

They both spoke at once and then the awkward moment turned into shared laughter. She stared up at him. Perhaps he wasn't quite as arrogant as she'd thought. He looked unsure of himself.

"Can I make you a cup of tea?" she enquired politely as she put the instruments into the autoclave and closed the door.

He shook his head. "No thanks. I could do with something stronger. Come out for a drink. The Fox and Pelican is just down the road. You can have half an hour to change and I'll meet you there."

The arrogance of the man! She hadn't misread him. Why couldn't he have *asked* her? If he had, she might have been tempted. But his automatic assumption that she would immediately do his bidding riled her.

"I'm sorry," she said coolly. "I'll have to decline your pressing invitation. I have another engagement."

"Oh." To her surprise he looked disappointed and briefly she felt sorry for him.

"Perhaps another time then." He walked swiftly away and she stared after him, almost regretting her refusal.

"Are you alone?" Carol stuck her head round the door. "I saw the dishy David going up the corridor. Have you had words?"

"No. As a matter of fact he asked me out."

Carol did a goldfish impression. "He didn't."

"He did."

"Are you going?"

"No."

"Why not? He really is rather gorgeous even if he does think he's God gift to women and to the medical profession."

"That's the trouble. He just assumed I'd got nothing better to so I …"

"I expect he'll try again. Now what did you think of Chris? I've been dying to ask you."

Eleanor gazed at her friend in exasperation. She was very fond of Carol but her inability to listen to the end of a sentence without interrupting and changing the subject was often irritating. And she didn't want to discuss Chris. She felt embarrassed about him. She realised Carol was still waiting for her answer. She turned away, annoyed that her usual blush was appearing.

"He seemed very nice. I'm sure your tennis has …"

"He's incredible, isn't he? I couldn't believe it when he asked me out. We get on so well together and he's taken me to some lovely places. Perhaps if you and David get together, we could make a foursome."

"I don't think there's much chance of that," retorted Eleanor tartly. "Look, Carol, I really have to go. I'm going to Jenny's for supper."

"I've got to go as well. Chris is taking me out for dinner. Give Jenny my love and ask her what she thought of Chris, won't you?"

I certainly won't, reflected Eleanor as Carol whirled out of the door.

"Well, what's he like?" Jenny handed Eleanor a much needed gin and tonic.

"Who?"

"Don't be obtuse. The new surgeon, of course."

"He might be OK if he didn't behave as though the rest of us were put on this earth merely to do his bidding."

"Well he *is* a surgeon. Presumably you do have to jump when he says so."

"Not when I'm off duty, I don't."

"Oh? What's that mean?"

"He asked me out for a drink. No. Correction. He didn't ask. He told me he'd meet me in the *Fox and Pelican*."

"Did you go?"

"No. I said I was coming here."

"That's no excuse. You know I'd have understood."

"All right. I might have gone if he'd asked me nicely but he didn't so I said I had another engagement. For goodness' sake, let's change the subject. Where's Peter?"

"He's working late. Said he'd send out for something and join us for coffee. So it's just us."

"That's nice."

"Yes I'm quite glad really 'cos I wanted to ask you about IVF."

"Oh Jenny, you're not still thinking …"

"Ellie, I'm desperate. I won't give up until we've tried everything."

"What does Peter say?"

"He won't adopt."

"I know that. Do you know why he's so set against it?"

"Not really. He just clams up when I ask him for a reason. I wish we could adopt. It would be the easiest option."

"I think it's quite difficult to adopt babies now," said Eleanor thoughtfully. "Most adoptions are of older children, I think."

"I find that hard to believe. England has the highest teenage pregnancy rate in Europe. Some of those girls must want the babies adopted."

"Mm. You'd think so, wouldn't you?"

"Anyway that's beside the point. Tell me about IVF."

"What do you want to know?"

"How it works. How expensive it is. Its success rate. How quickly I can have it."

"Hold on. I'm not an authority on it. I work in the theatre, remember."

"But you're a nurse."

"And you're a teacher but I don't expect you to know everything about everything."

Jenny smiled wryly. "Sorry. Could you please find out about it for me?"

"I'll try. I assume you've talked to Peter about it."

"I must check on the food." Jenny leapt up and headed for the kitchen. Eleanor followed her.

"*Have* you talked to Peter about it, Jenny?"

"Well ….I was waiting for the right moment."

"You'd better hurry up and find it then, hadn't you? After all, you'll presumably need his sperm."

"I suppose so."

"What on earth do you mean? You *suppose so*. You weren't thinking of going to a donor bank, were you?"

"No, no of course not." Jenny lifted the casserole out of the oven. Eleanor thought that her sister's flushed cheeks were not only the result of her close proximity to the oven. She looked flustered.

"Do you know *why* you can't have children, Jenny?"

"Not really. Peter's sperm count is low but none of the tests were really conclusive." She placed the casserole on the kitchen table. "You don't mind eating in here, do you?"

"Of course not. It's cosy." She looked around the dark panelled designer kitchen that Peter had insisted on when they moved into their eighteenth-century cottage. When they had bought it three years ago, they'd been told they could make alterations to the inside but the outside must remain the same in keeping with the others in the road. Practically every house in the small village of Goldham near Hazelford had a history and theirs was no exception. It had originally belonged to the wheelwright and there was a large wheel in the garden. Not surprisingly it was called 'Wheelwright Cottage'.

"What did you think of Carol's new boyfriend?" queried Jenny as she spooned vegetables onto Eleanor's plate. "Did you speak to him?"

"Mm." Eleanor was glad her sister wasn't looking at her. The thought of tall, handsome Chris had been invading her mind at frequent intervals since she'd met him. She wondered if he would contact her. She didn't want Jenny prying so she hurriedly changed the subject. "This looks delicious. I'm starving."

But Jenny was not to be deflected. "I thought they looked really well together. Who is he?"

"His name's Chris and he works at the Health Club. That's all I know."

"I wish you'd find someone, Ellie. I worry about you. I wish you'd marry and settle down."

"For goodness sake, Jenny, this is 1999. Marriage isn't the only option open to women today."

"I hope you've not planning to live with one of your boyfriends," retorted Jenny, tartly.

"Jenny, don't be absurd. You know that wasn't what I meant. I enjoy my job, you know. You've got a career; you should understand."

"I'd give it up if I could have children," said her sister wistfully.

"Sorry. I didn't mean to remind you."

"It's all right. More wine?"

"No thanks. I'm beginning to feel sleepy. I mustn't stay too long. I have to be up early in the morning."

Later, as she drove home, she thought about what Jenny had said. Of course she wanted to get married some time. But she was in no hurry. She had had various boyfriends but she had never felt more than friendship for any of them. Apart from a couple of disastrous infatuations in her teens, she had never felt deeply for any man and was beginning to wonder if she was capable of "falling in love". Until now! She hoped Chris would contact her. The very thought of his dark good looks made her heart pound.

Chapter Three

The shrilling of the phone penetrated Eleanor's deep sleep. She sat up too quickly and the room whirled around her. She groaned and lay down again squinting at the alarm clock which she had not set. It was only eight o' clock. Who on earth was ringing her so early on a Saturday morning when for once she could have a lie-in? She had planned a long leisurely bath followed by a browse round the shops. The insistent ringing continued. She really must have a phone by her bedside.

Sitting up gingerly, she was relieved to discover the furniture had realigned itself in its proper place. She felt for her slippers, dragged on her dressing gown and staggered towards the phone which ceased to ring as soon as she reached it.

"Blow." She collapsed on the chair beside the phone table; she might as well find out who here early caller had been. She dialled 1471 and frowned as she listened to the number. She didn't recognise it. Putting the phone down, she picked up a pencil and pad and dialled again making a note of the number. She stared at it.

"To return the call, press 3." Eleanor sleepily obeyed. It was probably a wrong number.

"Hullo." A male voice answered.

"Did you just phone me? It's Eleanor Bradley."

"Eleanor, it's Chris. I met you at your parents' anniversary party. Thanks for ringing back. The phone rang for ages so I gave up."

Her heart did a somersault and landed in her slippers. She gripped the phone. "I'm sorry. I was still in bed. I usually have a lie-in on Saturday if I'm not working."

"I wondered if you were free today."

"Yes, yes I am." Had she sounded too eager?

"It's a lovely day. I thought we could go for a drive and find a pub for lunch and then go out somewhere for dinner."

She hesitated. "What about Carol?"

"What about her?"

"I thought you and she … er … Won't she … mind?"

"Don't worry about Carol. It's only a casual relationship. We're just friends."

Carol hadn't given that impression but Eleanor wanted to believe him. She'd never felt like this before and she'd just have to lock up any guilt feelings.

"Well? Will you come?" He sounded impatient.

"Yes. I'd love to. Thank you."

"I'll pick you up about eleven? Will that give you time to get ready?"

"That's fine. Do you know where to find me." She gave him directions and hung up. What *was* she doing? She prayed that Carol wouldn't discover her treachery.

As she lay cocooned in froth, she contemplated her wardrobe. She would have to wear something suitable for a day out in the country and for dinner. She settled on a pair of reddish trousers and a purple blouse. She surveyed her shoes and then decided to wear flat sandals and to take a pair of heels to change into. She inspected her face in the mirror and jumped as the bell rang. Chris looked handsome in smart black jeans and a white shirt covered by a maroon jumper.

As they drove off, he said, "I thought we'd drive out to Newcombe Downs and perhaps have a walk and then go on to Castleford."

"There's a lovely pub there. It's very historic. Have you been there?"

"No. I've passed it and always wanted to go in."

At Newcombe Downs they indulged in cornets and laughed when the ice cream dripped down their chins as they walked down the hill. A hazy mist hovered over the Downs in the distance and there were a lot of cars in the car park. The beautiful weather had obviously tempted others out as well. But when they reached the wooded area at the bottom of the slope, they met only the occasional dog walker. Once Eleanor tripped and Chris put out his hand to steady her. She felt his warmth through the thin cotton of her sleeve and her insides started to melt, like the ice cream.

"All right?"

"Fine," she gasped, hoping her shortness of breath would be attributed to the slight incline. They walked for over an hour and then returned to the car feeling exhilarated.

"Ready for some lunch?"

"I think I am."

"Do you want a coffee before we leave?"

"No, I'm fine. What about you?"

He glanced at his watch. "It's nearly one. I think we should push on."

They met few cars on their journey through the country lanes and eventually pulled up beside the green on which Edward VI's retinue of four thousand men had camped over four hundred years previously because they could not all be accommodated in the Crown Inn which oozed history. A recent magazine article was framed inside the doorway. They stopped to read it.

"Goodness!" exclaimed Eleanor. "They actually plotted to get rid of poor little Jane Grey in one of the rooms here."

"I always felt sorry for her."

"So did I."

"Let's go and find something to eat."

The bar was fairly busy but they managed to find a table by the window and when they had pored over the menu, Chris went to order their food. Eleanor wanted to find out more about him but she didn't wish him to think she was prying.

"So how long have you worked at the Health Club?" she queried as he handed her a gin and tonic.

"About six months. I was working in America before that."

"Oh. Whereabouts?"

"In Colorado. I learnt a lot of useful tips."

"How long were you there?"

"A year."

"You weren't tempted to stay?"

He shook his head. "It's too modern. No history. Everything's so new. I prefer this." He waved his hands at the oak beams and stained glass windows sporting crests of long dead knights. "Have you been to the States?"

"No. I haven't been anywhere much. Just the odd holiday in France and Italy. I've never really felt the urge to travel. I guess we're a stay at home family."

"Well someone's got to remain at home to welcome the travellers back." He grinned at her. "I'm afraid I'm a travelholic. My father says that giving me travel brochures is like giving alcohol to an alcoholic."

She laughed and sipped her drink. "So will you soon be off on your travels again?"

"That depends." His brown eyes gazed into hers but further conversation was prevented by the arrival of their sandwiches. "Mm, these look good. I'm starving after all that exercise."

"Yes," agreed Eleanor, trying unsuccessfully to match his enthusiasm. Her appetite had vanished. Only trivialities were exchanged while they ate. When they'd finished, Chris went to order coffee and when he returned with the cups, he said, "Now where shall we go this afternoon? Have you been to Hatton Place? It's a National Trust property. Do you like that sort of thing?"

"Yes I do. I haven't been there. It's been on my list of things to do for ages."

"Right." He glanced at his watch. "I think it opens at two. And I've booked dinner at The Mill for later. Is that all right?"

"Lovely." The Mill was a very expensive restaurant where the old water mill could still be seen. It overlooked the river. She'd never been there.

By the end of the evening Eleanor knew that she was falling in love. To her delight Chris had told her he was a Christian but didn't attend a regular church as he often had to work on Sundays. Outside her flat, he gave her a chaste goodnight kiss and she let herself into the house waving as he walked back to his car. She would have preferred a more lover-like kiss but there was plenty of time. Her guilt was still firmly locked away and she was determined not to think about Carol. But that was not easy as she lay in bed thinking over the events of the day and wondering what the future held.

Melanie stared at the computer screen. Simon was away for the day but he had left her with a mountain of work. He hoped to publish three titles in time for the Christmas market but she felt he was optimistic. Discouraged, she glared at the two typescripts on her desk. She had promised to proofread them for him. As a small publisher, he tried to keep expenses down and it was cheaper to use Melanie rather than to send the work to an outsider. At least he had sent her on a proofreading course, she reflected.

Her brain wouldn't function properly this morning. She kept remembering the ugly scene at the restaurant. She wished now she'd ignored Lorna's needling instead of being upset by it. Stepping carefully over the files and magazines that littered the floor, she headed for the coffee machine. The office was small and Simon used the floor as a filing cabinet. It was like walking an obstacle race, she thought crossly. Obsessively tidy herself, Simon Rawlins' slapdash method of working infuriated her. The only major row they'd had was when she'd tidied up the office during one of his frequent absences.

He'd been furious when he returned. "I shan't be able to find anything," he had stormed. "I know it looks chaotic but it's *organised chaos*. You can keep your own desk as tidy as you like but don't *ever* touch mine again. And those files are on the floor for a reason."

Chapter Three / 31

"I don't know why you don't let me put everything on disk. They'd take up much less room."

"And what happens if there's a power cut or the computer crashes?"

"But …"

He'd become even angrier. "I'm the boss, here, Melanie. You either do as I say or you can find another job. OK? Now put everything back where it was."

She had cringed as he slammed out of the office. It had been seven o' clock in the evening and she'd been exhausted after a long day. She sobbed as she tried to remember where everything had been. She never made the same mistake again. That had been two years ago – soon after she'd started to work for him. He still preferred to receive typed manuscripts rather than disks. He said he could deal with them anywhere not just at his desk. Melanie pointed out he could invest in a laptop but he wasn't interested. *She* was the computer buff and he was happy to let her get on with it.

She plugged in the kettle and looked with disfavour at the cluttered floor. Simon refused to have a cleaner because "she'd move everything" so it was left to Melanie to manoeuvre the carpet sweeper around the floor and give the room a superficial dust occasionally. She'd borrowed a vacuum cleaner from one of the downstairs offices at first but had been terrified of sucking up some vital piece of paper by accident. Perhaps she should do her cleaning stint today. But she had too much work to do. It was already ten o' clock and she'd only typed one letter.

She made her coffee and carried it over to the small window beside her desk. That needed cleaning too. The sun striking through it emphasised the smears. It was time the contract cleaner cleaned the outside. She must check when he was due. Taking a sip of the scalding coffee, she stared down at the incessant traffic streaming and stopping along the high street. The office was on the third floor so the sound was muted. When she opened the window, the noise increased. Pulling the curtain across to shield both her and the computer from the blazing sun, she sat down and tried to focus on the letters she had to type.

By lunch time, she'd completed part of her work and decided to take herself and her sandwiches into the park where she could find a shady spot and concentrate on proofreading one of the novels that was due at the printer's in a month's time. On this warm September day other people had the same idea but she found a seat beside the lake and was soon deep in the adventures of an eighteenth-century heroine.

"Hullo Mel."

"Kate, what are you doing here? Shouldn't you be at school?"

"It's lunch time, silly. Anyway it's the first day and we're finishing early. The first day's always chaos."

"Want a sandwich? I'm afraid they're ham."

"You know I don't eat meat."

"Sorry."

"Anyway I've decided to give lunch a miss today. I'm getting too fat."

"Oh Kate, don't be ridiculous. Of course you're not."

"Well, I want to lose some weight."

"Don't do anything silly. Sorry, Kate, I really have to get on."

"Lover boy away?"

"Excuse me." With dignity, Melanie collected her belongings and moved to the next seat which had just been vacated.

Her sister followed her. "Sorry, Mel. I know how touchy you are about him."

"Never mind. I don't want to talk about it and I really do have to get on."

"Pardon me for speaking." Kate flounced off and Melanie sighed. Kate's mood swings were getting worse.

As she wandered back to the office, she thought about Simon. He was the first person she had properly fallen in love with. She'd had crushes on some of the boys at the Youth Club at church but this was a more mature feeling – at least she thought it was. After all she *was* twenty – old enough to know her own mind. She remembered again the scene at lunch the previous day. She wouldn't forgive Lorna. Now her parents would worry about her and Eleanor would lecture her.

She reflected bitterly that they had nothing to worry about. Simon had never shown the slightest interest in her. Why should he? No male had ever made any overtures. She gave out the wrong signals. She was obviously clever and she made no attempt to make the most of her appearance. She had never been interested in clothes and she tended to grab the first thing that came to hand in the morning. Tidy though she was at work, at home she left her dirty clothes for her mother to wash and bundled her clean things into a drawer.

She was aware that she took advantage of her mother and sometimes she thought she should find a flat of her own but her lifestyle was comfortable and she didn't know where her future lay. She had daydreams of setting up a love nest with Simon. Perhaps he would even leave his wife and marry her. But she knew this would never happen. She hadn't needed Eleanor to warn her of the dangers of falling in love with a married man. She knew it was wrong and against her Christian principles but sometimes her heart overruled her morals and she imagined running away with him and living happily ever after. The thought of a messy divorce and a tussle over his two children, Darren and Chloe, she pushed firmly into the bottom of her mind box and locked it.

She was so deep in thought she almost walked past the office door. She hadn't done much proofreading. Meeting Kate had unsettled her.

Simon was pleased with himself when he walked in the next morning.

"Successful trip?" asked Melanie, heading for the kettle. Coffee was always his first priority.

"Excellent. I persuaded Maria Knowles to write for us."

"My goodness, you have been busy. How did you manage to prise her away from her current publisher? She's been with them since she started, hasn't she?"

"Mm. She's written five books for them but apparently her editor's left and she doesn't like her new one. I contacted her at the right time."

"Great. Shall I send her a standard contract or do you want anything added?"

"She's promised to sign for two books so you'll have to alter it."

"I'll do it today."

Simon threw a manuscript on her desk. "When you've done that, can you typeset the corrections on this. Joy finished proofreading it yesterday. Here's a list of alterations. It's due at the printer's tomorrow."

"Right."

The contract was soon done and two copies signed by Simon were ready to post to Maria Knowles for her signature. Then Melanie turned her attention to *Down Memory Lane*. She'd already scanned it into the computer and she called up the file and prepared to make the alterations. She didn't usually read the script at this stage. The proof copies had already been checked by the author and by her or Joy, Simon's wife. This one had been done by Joy but for once her mind had apparently not been on her job. Melanie frowned and read the page again. It didn't make sense. In the middle of the page were two identical paragraphs and the following one bore no relation to them. Deborah Keene was such a conscientious worker that it was unusual to find many errors in her original typescript. What had gone wrong? Why hadn't Joy picked it up?

Melanie rolled the screen up to the next page and then back. The first page she was looking at ended in the middle of a sentence and a new paragraph started on the following page. She sat back staring at the screen with her brain clicking into overdrive. Obviously there were sections of the text missing and Deborah had typed one paragraph twice instead of the following one. As the disk was due at the printer's the next day, there was a big problem. Simon had disappeared but she hoped he had his mobile with him. About to dial him, she paused. Could she sort this out herself? If she could contact Deborah, all was not lost.

Closing the file, she called up the address book and dialled Deborah's number. A disembodied voice informed her there was no one available to take her call but if she would like to leave a message … She replaced the phone. Should she ring the printers or would that be taking too much on herself? She chewed her lip, thinking furiously. Then she picked up the phone again and dialled her employer. Fortunately he hadn't switched off his mobile as he had a habit of doing!

"Simon, we have a problem. There are sections of the text missing in *Down Memory Lane* and I can't get hold of Deborah. Shall I leave her a message? Or shall I put off the printer?"

"What!" Simon's voice boomed down the wires and Melanie held the headpiece away from her. "But Joy's proofread it. She can't have missed such an obvious thing?"

"Well, she has," said Melanie tartly. "So what do we do to limit the damage?"

"Leave a message for Deborah and ring Dave to tell him we'll be late with the disk."

"How much later?"

"We can't leave it long. It's due out at the end of October."

She put the phone down and immediately picked it up again to dial the author. It was still the answerphone. She left a message identifying the problem and asking Deborah to ring as soon as she got in. Then she rang the printer who grumpily said he was very busy and didn't like having his schedule disrupted by temperamental publishers. Melanie was outraged.

"Dave, that's not fair. We've always kept to deadlines. This has never happened before and I don't understand why it wasn't spotted earlier. We'll let you have the disk as soon as we possibly can."

"OK. Sorry I yelled at you, Mel, love. That's the second thing that's gone wrong today. I'm just waiting for the third thing to happen."

"Perhaps it won't."

"With my luck, I'm sure it will."

"Hope it's not too bad then." She rang off and returned to the computer screen, hoping she wouldn't find any more complications. She worked through her lunch break eating her sandwiches when she could. It was nearly seven when Deborah finally phoned. She was upset.

"Oh, Melanie, I don't know what I was thinking of. I've never done that before. I missed six pages and I'd put my handwritten manuscript in the loft and I couldn't find it."

"Have you found it now?"

"Yes, just this moment so I thought I'd better phone you straight away. What shall I do? You won't be able to read my writing. I'll have to type it out."

"Fax me the handwritten sheets and I'll call you if I can't read something."

"Darling, you know I don't have a fax."

Melanie groaned. Of course she knew. She'd forgotten. Deborah was a sweet elderly lady who had never caught up with modern technology. It was amazing she'd actually invested in an answerphone. She wrote her novels by hand and typed them up on a typewriter. At least it was an electronic one but she would have nothing to do with computers or faxes. Sighing, Melanie resigned herself to a long night.

"I think you'd better read it to me and I'll type it in. Hold on while I reorganise the phone so I don't have to hold it." She put it down and pressed a button. Then she rolled back the novel that was still on the screen to the required page. "Right. Off you go."

It was a long process because Deborah found it difficult to read her own writing and it was so long since she'd written the book, she'd forgotten what she'd written. Melanie had to call up frequent toppings of patience as she waited for Deborah to find the right word.

"Now should that be 'in' or 'on'? I think it's 'on' dear …I don't like that expression. What can I put instead? Let me see … Ah yes …"

And so it continued through the long evening. Melanie hoped that Simon wouldn't notice the exceptionally high phone bill but she couldn't think of what else she could have done. He came in while she was still on the phone. He was in a foul temper so his day obviously hadn't been very satisfactory either. He glared at her and flung himself down in the chair in front of his cluttered desk.

When she eventually put down the phone, he snapped, "Why are you still here? You should have gone hours ago."

"I've been working on *Down Memory Lane*. Deborah hasn't got a fax and I didn't want to wait for her to type it and send it so

Chapter Three / 37

she had to dictate it to me." She hesitated. "There were six pages missing."

He exploded. "Six pages. However long have you been on the phone?"

"I don't know. I didn't look at the clock."

"It'll come out of her royalties. Stupid woman. And what Joy was thinking of, I can't imagine. She's had the wretched book for a month. I'm furious with her."

"Would you like a coffee?" asked Melanie to soothe him. She'd never heard him criticise Joy before. He was still glowering but suddenly he looked at her and the anger died out of his eyes and was replaced by something else. She stared back at him, her heart suddenly starting to thump. He was looking at her as though he cared. She stood up and blundered towards the kettle but caught her foot in the bundle of manuscripts beside his desk and would have landed on her face had he not grabbed her arm.

She gasped. "Sorry. Clumsy of me. I've never done that before."

He was still holding her and slowly he turned her round to face him. She became still. Her head was in the right position to rest on his shoulder but she didn't dare. She looked down, noting that his shoes needed cleaning.

"Melanie, look at me." She looked up and he released her so that he could remove her glasses. She blinked. Without them everything was a blur but she didn't care. He was going to kiss her. She shut her eyes and raised her face to his, revelling in the feel of his arms around her. This was the moment she had dreamt of. His lips gently touched hers and she flung her arms round his neck.

The phone shattered into a thousand fragments the fragile moment that had been the best of her life. She felt his arms drop away and heard his voice.

"Yes Joy. Yes. I'm just coming. I got held up. I've had a bad day. Yes, all right. I couldn't help it. I'm sorry I didn't phone you." He slammed down the receiver.

Melanie gradually surfaced from the warm cocoon in which she had been luxuriating. She groped for her glasses but knocked them off the desk where he had placed them. He picked them up and handed them to her and she put them on, peering at him uncertainly. He looked embarrassed.

"I'm sorry, Mel. I shouldn't have done that."

"Why not? I liked it." Melanie was horrified to hear her words. She clapped her hand over her mouth.

"You're very sweet. I could ..." He stood up and said formally, "Thank you for staying so late today. Let me drive you home. We can finish off the work tomorrow."

"It needs proofing. She didn't seem to know what she wanted to say half the time. I'll sort it out tomorrow."

It was still warm when they left the building and walked out to the office car park. Neither of them spoke on the short journey. Melanie was still bemused by the kiss. She wondered what would have happened if Joy hadn't phoned. Simon made no attempt to kiss her when he stopped outside her parents' house. He didn't even go round to open her door. She felt deflated – like a balloon that a child has started to blow up and left to fly undirected until all its air has been expelled.

She slammed the door and ran up the path. She didn't even say goodnight. If she had, her voice would be thick with the tears that were waiting to overflow. She let herself into the house and quietly shut the door. Her parents must have gone to bed. Through blurred eyes, she glanced at her watch which showed her it was nearly eleven o'clock. Leaning against the door, she shut her eyes, letting the tears seep through her lids. She felt exhausted as though she were convalescing from a long illness.

Dragging herself towards the stairs, she crept up to her bedroom holding on to the banisters and feeling her way along the wall. The trickle of tears became a flood and she had to bite back the groans that filled her mouth and were waiting to erupt into a volcano of howling. Safely in her room, she flung her glasses on the bedside table and hurled herself on the bed, burying her face in the pillow which was soon saturated. She banged her fists on the bed and drummed her feet. Eventually exhausted, she rolled over and blinked myopically at the ceiling, occasionally hiccuping a sob.

She sat up, swinging her legs to the ground and frowned. *Why* was she so upset? She thought back to the kiss. It *had* meant something; she was sure of it. She pushed away the thought of Simon's pretty little wife, Joy. She had come into the office once or twice and Melanie had tried hard to be civil to her. It was difficult to dislike Joy. She tried so hard to please and she was obviously devoted to her husband. The way she always clung to him irritated Melanie but she had to admit she was jealous.

What *was* she thinking of? Simon was happily married and everything that she had learned from her parents was shouting at her to leave him alone. Nice Christian girls didn't steal other people's husbands. But she wasn't sure she *was* a Christian. Oh she went to church and paid lip service to the creed but she wasn't sure how deep the roots were. She suspected that her upbringing had fallen on stony ground and was likely to be swamped by the weeds of the world. Her mind suddenly shot off at a tangent and she reached for the notebook that always lay beside her bed.

"Weeds of the world," she muttered as she wrote it down. "I like the alliteration. Perhaps I'll use it."

She'd done six chapters of her romantic novel but had then faced the inevitable blank wall known as "writer's block". She hadn't let Simon see it. She wanted to finish it first. Thinking about it restored her a little and, late though it was, she decided to do some writing. Perhaps it would help her to go to sleep and writing was supposed to be therapeutic – or was that only keeping a journal?

Changing into her pyjamas, she sat at the desk her parents had bought her for her eighteenth birthday and unlocked the drawer containing her masterpiece. It was a warm night and she hadn't drawn the curtains but she didn't open the window in front of her as she didn't want any inquisitive small visitors peering at her work. She'd open it before she went to bed.

She wrote steadily. The traumatic experience of the evening gave her pen wings as she empathised with her heroine who had just been cruelly rejected by her lover. Melanie knew exactly how Lucinda had felt. The feelings were hers. It was the best time to write, she felt. The world was so quiet and there were no interruptions. She must do it again. She almost forgot Simon as she plunged Lucinda into more and more difficulties without any idea of how she would be rescued.

As she wrote, she gradually became aware of sounds outside the window. Subconsciously she'd been aware of them for some time but now having satisfactorily reached the end of a chapter, she laid down her pen and stretched. Surprised, she looked out of the window. When she had started to write, she could barely see the silhouettes of the trees in the garden. Now they were sharply etched against a watery blue-grey sky edged with candy floss pink.

"Oh my goodness." She looked at her watch. It was after four o'clock. The sound she was hearing was getting louder. It was the singing of the birds heralding the dawn. She was jerked back to reality. She had to leave for work at eight. She had less than four hours. She must get *some* sleep!

Her alarm went off as soon as her head touched the pillow. But it said seven o'clock so she must have slept for three hours. The events of the previous evening pattered into her mind shovelling thoughts of her novel into the corner. She groaned. Her mouth felt like a sponge that hadn't felt water for months, her eyes wouldn't open properly and even with her glasses, she couldn't focus. Shutting her eyes, she flopped back on the bed. She rarely took days off but she didn't feel at all well. But if she didn't go in, Simon might think she was upset about the previous evening. Well she was but had she slept, she would certainly have been at her desk.

"Melanie. It's seven-thirty. Are you up? You'll be late." Her mother knocked at the door and promptly opened it. "My goodness, child. You look awful. What's the matter?"

The kind words triggered the tears again. "Oh Mum, I don't feel well. Can you phone Simon for me?"

"Of course I will." Dorothy put her arms round her daughter. "What's the matter, dear?"

"Nothing." Melanie's reply was muffled and her mother didn't pursue it.

"Would you like some breakfast? Are you hungry or do you just want to sleep. Oh …" She broke off and stared at the desk.

For once Melanie had forgotten to lock up her manuscript. "Melanie, you weren't writing all night."

"I didn't mean to. I ... I was late in and – and, well, I supposed I was suddenly inspired and – and, well, suddenly I heard this noise and it was the dawn chorus."

"Oh Mel, what are we going to do with you?" Dorothy was laughing. She suspected it wasn't the first time Melanie had written through the night but it was the first time she had proof. "I'll bring you some tea and toast and then I'll ring Simon."

"Thanks, Mum."

✣ ✣ ✣ ✣

"Carol, are you all right?" It was the end of the day shift and Carol continued to clear up with her back to Eleanor. There was the sound of a sob. "Sit down. I'll make you a cup of tea." Did Carol know her best friend was deceiving her?

Carol grabbed a handful of tissues from a handy box. "I think Chris is seeing someone else, Ellie."

Eleanor was glad she had her back to Carol as she held the kettle under the tap. She could feel the prickles start to pierce her neck and knew that blood was flooding her face and neck. She gave an exclamation of annoyance as the water overflowed over her hand and sleeve; she hoped her colour would recede more quickly than it usually did. She mopped herself up and emptied out some of the water before switching on the kettle and busying herself with the mugs.

"What makes you think that?" she asked trying to sound casual. She had to find out whether Carol had identified the "other woman".

"We went out last night but he ... he seemed preoccupied. He took me home early and ... and he didn't even kiss me goodnight properly." She dissolved into tears.

Eleanor continued to probe. "Did he say anything about anyone else?"

Carol shook her head. "No but I – I'm sure there is someone. Oh Ellie, What shall I do? I love him so. I've never felt like this about anyone before."

Nor have I, reflected Eleanor. Oh dear! Why did Christopher Davenport have this devastating effect on her? The guilt which had been firmly locked away now probed through every pore and her hands shook as she poured water over the tea-bags in the mugs. Why was she being so wicked? How could she deliberately steal Carol's boy friend? But she couldn't help how she felt, she consoled herself. She was besotted with the dark handsome tennis coach.

She was relieved that Carol appeared too wrapped up in her own despair to notice her friend's discomfiture. When Carol had left and Eleanor was washing up the mugs, she tried to think rationally about the mess she had created. She knew she should refuse to go out with Chris again and send him back to Carol. That would be the Christian thing to do. But would it work? He'd said they were "just friends". She hated the deceit. If she told Carol, she'd lose her friendship and she didn't want that. She tried to pray for help but no answer came. While she was always happy to give advice to her sisters, she wasn't able to sort out her own problems so easily.

✥ ✥ ✥ ✥

"There's a visitor for you, Melanie." Dorothy Bradley opened the door of the sitting room where Melanie sat slumped in an armchair staring at nothing. She'd been like that for the past two days and the family had been very concerned about her. She'd resisted any attempts to see the doctor, saying she wasn't ill but she'd refused to return to work. Simon had phoned several times but she always gave an excuse for not talking to him.

Now he followed her mother into the room and Melanie stared at him in horror, her tongue tying itself in knots.

"I'll leave you to talk." Dorothy went out, shutting the door quietly behind her.

"I've been worried about you, Mel. Why wouldn't you talk to me on the phone?"

"I ... I felt embarrassed and hurt and – oh I don't know."

"I'm sorry, Mel," he said gently. "I think you're very sweet and I wouldn't have hurt you for anything." Her eyes flew to his face and she blinked away tears. He sat down opposite her. "I've been thinking a lot over the past few days and although I'd miss you a great deal, I think it might be better if we didn't work together any more."

"But I don't want to leave you." She started to cry. How stupid she was! For the past two days she'd been trying to find the strength to send in her notice so she could make a fresh start. Now that *he* had taken the initiative, she knew she didn't want to leave him. She would be happy if she could only see him every day.

"Don't cry, Mel. Just listen to me. When I was at a Book Fair recently, I met this chap who's just starting up a new publicity venture. He's looking for someone reliable to train as his personal assistant with a view eventually to running it for him. He's a very successful businessman with pots of money and fingers in all sorts of pies. I think the job would be ideal for you. Eventually you'd be running the whole show as once a business is off the ground, he usually leaves it to his PA to run while he searches for pastures new."

Melanie had stopped crying and her mind was functioning again. She glanced at him. Was she imagining the tenderness in his eyes? Perhaps he did care for her. The seed of an idea embedded itself in her mind; she would water it later.

"It sounds interesting," she admitted, "but there must be hundreds of people after a job like that."

"He likes to have a personal recommendation. I've told him about you and what a brilliant organiser you are and he sounded really keen." He looked embarrassed. "Actually Mel, I've arranged an interview for you on Wednesday morning."

"Without even asking me?"

"I phoned several times and you wouldn't talk to me," he reminded her. "At least go and see him. I think it would be an ideal opportunity for you and you've always been ambitious, haven't you?"

"Have I?" she asked, bemused. Things were going too fast. "I'll think about it."

"Don't take too long. Ring me this afternoon."

"How would you manage without me?"

"Don't worry about me. I'd cope." He hesitated. "You could still do some proofreading for me, couldn't you?"

So he wouldn't want to lose her completely. She smiled for the first time. The seed she had planted started to germinate. "Of course I could."

✥ ✥ ✥ ✥

"What are you doing?"

Jenny hurriedly bundled up the booklets she'd been perusing and looked up.

"Hullo, darling. I didn't expect you so early."

Peter crossed the room to kiss her. "What's this. IVF treatment. Jenny, you're not seriously considering …."

"Oh Peter, why not? It would give us a chance to have a child of our own."

"And it might not. The chances of success are about one in five."

"How do you know?"

"I think I read it somewhere. Would you like a sherry? What are we eating? Shall I go and get some wine or have we got some?"

"Oh dear. I haven't really thought. I was so engrossed." Flustered, Jenny stood up scattering leaflets all over the floor.

Peter stooped to help her pick them up. "You've got a library here. Where did you get them?"

"I wrote to the Human Fertilisation and Embryology Authority."

"Without discussing it with me? I *am* involved, you know."

"Oh darling, I know. I'm sorry. I should have asked you but I thought I'd find out about it first so I could tell you about it."

"Well don't bother. I've no intention of taking part."

"Oh Peter, please."

"Jenny, I've been in court all day. I'm tired and all I want to do is relax. I don't want an argument as soon as I come in."

"I'm sorry," she said contritely. "I didn't mean to badger you. I was going to have a meal ready for you but … I didn't realise it

Chapter Three / 45

was so late. I'll see what I can find in the freezer. And yes, I would like a sherry please."

How could she have been so stupid? She reflected crossly as she left the room. She'd intended to marshal her facts together and pick her moment to broach the subject of IVF with her husband. Now it would be very difficult to get him to agree. She sighed. He could be so stubborn sometimes. She opened the freezer door. It needed defrosting. She'd have to do a big shop soon. There was a chicken Kiev or a lamb casserole that she'd cooked the previous week.

"Chicken Kiev or lamb casserole?" she called.

He appeared at the kitchen door with her sherry. "Why don't we go out instead?"

"Do you really want to?"

"Why not?"

"All right."

"I'll book for eight at Mario's. But no discussion of IVF."

"I promise."

But they would have to discuss it some time. She could be as stubborn as he was and she was determined to explore all possible avenues before she accepted the fact that they would not have a family.

Over the next few weeks Jenny tried unsuccessfully to pin her husband to his chair so he would listen to what she considered her very convincing arguments for visiting their GP to discuss the possibility of IVF treatment.

Eventually she managed it. She had returned early from school and decided she would wait no longer. She cooked his favourite meal – steak with fried onions, mushrooms, tomatoes and scalloped potatoes. When he returned soon after seven, she'd already had a shower, dressed in an attractive lime-green trouser suit whose flared legs suited her slim figure and drenched herself in his favourite Anais Anais perfume.

"Hullo darling. Would you like a shower before you have a drink? Dinner will be about eight."

He kissed her. "You look very smart. Is it a special occasion?"

"No, I just felt like dressing up and cooking you a nice meal."

He looked suspicious. "No ulterior motive?"

"Of course not," she lied, quickly turning away. She was relieved she didn't blush as easily as Eleanor did.

"I'll have a quick shower and join you. Mix me a whisky and soda, will you?"

"Your wish is my command, oh, master."

He grinned and disappeared upstairs. She returned to the kitchen to inspect the frying pan. The onions were browning nicely. She'd do the steak under the grill. It shouldn't take long. They both liked it medium rare.

When he came down, she'd mixed his drink and poured herself a sherry. Appetising smells drifted in from the kitchen.

"This is nice." He stretched out his long legs and took a sip of whisky. "Perfect."

She smiled. She'd raise the thorny subject afterwards. She didn't want to spoil the meal. He ate with gusto but she'd only given herself a small portion of steak which she pushed around her plate. It was some time before he noticed her lack of appetite.

"Aren't you hungry?" he asked, concerned.

"Not very. I had lunch at school today. It filled me up. Would you like some dessert? I could find something in the freezer. Or just coffee?"

"Coffee's fine. That was a huge piece of steak and my plate was swamped with vegetables. I don't think I could eat another thing. It was delicious. Thank you, darling."

"My pleasure." She took the plates out to the kitchen and thoughtfully spooned coffee into the *cafetière*. She'd never have a better time to talk to him but she was nervous. She was beginning to think he didn't share her fervent desire to have a family.

When she returned to the lounge, he had his head back in the armchair and his eyes closed. He didn't stir and she realised he was asleep. Bother! She looked at him. His long lashes about which he was so embarrassed were more noticeable with his eyes closed. Her heart lurched. He was so handsome and she loved him so much but her desperate desire for children was starting to drive, perhaps not a wedge, but certainly a large splinter between

Chapter Three / 47

them. She said a quick prayer for guidance as she poured the coffee and set it down on the occasional table beside him. He stirred and opened his eyes.

"I wasn't asleep."

"Of course you weren't."

"This is cosy." He took a sip of coffee and sighed contentedly. "Just as I like it."

Could she risk adding another splinter to the crack? But perhaps he would be more amenable after a good meal and more than half a bottle of wine.

"Peter."

"Yes?"

She hesitated but she *had* to speak. "Peter, I really *do* want to try this IVF treatment. Won't you *please* look at the leaflets and come and talk to Dr Reynolds."

She watched a shutter come over his face; his lips tightened into the stubborn expression she knew so well. He looked like a little boy who was about to have a temper tantrum if he couldn't get his own way. She sighed.

"I don't want to do it, Jenny. I've told you. If we can't have children in the normal way, then I don't believe God wants us to have them. Besides, I think IVF is a most unnatural process. I wouldn't feel like a proper husband."

✣ ✣ ✣ ✣

"Simon? It's Mel. I got the job!"

"Congratulations. I'll miss you."

"Well you'll have to put up with me for a bit longer. I don't start till next September."

"Oh."

Did he sound relieved or disappointed? Was *she* relieved or disappointed? She wasn't sure but she was certainly excited about the new job and relieved she would have several months to prepare for it. Meanwhile she would still see Simon every day and the seed she had planted had now been watered and was sprouting leaves. It was time to take a cutting and transplant it in *his* mind. She took a deep breath.

"Simon, I've been thinking. I'm sure it's time I moved out of my parents' house. I'd love you to help me find a flat. Would you have time?"

"Of course I would." His voice sounded warm.

"I've found some flats in the local paper. Are you free this afternoon?"

"Just let me check. Yes, I haven't got any appointments. I was going to look at the slush pile to see if there was anything worth salvaging but that can wait. Why don't I treat you to lunch first to celebrate your getting the job?"

"Wouldn't Joy mind?" She held her breath.

"Why should she? It's a perfectly legitimate reason for taking you out." He sounded defensive.

"So it is." She smiled into the receiver. Her first 'date' with Simon! Would it be the first of many or was she deceiving herself?

✣ ✣ ✣ ✣

Eleanor pushed open the door of the gym bar and looked round appreciatively. Candles on each table cast a soft light and the log fire in the middle contributed to the cosy atmosphere. After her workout she'd treat herself to a drink and perhaps a snack. She hadn't had anything to eat before she left. Readjusting her backpack, she headed for the changing room. Then she stopped, frowning. Surely she recognised the back of that head. She hesitated briefly and then moved purposefully towards a table where a lone man sat morosely sipping a beer.

"Hullo, Peter." Her brother-in-law looked up and made a half-hearted attempt to rise to his feet. "Don't get up. I'm just on my way to the gym. Have you just had a session?"

He shook his head. "I was going to and then I couldn't be bothered so I decided to have a drink."

"How's Jenny?"

"All right, I suppose."

She looked sharply at him. "Is everything all right, Peter?"

"No, it damn well isn't!"

Eleanor removed her backpack and sat down opposite him. "Do you want to talk about it?"

"I don't want to bore you."

"Don't be silly. You're my brother-in-law. I want to help."

"Have you talked to Jenny recently?"

"Yes." She didn't elaborate.

"Has she told you about this daft idea she has?"

"You mean the IVF treatment? You know, Peter, it's not really so daft."

"I might have known you'd take her side."

"I'm not taking anybody's side but have you really thought about it? It might be the answer you know. She said you wouldn't even discuss it."

"Well can you blame me? It's an admission of failure."

"Oh Peter, of course it isn't. How can you be so negative? Why don't you at least give it a try?"

He looked sulky. "I don't like the idea. I'd be embarrassed."

She bit her lip but managed to control her features. Fortunately he was glaring at his pint so he didn't notice her attempts to hide her smile. How could she convince him to change his mind? The cracks in her sister's marriage were becoming wider every day. She hated to see the coldness that was growing between hem.

"It would be much worse for Jenny, you know," she said gently.

"But she wants it so desperately. I want kids too, Eleanor, but she's absolutely obsessed. I don't know how she ever manages to concentrate on her work. As soon as I come in, she's nagging at me. I can't take much more. It's ruining our sex life. I feel I have to make an appointment with her to make sure it's the right time of the month. It's become so – mechanical." He suddenly buried his face in his hands and Eleanor was overwhelmed with compassion for him. *Why* hadn't God allowed Jenny to conceive?

"I'm so terribly sorry, Peter," she said inadequately.

He looked up. "What do you really think, Eleanor? Don't you think IVF is going against nature and not what God intended us to do? Surely if he'd wanted us to have children, we'd have had them by now. Not everyone is blessed with a family."

She considered carefully before she answered. She had to say the right thing. Perhaps she might be able at least to make him reconsider.

"At one time, I think I'd have agreed with you. But there is another side to the argument you've put forward. Surely God has allowed medical science to move forward and has given doctors the ability to help infertile couples. This knowledge comes from him, doesn't it? Of course it can be abused and misused but I know a Christian couple who used IVF and now have two delightful children and are very happy."

He looked startled. "Really? So Christians do use it."

"Of course they do." She decided to push her advantage. "Is your Christian moral stance just an excuse? Perhaps you didn't want to have the tests and go through the process because of embarrassment, so you found an excuse."

He gave a sheepish grin. "Maybe. I don't really know. I feel so mixed up about it and she keeps attacking me when I'm tired and can't think properly."

"I don't want to interfere but shall I have a word with her and suggest she leaves it for a while? Then *you* can talk to her when you've thought it through and you can both discuss it rationally."

There was a long pause and she wondered if she'd gone too far. He picked up his glass and drained it. Setting it down, he looked straight at her.

"You're a sweet girl, Eleanor. It's helped to talk to you. I felt almost suicidal when I came in here this evening. I just had to get out of the house. Jenny kept on and on at me. In the end I yelled at her and told her I was fed up and perhaps we should separate."

"Oh Peter, I'd no idea it had gone so far. I'm so sorry. She must be feeling awful."

"I think part of me hoped it would bring her to her senses. But I was so angry. I just wanted to hurt her as much as possible."

"Do you still feel the same?"

He shook his head. "I've been sitting here trying to pluck up the courage to go home. I love Jenny, Eleanor. I'd never do anything to hurt her."

Chapter Three / 51

"Of course you wouldn't," she said bracingly. She stood up. "Why don't you go home and make your peace with her and tell her you'll talk about IVF when you've thought about it."

"Do you think she'll listen to me? She was angry too."

"I'm sure she will." She waited for him to move but he still sat slumped in his seat. She sighed. "Do you want me to go round and smooth your path for you?"

He looked at her eagerly. "Would you? Please. You said you'd talk to her."

She laughed suddenly. "You *are* a coward, Peter. I believe you're afraid of your wife."

He grinned ruefully. "Don't be ridiculous."

She picked up her backpack. "I *was* going to the gym."

He was immediately contrite. "Oh Ellie, I *am* sorry. What a selfish creature I am. And I never even offered you a drink."

"Don't worry; it's all in a good cause." She glanced at his glass. "But I shouldn't have any more beer. Have a coffee to sober you up."

"I'm not drunk!" he exclaimed indignantly.

"I know you're not but you'll need to be stone cold sober to talk to Jenny. You don't want her to find another excuse for attacking you, do you?"

"OK. You win. I'll have a coffee and you'll talk to Jenny?"

"I will." I just hope I find the right words, she reflected as she left him at the bar ordering, she hoped, a strong cup of coffee.

Chapter Four

"Are you quite sure about this, dear?" Dorothy looked anxiously at her middle daughter. You know you're welcome to stay here as long as you like."

"I know, Mum, but this flat's come up and, well, it seemed a good idea," Melanie assured her parents. "Simon came with me to look at it and he thought it was great."

Eleanor glanced quickly at her sister. Melanie stared boldly back at her and then returned to demolishing the lamb casserole their mother had cooked.

"When are you moving in?" asked her father. "Would you like some help?"

"It's OK thanks, Dad. Simon is going to help me."

"That's very kind of him. Are you sure he doesn't mind?"

"No, he offered."

"Do you need furniture?" Dorothy was always practical.

"No it's furnished. I'm renting it. But I'll take my desk with me – and that little rocking-chair. If you don't mind."

"That's fine. Let us know if you need anything else, won't you, dear?"

"Yes, thanks, Mum."

"I think it's brill. Can I come and stay with you?" Kate was bubbling with enthusiasm.

"There's only one bedroom."

"I could bring a sleeping-bag."

"We'll see."

"I'll be the only one left at home. Can I move into Mel's room, Mum? It's bigger than mine."

"I don't see why not."

"I do." Melanie was flushed. "I might want to come back. Where would I sleep if I come for the weekend?"

"In my room." Kate sounded smug.

"But ..."

"We can talk about it later," said Dorothy hurriedly, sensing a family row. "Eleanor, will you help me clear the dishes and bring in the dessert?"

Melanie looked surprised; that was usually Kate's role. No doubt her mother and sister were going to talk about her, she thought crossly.

She was right.

"What do you think about this move, Eleanor?" Dorothy sounded worried as she took the trifle out of the fridge.

"It's what she wants and she *is* twenty. She'd go sooner or later. Don't worry."

"I can't help it. If she's by herself, she won't eat properly and she'll stay up half the night writing that novel of hers."

"I'm sure she'll be all right. I'll keep an eye on her. The flat's quite near the hospital."

"Oh would you, dear? That would relieve my mind."

"How's your course going? Are you still enjoying it?"

"Yes, I am but it's hard going back to nursing after twenty years. Everything's so different. I'm working on the children's ward next week. I'll enjoy that."

"Nurses are still in demand. I think this Return to Nursing course is a wonderful idea." Eleanor picked up the trifle and carried it into the dining room.

"Great!" exclaimed Kate. "My favourite dessert."

"Mine too," agreed Eleanor.

"That's why I made it," laughed Dorothy.

After a second helping had been forced on her, Melanie announced she wanted to sort out the things she needed to take to her new flat.

"Like some help?" Eleanor offered.

Melanie hesitated. "If you like. Thanks. Do you mind, Mum? Kate can help you, can't she?"

"Thanks a bunch." Kate glared at her sister. "Why is it always me?"

"Because you're the youngest, of course." Melanie grinned at her. "Anyway you'll have to get used to it now. You'll be the only one left."

"There's no need for that, Melanie," said her mother crossly. "It won't take us long to put the things in the dishwasher and I'll make some coffee later."

"I don't really need any help, you know, Ellie," said Melanie as the two girls ascended the stairs.

"I wanted to talk to you."

"Yes, I thought you probably would." Melanie sighed as she opened the door; Eleanor followed her in and sat on the bed. She stared out of the window. The remaining leaves on the apple tree were stirring but there was no breeze. She caught a glimpse of a bushy tail dancing round the trunk of the tree. She smiled.

"Sammy Squirrel is still in residence, I see."

"What?" Melanie followed her sister's gaze. "Oh yes. I see him most days. I'll miss him."

"Are you sure you're doing the right thing, Mel? Why don't you stay at home until you start your new job?"

Melanie shook her head. "I've got the flat now. It's time I cut the parental apron strings, Ellie."

"I suppose so. I worry about you, though."

Melanie gave her sister a quick hug. "You're like a mother hen always clucking around your chicks. I'll be fine."

"Mum thinks you won't eat properly."

"I will. All I'll have to do is to stick a meal for one in the microwave. Now stop worrying. Go down and reassure Mum that I won't starve and I'm not going to Outer Mongolia."

Chapter Four / 55

Eleanor laughed and stood up. "All right. But you will tell me if you need any help, won't you? And I'm always available if you need to talk."

"I know."

After she'd gone, Melanie sat on the bed thinking. She was sure Eleanor had guessed there was an ulterior motive for her moving. But would things work out as she planned? She loved Simon and she hoped her flat would a haven to which he would come when his wife was being difficult. She would show him how much better she understood him than Joy did. Her cheeks grew hot and she could feel her body responding to her adulterous thoughts. Was she, a girl brought up in a Christian home, really contemplating an affair with a married man? She shut her eyes and tried to pray but there seemed to be a blockage between her and God. That shouldn't surprise her, she reflected; God would certainly not approve of her thoughts. But Jesus hadn't condemned the woman taken in adultery, had he? But he *had* told her to 'sin no more'.

'Sin' was a horrid word, she thought. Hardly anyone outside church used it nowadays. And she was hoping to 'live in sin' – or almost. That was an old-fashioned expression too. 'Living in sin' was so common nowadays that it was no longer regarded as a 'sin' any more. In fact to use the word at all was almost 'politically incorrect'. She suddenly giggled. If you accused someone of 'living in sin', you could probably be accused of discrimination. She sobered. Her conscience told her that what she was going to do was wrong, but in spite of that she was determined to go ahead.

✤ ✤ ✤ ✤

"Hi. Mind if I sit here?"

Lorna glanced up from her coffee. "Feel free."

"I'm Will."

"Lorna."

"First year?"

"Yes. I'm very new. Feel a bit bewildered actually."

"What are you reading?"

"History of Art and Publishing. And you?"

"French and History of Art. I'm third year but it's a four-year course. I have to spend a year in France."

"That should be fun."

"Maybe."

There was a pause while they both sipped their coffee. Lorna scrabbled around in her mind for something to say. She didn't usually have any problems in that direction. She usually spoke before realising it would have been better to sort out her thoughts first. Tact was not a trait that one associated with Lorna. However, on this occasion she didn't want to put her clumsy foot where her mouth should be.

She rather liked the handsome young man opposite her and she didn't want to frighten him off as she'd sometimes done with others who'd shown an interest. As they became more interested in her, she relaxed and so did her unruly tongue. It was delighted to find no curb on it and ran merrily along, horrifying Lorna who was frequently mortified at what she heard herself say.

"Where do you …?"

"Are you going …?"

They both spoke at once and then laughed. He waved courteously at her. "You first."

"I was going to ask where your home was."

"I'm from Bristol. What about you?"

"I'm from Hazelford in Surrey. I'll probably go home most weekends as it's not far." Now why had she said that?

"Have you brothers and sisters?"

"Four sisters."

"My goodness."

"What about you?"

He shook his head. "My parents decided one of me was quite enough."

"I'm sorry."

"Don't be. I don't regret not having to share everything."

Chapter Four / 57

She wondered if he were joking but somehow she didn't think he was. She sipped her coffee. The noise in the student canteen increased as more students clattered in and demanded sustenance.

"Are you going home this weekend or do you fancy a club on Saturday?"

"What?"

"Would you like to go to a club on Saturday night?"

A club. She was sure her parents wouldn't approve. It sounded decadent somehow. The noise was too loud to request details but she quite liked him. If she didn't like it, she'd ask him to take her back to her lodgings. When she'd come up in the holidays, she'd been lucky enough to meet Tina whose flatmate had just got married so she'd been looking for a replacement for the rented two-bedroomed house on the outskirts of Hazelford. Lorna had moved in but saw little of Tina and she hadn't been out much since she'd arrived. She made up her mind.

"I'd love to go."

"I'll pick you up about nine. Have to go now. I've got a lecture. See you on Saturday. 'Bye." He stood up, started to walk away and turned back with a grin. "Forgot to ask where you live."

She gave him her address and watched him leave the room. Was it possible to fall in love at first sight? She thought she had. Her coffee was cold and the thought of allowing anything to approach her churned-up stomach made her feel sick. She could hardly wait for Saturday.

✤ ✤ ✤ ✤

"Eleanor, it's Chris."

"Hullo." Her heart did its customary somersault.

"How are you?"

"Fine. You?"

"Fine. I wondered if you'd like to come out for dinner tomorrow."

She hesitated. Did she really want to start up a relationship with Chris? Yes, of course she did, but Carol considered him her property. She felt as though she were being savaged by a particularly vicious dog. She desperately wanted to go out with

Chris. Every time she saw him, she turned to jelly. But how could she so hurt her oldest friend? And this was *not* the behaviour of a Christian.

"Well? Please say yes, Ellie. I can't wait to see you again."

"What about Carol?" She had to ask again.

"Carol's fine. We went out last night."

So he was two-timing her friend – and her. How could she possibly love someone like that? But she suspected that she did.

"You haven't told Carol about us, have you?"

"Of course not. I'll let her down gently."

"I think she suspects something."

"It's your imagination."

She sighed. Why did men bear such a striking resemblance to ostriches? She firmly bolted the door on her guilt. "Thank you. I'd love to come."

She tried to keep out of Carol's way for the rest of the day. But as she sat opposite Chris in the restaurant the next day, she forgot all about her friend. Her companion was amusing, witty and, she was sure, falling in love with her. She knew by now she was in love with him and scarcely noticed that her wine glass was always full although she was constantly sipping from it.

He drove her back to her flat and leapt out to open the door for her. She was glad of his arm to steady her as she climbed out; her legs seemed reluctant to respond to messages from her brain.

"Are you going to invite me in for a nightcap?"

She giggled. "Why not?" She fumbled for her key but he took it from her and opened the door.

"I'll make s–some coffee." She meandered into the kitchen and leant on the kitchen table. She felt decidedly odd. Surely she wasn't drunk. She'd drunk very little – hadn't she? But they'd finished a bottle of wine between them and he'd insisted she had a brandy with her coffee. Taking some deep breaths, she carefully filled the kettle. Some coffee would restore her.

As she set out the mugs on a tray and made the coffee, an overwhelming sense of depression suddenly descended upon her. The guilt she had locked away escaped and flooded over her. What *was* she doing? How could she deceive Carol in this way?

She must end it. Slightly unsteadily, she carried the tray into the lounge but as she tried to place it on the coffee-table, her legs finally rebelled and she collapsed on to the floor tipping the hot liquid over the carpet, the coffee-table and Chris' trousers.

"Oh, I'm sho … sh … shorry." The tears which had been threatening now cascaded down her cheeks and she covered her face with her hands and sobbed and sobbed.

"Ellie, Ellie, darling, don't." She felt his arm round her shoulders and her insides melted. Pulling her hands away from her face with his spare hand, he tilted her face towards him and bent his head to kiss her gently on the lips. Her eyes flew open and suddenly her arms were wound tightly round his neck. Gently lifting her up, he laid her down on the sofa. Then suddenly he was on top of her, breathing heavily and kissing her face and neck. She returned his kisses reflecting his passion. Her depression vanished. She thought of nothing but the man who was awakening her body in a way she had thought would never happen.

It was when she realised that her blouse had been unbuttoned and his hands had moved towards her breasts that her brain started to function again. Suddenly she was ice-cold sober. She tried to push him away and twisted her head away from him.

"Chris, no – please." She was gasping. She wanted him to continue his exploration but now her conscience was battering her.

"Ellie, you're lovely. You skin is so soft. Let me love you – please, Ellie."

"No." Her scream startled him and enabled her to push him away and sit up. She hurriedly pulled her blouse together as he rolled on to the floor. She almost giggled as she looked at him. He looked so ridiculous with his mouth open – like a little boy who'd been promised a sweet and then had it snatched away. Flustered, she started to rebutton her blouse with trembling fingers.

He regained control of himself and stood up. "I apologise. I got carried away."

"I'm sorry, Chris. But I don't – I won't – I …"

"You don't need to explain." His voice was cold.

"I didn't mean to lead you on," she said in a small voice.//
"But you did."

"Yes," she whispered. "But it would have been wrong. I'm a Christian. I want to save myself for my husband." Goodness, how pompous she sounded.

"I'd better go before I upset you any more."

He was out of the door before she'd even finishing buttoning her blouse. She lay back and shut her eyes. It felt as though a liquidiser was whirling around in her head. How could she have let things go so far? He'd probably drop her after this. And she was no longer sure how she felt about him. Was it possible to fall out of love as quickly as one fell into it. She tried to stand up but groaned and fell back. She couldn't solve any problems tonight. Perhaps things would become clearer in the morning.

But the next day her thoughts were still in turmoil. She was relieved that Carol had phoned in to say she was unwell. She tried not to think of the reason for her friend's "sickness". She was kept busy all day as the list of operations was exceptionally long. As she handed the surgeon the appropriate instruments, she was aware of a pair of blue eyes above a surgical mask glancing at her occasionally. Was she imagining it or was there sympathy in his gaze? She felt uncomfortable and hoped he would attribute any redness in her cheeks to the heat of the operating theatre.

Her head felt as though an army of dwarfs was playing bowls inside it and at any moment a large bowl would burst out of her skull. She found it difficult to concentrate but David Baines seemed remarkably patient. Perhaps she'd been wrong about him. She was relieved when the last patient had been wheeled away and she could escape to the staff room for a much needed cup of tea. She was alone and was just savouring the taste of the welcome brew when a familiar voice said, "May I join you?"

Startled, she jerked the cup and some hot tea trickled over her hand.

"Here." The surgeon handed her a towel.

"Thanks. You startled me."

Chapter Four / 61

"I'm sorry. I wondered if you'd like to come out for a drink. You look as though you could do with something stronger than tea."

He looked quite at home in this usually feminine stronghold as he poured himself a cup of tea. She surveyed him; he had *asked* her this time.

"I've got a bad headache," she informed him, aware that it sounded as though she craved sympathy.

"I thought you weren't your usual self today. Perhaps alcohol isn't a good idea. You could always have orange juice."

She shut her eyes. She was too tired to make decisions. On this occasion she would have been quite happy for him to make it for her but he showed no intention of doing so. He sipped his tea in companionable silence and waited for her answer. Why not go? She'd probably turned Chris completely against her and she wasn't even sure now if she cared. Perhaps some more alcohol would counteract the result of the previous evening's carousing. She made up her mind.

"All right, I'll come. But I'm not dressed." She knew she sounded ungracious.

He grinned. "You look very smart but I wasn't suggesting taking out a theatre nurse still wearing her cap."

"Oh dear." She snatched it off pulling out the pins that held her hair in the formal bun she wore for work. Dark ringlets cascaded untidily over her shoulders. She glanced at him. His blue eyes were twinkling with amusement.

"How about if I give you half an hour to change and then meet you at the main door of the hospital?"

"All right."

After he'd left, she stood in the middle of the room, feeling bemused. Then she hurtled across to her flat. The sun still shone from a blue sky and promised a beautiful evening. Hurriedly she showered, pulled out her entire wardrobe and then put on the first dress she had pulled out. Pink and white cotton, it matched her flushed cheeks. He was already waiting when she hurried up, out of breath.

"There's no need to rush," he said, amused.

"I know," she gasped. "It's just that I hate being late and keeping people waiting."

The Fox and Pelican was crowded. David steered Eleanor to a seat in the corner. She wrinkled her nose. Why didn't pubs have non-smoking areas?

"What will you have?"

"Dubonnet and lemonade please. It doesn't have such a devastating effect on me as gin and tonic."

"Do you want a sandwich? You haven't eaten all day."

She shook her head. "I'll eat later. But some roasted peanuts would be nice."

"Coming up."

He disappeared and she surreptitiously abstracted her mirror from her handbag. It showed her that she *had* remembered to put some lipstick on and that none of it had seeped onto her teeth. Snapping her mirror shut, she looked around her. It was a favourite haunt of medical staff from the hospital so she was not surprised to see a number of faces she recognised.

"Hullo, Sister. Don't often see you in here." Anne appeared before her, balancing a tray of drinks. Eleanor nodded and smiled. She decided against competing against the volume of sound and hoped Anne would take the hint and not notice her incriminating blush.

"Here you are. Hullo, Anne." David deposited her drink in front of her and Anne's eyes opened wide. No doubt news of her "date" would be all round the hospital by tomorrow, Eleanor reflected. She glared at Anne's back as her colleague wove her way across to a table containing a gaggle of nurses. She wished she hadn't come. It was too noisy to talk and she didn't want alcohol. Why on earth hadn't she asked for an orange juice as David apparently had? He'd collected a sandwich as well. She wondered whether he cooked for himself or usually ate out.

"Don't you drink?" she asked, surprised.

"Very rarely. I don't like the taste."

"Oh." She sipped her drink thoughtfully.

"It's a bit noisy, isn't it?"

"Mm."

Chapter Four / 63

"I didn't realise it would be so crowded. I don't usually come in here. Shall we go somewhere else?"

"Oh no, this is fine." She took another gulp of her drink. She blushed again as she felt his eyes on her. Her heart started to beat faster and she said quickly, "Do you have a long list tomorrow?"

He shook his head. "I'm not working here tomorrow. I'm going to St Lukes. I operate there as well."

"You're very good," she said shyly.

"Thank you. You're very competent, too. I know I can rely on you."

She smiled. "I enjoy theatre work."

"What else have you done?"

"I worked for six months in Intensive Care. I found that quite difficult. I preferred my stint in A and E."

"You obviously like to be busy. But I didn't ask you out to talk shop. I wanted to find out more about you but I don't want to shout."

"The noise does seem to be getting louder. Why don't they turn the music down?"

"Would you like to find somewhere quieter for a meal?"

She shook her head. "I wouldn't be very good company tonight. I'll go home and have an early night."

"Perhaps another time then."

She hesitated. He certainly improved on acquaintance. She made up her mind. "Thank you. That would be nice."

"Give me your number and I'll give you a ring. Have you got a pen? I left mine in my jacket."

"I think so." Eleanor opened her handbag and rummaged in it. "I haven't got anything to write on."

"Write it on the beer mat." He pushed it across to her.

"I'll give you my parents' number too. I'm often there at weekends." She scribbled on the mat and he put it in his shirt pocket.

"Would you like another drink?"

She glanced at her watch. "No thank you. I must be going."

"I'll walk you back."

"Thanks."

✣ ✣ ✣ ✣

"You're really sure about this, Peter?"

"Jenny, don't keep asking me. I've said I'll see Dr Reynolds with you and we'll take it from there. Please don't keep nagging me."

"I'm not nagging," said Jenny, hurt. "I just want it to be a joint decision."

"Well it is. So if you're ready, we can go." He picked up his keys from the hall table and Jenny followed him out of the house. She felt as if she were in a dream. Was this really happening? Had Peter really agreed to think about IVF? She watched him set the burglar alarm and double lock the front door and then walked down the drive to wait for him to retrieve the car from the garage.

She shivered although she wasn't cold. It was a bright October day but the sharpness of autumn was in the air. She was excited but she knew she mustn't expect too much. It might not work. If the treatment using her eggs and Peter's sperm wasn't successful, she, like her husband, had no intention of using a donor. Desperate she might be but there *were* limits and the thought of another man's sperm being implanted in her womb made her squirm. Peter had agreed to try this method only on condition that *his* sperm was to be used. She'd been quite hurt when she realised he thought she might consider a donor.

Sliding into the passenger seat, she clasped her hands together. Both she and Peter now had some idea of what was involved but they would have to convince Dr Reynolds that IVF was the right choice for them.

The waiting room was crowded with a variety of patients. Two toddlers were engrossed in emptying the toy box and strewing the contents all over the floor. Jenny looked longingly at them. Would she, one day, bring her offspring to the surgery? Opposite her, a young mother cradled and rocked her crying baby and Jenny yearned to hold the tiny body in her arms.

She felt an arm nudge her and moved closer to Peter. But the movement had been deliberate and she was being addressed in a voice intended to be quiet but carrying round the room.

"Would you like to see the pictures of me little granddaughter? Do look. Ain't she cute?" A photo of a tiny red-faced infant was thrust under her nose. "I only got the pictures this morning. I 'ad

Chapter Four / 65

to show them to someone. You don't mind, do you, dear? That was taken soon after she was born. Oh do look at this one with her proud mum. Can see the likeness, can't you? At least I can. And this is the latest. She's just a month old now. I'm going down to see them next week. I can't wait. You got any kids, dear?"

Jenny felt as though she were suffocating. She didn't even want to look at her questioner. She felt as though the whole room was waiting for her answer. Even the baby had stopped crying. Why had *she* been this awful woman's victim? Slowly she turned to look at a plump, motherly woman who was just starting to show signs of embarrassment.

"No," she said, enunciating clearly because her lips felt like blobs of plasticine. "I don't have any children and I am not interested in seeing pictures of your grandchild. Please leave me alone."

She watched the woman's mouth drop open as a mottled flush spread slowly over the friendly face. Her tormentor turned away in a huff. "Sorry, I'm sure. I won't say another word."

"Good," muttered Jenny who was already regretting her rudeness but couldn't face explaining why she had been so impolite. The embarrassment was broken by the ping of the bell and, hopefully, she looked up. But it was the blue light for the practice nurse. The young woman with the baby hung up her blue disc and disappeared through the door. The last red disc bore the number five.

"What number are we?" whispered Jenny.

Peter glanced at the disc the receptionist had handed him. "Eight."

Jenny glanced at her watch. "Our appointment was for ten-thirty. It's a quarter to eleven now."

He put his hand over her restless fingers where were lacing and unlacing themselves.

"We're not in a hurry, are we? I haven't got to work today and you're on half-term."

"I know. It's just that I want to get it over with. I'm so nervous, Peter."

"There's nothing to be nervous about, dear. We're just going to talk to him." He squeezed her hand. "Shall we find somewhere nice for lunch afterwards? It's a lovely day."

"Oh Peter, I can't think beyond our appointment." She withdrew her hand and continued to link and unlink her fingers.

He picked up a magazine from a table in the middle of the room and flicked over the pages. But he couldn't concentrate either. He was too aware of his wife's nervousness.

It was another half hour before patient number seven red disappeared through the door. His appointment was short and Jenny's heart lurched as the pinger at last sounded for them. Hurriedly she got up, dropping her handbag and spewing out some of its contents. She looked down, bewildered. Why on earth hadn't she fastened it?

Peter swept up her make-up bag, a packet of tissues and purse and bundled them back into the black bag firmly zipping it up before returning it to its owner. The bell pinged again.

"Oh dear." Jenny, flustered, pushed opened the door and almost ran down the corridor to the door marked "Dr Reynolds". Peter followed more slowly.

"Jenny, my dear, how are you? And Peter. Do sit down." He drew forward another chair for Peter and beamed at them over the top of his spectacles. "Now what can I do for you?"

Jenny cast a terrified glance at Peter. Now that the moment had come, she couldn't think of what to say. The doctor waited calmly. She had known him all her life and he was a family friend but all her rehearsed speeches had gone walkabout and her mind was a void.

Peter cleared his throat. "As you know we – er – we've been trying to start a family for some time now but we – er – can't seem to manage it so we wondered …"

"I want to try IVF treatment," Jenny burst out. "I've been reading about it and I think it might work."

"And you, Peter?" Dr Reynolds picked up a pen and made some notes. Peter's mouth had tightened at Jenny's use of the singular pronoun.

"Yes. I agree." He was short.

Chapter Four / 67

"How old are you, Jenny?"

"Twenty-six."

"That's quite a good age to try. Now let's see …" He turned to the computer on his desk and typed in some words. It seemed an age to Jenny before the screen buzzed into life but it was at an angle and she couldn't read it. "We've done all the standard tests, haven't we? You know you have a low sperm count, Peter?"

"Yes. Would that make a difference?"

"Not necessarily."

"We've thought about it," said Jenny eagerly. "And we want to go ahead with it."

Dr Reynolds turned to them. He leaned back in his chair and surveyed them kindly. "It's not as simple as that, my dear. IVF is not suitable for everyone. And it *is* expensive." He put the tips of his fingers together and looked straight at Peter. "Would that be a problem?"

"Probably not but can't we get it on the NHS?"

"There is very little funding for this from the NHS today. And even if there were, you still have to pay for the drugs and some of the tests. It doesn't come cheap."

"We're not poor. I'm sure we can manage."

"How much do you know about it?"

"I wrote to the Human Fertilisation and Embryology Authority and they sent me a packet of stuff. We've both looked at it, haven't we, Peter?"

He nodded.

"Did you receive a list of clinics offering IVF?"

"Yes. There's one in Hazelford, isn't there? I wrote for information from them and they were very helpful." She looked hopefully at the doctor. "So we can try it, can't we?"

"I don't see why not. But you must be patient. I'll write to the consultant but it may be some time before you get an appointment."

"Even if we go privately?"

"I'm afraid so." He turned back to the screen. "Now I've got some details about you both but I need to ask you some questions.

Do either of you smoke?" They both shook their heads. "What about drink?"

Jenny laughed. "We're not teetotallers; we only drink socially."

"How much?"

"We usually have a drink before dinner and some wine with the meal."

"It might be better for you to cut down a little, Jenny."

"I'll stop altogether if necessary."

"Perhaps later. Have either of you ever used drugs?"

"No!" exclaimed Jenny, horrified.

"Peter?"

He was finding something very interesting on the floor. He didn't look up. "When I was at university, I tried cannabis – only once."

Jenny went cold. He had never told her. But why should he? Had this contributed to their infertility? Questions and answers tumbled over themselves in her mind trying to find a match. It took her a while to realise that Dr Reynolds seemed unconcerned and was asking another question. His eyes were on the screen.

"Sorry," she murmured. "What did you say?"

"I asked if either of you have ever had any other partners."

"No." Jenny's reply was prompt but once again Peter was slower. She glared at him. He was looking embarrassed.

"Years ago, I had a relationship with a girl. It – it only lasted a few weeks."

"You never told me." Jenny was outraged.

"It didn't seem relevant."

"The girl didn't become pregnant?" the doctor queried. Peter shook his head. "Jenny, you've never had a miscarriage, have you?"

Tears flooded her eyes. "No," she whispered. There was a pause while the doctor inserted the information into the machine. She wondered if he was giving them time to recover. She felt as though she'd been punched. What else had Peter not told her?"

Chapter Four / 69

Eventually the doctor deserted the screen and leaned back, his hand together in their customary pose. "So you'd like to try IVF?"

"Yes."

"Very well. I'll write to Mr Coombes and the clinic will be in touch with you about an appointment. But it may take some time. One last thing. It might be an idea to keep a diary of your periods and also make a note of when you have sex. The consultant might find that useful."

✤ ✤ ✤ ✤

Lorna stared at the clothes she'd laid out on her bed. Would she be dressed suitably for her first visit to a night club. She pulled on the stretched lycra cropped top that Tina, her flat mate, had lent her and stepped into her short black leather skirt. Easing it over her slim hips, she zipped it up and turned to gaze critically at herself in the mirror.

The turquoise top suited her but was it too low? Was she showing too much of her cleavage – what there was of it? Tina had assured her that most of the girls would be showing more flesh than usual but she would feel uncomfortable. She stepped into her high-heeled black sandals and took a few tentative steps. It was the first time she'd worn them and they'd cost more than she could really afford. She wondered if she'd be able to dance without falling over. She experimented. If she moved her body more than her feet, she should manage it.

Sitting down at the dressing-table, she applied her make up and painted red varnish on her nails. After they'd dried, she swept up her long fair hair and pinned it on top of her head. She thought she looked very sophisticated. She hoped her hair wouldn't collapse if the dancing was too energetic.

Will was prompt and she looked hopefully for a car but there was no sign of one. She dragged on her black jacket and shut the door behind her.

"You don't mind walking, do you?" he queried. "It's not far."

"Of course not," she lied, teetering down the street on her high heels. She wished he'd slow down. She was having trouble keeping up with him. He eventually realised she was about five steps behind him and waited for her to catch up.

"Sorry," he grinned.

"It's OK. You're not wearing heels. I don't want to twist my ankle before I get there!"

"Here, take my arm. I don't want to have to carry you home."

She giggled as she slipped her hand into the crook of his arm. She could feel his warmth though his jacket. It sent electric shock waves through her body. She knew it was going to be a night to remember. She had never felt like this about anyone before. They walked down the main street. Most of the shops were shut but their windows still blazed with light.

"Here we are." She glanced up at the flashing lights. The Oyster Shell. Strange name, she thought. She associated oysters with pearls but then remembered that they were also supposed to be an aphrodisiac. Will had gone ahead of her down the narrow steps so she was glad he couldn't see her blushes.

The music blaring out made her heart beat faster and when they reached the floor, she could feel the beat through her high-heeled sandals. She tapped her foot as Will paid their five pounds entrance fee.

"Where's the band?" she asked as they wove their way across the floor around gyrating bodies.

"What?"

"Where's the band?" She raised her voice. Carrying on a conversation was obviously a non-starter.

He shook his head and took her hand. She was grateful, as she was beginning to feel very disorientated; the loud music, the flashing lights, the mass of bodies and the heat all combined to make her feel sick. For a moment she wished she hadn't come. It seemed an age before Will deposited her on one of the few chairs to be found. Most of those who weren't dancing were propping up the walls and the bar or standing around in groups. Hardly anyone was sitting down but Lorna was glad to. She removed her jacket and gave it to Will who jerked his head towards a sign that said "Cloakroom" and disappeared. For a moment she panicked at being left alone. Then she saw him emerge from the cloakroom

Chapter Four / 71

and head for the bar. She wondered what he'd get her to drink. He hadn't asked her what she wanted but he wouldn't have heard the answer. Her head was starting to throb and she closed her eyes. That was a mistake as she felt her head starting to spin. Opening them, she took some deep breaths. That was better. Will had disappeared into the crowd surrounding the bar and she looked around her.

Tina was right about the dress code. Most of the girls had tops that barely covered their essentials. Sparkling nostrils indicated pierced noses and some were even exposing pierced belly buttons with a variety of decorations. Leather was popular and Lorna's eyes became riveted to one girl wearing a very tight vivid pink top over a matching short leather skirt. As she twisted and turned Lorna thought she looked like a very shapely sausage about to burst out of its skin. Most of the men, like Will, were wearing trousers and shirts. They were not as decorative as the girls although some sported earrings and nose rings.

"I've got you a Bacardie and Coke." Will emerged through the crowd and shouted in her ear.

"Thanks," she mouthed as she took a sip.

She could taste the coke but there was another taste overlying it. It was smooth – like velvet. She liked it but was determined to make it last. She had no intention of getting drunk. Naive she might be but she wasn't stupid.

"Like to dance?" Will stood up and held out his hand and she followed him onto the dance floor. He let go of her and soon they had joined the mass of whirling, jumping, twisting, gyrating bodies. Lorna found it stimulating. The beat she could still feel through the floor gradually insinuated itself into the rest of her body. She could feel her hair pins dropping on the floor but she didn't care. She laughed and tossed her hair as it descended to her shoulders. Will grinned at her and gave her a thumbs up sign. She hoped no one would slip on the hairpins and do themselves an injury but the bodies were so tightly packed there was no room to stoop and pick them up.

Breathless, at last, she indicated to Will that she wanted to return to her much-needed drink. He nodded and they wove their way back. Collapsing on the chair, she gulped down the rest of her drink and then wished she hadn't. She stood up, swaying slightly and Will put out his hand to steady her before she headed for the nearby Ladies sign.

Opening the door to the Ladies, she retched. The smell of vomit was overpowering and she tried to hold her breath. In front of her a girl was hunched over a toilet with the door wide open. She seemed to be regurgitating the entire contents of her stomach if not her whole body. Lorna averted her eyes from the sickly mess that had spilled over onto the floor.

She headed for the door farthest away from the sufferer and afterwards stayed only to wash her hands perfunctorily before rushing out of the door and taking some deep breaths of vomit-free air.

"I'll *never* get in that state," she vowed to herself. "It was revolting."

When she returned to her chair, Will put his mouth close to her ear and yelled, "Would you like to go upstairs? It's quieter up there."

She nodded. Her eyes were starting to sting. Although there were not many people smoking, those who were, seemed to be chain-smoking and one of these couples was standing near them. They squeezed past the crowd to the spiral staircase and ascended to the upper floor. The music was not so loud and it was more spacious. There was also not so much smoke in the air. She looked at the tall tables with high stools around them as well as chairs around the outside.

"Would you like another drink?" Will still had to raise his voice but at least the decibels were considerably lower than they had been downstairs.

"Just a coke please." She wasn't going to descend to the depths of the girl she'd recently seen. Already the Bacardie had gone to her head. It had obviously been stronger than she'd thought.

The rest of the evening she enjoyed. Upstairs there was only a small dance floor. As the evening wore on, the music became slower and they danced together. She felt light-headed and safe as he held her tightly. She rested her head on his shoulder and shut her eyes. She wanted the evening to go on for ever. This was love, she was sure. She hoped he felt the same but where it would lead, she had no idea. She would live for the moment only.

She was surprised when it was time to leave as the club was closing. She had really enjoyed herself and felt dreamy until they stepped outside. The chill air of winter was nudging away the autumnal balm. She shivered and Will put his arm round her and she snuggled up to him as they walked up the street.

"Can I come in for a nightcap?" he asked as they stopped outside her door.

Lorna looked at him. His fair hair gleamed under the street light and she was sure her eyes were shining but she was high on excitement and love, not drugs. She wanted desperately to invite him in but her irritating conscience *would* get in the way and remind her of the dangers. They had both drunk more than they should have done and she didn't want to spoil their relationship before it had even started properly.

"I don't think that's a good idea, Will. I've had a lovely evening but it's late and I have to get up early tomorrow."

"But it's Sunday," he objected. "No one gets up early on Sundays."

"I have to go to church and I'm going to lunch with my parents."

Oh dear! She hadn't meant to say that. Why did she never think before she spoke? She struggled to redeem herself in his eyes.

"My parents always go so I usually go with them if I have lunch there."

He still looked bemused. She wasn't surprised. Was he having difficulty reconciling the Lorna he'd just taken to a night club with the dutiful daughter who went to church with her parents? She hoped she hadn't put him off. *Why* didn't she learn to guard her tongue? If she wasn't upsetting other people, she was making difficulties for herself.

She shivered suddenly. "I'd better go in." She lifted her face. Surely he'd kiss her or did he feel she might "contaminate" him with her "religion".

Suddenly he smiled down at her. "You're a strange girl, Lorna Bradley," he said. "I'm glad we went out. I had a great time. We must do it again."

"Oh yes," she whispered as he bent his head and she felt his lips on hers. Her insides started swimming around out of control as she responded, clutching her arms round his neck.

"Let me come in Lorna. Just for a moment. I can't kiss you properly out here." He nibbled her ear and little shafts of pleasure trickled down her neck. She started to weaken but then memories of her upbringing started to form an invisible barrier. She shook her head.

"No. I can't, Will." She hurriedly detached herself and fumbled for her key. She must get inside before she changed her mind. She looked back before she closed the door. He was already walking down the road. Would he ask her out again or had she wrecked her chances?

❖ ❖ ❖ ❖

"There's still nothing from the clinic. Do you think he forgot to write to them? Or perhaps the letter got lost in the post. Do you think I should phone them to ask if they got it?"

It was Saturday morning and Peter lowered the paper to look at his wife. "Jenny, it's less than two weeks since we saw the doctor. Give them a chance. Leave it for another couple of weeks."

"But that will be a month."

"It'll give you time to have a period, then, won't it? Dr Reynolds did tell you to keep a record."

"I've had it. You know I have," said Jenny sulkily.

"Well, keep a note of how long it lasted and remember to put down that we had sex last night."

"Are you thinking of changing your job?" asked Jenny sarcastically. "Of course I've kept a record. Oh there's the post now."

She rushed out but returned a few moments later. "Nothing but bills." She threw them on the table before sitting down and pouring herself another cup of coffee. "I hate waiting."

Chapter Four / 75

"I know patience isn't one of your virtues but you'll just have to try to learn some, my dear."

She grimaced at the back page of the paper that hid his face. She knew her failings. She didn't need to be reminded of them.

✤ ✤ ✤ ✤

Melanie sat in the small rocking-chair she had brought from Highfield and glared at the television. The nine o'clock news had just come on but she wasn't watching it. Thoughts were churning round in her mind like clothes in a washing machine. How she wished she could take them out, iron them and fold them neatly away. Her brain definitely needed ironing. It was so creased she wondered if it would ever be smooth again.

Sighing, she shut her eyes and let the newscaster's words wash over her. There had been another earthquake in Turkey and war was simmering again in the Balkans. Nothing changed, she thought. "There shall be wars and rumours of wars". Unbidden, the Biblical quotation jumped into her mind. Perhaps they *were* nearing the end of the age. How close was the final battle of Armageddon? Her eyes snapped open. Why add yet more mess to the turmoil that was in her mind?

She was bored. She'd thought it would be so wonderful to have a flat of her own where Simon could come to visit her every day. She knew now she'd been living in a dream world. Soon after she'd moved into the flat, she'd invited her employer for a meal to thank him for his help. But she'd had an ulterior motive; having plied him with wine and brandy, it wasn't difficult to persuade him that he was in no fit state to drive home. She knew his wife had taken the children away so there was no one waiting for him. Then in the cosy after dinner atmosphere, one thing led to another and he ended up in her bed. In the morning he'd left before she'd woken up but she hadn't felt at all guilty. Since then, his visits had been rare and he'd refused to take her out "in case anyone sees us". Melanie had been furious. She didn't want him to hide her away. She wanted him to flaunt her. Why shouldn't the whole world know she was his mistress?

But she wanted more than that. She had hoped they would become closer and she could prise him away from Joy. She hated that clinging little doll. It was becoming very hard to be civil when Simon's wife made one of her rare visits to the office. She was so smug and Melanie felt Joy was patronising her. She was sure Joy didn't know her husband was being unfaithful. Switching off the television, she sat, thinking. Perhaps she should drop a hint. If Joy knew, things might come to a head. But would Simon ever leave his family for her? The negative answer she pushed as far away from her as she could. She was obsessed with her employer. Eleanor's words about ruining four lives bowled into her mind but she viciously batted them away to join all the other unwelcome thoughts on the boundary.

She hadn't visited her parents for months. Her mother phoned her every week but their conversation was stilted. She knew Dorothy suspected her daughter had problems but assumed they were work related. She glanced at her watch. It was nearly half-past ten and Simon had not visited her. Dragging herself out of her chair, she crossed to the window. A watery moon tried to smile from a dark star-encrusted sky. The world looked so still and peaceful but her thoughts were too tangled to straighten out at the moment. She would go to bed and hope her subconscious mind would provide some answers in the morning.

It was the end of October and the following morning produced another bright clear day. Melanie had not slept well and the beautiful day did not at all suit her mood. But she had at least made one decision. She would speak to Simon and persuade him to visit her that evening. She would prepare a special meal and prove how essential she was to him. She knew his business wouldn't be so successful without her. It was she who often suggested he took risks with new authors and some of them were doing well. She was far more use to him than his wife who only proofread. She wondered how he would manage without her when she started her new job.

She dressed more carefully than usual but was aware that in an elegance contest she could never hope to compete with chic Joy who always looked as though she'd just left a beauty salon. Perhaps she should do something about her appearance. She wasn't bad looking but she had never been interested in clothes. However, she had made an effort when she first realised Simon

Chapter Four / 77

was interested in her. She'd even invested in contact lenses but she wasn't very happy with them.

The following day she reached the office before Simon and after making herself the inevitable cup of coffee, she sat down to sort through the day's post. She frowned over one letter. It was from Hilda Bowen, a writer who'd been with Simon since he set up on his own. She was a delightful lady in her fifties. Thoroughly professional, she always kept to deadlines and listened to advice. It was unlike her to complain about anything. The letter was polite but Hilda was "disturbed" that she had not yet received the proof copy of her latest book which had been due at least four weeks previously.

Where was it? Switching on the computer, Melanie keyed in her password and brought up Hilda's file. The typescript had been given to Joy six weeks ago. What *had* she been doing? Proofreaders usually had two weeks to return the work to the publisher who then sent the corrected copy to the author for a final check. Melanie was surprised Hilda had not been in touch before.

She would have to phone Joy. Stretching out her hand to the phone, she realised that, after her mental debate of the previous night, she didn't want to talk to Simon's wife. If she did, she might say something she would regret. Upsetting Joy would not be a good move. Simon wouldn't like it. If anything was to be said to Joy, *he* would have to say it. Trying to blot out her personal feelings, she picked up the phone but before she could dial, Simon burst in.

"Sorry I'm late, Mel. The traffic was diabolical this morning. There was an accident in the high street so that didn't help."

"We've got a problem. I was just going to phone Joy but I think it would be better if you did it."

"What's the matter?"

"Hilda Bowen hasn't had her proof copy. Joy's had it for six weeks. Do you think she's lost it?"

He glared at her. "Don't be ridiculous. Joy's very conscientious."

"I know she is usually but this time she's boobed."

"There's probably a rational explanation."

"There'd better be. We don't want to upset Hilda, do we?"

He sat down at his desk and dialled his home. "There's no answer. She's probably not back from taking the kids to school. I'll phone later. How about some coffee?"

It would be nice, she thought sourly, if just occasionally he would make his own coffee or even make some for her. By the time she'd made it, Joy had obviously returned home and he was in the middle of an acrimonious conversation. "Well find it, for goodness' sake. What's the matter with you, woman? Hilda's one of our best clients and I don't want to lose her. Oh do stop crying. You know how I hate it. Ring me when you've found it."

Melanie smiled sweetly as she deposited his coffee – milk and two sugars – on his desk. She wasn't averse to her boss falling out with his wife. But his scowling face didn't encourage questions about his non appearance the previous evening. She returned to her place and there was silence. She kept glancing surreptitiously at him. Finally she caught his glance and hastily looked away. She could feel a blush starting to stain her neck. She hated blushing. Eleanor did it all the time and it made her look even prettier. *She* looked like a ripe tomato past its sell-by date! She turned her head away.

"What on earth's the matter, Mel? You look as if you've lost a diamond and found a piece of glass." He glared at her.

"How poetic." She didn't want to have a row with him but she was terrified that he was losing interest in her. "You didn't come round last night."

"Joy had prepared a special meal for the kids. I couldn't leave them, could I?"

"They always come first, don't they? Your precious wife and kids. What about me?" To her horror she realised she was shouting. She shouldn't have said that. Clapping her hand over her mouth, she stared at him with round eyes. He stared back but she couldn't read the expression in his eyes.

She'd often wondered what "a pregnant pause" would feel like. Now she knew but perhaps the expression was not very appropriate. The pause degenerated into misery and Melanie shut

Chapter Four / 79

her eyes to imprison the threatening tears. She had made a ghastly mistake. Hot needles of fear were about to force her over the precipice of despair. She couldn't move.

"It's all right, Melanie." She felt his hands on her shoulders and shuddered. Her eyes flew open releasing the trickle of tears. He drew her up into his arms. She sobbed and buried her face in his shoulder.

"I'm sorry. I shouldn't have said that."

"No, you shouldn't. You must understand I can never leave Joy. I love her."

"Don't you love me?" Her voice was a muffled plea.

"You know I do. But in a different way."

"So I'll have to settle for second best."

He released her abruptly and she collapsed onto her chair. He towered over her. "Is that how you see it?"

"No, I ... no, of course not." But it *was* second best. She knew Simon would never leave Joy and her conscience, prompted by her Christian upbringing, was shouting at her to leave him alone. But she couldn't. She was obsessed with him. She gazed adoringly up at him. "I love you, Simon. I don't want to lose you. I – I'd rather share you than not have you at all." He looked uncomfortable and she tried to return to normality. "Please come round tonight."

He hesitated. "I'll see if I can get away."

"Please do." She stood up and putting her arms round him, lifted her face. His arms tightened round her and he bent his face to kiss her.

The door burst open. "Simon, I've found ... Oh!" Joy stopped in the doorway.

As Joy stared at the guilty couple, it seemed to Melanie that everything went into slow motion. Simon released her but every muscle seemed to have petrified; she couldn't shut her mouth, her legs were numb and her eyes gazed, horrified, at Simon's wife. She had so often dreamed of Joy finding out about their affair. But not like this. Her legs started to tingle; they felt like spaghetti suddenly plunged into boiling water as she collapsed onto her chair still unable to drag her eyes away from Joy.

"It's not what you think," Simon croaked. But Joy wasn't listening. Dropping the envelope she held, she hurtled out of the door. "Joy, please – listen to me."

Galvanised into action, he rushed after her and through the glass wall that was now enshrouding her, Melanie heard his footsteps clattering down the stairs as he tried to catch up with his wife. She started to shake and her teeth rattled against each other. The hot needles had been replaced with icy fingers probing into every part of her body. Nothing would ever be the same again. Her mind was blank. She couldn't concentrate. Black thoughts, like mud, oozed into her mind. She wondered how Simon would explain to his wife that being wrapped cosily around his assistant at ten o'clock in the morning really meant nothing.

If she were a "nice girl" and followed the prompting of her conscience, she would pack her things and leave the office so that she caused no more upheavals in the Rawlins household. But she decided she wasn't at all "nice". She was totally selfish and all she wanted was Simon. She hoped Joy would go away and take her children with her, leaving the field clear.

Chapter Five

"More wine?" Will held the bottle poised over Lorna's glass.

She giggled. "You're trying to get me drunk."

"Why not?"

"You know why not. All right. Just a bit."

"You can't have a 'bit' of wine. It has to be a 'drop'."

"Sorry." She leaned back in the armchair resting her head on the back and curling her legs up under her.

"You've got nice legs," he remarked appreciatively.

"Thanks."

They'd been out again to The Oyster Shell and Will had insisted on buying a bottle of wine on the way home. Reaching her door, Lorna felt she had to ask him in for the first time. It was Friday night and for once she was up to date with her work so could have a lie-in the following day. She was sure he'd calculated that she would be unable to refuse him on this occasion. But she was determined that it was only the entrance to her house she was offering – not her bed. She hoped she'd be strong enough to refuse because she was sure that was where he intended the evening to end. She was beginning to feel light headed and her glass of wine and Will seemed to be a long way from her. She leant forward to take a sip of wine and then thought better of it. She pushed it away.

"I think I've had enough. I'm starting to feel squiffy."

"What a lovely word. But it doesn't matter, does it? You haven't got to drive anywhere."

She giggled again. "Nor have you." She was immediately annoyed with herself. Now she'd given him the opening she was sure he'd been waiting for. He took it.

"No. I haven't. I needn't even *walk* anywhere, need I?"

She swung her feet down and pulled her short skirt down towards her knees. "I don't know what you mean."

"Yes, you do. Come on, darling. Be nice to Will." He came over and sat on the arm of her chair. She felt his hand caressing her neck and she gave a wriggle of pleasure. Slowly his hand slipped down further and reached her breast. She didn't want him to stop. She twisted her head to find his lips.

Suddenly he released her and stood up leaving her briefly bereft. "What is it?" she whispered.

He took hold of her hands. "It's not very comfortable here. Let's find somewhere else. Where's your bedroom?" He pulled her up to stand facing him. Suddenly he was a stranger who had doused her in cold water.

She wrenched her hands away. "No."

"Oh come on, Lorna. You know you want it. All girls do."

She glared at him. "I'm not 'all girls' and even if I did 'want it', I won't do it. It's wrong."

"Little Miss Goody Two Shoes, aren't you? I suppose that's what they teach you at church. Well that's all out of date now. No one's a virgin when they get married any more."

His arrogance infuriated her and she hit back. "And you'd know, of course. That's all you want, isn't it? Well you're not getting it here."

His eyes pinned her rigid. She couldn't move, only stare at his eyes now smouldering with anger. "If that's how you want it, it's up to you. There are plenty of others who'll be only too happy to oblige."

Chapter Five / 83

She remained immobile as she watched him leave and heard the front door slam. Then she collapsed on the floor shivering and sobbing.

✤ ✤ ✤ ✤

Melanie glanced surreptitiously at Simon. He hadn't been to see her since Joy had discovered them kissing. He was polite to her but they hadn't really talked. She decided to leap in where even an angel might have had second thoughts. She wasn't going to give him up without a fight.

"Simon."

"Mm." His eyes were still fixed on the screen and he was frowning.

"I think we should talk."

"Oh not now, Mel. I'm busy."

"When then?"

"I don't think we have anything to say to each other, do we?"

Melanie felt her blood pressure rising. "Oh I think we do, Simon. We can't just leave it there. I know Joy saw us but …"

"I've explained it to her. Nothing happened. You were upset."

She stared at him. She couldn't believe what she'd just heard. How could he be so cruel?

"How can you say such a thing? You know we've slept together. You helped me find a flat so you could visit and …"

"It's over, Mel. We can't go back. I always told you I'd never leave Joy. I meant it."

"But she might leave you." Suddenly Melanie didn't care what she said. If he hurt her, she would retaliate and hurt him in the only way she could. He didn't react to her words and this made her even angrier. "Don't you understand? I love you more than she can possibly do."

"You're talking nonsense, Melanie. Just forget it, will you? I've told you it's over."

"Oh no, it isn't!" she snarled. "I won't let you go."

"You're going to have to. I'm going out. I'll leave you to calm down."

When he had gone, she sat down at her desk. Her brain was busy and she was breathing deeply. Anger was still driving her and fighting with her conscience. She felt as though a battle between good and evil were taking place inside her. Her conscience was directing her away from Simon but her evil angel was pulling her towards a road from which there would be no turning back without disaster. Pulling a sheet of paper towards her, she started to write.

> Dear Joy,
> I know Simon has told you nothing has happened between us but he is lying. Our affair has been going on since September. I moved from home to a flat which he helped me find so he could visit me in the evenings. Didn't you wonder why he was 'working late' so often?
> He still loves me, you know. Why don't you leave him alone? You know you can't make him happy.

She chewed the end of her pen. Had she said enough to sow doubt? She read it through hastily and signed her name at the end. Then before her conscience could start working overtime, she sealed it in an envelope, grabbed a first class stamp and rushed out of the office.

✤ ✤ ✤ ✤

"We've got an appointment at the clinic next Wednesday morning at ten," Jenny gushed as soon as Peter came through the door. "They've just phoned. You will be able to come, won't you?"

"Give me a chance to get in, Jenny. I'll have to check my diary but it should be all right. I know I'm in court on Thursday."

"Check it now – please." She hung up his raincoat and practically pushed him into the study, the small room off the hall that he had commandeered.

"All right, all right." He opened his briefcase and removed his laptop. Jenny watched him impatiently as he keyed in the letters to bring up his diary. "It was a lot quicker when you just opened a book," she grumbled.

Chapter Five / 85

"This is more accurate."

"Until something goes wrong."

He stared at the screen. "I have an appointment at nine in the office but I should be able to get to the clinic by ten. It's in Bridge Road, isn't it?"

"Yes, at the end. It's on the corner of Green Lane."

"I know it. I've often gone past but haven't been in."

"It's a private hospital with an IVF clinic. Ellie says it's best to go to a clinic where they do IVF all the time."

"I suppose it's the most expensive, too."

"Probably. But that isn't a problem, is it? We *can* afford it and it would be so marvellous if we could have a baby."

"Don't get your hopes up too high, Jenny. The rate of success is pretty low, you know."

"I know that but I don't want to think about it."

It was raining on Wednesday morning – a steady drizzle from a uniform grey sky. Jenny felt depressed as she locked the front door and went to get her car. Raindrops sprinkled her hair and dripped onto her face as she hurried to the garage. Once in the car, she was relieved that the remote control enabled her to shut the door without getting out. The spray produced by the car wheels hissed as she drove out of the drive and onto the road. The short journey was relatively traffic free as she had missed the rush hour. She drove slowly along the tree-lined road, thinking about the future. She didn't want to think too far ahead. The first hurdle had been overcome but the clinic had to be persuaded that they were a suitable couple for IVF.

It was still raining when she drove into the car park. To her horror it appeared full.

"Oh help!" she muttered as she drove round the corner to the end of the parked cars. "Oh thank you, Lord."

She manoeuvred the car into the one minute space remaining and squeezed herself out of the door. The rain had become heavier and she dived into her handbag for her micro-light umbrella. Having ensconced herself beneath it, she looked around. Where was the entrance? There were several doors but they all looked firmly closed. She walked round the corner retracing the way she had entered. The only hopeful looking door had a large bell but was marked: Deliveries only.

"Well here goes," she murmured as she pressed the bell.

The door opened promptly. "I'm very sorry," she said to the grinning porter. "I'm not a delivery. I can't find the entrance to the hospital."

"You're in the wrong place, love," he told her. "This is the staff car park. The hospital's the next entrance. There's a huge car park there." He pointed down the road.

"Thank you." Jenny was relieved she was early. Someone had parked in a non parking space behind her and she had difficulty getting out. By the time she'd managed a "hundred point turn", her arms ached in spite of the power steering.

The porter had been right. There was plenty of room in the hospital car park and she chose a place near to the entrance which had RECEPTION emblazoned over it. She pushed open the door to find a receptionist sitting behind a circular desk. Jenny shut her umbrella and tried to reach the desk without dripping rain onto the elegant pink carpet. The atmosphere was hushed.

"I have an appointment to see Mr Coombes at the Alexandra Clinic," she whispered.

The receptionist pointed to a door. "Go down that corridor and up the first set of stairs. The clinic's on your left."

It seemed a very long walk along the carpeted corridor. Jenny glanced at the pastel landscapes on the walls on either side of her. Some of them were beautiful and helped her to forget the rain outside and her nervousness. Through the doors she found yet another receptionist who offered her coffee and indicated the waiting room. Carefully juggling her coffee cup, umbrella and large handbag, she walked into the room, her feet sinking into the green pile carpet before she lowered herself into one of the luxurious armchairs and deposited her cup and handbag on the coffee table in front of her. After some thought, she placed her umbrella there as well. It had dried off a little during her walk.

She gazed around her as she sipped her coffee. The walls were pale green and a chandelier hung from the ceiling. The rain was still pattering against the large bay window overlooking a pristine lawn bordered with autumnal chrysanthemums and dahlias.

Chapter Five / 87

Someone must work hard on it, she reflected. She turned her head to become mesmerised by tiny golden and silver blue fish gliding around in a large aquarium. The slight ripple of the water and the smooth, silent movement of the little creatures calmed her and she started to relax. Beside the tank a large notice read: *Patients with appointments for a scan are requested not to arrive too early in order to avoid overcrowding in the waiting room.* Soon, she hoped, *she* would be one of those patients. Peter had not arrived but she was early and she was sure he'd be in time. Shutting her eyes, she leaned back in the chair trying to think of the forthcoming interview.

"Darling, I'm not late, am I?" She felt a light kiss on her forehead and smiled up at her husband.

"I don't think so. We haven't been called yet."

He looked round appreciatively. "Very plush."

"There's a tranquil atmosphere, isn't there?"

"Probably created by the fish." He nodded at the tank. "I can see why they have them in waiting rooms – very therapeutic."

"Mr and Mrs Adams, will you please follow me. Mr Coombes will see you now." The receptionist appeared at the door and beckoned them. The room they entered was wood-panelled with a matching desk and two comfortable chairs in front of it. The doctor peered at them over his half spectacles and waved them to the seats. He had a round plump face, very little hair and was slightly stooped. Jenny thought he resembled Mr Pickwick and repressed a giggle. He beamed benevolently at them.

"Dr Reynolds thinks I may be able to help you," he said in a soft voice. He picked up a letter and Jenny noticed his hands were long and elegant – a surgeon's hands, she thought. They sat strangely on his rotund body.

She smiled at him. "Oh I do hope so!" she exclaimed.

He put the letter down and clasped his hands together. "I don't know how much you know but I usually like to explain the procedure," he said gently. "In Vitro Fertilisation means that fertilisation takes place outside the body. At one stage it was done in a test-tube – hence the term 'test-tube babies'. But I don't like that expression. Today we use a 'culture dish'. You will be given something to stimulate ovulation, Mrs Adams, and at the right time we will collect a number of eggs from you. Just before we do, your husband will be asked to produce a sperm sample. The individual eggs and sperm will be combined in a culture dish." He paused and looked thoughtful.

"What happens then?" asked Jenny impatiently. "When are they implanted in me?"

"You mustn't be impatient, my dear Mrs Adams. I'm afraid patience is of the essence in this treatment."

"I'm sorry," murmured Jenny.

"If any of the eggs fertilise with the sperm, they are left to grow for about two days. After that they are transferred from the culture dish into your womb."

"All of them?"

He shook his head. "We never implant more than three."

"What happens to the others?" asked Peter.

"The ones that have fertilised can be frozen for possible future use. You have to give your permission for this."

"So if it doesn't 'take' the first time, I can try again?"

"That is correct."

"How long would it be before I knew if I was pregnant?"

"About two weeks. We'll be monitoring you and there are other tests we will need to take."

"Is there a greater risk of a miscarriage with IVF?" asked Peter.

"If your wife becomes pregnant, the chances of a miscarriage are no greater than in a normal pregnancy."

"What is your success rate?"

"The average is about seventeen per cent for each treatment cycle – less if a frozen embryo is implanted."

"That's not very high," commented Peter.

"But we knew that," Jenny reminded him. "We do want to try it, don't we, Peter?"

He nodded. "Yes, darling. We'll try it."

"I'm afraid it's not quite as simple as that, Mr Adams. We have to be absolutely certain that this treatment is right for you so I have to ask you some very personal questions."

For the next half hour Jenny felt as though every aspect of their lives was being put through a mangle and squeezed out of them. Their medical history was examined in detail, any genetic problems queried, their sex life detailed and their life-style described. After the surgeon had completed his notes, he looked up and said, "I assume you will have no objection to my contacting Dr Reynolds and asking for a full report on your medical histories. I need to be sure that he fully supports you in this."

"You are welcome to find out his views," agreed Peter as Jenny nodded.

"You must also discuss this fully and be prepared to give your written consent before any treatment commences."

"Of course."

"Phew!" said Jenny as they left the clinic. "They don't leave much to chance, do they? I feel like a wet rag after all that grilling."

"It's nearly lunch time. Let's find a pub and have a quick snack. I need to be in the office for an appointment at two. Leave your car here and I'll drop you back."

❖ ❖ ❖ ❖

Eleanor had been feeling depressed and confused for several days. She was uncommunicative with Carol because she felt an overwhelming sense of guilt about her friend. She was also aware that her feelings towards David had changed since their brief drink together. She felt she had misjudged him and would like to get to know him better. But although she saw him frequently, he made no attempt to renew his invitation. She had heard nothing from Chris and since she avoided Carol, she had no idea whether their romance was now blossoming after her rejection of his advances. She felt as though she were in limbo waiting for something to happen.

It was a fortnight since she had been out with David, and as she had a free weekend, she decided to spend it with her parents. She had just climbed out of a leisurely bath when her mother called her to the phone. Draping herself in a towel and dripping water over the carpet, she hurried downstairs.

"Hullo."

"Eleanor. It's David. I'm sorry I haven't been in touch before. I've been busy but I wondered if you were free to come out to dinner this evening."

"Yes. I am. I'd love to." It was true she realised.

"I'll pick you up about seven. Where's your parents' house?"

She gave him directions and hung up. Dorothy appeared at the kitchen door. "I've just made some fresh coffee. Do you want toast?"

"Thanks, Mum. That was David, the new surgeon. He's invited me out for dinner tonight."

"So you've changed your mind about him."

"I suppose I have but I don't really know him very well yet."

"Is he a Christian?"

"Oh Mum, I've no idea. No doubt I'll find out more about him tonight."

Dorothy looked worried. "Do take care, Ellie, won't you? I'd hate you to be hurt. I wish you'd marry and settle down."

"That's what Jenny said. Really I think you're both still living in the nineteenth century."

"It's only because we care about you."

"I know." She gave her mother a quick hug. "I'll take my coffee up with me."

"Don't you want any toast?"

"I'll have some later."

"You look very glam." Later that evening, Kate passed Eleanor's room as her sister was emerging. "Going somewhere nice?"

Eleanor blushed. How she wished she could control the flow of colour to her cheeks. "I'm going out for dinner."

"Got a new boyfriend, have we?"

Chapter Five / 91

"Oh shut up, Kate," sighed Eleanor. "Why don't you grow up?"

"All right. I'm going." She ran down the stairs turning at the bottom to say in a mock American accent. "Have a nice evening."

Eleanor put her hands to her cheeks. She hoped the colour would subside before David arrived but the doorbell went almost immediately and she and Dorothy arrived at the front door simultaneously. Eleanor opened the door.

"Hullo, David." She introduced her mother.

"How do you do, Mrs Bradley. Hasn't it been a beautiful day?"

Dorothy shook hands warmly. "It certainly has. I hope you have lovely evening. See you later, Ellie."

"Don't wait up for her. She may be late." David's eyes were twinkling and Dorothy laughed.

"I'll see you tomorrow then. I assume you'll be coming to church with us."

"Of course." Eleanor hid her annoyance. Why did her mother have to say that? She had no intention of hiding her faith from David but she wished to tell him in her own time. They were silent as they walked down the drive to his car.

"Which church do you go to?" he asked casually as he drove smoothly off.

"St Peter's. My parents have gone there for years and my father's a churchwarden." Now why had she said that? She knew from experience that any suggestion of "religion" was an excellent way of losing unwanted followers. But she didn't want to lose David. She liked him and wanted to get to know him better. She glanced at him. He didn't look "turned off" and the silence seemed a comfortable one.

After a short pause he said, "I go to the New Wine Fellowship when I'm able to."

"Oh!" She gasped. The New Wine Fellowship was a lively new church that had attracted a number of worshippers from the more staid Anglican churches in the community. They certainly didn't cater for "hangers on". Their members were fully committed.

It was his turn to glance quickly at her. "You're surprised."

"Oh – no of course not." She was flustered.

"Yes, you are. You were wondering whether to tell me you were a Christian."

"I *was* going to tell you," she said defensively.

"I'm sure you were."

After a pause to adjust her thoughts, she queried, "How did you know I was?"

"Well you don't exactly make a secret of it, do you?" He was very easy to talk to but so far he'd told her very little about his background and she was intrigued to discover how he had become involved with the New Wine Fellowship. As she sat facing him in the Italian restaurant, she asked, "How long have you been going to the New Wine Fellowship?"

"A couple of years." She waited and, glancing at him, she was sure he knew what she was thinking and was amused by it. At last he relented. "I got friendly with a colleague who introduced me to it. I was baptised into the Church of England and my mother was horrified when she heard I'd joined a 'happy clappy' congregation."

"Do you like it?"

"It's different. I'm not sure it's really my spiritual home but I'm still learning. How about coming with me one day?"

She hesitated. She had occasionally attended charismatic church services but had never felt very comfortable. While she recognised others' right to enjoy a more lively type of worship, she disliked the feeling that she was "odd" because she didn't wish to join in.

"Well?" He was waiting for her answer.

She made up her mind. "Yes, I'd like to."

"Have you been to that sort of service before?"

"Yes, but I really prefer a more traditional service."

"Like the good old Church of England."

"It's got its good points," she said defensively.

"Oh I wasn't criticising it. It's a bulwark of the establishment."

She glared at him. "I'm not sure that's true any more."

"Probably not," he agreed. "How about next Sunday? Or are you working?"

"No, I'm working the following one. Thanks. I'd like to come."

"The service is at eleven so I'll pick you up about ten-thirty. It gets quite crowded."

It certainly did. When they arrived at the church soon after half-past ten, the car park was nearly full but David managed to find a space. People of all ages were milling around the entrance to the church. Many of them greeted David and grinned at Eleanor who was beginning to feel rather claustrophobic. The noise was accelerating and she felt rather sick.

David led her into the church where rows of chairs faced a middle aisle. She found it strange not to face the front where a huge screen covered most of the wall. In front of it was a table covered with a green baize cloth and bearing a large open Bible. There was no cross on the table and the only decoration was a group of banners containing Bible verses: "Christ is the light of the world": "Jesus Christ, the same, yesterday, today and for ever".

"Don't we need service books?" she asked.

"What?" he bent his head to hear her.

She raised her voice above the noise and repeated her question. He shook his head.

"We don't use them. You'll see."

She was intrigued and cast a surreptitious glance at her watch. Ten minutes to go and the church was already full but there was no stillness. People were moving around and greeting each other with hugs and cries of excitement. It was nothing like anything Eleanor had ever attended before. She was fascinated by the congregation. The young people wore the usual uniform of jeans and tee-shirts while the older members wore a variety of garments. Some of the men were formally dressed in suits and ties while others, like David, wore casual pullovers and trousers. A number of the women also wore trousers but some of the older ladies wore long skirts and even hats. Eleanor wondered if she looked out of place in her cream linen suit.

Suddenly the congregation broke into song. The chattering voices were lifted in unison as the words of a hymn that Eleanor didn't recognise appeared on the screen. The singing was lusty and some members of the congregation not only waved their arms around but even danced up and down the aisles. Eleanor watched bemused but she was swept along by the euphoria. David, beside her, was singing loudly and by the last verse, she found she was joining in.

The service proceeded in what to Eleanor seemed a rather chaotic fashion. However, there were few pauses and one item followed swiftly upon another. One woman asked for prayer because she was going into hospital and a group congregated in the aisle and prayed for her. Eleanor found herself unexpectedly moved. A man read a passage from the Bible and spoke at length about it. Unannounced hymns were sprinkled throughout the service; she recognised some of them.

It was a long service. By the time they were finally able to drive away it was nearly one o'clock. Eleanor had difficulty restoring her face to normal after the smile with which it seemed she'd greeted the entire congregation.

"Well what did you think of it?" David asked as they drove away.

"It was certainly different. There didn't seem to be any order and yet there was an underlying pattern."

"They would say God's Holy Spirit was influencing it."

She looked quickly at him. "And you?"

He hesitated. "I'm not sure. I think any group that has no official leader tends to produce leaders and sometimes things can go wrong."

"In what way?"

"I met someone once from a group that had started well – very Bible based. Then one of the leaders started introducing his own ideas and eventually caused friction and division. It can get very authoritative."

"And you think the New Wine Fellowship might go the same way."

"I hope not. There are no signs of it yet."

"Would you like to come to St Peter's with me one Sunday?"

"Return to my roots, you mean," he teased with a grin.

She laughed. "I didn't mean that. I came to your service so I thought you might like to come to mine."

"Sorry. Yes. I'd love to. Shall we find somewhere for lunch?"

"I meant to invite you home. We usually have a family meal on Sundays."

"It's a bit late, isn't it? It's nearly half-past one. I'd love to come some time. Let's find a pub and you can phone your mother. Will she be put out?"

"Oh no. She's very laid back. We never know who's going to turn up for Sunday lunch. But I'll phone her anyway."

He turned off the main road and headed for a nearby village. They soon found the Stag and Hounds which offered a "Sunday roast".

After Eleanor had phoned home and they were waiting for the meal, David said, "Do you mind if I ask you something?" Her heart raced but calmed down when he continued, "I wondered what your views were on abortion."

"I'm against it," she said quickly. This emotive issue was not one she would have chosen to discuss with an attractive man over Sunday lunch.

"I expected you would be but are there any extenuating circumstances in which you would feel it was the only alternative?"

She thought for a moment. "If the mother's health were threatened, I suppose it might be acceptable. But I don't agree with abortion on demand. I think it's frightening. Just think of the number of geniuses who may have been killed because someone was too selfish to have a baby that was probably the result of a few moments' pleasure." She warmed to her theme. "Do you know that one in five pregnancies is now aborted? That's nearly two hundred thousand per year. And sometimes pressure is put on the parents to abort a foetus that might be disabled. Only God has the right to take life." She stopped, suddenly embarrassed. "Sorry. I got carried away."

"You're preaching to the converted, you know."

"You wouldn't do an abortion?"

He shook his head. "No. And like you I don't approve of the ease with which they're available."

"I'm glad. I've refused to assist at them and fortunately Manor Hospital respects conscience views but I have heard of nurses in other places losing their jobs because they refused to assist."

"I'm afraid Christian values are being eroded all the time."

"Why did you ask me what I thought about it?"

"I've been invited to speak on the subject at a university debate and I thought you might have some views."

"Oh." She waited for him to elaborate but he changed the subject and for the rest of the evening anything to do with their work was not mentioned.

✣ ✣ ✣ ✣

"Well tell me all about it." Carol tucked her long legs underneath her on Eleanor's sofa and waited. Eleanor didn't reply at once. Did she want to talk about her dates with David? Carol wasn't known for her discretion and Eleanor didn't relish providing titbits for a gossip-deprived hospital. On the other hand, if Carol knew she was going out with David, it might prevent her reaching the right conclusion about "the other woman". She pressed down the plunger on the *cafetière* and glanced at her friend. Carol looked tired and unhappy. She hadn't mentioned Chris lately and Eleanor couldn't bring herself to ask. She had heard nothing from him and she was relieved. Her infatuation seemed to have died a natural death since she had rejected his advantages and been out with David. She hoped Carol never learnt of her perfidy. She had certainly not behaved at all like a Christian.

Carol was becoming impatient. "Come on, Ellie. I'm dying to hear about our handsome surgeon. He really is drop dead gorgeous."

"Yes," agreed Ellie. "He is. We went out for dinner and then last Sunday I went to the New Wine Fellowship with him."

"Ellie, you didn't," gasped Carol. "I wondered why you weren't at St Peter's. I thought you didn't like all that 'happy, clappy' style of worship."

"Well I don't really but it was interesting." She poured some coffee into a mug and handed it to Carol.

"Did the dishy David dance in the aisles?"

"Don't be silly. Of course he didn't" She hesitated. "I must say I prefer a more formal service but they're really sincere, you know, Carol. I don't think we should criticise people because they do things in a different way."

"No, you're quite right. I didn't mean to criticise. Well go on."

"That's all really." For once Carol was obviously listening but Eleanor didn't want to go into details. "Oh he's coming to St Peter's with me next Sunday and I've invited him to lunch with the family afterwards."

"Is he coming?"

"I think so."

"Lucky you. Chris seems to have cooled off." Eleanor looked sharply at her friend. Her heart started to pound. But Carol seemed lost in her own thoughts. She obviously had no idea of her friend's treachery.

✤ ✤ ✤ ✤

"What on earth's the matter, Mel? You look awful."

Melanie was standing forlornly outside Eleanor's flat when she returned home. Tears cascaded down her cheeks when she saw her sister.

"Oh Ellie, I've been so wicked."

"Come in and tell me about it." Eleanor opened the door and shepherded her sister in. "I'll make you a cup of tea. There's a box of tissues on the table. Sit down on the sofa and relax. It's more comfortable than the chair."

She bustled into the kitchen. What had happened now? She hadn't seen her sister for some time and had intended to visit her but she'd been so tired after work. Thoughtfully she made the tea and opened the biscuit tin. Thank goodness. It still contained a few of the chocolate digestives that were Melanie's favourites.

Carrying the tray into the small living room, she was relieved to see that her sister had stopped crying. But her reddened eyes suggested that weeping had been a constant activity for some time. The dying sun shone on her lank hair which looked as though it needed a wash. In fact, Eleanor thought, Melanie looked as though she needed to be remade completely. She was a mess. Eleanor drew the curtains slightly so the sun didn't glint directly into her eyes. She poured out the tea and handed over a cup.

"Do you want to tell me about it? I assume that's why you're here. Is it Simon? I did warn you."

As soon as she had uttered the last sentence, she wished she could recall it. Melanie's eyes flashed.

"I knew you'd say that. You're so pompous, Eleanor. And it's all right for you. Everything always works out for you. I knew I shouldn't have come." She jumped up, knocking over her cup; the tea flooded the table drenching the box of tissues and trickling on to the plain fawn carpet that was standard issue. She headed for the door.

Ignoring the mess, Eleanor grabbed her arm. "I'm sorry, Melanie. I didn't mean to say that. It just slipped out. Please sit down again. I'll get you another cup of tea."

Melanie hesitated and then obeyed. "I'm sorry about the mess. Shall I clear it up?"

"No, I'll do it. Here have my cup and I'll pour another one when I've mopped up. Would you like some sugar in it? It might be a good idea. You've obviously had a shock."

"Ugh! No thanks. I can't bear the taste."

"Well have a choccy bikky to go with it." She held out the tin and Melanie took one.

By the time the damage had been repaired and they were both sipping freshly brewed cups of tea, Eleanor felt exhausted but she tried to hide it.

"Now," she said cosily. "Do you want to tell me about it?"

Melanie nodded. She took a sip of tea and then carefully put her cup down on the table. It was obvious she didn't know where to start but Eleanor knew she couldn't be rushed.

At last her sister spoke, "Joy found out about us. She came into the office and we – we were kissing." There was another long pause but Eleanor didn't want to interrupt in case she said the wrong thing again. "She – she rushed out and – and Simon went

Chapter Five / 99

after her. He – he told her it … it didn't mean anything and there was nothing be – between us. Oh, oh …" Grabbing a handful of tissues Melanie gave vent to her grief. She howled and howled.

Eleanor went and sat beside her. She put her arms round the distraught girl and Melanie sobbed into her shoulder. Although she was sorry her sister was so upset, she couldn't help thinking it was the best thing that could have happened. But she hadn't heard the worst. Melanie suddenly broke away from her. Suddenly she looked much older than her twenty years and Eleanor was reminded of a Greek tragedy mask with the corners of its mouth turned down and tears seeping out of its eyes. Hairs prickled on her neck. She remembered that Melanie had said she had been wicked. What *had* she done? Ghastly thoughts tumbled around in her mind but she tried not to focus on any of them. She waited.

"I wrote Joy a letter telling her that Simon had lied and we *were* having an affair. I posted it two days ago and … and I haven't been able to think of anything since. I wish so much I hadn't done it. But I was so angry and – and I love Simon so much more than she could and …" She dissolved into tears again and looked up at Eleanor through the watery curtain. "I wish I hadn't done it. Will God ever forgive me?"

"Of course he will – if you're truly sorry."

"Oh – I am. But – but I still love Simon. Oh, Ellie, what am I do do?"

Eleanor became the practical nurse. "You could write another letter to Joy saying you are sorry and it wasn't true."

"But that would be a lie. It *was* true. Simon and I *were* having an affair but … but he seems to have cooled off lately."

Eleanor debated whether to reiterate the reasons for forgetting Simon but she didn't think Melanie would listen. She was horrified at the depths to which her sister had sunk. She must be obsessed with the man.

"Would you like to stay here tonight? That sofa folds into a bed. It's quite comfortable and I can lend you night things."

Melanie shook her head. "No, I'd better get back. Simon might come and I must be there if he does."

After what she'd just heard, Eleanor doubted if he would want anything more to do with his assistant. She had obviously done an excellent hatchet job on his marriage and she reflected that it was extremely unlikely that he would ever have left his wife for Melanie. By her own admission, he had already cooled off before Joy discovered them. She couldn't understand how Melanie, brought up to observe Christian moral standards could have behaved in such an utterly selfish way. But had she herself behaved any better by going out with her best friend's boyfriend?

✤ ✤ ✤ ✤

"So will you do it for me?"

"Every day?"

"Yes please." Jenny looked pleadingly at Eleanor. "The clinic said I could do the injections myself or get Peter to do them but I thought it would be nicer if you did them for me."

"I work in the theatre. I don't give many injections."

"I'm sure you'd be better than Peter – or me."

"Oh all right. Does it have to be at the same time each day?"

"Yes, I'm afraid so. Apparently the drug will give me a sort of menopause and then stimulate the follicles so that I produce lots of eggs that they can harvest." She giggled. "Makes me sound like a wheat field, doesn't it?"

"When do we start?"

"I've got the syringe and stuff. Can you do the first one now? Then you could come in after work every day, couldn't you?"

"I see you've got it all organised. I'll try but you'll have to do it yourself if I can't make it any time."

Jenny nodded. "I'll go and get it."

She returned with a small box which she handed to Eleanor who opened it and removed its contents.

"It's a subcutaneous injection – just below the skin."

"I do know what that means."

"Sorry."

Chapter Five / 101

Jenny watched apprehensively as her sister drew the liquid into the syringe. She winced as the needle was inserted carefully under the skin of her thigh..

"I'll be like a pin cushion before this is over," she grumbled as she rearranged her clothes.

"You'll probably feel a bit bloated in a few days," Eleanor warned her. "When do you have to go back to the clinic?"

"I have to have a scan in a few days to see how I'm doing."

Eleanor was right. Jenny started to feel bloated but she felt the discomfort was worth suffering if eggs were flourishing inside her. She wondered how many there were. It felt as though she were carrying a whole army.

On her second visit to the clinic she found her way easily, bypassing the receptionist in the main part of the hospital and marching down the long corridor and up the stairs to the Alexandra Clinic.

The receptionist smiled at her. "It's Mrs Adams, isn't it?"

"Yes. I've come for a scan. I hope I'm not too early." She remembered the notice in the waiting room.

"No you're fine. The nurse will be with you in a moment."

The waiting room contained only two occupants, both about Jenny's age. They ignored her. She sat down trying to calm herself. Nervously she twisted her wedding ring until she felt she was rubbing away her skin. She folded her hands in her lap and tried to keep them still.

"Mrs Adams, please follow me." A young girl in a white coat appeared at the door.

Jenny jumped up shooting her handbag onto the floor. Fortunately on this occasion it didn't fly open. Apologising, she picked it up and followed her guide out of the room.

"I'm the nurse who'll be looking for your eggs," the girl said with a smile. "My name's Debbie." She ushered her patient into a small room containing a couch to the end of which were attached two black saddle-shaped leather leg rests. Jenny turned her eyes away. Beside the bed was a table containing a television monitor.

"That's so you can see what's going on," Debbie explained. "Now I'd like you to use the loo through there and take off your panties and tights if you're wearing them. Then come back and sit on the end of the bed and I'll explain what happens. There's nothing to worry about."

Of course there was, thought Jenny nervously, but she managed a weak smile as she went through the door beside the bed and closed it behind her. Having divested herself of her lower garments and used the facilities, she opened the door and returned feeling slightly embarrassed at her half naked state.

"Put this blanket over your legs while I explain what I'm going to do. There's nothing to worry about. I'm going to have a little look around inside you. This is what I use." Debbie held up a long plastic instrument covered at one end, Jenny was amused to notice, by a condom. Debbie pointed to it. "There's an ultrasonic eye which will show us how many eggs you are producing. Now if you'll just lie down."

She took the blanket and helped Jenny to lie back on the couch. Gently she lifted her patient's legs so that they rested comfortably on the "saddles". Jenny tried to ignore the indignity she was suffering. Why am I doing this? she thought. But she knew it would be worth it if she could only become pregnant.

"If you want to see what's going on, you can watch," Debbie told her, turning the monitor to face the bed.

"Thank you."

The insertion of the ultrasonic eye felt like any other internal examination and she'd had plenty of those over the years she'd been trying to get pregnant. She gazed at the screen but found it hard to focus on anything. At first there was only a grey and black amorphous blur. Then, as she continued to stare, it was transformed into a squelchy blackcurrant jelly which hadn't set very well so the slightest movement was causing it to wobble. She hated blackcurrant jelly!

"That's coming along nicely." Debbie removed the ultra sonic eye and laid it down. "The treatment seems to be working. "We'll have another look in a week's time, Mrs Adams."

❖ ❖ ❖ ❖

"Rosa, can I have a word please?" Jenny beckoned her deputy into her office.

"Are you all right, Jenny? You look a bit flushed."

"I'm fine. Take a seat."

Rosa sat down opposite the desk and Jenny looked at her affectionately, knowing she could trust her. Her black hair was tidily plaited into a pigtail which hung almost to her waist; her straight black skirt and fitted jacket emphasised her slim figure and made her look even taller than she was. The pale blue reveres of her blouse lay against those of the jacket in the current fashion of business women. She looked more like a company director than a teacher in a comprehensive school. She would still look elegant at the end of the day.

"What did you want a word about?" queried Rosa when Jenny didn't speak. "Have I got a smut on my nose or something? Why are you staring at me?"

"Oh sorry." Jenny laughed. "I was just thinking how glamorous you always look, even at the end of the day. By then I've lost all my lipstick, my hair's all over the place and I can't even be bothered to comb it. What's your secret?"

"No idea. Is that the 'word' you wanted to have with me?"

"No, of course not. I want to tell you something in confidence. I know I can trust you."

"Of course you can."

"You know Peter and I have been trying for a family for ages. We've decided to go for IVF."

"Oh that's marvellous, Jenny. I do hope it works for you."

"Thanks. The thing is I've only just started the treatment and I have to go to the clinic for some scans. I've tried to arrange them for when I'm free so I hope I won't have to ask for much cover. I don't want everyone to know but I'd be happier knowing that I'd told you because I'm going to need a lot of support. I don't know how I'll react and it's bound to be very stressful."

"I'll always be here for you, Jenny. You know that. Just let me know if there's anything at all I can do. When's your next appointment?"

"It's on Friday. And then, if things go according to plan, I have to have scans on the following Monday and Wednesday. I've checked the timetable. Friday's no problem. My appointment's at nine and I'm not teaching till eleven. On Monday and Wednesday I'm free last period so I'll see if I can get afternoon appointments. If I can't, can I try to arrange it for when you're free so you could cover for me? I'll leave some work of course."

"No problem. Of course I will."

"Thanks." The shrieking of the bell followed by the stampede of a thousand pairs of feet effectively prevented any further conversation as they fought their way through milling bodies to their respective classrooms.

❖ ❖ ❖ ❖

"Hullo, Eleanor. I'm glad I've bumped into you. How about a coffee? I want to talk to you."

"I'm in a hurry, Chris. I only came out to buy some food. I'm on duty at twelve."

"How about dinner tonight?"

"I'm working late."

"Tomorrow then. Please. I really do need to talk to you."

She glanced up at him. He appeared to have forgotten their last encounter. And she was intrigued to know what he wanted to talk to her about.

"All right. Pick me up about seven."

"See you." He strode off and she stared after him. She'd decided to finish with him so why on earth had she agreed to go out with him again? Her heart was still firmly anchored in its place. Tomorrow she would definitely tell him she wouldn't go out with him again and she would persuade him to go back to Carol.

That problem solved, she returned to her shopping, but the thought of the following evening kept insinuating itself into her mind. He had something to say to her but she definitely had to talk to him.

The dinner was not a success. They had hardly sipped their drinks before Chris started.

"How's lover boy then?"

"What?" Her hand jerked and gin and tonic splashed over the top of the glass. She put it down carefully knowing colour was flooding her face.

"Mr David Baines. You *are* going out with him, aren't you?"

"I don't think it's any of your business."

"I think it is. I don't want you to get hurt."

"What on earth are you talking about? Is that why you've asked me out? To find out about David."

"Partly," he agreed shamelessly.

"I don't think you have any right to pry into my private life."

"I suppose not. But I've heard things about the gentleman. Just be careful, Ellie."

Prickles ran up her spine. "What 'things'?"

"Even I can see he's attractive to women. You're not the first you know."

"I didn't think I was," she said crossly. "Why are you so bothered? I thought you … Anyway, I haven't felt the same about you since …" She broke off, embarrassed.

He finished the sentence for her. "Since I tried to get you into bed."

"Yes. You really shocked me, Chris. I thought you were a Christian."

"I'm only human."

She glared at him. "So am I but I hope I can exercise more self-control."

"Men are different."

"Oh really, Chris. I do know that but there are plenty of men who do manage to control themselves."

"All right. All right. What are you going to eat? You haven't even looked at the menu."

She glanced at it. "I'm not very hungry. I'll just have a chicken salad."

"Are you sure?"

She nodded and he beckoned the waiter and gave their order. When he had left, Chris said, "You like David, don't you?"

"What if I do?"

"Just be careful. He's not worthy of you."

"Oh Chris, don't be so old fashioned."

"I just don't want you to be hurt."

She stared at him. "You're not jealous by any chance, are you?"

"Of course not."

"I think you are."

"Rubbish."

"You are."

"All right then, I am. I love you, Ellie and you'd be wasted on him. He wouldn't appreciate you. Marry me."

"What did you say?"

"I know it's a bit sudden but I really do love you, Ellie."

"You hardly know me."

"I fell in love with you the first time I saw you. I know I want to spend the rest of my life with you."

"It's not just because of David, is it?"

"What do you mean?"

"You don't want me just so David can't have me."

"Ellie, that's an awful thing to say."

"Yes, I suppose it is but – you're so odd about him. And you don't even know him. Do you?"

"I know enough about him. He's hypocritical. Oh he goes to church and pays lip service to Christianity but he doesn't seem to practise it."

"How on earth do you know that?"

"I've heard things."

"You keep talking about 'things'. What 'things'? Is there something you've not telling me – that I should know."

He burst out, "He's a ladies' man. I think you're infatuated with him."

"I'm not. I just like him."

"Infatuation isn't the same thing as love you know."

"I do know that. Will you stop going on about it. What's the matter with you?

Chapter Five / 107

"I told you. I love you."

She glanced at him. Did he really love her? He hardly knew her. She still felt that jealousy was lurking somewhere behind him waiting to pounce. Her chicken salad was placed before her and she picked at it. For a while they ate in silence.

Suddenly he said, "There's something else, Ellie. I think he performs abortions. In fact I know he does."

She went pale. "Chris, don't say things like that. I don't believe you. His views are the same as mine. He told me so and I believe him."

"He works in a private clinic and I'm sure he does them there."

"How do you know?"

"Never mind how. Just believe me."

"You're only saying it because you want to put me off him."

"You haven't answered my question."

"What question?"

"Will you marry me?"

"No."

"At least think about it. Do you really think David will propose? You might not get another offer."

She stared at him in amazement. Then she burst out laughing. "Oh Chris, don't be so arrogant. This is the end of the twentieth century. I don't *have* to get married. I could have a perfectly fulfilled life without."

"Oh, but think how much better it would be *with* a man."

"You're impossible." Against her will, she laughed again.

"That's better. I thought I was going to stay in the dog house. Will you marry me? Please." He stretched his hand across the table to her. The look on his face almost made her soften. But she could not forget what he had said about the surgeon. And she was not sure he was telling the truth. She hardened her heart and ignored his hand.

"I don't think you've thought about it carefully enough. I don't think I'd be a good wife for you."

"Let me be the judge of that."

"I'm sorry, Chris. I can't eat this. Please take me home."

"I will when we've finished."

She stood up. "I'll get a taxi."

"Oh all right." He threw some money on the table. "I hope that will cover it. I'm not used to having my dates cut short."

"Don't sulk, Chris."

"I'm not."

"Don't shout."

"I love you, damn it."

"Don't swear."

"Oh, stop nagging."

"There you see. You wouldn't want to marry me. I'd nag you all the time."

"Oh get in the car," he said, exasperated. "You really are the most infuriating woman. I wish David joy of you."

"Thanks."

He drove her to her flat in silence and didn't even open the door for her.

"Goodbye Chris. Thanks for the meal."

"You didn't eat it."

She ignored him and stalked into the building. In her flat she kicked off her shoes and flung her bag and keys on the table. Then, collapsing into the armchair, she stared ahead of her, thinking. Through no fault of her own, she seemed to have been instrumental in opening a very nasty can of worms. *Was* there a germ of truth in what Chris had said? How well did she really know David? Or Chris?

"Oh bother both of them," she muttered. She switched on the television and watched a news update. It was as depressing as usual. Switching it off, she decided on an early night although sleep might be a long while coming. She had to work the following morning but she'd go home for the rest of the weekend.

Chapter Six

"I feel so muddled, Ellie. I'm sure I'm in love with Will but ..." Lorna hesitated.

"But what?" Eleanor sighed and put down the Sunday paper she was reading. Lorna wondered whether to continue or not. Obviously Ellie didn't want to hear her problems but there was no one else to talk to. Their mother had refused all help in the kitchen and their father was pottering in the garden pruning his beloved roses. Kate was in her room trying to finish an essay she should have completed the previous day and there were no other visitors on this particular Sunday. It seemed an ideal time to confide in Eleanor but now she wasn't sure it was such a good idea. She'd probably get a sermon. But she had to tell someone.

"Will wants me to sleep with him," she blurted out at last.

"I hope you refused."

"Of course I did but, oh Ellie, he says if I won't he'll find someone who will and everybody does it before marriage and – and I'm old fashioned and ..." She paused, blinking. She would *not* cry.

"He's probably got a point even if he is exaggerating, but just because 'everybody' does it, doesn't mean it's right, you know."

"I know but I don't want to lose him."

"If that's all he wants, you'd be well rid of him. You can't build a relationship on sex alone."

"But we get on so well," objected Lorna. "It's not only sex."

"In that case get to know him better. You're only nineteen, Lorna. You've got your whole life ahead of you. It would be stupid to foul it up."

"But I know he'll find someone else," wailed Lorna.

"I suppose he isn't a Christian," said Eleanor thoughtfully. She laid the paper down and gazed at her sister.

Lorna laughed scornfully. "I shouldn't think so."

"Doesn't that worry you?"

Lorna shrugged and scowled at her sister. "No, it doesn't. Oh I might have known you'd preach at me. I thought you'd help me."

"Well what do you want me to say? I'm hardly likely to condone you going to bed with Will, am I?" Eleanor's voice had risen and to Lorna's astonishment, she had started to blush. Had her older sister had a similar problem?

"Ellie, have you …?"

"Isn't lunch ready yet?" Kate hurtled into the room and flung herself down on the sofa which creaked beneath her. "My essay's rubbish. I expect I'll have to do it again."

"Why do you always leave everything to the last minute?" asked Eleanor. "I'm going to see if Mum wants any help." Her colour was still high and Lorna gazed thoughtfully after her.

After she'd left, Kate said shrewdly, "What's the matter? Did I interrupt something?"

"No of course not." Lorna and Kate had always got on well and often shared "girlie" confidences but for the first time, Lorna felt the age gap between them. She couldn't share her problems with sixteen-year-old Kate – could she?

"Boyfriend trouble? How's the gorgeous Will?" Was she a mind reader? "Aha. I knew there was something. Tell me all."

Lorna glared at her. "It's nothing to do with you."

"Oh come on, Lorna. Don't be a spoilsport. You know you always tell me everything. Go on. Please."

"Will wants to – well, go further than I do."

"You mean he wants to sleep with you?" Kate's voice was a squeak.

Chapter Six / 111

"Keep your voice down. I don't want Mum to hear."

"Are you going to?"

"No – at least I don't think so."

"You can always go on the pill. I'll let you have some if you like."

"Kate!" Lorna was horrified. She hadn't even contemplated taking precautions because she'd never intended to submit to Will's pressure. But she was shocked to discover her younger sister was organised in that department. Surely she hadn't ...she had to find out. "Kate, you haven't ... you know."

"No, not yet. But I wanted to be prepared in case it happened."

"Oh Kate no – you mustn't. Whatever would Mum say? How did you get the pills?"

"From the school doctor. And Mum knows."

"She knows!" Lorna felt that at any moment she would emerge for this bizarre scene they were acting out and return to normality.

Kate grinned. "She found them. There was an almighty row as you can imagine. Ellie had to pour oil on troubled waters."

"She was there too?"

"She'd dropped in after work and heard the racket. I think she thought murder was being committed."

"I'm not surprised Mum was mad. How could you, Kate? You're only sixteen."

"So?" Kate's lips tightened. "Lots of girls my age are married."

"Is that what you want? Have you got someone in mind?"

"No, not yet. Well, do you want some of my pills or not?"

"Didn't mum confiscate them?"

"She didn't find them all."

Lorna shook her head to try to dislodge the ball of shock that was clamped to it. She was badly shaken. They had been brought up so carefully. She must try to talk Kate out of doing something she'd regret. Perhaps if she took all Kate's pills, Kate would change her mind.

"All right. Give me your pills then – all of them. And Kate, you're not to get any more and you're not to do anything stupid. Do you understand?"

Kate giggled. "You sound just like Ellie. Except that you're as bad – aren't you? You'll use the pills."

"No. No. I won't. You've made up my mind for me, Kate. Will said he'd find someone else if I wouldn't sleep with him. Well he can as far as I'm concerned. I won't be blackmailed into sleeping with him."

She saw dawning respect in Kate's eyes. She was only a child after all. Kate nodded solemnly. "It *is* wrong, isn't it, Lorna? I don't think I'd really have done it. But all my friends were getting the pill so I … I had to keep up with them – didn't I?"

"Lunch is nearly ready, girls. Kate, go and call your father, please." Dorothy bustled in bearing a dish of roast potatoes and Eleanor followed with another one of broccoli and carrots. Her colour had returned to normal but she avoided looking at her sisters. Lorna suddenly realised how hungry she was. The roast beef smelt delicious. It was good to be part of a close family. How could she ever do anything to hurt them?

✥ ✥ ✥ ✥

Eleanor had had little time to talk to David since she'd seen Chris. Part of her didn't want to tackle him about the thorny issue of abortion. She thought about their discussion. He had been *so* convincing. But Chris said he was a hypocrite. Could she believe anything Chris told her? He said he was in love with her but would he have said it if she hadn't been so obviously attracted to David? She must talk to her colleague but when?

Perhaps she could cook him a meal. He'd taken her out several times. They would be private in her flat. She didn't want to talk to him in the theatre in case they were interrupted. Yes. That was what she would do. She rang him up and left a message on his answerphone.

The following day he waylaid her as she was coming out of the locker room. "Thanks for your message. I'd love to come to dinner with you. This Friday's fine."

"Good. About seven-thirty."

"I'll be there."

She prepared a casserole so all the work could be done beforehand. When he arrived, he brought her a huge bouquet of flowers and a bottle of wine.

"Oh thank you. They're beautiful. I'll just put them in water. I have some wine cooling in the fridge. Would you like a glass?"

"Please."

She was all fingers and thumbs as she opened the bottle and the cork broke before she finally managed to pour a glass. She moved some floating cork fragments from the glass and took it in to him.

"I'll be with you in a moment."

The food smelt good but she wished it didn't permeate the entire flat. She found two vases for the flowers and carried one into the living room and put it on the table.

"I didn't have a centre piece. They look lovely."

"You've made your flat very nice," he said appreciatively.

"Thank you. Dinner's nearly ready."

She returned to the kitchen and poured herself a glass of wine. She didn't want to drink too much as she needed to keep her mind clear. But she also needed some artificial courage.

It wasn't till they were having coffee that she was able to raise the issue. She'd been tense all evening but if he had noticed, he'd made no reference to it, merely praising her cooking and chatting comfortably.

As she handed him his coffee, she blurted out, "Someone told me you did abortions at a private clinic." That wasn't what she had intended to say. In horror she waited for his response.

He looked startled and then angry. "Well I don't. I told you I didn't approve. I thought you believed me."

"I wanted to but …" Her lips trembled and she looked up at him with her eyes awash with tears. "Oh you don't do them, do you?"

"No, I told you I didn't. I'm sorry you believe rumours rather than me." He stood up and walked over to the door. "I think I'd better go."

"Oh no, please." She put out her hand but he ignored it and stalked towards the door. She didn't want him to go but now it was too late. *Why* had she ever listened to Chris?

"I'm sorry, David." She caught up with him as he opened the front door.

He looked at her coldly. "I'm sorry too. I thought we were getting on well but I don't like having my word doubted. Goodbye, Eleanor."

He shut the door behind him and she realised she was shaking. She slunk back to the living room and slumped on to the sofa. Covering her face with her hands, she indulged in a hearty bout of weeping. Of course she believed him. She was sure he was far more trustworthy than Chris. Would he ever forgive her?

✣ ✣ ✣ ✣

Debbie had been pleased with Jenny's first three scans. Now it was time for the important last one. Jenny was nervous as she drove to the clinic for her fourth scan. Would they find enough eggs to collect? It was Wednesday afternoon and she'd had a bad day. In the morning she'd had to deal with an irate parent whose child was having a personality clash with the probationer. It had upset Jenny who hated scenes. She had then been late for her GCSE class and realised she'd left their carefully marked essays at home. They were *not* pleased and her attempts to stimulate some interest in Walter de la Mare's poem *The Traveller* had fallen on stony ground.

Her lesson with her grade eight class in the afternoon had been a disaster and by the time she finally drove out of the car park just after three she felt like crying. The morning rain had drizzled itself out and sheets of blue sky were appearing above her so as she drove, her spirits lightened.

She was used to the routine now and made her way quickly to the clinic reception area. To her relief she was told to go straight to the scanning room where she prepared for the all-important scan.

"Good afternoon, Mrs Adams." Debbie breezed in as Jenny came out of the bathroom.

Chapter Six / 115

"Good afternoon, Debbie. Do you think it will be all right?"

"Well let's have a look, shall we? Just relax."

It was hard but Jenny did her best and was relieved when Debbie said, "That's coming along nicely. I can see a number of eggs so I'm sure we'll be able to collect some." She sounded like a farmer's wife talking about her hens, reflected Jenny as Debbie replaced the scanner on the table. "After we've checked with Mr Coombes, the gynaecologist, we'll let you know when the eggs can be collected."

"Thank you. I'll give you my mobile number so if it's switched off you can leave me a message and I'll get back to you as soon as I can. I'd rather you didn't phone the school."

"I can understand that. Just tell the receptionist when you leave."

She'd be relieved when the eggs had been removed, Jenny thought as she dressed. Perhaps she wouldn't feel so bloated then. She wondered how many there would be. If there were too many, perhaps it would be difficult to collect them. She felt as though she was carrying a football team inside her. Surely some of them would be suitable.

✥ ✥ ✥ ✥

Lorna stared at the phone. Her heart was beating and she could hardly breathe. Her good resolutions were rapidly dispersing like droplets of dew in the sun. She didn't want to lose Will. She loved him. Or was she being a dog in the manger and not wanting anyone else to have him? Should she ring him? What had she got to lose? Her virginity probably! But that was the price she would have to pay for being in love. She didn't think beyond the fact that she wanted to see him again. She was unaware of the chasm beginning to open under her feet. Would she have drawn back if she could have seen what the future held for her?

She grabbed the phone and hurriedly dialled his mobile number. *This is the BT answering service. Please leave your message after the tone.* Of course he would have switched it off! But the die was cast. She couldn't back off now. She gabbled, "Hi Will, this is Lorna. It's Saturday morning. I'd like to see you. Please ring me sometime."

She hurriedly put the phone down. Now she had the rest of the day to wait. She must do something. She wandered aimlessly round the flat. Tina had gone to her parents for the weekend so she was quite alone and she had nothing planned. She couldn't even go out now in case Will rang. She made herself a coffee in the tiny kitchen and carried it back to the equally small living room. The autumn sun was glinting through the windows and she could see golden dust motes dancing in front of her.

The round table in the centre of the room, donated by Tina's parents, was littered with papers and files. Lorna grimaced. The area not covered by paper was layered with a delicate film of dust. So was the television table and the scattering of crumbs on the plain grey carpet had been there so long they looked like a pattern. Lorna wrinkled her nose. The place was filthy. Neither she nor Tina ranked housework very highly on their list of priorities. Perhaps she could give the place an "autumn clean" while Tina was out. But she couldn't really be bothered. What was the point? It was more important to get her work done, wasn't it? But she felt no incentive to revise or write essays either. In fact she felt very bored. Her coffee had become cold and she contemplated making another one. It was nearly lunch time but she wasn't hungry. She hadn't had any breakfast either. By the time she was dressed, it had seemed too late.

The shrilling of the phone sliced the silence and she rushed to answer it. "Hullo … oh hullo, Mum. Yes, I'm fine. No, I can't come tomorrow. I'll come next week. OK? Yes ….. Yes. Really …." She cast her eyes up to the ceiling. Her mother was a dear but once on the phone, it was difficult to cut her off. It was ten minutes before she finally replaced the receiver. She hoped Will hadn't been trying to phone.

She drifted back to the kitchen. Glaring with distaste at the grease on the top of the cooker, she picked up the dishcloth. The cleaner container was almost empty. She squeezed some cream onto the surface and desultorily rubbed the cloth over it. Some of the grease was resistant to her ministrations so she squirted the remaining cream onto it. The container burped at her and she tossed it into the bin.

Chapter Six / 117

It was late afternoon when Will finally phoned. Their disagreement might never have happened. He sounded the same as he always had.

"Lorna, I'm sorry I haven't rung you. My tutor's putting the pressure on. I've missed you." Her insides did a somersault into her trainers. "There's a party at Bob's tonight. Fancy coming?"

"I'd love to."

"I'll pick you up about eight."

"Shall I bring anything?"

"I'll take a bottle. You don't need to worry. See you later."

The phone rang again as soon as she put it down.

"Yes?"

"Hullo, Lorna. It's Ellie. I wondered if you'd like to come and see *An Ideal Husband* tonight. It's only on for four nights and I've been given some complimentary tickets."

"Who's doing it?"

"One of the local amateur societies. Quest, I think. They're very good."

"Sorry, Eleanor, I can't. Will's taking me to a party tonight."

"Oh." The single syllable was swollen with disapproval. "Well be careful, Lorna. Don't do anything stupid."

"Oh don't nag." She hurriedly put the phone down denying her sister the chance of digging up her hibernating conscience. But the soil had been loosened and the guilty worm was wriggling its way to the surface. She scowled at the phone. Why did Eleanor always have to spoil everything? She'd managed to bury her doubts quite efficiently until the phone call had acted as a sharp spade. Why on earth had she given a reason for refusing the invitation? She could easily have said she was washing her hair. Of course Eleanor wouldn't have believed her.

"Oh bother," she muttered. "We're only going to a party for goodness' sake."

And she knew how to behave – didn't she?

✤ ✤ ✤ ✤

Jenny was marking in her office when she heard the muted tone of her mobile phone. She froze. She'd left it switched on hoping the clinic would phone before she had to teach. Where was it? Frantically she burrowed into her capacious handbag, retrieved it and hurriedly pressed the OK button.

"Hullo. Jenny Adams speaking."

"Mrs Adams, this is the Alexandra Clinic. Mr Coombes has checked your latest scan and you definitely have some eggs ready for collection … Mrs Adams? Are you still there?"

"Yes – oh yes. Thank you." Jenny's voice sounded like a squeak.

"Can you and your husband come on Friday at ten? We'll need to collect some sperm from Mr Adams to mix with your eggs."

"How marvellous," breathed Jenny. "I can't believe it's really happening."

"Don't get too excited, Mrs Adams," the voice warned. "There's a long way to go yet."

"I know but this is the first stage, isn't it? We'll be there on Friday. Thank you." She ended the call and hugged herself. At last! She must phone Peter. She dialled the number but he was in court. She decided against leaving a message; she'd try again later.

Reports and scripts lay thick on her desk but she couldn't settle now. She gently patted her stomach. "You little darlings," she whispered. "One of you is going to grow into a baby."

It wasn't until lunch time that she was able to phone Peter again but he was still in court so she decided to wait until the evening to tell him her news. The rest of the day was a blur as she tried to contain her excitement. Rosa and the rest of the department could cover her lessons. After much thought, she decided to tell the Head she had a hospital appointment and would be unable to return to work after it. As she'd covered her lessons within her department, he didn't ask any awkward questions.

As soon as she arrived home, she flung her coat and bag on to a chair and dived at the phone. Fortunately Peter had at last left the courtroom.

"Darling, my eggs are ready to collect and we've got an appointment for ten on Friday. You *can* make it, can't you?"

"Yes, I should be able to. The trial took longer than expected but the jury's out now. But why do you need me there?"

"Oh Peter," his wife said, exasperated, "I've explained it to you so many times.. You have to produce some sperm to be mixed with the eggs."

"Oh yes, of course. Right. See you later." The phone was hurriedly replaced and Jenny gave a giggle of relief. Thank goodness he was able to make it. But he would hate having to produce sperm to order. He said it was unnatural and she could see his point. She frowned. She hoped he would be able to oblige. If not, there would be a delay and they'd have to make another appointment. Perhaps they'd freeze her eggs until there was sperm ready to mate with them. But she was making difficulties.

Drifting into the lounge, she sat down and thought about the following day. She felt excited but also apprehensive. Shutting her eyes, she said a quick "thank you" prayer. She and Peter had prayed so often that God would bless them with children. Now that there was a possibility, she should at least say, "thank you".

On Friday they drove together to the clinic.

"Nervous?" Peter asked, as he drove into the car park and found a parking space.

She nodded. "Are you?"

"Of course. I just hope I can perform."

"You will. I know you will." She took his arm and squeezed it as they walked to the main door and made their way to the clinic where they were ushered into the empty waiting room. They didn't have to wait long. A nurse breezed in.

"Good morning Mr and Mrs Adams. I'll be looking after you. My name's Anne. Please follow me." She preceded them down a corridor and she stopped outside a door which she opened. "If you wait here, Mr Adams, I'll come back in a moment and take you upstairs. Please come with me, Mrs Adams."

Jenny's heart started to beat faster as they stopped outside the doors of the operating theatre.

"I'm really nervous," she whispered. "Will it be all right? Can anything go wrong?"

Anne patted her shoulder as she opened the door beside the operating theatre. "Don't worry, my dear. It's understandable to be anxious. You'll be fine. You'll be sedated and it'll all be over in a jiffy. Then I'll make you a cup of tea while you relax. Now change into this gown and put on these slippers while I take your husband up to do his duty."

She whirled out of the room and Jenny slowly undressed. The white gown had tapes to do up at the back. She would have to get Anne to tie them for her. Her fingers were clumsy from nerves.

"All ready then?" Anne was back. She competently tied the tapes and Jenny followed her through the swing doors into the operating theatre. An autumnal sun floated through the pale green Venetian blinds and the only furniture was the long white couch and a table. At one end of the couch were the familiar black "saddles". She felt like a prisoner about to be stretched on the rack as she hoisted herself onto the couch. Mr Coombes bustled in.

"Good morning, Mrs Adams. What a lovely day it is and you must be so excited. If you're comfortable, I'll explain what we're going to do."

Jenny nodded and Anne raised the top end of the couch so she could comfortably look at not one doctor but three.

"This is Dr Brown, the anaesthetist." A small wiry man nodded and moved towards her. She wondered if he was going to shake hands but then realised he was more interested in the equipment behind her. He was followed by a dark-haired girl in a white coat who smiled reassuringly at her.

"And this is Dr Fry, the embryologist. You've had a scan before so you're familiar with the procedure. Only this time we will be not only searching for eggs but sucking them out. Do you want to ask us anything?" Jenny shook her head. The gynaecologist held up something that looked like a piece of wire attached to a long needle. "This end," he pointed to the needle, "is what we use to collect the eggs. Each time we find one, it is sucked out and the nurse will take it into the lab through that

Chapter Six / 121

door." He pointed behind him. "Dr Fry will then put it with some solution in a culture dish ready to be mixed with your husband's sperm. Have you a culture dish to show her, Dr Fry?"

The young woman came to the door of the operating theatre and held up a small round plastic dish containing an inner and outer circle. She explained. "We put the eggs and sperm in the middle and after fertilisation we scrape off any extraneous matter on to the outer rim. Then the embryos are cleaned ready to pop back inside you."

It sounded so simple. Would it really work? Her mouth was dry and she wished they'd get on with it instead of talking.

"Just a little prick, Mrs Adams." The anaesthetist's voice startled her and she braced herself for the injection in her arm. At last!

She felt as though her body didn't belong to her and she was enshrouded in mist. A blur near her feet was probably Mr Coombes preparing to extract her precious eggs. She wanted desperately to stay awake but she found herself floating into a pleasant pale green haze; occasionally she was aware of a slight pain similar to a period pain but it didn't last. She was only vaguely aware of the murmur of voices around her although she thought the word "egg" appeared several times.

"There we are. All done. And we've a nice little collection of eggs to introduce to your husband's sperm." She drifted off again. Where was Peter? He should be here. Oh no he was upstairs. "Wake up, Mrs Adams."

"Oh." She opened her eyes. She was still in the middle of a green mist but she realised it had been created by the sun filtering through the green blinds. She wriggled her toes which now belonged to her again and remembered where she was. "Was it all right?"

Dr Fry came into the room. "It was fine, Mrs Adams. If your husband has performed satisfactorily, we can soon try to form an embryo."

Jenny sat up quickly, her dreaminess dispelled. "How long will it take?"

Mr Coombes laughed. "You *are* impatient, aren't you?"

Dr Fry answered her question. "We'll look at them tomorrow to see how many of the six eggs we collected have fertilised."

"Supposing none of them do."

The doctors exchanged glances. "I'm afraid we'd have to start again," said Dr Fry. "But don't let's think of that. If all are fertilised, we will put two back in your uterus and the rest can be frozen. You've both given your consent, haven't you?"

Jenny nodded. She was beginning to feel light-headed. She was relieved when Anne bustled in and helped her off the couch.

"Now you get changed, dear, and I'll take you to a room where you and your husband can relax for a while. You've earned it."

Suddenly Jenny wanted to cry. She had tuned herself up to such a high pitch that the taut strings of her mind and body were in danger of snapping. The tears relaxed her slightly and she at last allowed a shaft of optimism to sneak into her thoughts. She had done it! She shut her eyes, smiling as a tear trickled down her cheek; the light in her mind grew brighter and in the middle of it was a plump giggling baby. She gave a sigh of contentment as she edged herself off the couch and went to dress. It took her longer than usual and Anne had to help her.

"I'm sorry," she muttered. "I'm all fingers and thumbs."

"That's all right, dear. You're bound to be a bit woozy after the anaesthetic. Now, come along and relax for a while."

Dreamily she followed her guide down the corridor and into a small room containing a bed, a table and chair and another easy chair. Beside the bed another door led to the bathroom which Jenny realised she was desperate to use. When she returned, the nurse handed her a steaming cup of tea. It was the most delicious brew she'd ever tasted. As she sat sipping it, she wondered how Peter had got on. She'd almost forgotten about him. Briefly her spirits plummeted again. Suppose there were no sperm to fertilise with her perfect eggs.

"Darling, we're on the way." Suddenly her husband was beside her and he sounded excited. "You *are* a clever girl. Six eggs they collected and you'll be pleased to know I managed to produce some playmates."

"I never doubted it," she lied. "Can we wait until we know they've fertilised? How do they do it? I've forgotten."

"They prepare some culture – a sort of yoghurt and put that in a dish with the eggs and sperm and hope they get together. I think they're put in an incubator for a while."

She put down her cup. "Oh Peter, isn't it exciting? But I do hate waiting."

"I know you do. But it may not be for too long."

"Finished your tea?" The nurse was beside them again. "Stay and relax for a while. Don't go home until you feel up to it, Mrs Adams."

Jenny was disappointed. "Can't I wait to see if they're going to ... fertilise?"

"I'm afraid it might be a long wait. We don't put them together at once so it will be at least eighteen hours before we know if they've fertilised. You can phone us tomorrow. We'll be able to tell you more then. But don't phone too early and try to get a good night's sleep tonight."

"I don't think I'll be able to sleep a wink," said Jenny as they walked to the car. "I'll be far too excited."

But the tension over the past few days had taken its toll and, to her surprise, she slept well. When she woke, it was past nine o'clock. Although it was Saturday, Peter had gone to his Chambers and there was a mug of cold tea on her bedside table. She hadn't heard a thing.

Was it too early to ring the hospital? She decided to get dressed and have a fresh cup of tea first. It was still not quite ten when she sat in front of the phone. She couldn't wait any longer. Her hands were clammy with sweat and she wiped them on her jeans. Then, taking a deep breath, she dialled the number.

A few minutes later, she slowly put down the receiver. Her face was expressionless. Then suddenly she leapt from the chair and did an impromptu dance around the room.

"Yippee! Yippee! Yippee!" she shouted. "Oh thank you, Lord; thank you; thank you."

Racing back to the phone, she hurriedly dialled Peter's number but was told he was not available. She scowled. She wanted to tell him *now* that there was an embryo ready to be implanted in her.

"Where is he?" she demanded crossly.

"I really couldn't say, Mrs Adams," was the cool reply.

"Please tell him to ring me immediately. It's urgent."

"Yes, Mrs Adams. Not bad news I hope." The voice softened.

"No. It's … no." She clamped her lips together. She didn't want him hearing from someone else. "Just tell him to phone me, please." She should get on with some work but she couldn't settle. The sun beckoned her out but she didn't want to leave the house until Peter had phoned.

She had to wait for over an hour. The time crawled by and she was even reduced to watching television – something she *never* did during the day, even in holiday periods. At last the phone rang and she hurtled over to it.

"Peter? Great news, darling. They're going to implant two eggs in me on Monday."

"That's wonderful. What time's your appointment?"

"Ten o'clock again. Can you come?" She sounded wistful.

"I'm really sorry, darling. I'll be tied up in court all day. I don't want to upset our new lady judge by being late."

"A lady judge?" said Jenny, intrigued.

"Of course. Why not?" Why not, indeed? Did she have children? If so, how did she juggle a busy professional life with the demands of her family? But if she was a judge, she was probably older and her children were grown up. Perhaps she had grandchildren.

"Jenny, are you still there? You've gone quiet."

"Just thinking."

"I'll see you later. I should be able to get away about five."

"Have you really got to work all day? It *is* Saturday, you know."

"I'm sorry darling but my desk is piled high. I must clear some of it today."

"All right. See you then. Love you." Thoughtfully she replaced the receiver. Would she be granted maternity leave? Of

Chapter Six / 125

course it was statutory now, wasn't it? Did she want to go on working? She'd only just started her new job. She wouldn't be very popular when she asked for leave so soon. But she mustn't think of that now. It was a long way in the future. She was impatient for Monday to arrive.

She was used to the procedure now although she wished Peter could have been there with her. This time there was no anaesthetic. She didn't feel nervous any more as she entered the embryo transfer room – only excited. She shut her eyes; when soft music seeped into her being and relaxed her, she thought she was dreaming and hurriedly opened them again. She didn't want to sleep during this important moment.

"Does the music help?" Mr Coombes stood beside her.

"It's lovely," she sighed contentedly.

"Are you ready for your big moment?"

"Oh yes." She smiled at him and he moved to the end of the couch and gently lifted her legs onto the leather "saddles". Soon she would have a tiny baby growing inside her.

She squinted down as he inserted the plastic tube and gently placed her two beautiful fertilised eggs into her womb. As the plastic tube was removed, she imagined she could feel both of her eggs starting to grow. Perhaps she'd have twins. Dreaming of shopping for her new babies, she was only vaguely aware of the gynaecologist speaking to her. He had to repeat his words.

"I'd like you to stay here for a little while, Mrs Adams. I'll leave the music on and the nurse will come to collect you later. Just relax. Good luck."

She smiled dreamily. Luck didn't come in to it. Already she was in a world surrounded by babies. What fun it would be.

✥ ✥ ✥ ✥

"Have you tackled David yet."

Eleanor turned at the familiar voice. She was coming out of the bank on the Saturday morning after the disastrous dinner. She had nearly collided with Chris so she couldn't pretend she hadn't seen him. She didn't want to talk to him. Her encounter with

David was still too close. She was sure Chris would gloat if he knew David had walked out on her.

"I'm very busy, Chris. I've got a lot to do." She started to walk on but he fell in step beside her.

"You have, haven't you? What happened?"

"It's none of your business."

"Yes it is. I love you, Ellie. I shall keep on telling you until I wear you down."

"Oh go away," she said, exasperated.

"I'll ring you," he called after her retreating back.

She marched on, her arms aching from the bag she was carrying. She'd stocked up on library books and her arm felt as though it was being dragged out of its socket.

"He could have offered to carry it," she thought sourly.

As she walked to the bus stop, her mind was in turmoil. She hadn't wanted to think about David and now Chris had brought it all back. Bother him! Of course he'd be pleased if he knew what had happened. But she was definitely not about to leap into *his* arms – or his bed. She was angry with herself that she had accused David of being prepared to kill unborn babies. Why hadn't she trusted him?

She must talk to Jenny. Jenny was sensible and would give her some good advice. She'd ring her and see if she could go round. Peter would probably be watching football on Saturday afternoon, if he wasn't working.

❖ ❖ ❖ ❖

She had been right. Jenny was alone and delighted to put aside her marking to talk to her sister. She was much more relaxed now she hoped she had a baby growing inside her.

"How do you feel about David now?" she asked when Eleanor had related the story of the dinner fiasco. "Do you want to see him again?"

"I'll have to see him. I work with him."

"You know what I mean."

Eleanor hesitated. What did she feel? She still felt upset but was that because her pride had been hurt? "I suppose I do still like him. There's … there's something about him and we get on so well. I'd like to get to know him better, I suppose. But I've probably blown it now. I should have believed him. I don't think he'll want anything more to do with me." Tears threatened to spill out. "He said he didn't like having his word doubted."

"Oh Ellie, why on earth didn't you believe him? You do now, don't you?"

"Of course I do."

"I think you should tell him. He may have cooled down by now. It must have been a shock for him when you suddenly attacked him."

"I suppose so."

"Well I hope it works out. He sounds a nice chap."

✥ ✥ ✥ ✥

But it wasn't easy. The atmosphere between nurse and surgeon was strained. Neither felt comfortable with the other and at the end of the day Eleanor couldn't wait to leave the operating theatre for the safety of her flat.

One afternoon, thinking David had already left, she decided to relax over a cup of tea before going home. She made the tea and collapsed onto one of the utilitarian chairs. Kicking off her shoes, she put her feet on the table and took a sip of the reviving brew. She gave a sigh of contentment and shut her eyes.

"May I join you?"

"Oh!" She jumped, upsetting the tea which started to form a decorative pattern on the front of her plain pink jumper. This was getting to be a habit. "Ouch. That's hot. You startled me. I thought you'd gone."

"Sorry. Here, put this under your jumper." David handed her a tea towel from the rack. She glared at him and turned her back while she fumbled with the cloth and then picked up another one to try to removed the stains.

"I'll have to go home and change," she grumbled as she emptied the remains of her tea into the sink, washed up the mug and dumped it on the draining board. She made for the door but he was standing in front of it. "Please let me pass."

Instead of moving, he took a step towards her and pulling her close to him, he kissed her hard on the lips. For a moment she responded. She felt right in his arms but the physical side was only part of a relationship. She pushed him away, her mounting fury giving her added strength. Why was she so angry? She felt confused and her emotions were in a tangled heap. She was gasping for breath when he finally let her go.

"How – how dare you!" she exclaimed.

"You didn't seem to mind." To her annoyance, he seemed in complete control of himself. His reaction added more fuel to the fire of her anger. She was surprised it wasn't scorching him. Pushing past him, she wrenched open the door and rushed down the corridor ignoring the groan that suggested the wood had struck him as she flung it back.

The tea towel had slipped down in front of her jeans and attacked her feet; she just prevented herself from tripping over it. Annoyed, she grabbed it and continued her headlong flight, getting colder as the wet jumper clung to her. As she stepped outside, the wind slashed at her and she gasped. Winter had definitely arrived. Where was her coat? She'd left in such a hurry, it was still in the locker room. She couldn't brave the icy Siberian blasts without some protection. The cold would unerringly target her wet jumper and she'd end up with pneumonia. Perhaps that would be a good thing. She wouldn't have to work with David. She could stay in bed and mope.

She heard his footsteps in the distance and quickly dodged round a corner until he'd left the building. She returned to the locker room by a circuitous route in case he returned. Back in her flat, she wondered again why she had reacted in the way she had. But she'd been startled by his behaviour. He'd angrily walked out on her because she'd doubted him and today he'd kissed her and obviously expected her to respond. He *was* arrogant after all. She didn't want any more to do with him. So why did she feel so miserable?

✥ ✥ ✥

"My goodness, it's huge. I didn't realise we were coming to a stately home." Lorna gaped as Will drove through the open

Chapter Six / 129

wrought-iron gates in the wake of several other cars. Floodlights shone on a long rectangular building boasting three storeys and an abundance of lattice windows. The black timbers on the white stuccoed walls indicated a Tudor influence while two tall decorative chimneys stood sentinel at the front. They looked as if they'd been added as an afterthought. Perhaps they had.

Will eased the car up the gravel tree-lined drive past a small lake in the centre of which a fountain gushed out multi-coloured water by courtesy of strategically placed lights. They drove round the lake to the car park. In front of them, wide stone steps led up to the arched entrance of the house where the huge wooden door stood open in welcome.

"Does Bob really live here?" asked Lorna in amazement.

"His parents do but they're away for the weekend. Apparently the house has been in his family for generations."

"How old is it?"

"You'll have to ask Bob."

"I haven't met him yet. Will he mind me coming to his party?"

"Of course not. As you can see there's plenty of room. Come on."

They straggled up the steps with the other newcomers and the noise increased as they drew closer. At least the loud music wouldn't disturb the neighbours, Lorna reflected. It didn't look as if there were any for miles. Music and excited voices engulfed them as they entered a large hall filled with people.

"Will, glad you could come." A dark-haired young man with thick eyebrows that almost met across the bridge of his nose and a wide grin pushed through the crowd.

"Hi, Bob. This is Lorna."

"Hi, Lorna. Welcome to the ancestral pile."

"It's lovely," Laura enthused. "How old is it?"

"It was originally Norman but there's not much left of that part of it. It's rather a mongrel as bits have been added on over the years. But the main part was rebuilt in 1568."

"I thought it looked Tudor," said Lorna, pleased.

Bob grinned. "The beams give it away, don't they? Come and have some punch. It's my special brew. You must try some."

They followed him into a large kitchen where Mrs Beeton would have been at home. In the centre was a large square oak "island"; its black marble top was covered with a variety of dishes containing crisps and dips. Above it a motley collection of gleaming copper utensils hung from a metal contraption attached to the ceiling. Facing it on one side was a huge Aga, set in what had obviously been the original fireplace over which cooking had taken place. A modern stainless steel sink on the opposite side looked anachronistic but whoever was washing up would have a marvellous view over the lake. Fitted oak cupboards and drawers graced two of the walls while along the third a rectangular oak table bore a variety of bottles and glasses. In the centre reposed a huge silver punch bowl. Will added the bottle of wine he'd brought to the collection.

"Help, something's burning!" Bob suddenly yelped. He dived at the Aga from which smoke was beginning to ooze. Grabbing an oven cloth, he dragged out a huge pizza and dumped it on the black marble of the "island". "Just saved it. Cut it up will you, Jane. Thanks."

"I will when it's cooled down," retorted the girl he'd addressed. "You haven't got a drink, Will. And …?"

"Lorna."

"I'm Bob's sister, Jane. Are you going to try some of his special brew?"

"Yes please."

Slices of kiwi fruit and orange were floating on the top of the brimming punch bowl. Jane spooned some into a glass and handed it to Lorna. It was delicious. There was a hint of cranberry and orange and some other fruits she couldn't identify. She realised she was thirsty; her glass was soon empty and promptly refilled. Will led her towards the huge drawing room where the elegant green upholstered chairs had been pushed to the sides of the room and the carpet rolled back exposing a wood floor now covered with dancers. Lorna looked around but didn't see anyone she recognised. Dress appeared to be a little more conservative than that worn in the night-club and not so much bare flesh was on show; but the colours were as bright and skirts as short.

Chapter Six / 131

Will and Lorna joined in, still holding their drinks as there didn't seem anywhere to deposit them. Lorna was glad of hers as the heat and the dancing made her even thirstier.

"Let's go and find something to eat," Will gasped when they had worn themselves out and Lorna was starting to see double. "I'm starving."

"So am I." Her words were a little slurred but perhaps Will hadn't noticed. She held up her glass. "I'd … I'd like another drink too."

"I'll get you one."

They crossed the entrance hall and proceeded down the stone-flagged corridor past several closed doors. The noise from the drawing room had receded but more noise was issuing from beyond an open door in front of them.

"This must be the dining room."

"It's beautiful."

"You find some food and I'll get the drinks." Will disappeared and Lorna edged her way into the room. Portraits of bygone inhabitants gazed benignly down on the youthful crowd representing an innovative century they could never have imagined. At one side of the room the large ornately carved fireplace was not only for decoration as a huge log fire blazed in it.

The flames appeared to be slightly blurred but it was probably the heat Lorna decided as she wove her way through the crowd. Jane waltzed in bearing a tray of tortillas with a selection of fillings. She dumped it on the long refectory table which dominated the room.

"Now you lot had better eat these. I learnt how to make them when I was in Mexico. They're not from the local supermarket, you know. Eat as many as you can. I've made plenty and we don't want any left. There are some more in the kitchen. Have you had tortillas before?" she asked Lorna who shook her head. "I'll show you what to do." She spooned some filling on to the flat tortilla and, rolling it up, handed it to Lorna. "It's very hot," she warned.

Her guest took a bite and her eyes watered. "My goodness, it is. But it's nice."

"Have another. This filling's not quite so hot."

"I must take one for Will as well."

"Take a couple with different fillings." Jane competently rolled the tortillas and handed them to Lorna.

"Thanks. It's a lovely party. Thank you for letting me come."

"You're welcome. Excuse me." Jane flitted off to greet more guests.

"Here you are." Will returned with two brimming glasses. He stared at the food. "What's that?"

"Tortillas. They're Mexican and they're very hot."

"Great. Let's find somewhere to sit. I've got an idea. Come on."

He led her back down the corridor to the entrance hall from which a wide peach-carpeted staircase led to the floors above. Other guests had had the same idea. The lower stairs were crammed with couples eating, talking and, in some cases, using the opportunity to twist themselves into single entities. Lorna felt embarrassed but no one else was taking any notice of the embracing couples.

"Let's go further up." Will nodded at the staircase and, carefully stepping over bodies and occasionally causing a yelp from one of them, Lorna followed him up. She was having difficulty focusing and was glad of the help afforded by the decorative wooden banisters to which she could cling. The staircase curved but it was still crowded. Higher and higher they went until at last they were able to cram themselves into a space created by another couple moving closer together. Lorna was glad to sit down. She was beginning to feel giddy.

She had lost her hunger but her thirst was becoming stronger. She gulped at her drink and then decided she would start to attack the tortilla. She munched slowly because it was very hot and her eyes started to close. She was so tired. How long had they been here? Her bed was beginning to beckon enticingly.

Chapter Six / 133

She dropped her head on to Will's shoulder and he put his arm round her. She sighed contentedly and snuggled closer. She could stay like this for ever. The music and the voices had blurred to a drone and although her head was spinning gently like a top running down, she found it quite a pleasant sensation. She drifted off to sleep.

Chapter Seven

"Lorna, Lorna, wake up, darling."

She felt a butterfly kiss on her cheek and turned happily to put her arms round the kisser. "Mm. What time is it?"

"It's nearly eleven."

"I thought it would be much later than that," she murmured sleepily. "It's been a lovely party, Will, but I think I'd like to go home now."

"Darling, you *are* home."

"What?" Sleep shattered in a thousand fragments and she sat up with a jerk. She groaned and put her hand to her head. "I've got such a headache. What on earth did Bob put in that punch?" Then, bewildered, she looked around. She was lying in her own bed with Will beside her and a motley collection of clothes littering the floor. She looked at Will with wide horror-stricken eyes. "What happened?"

"We came home and – and I put you to bed. You were very sleepy but you didn't want me to go. You were so sweet, Lorna, and it was lovely to make love to you. I think I love you."

She burst into tears. Once she had wanted to hear those words but now they hardly registered a dot in her mind.

"Darling, what's the matter? I thought you wanted it too. You seemed to."

"Oh, I've been so wicked. How could I do something like that? Will, you *knew* I didn't want to … to …" She broke into sobs again.

He looked bemused. "But last night you seemed …"

"I don't remember anything about last night," she screamed. "At least – at least – I thought I was dreaming and I … I …"

"So you did like it really?" He sounded anxious.

She gulped. "Yes – I suppose I did." Suddenly she clutched the duvet to her in horror. "Oh Will, suppose I'm pregnant."

He looked startled. "You *are* on the pill, aren't you?"

"Of course I'm not. I didn't think I'd need to be."

She watched his face whiten. "You probably won't get pregnant."

"You can't know that." She was still sobbing.

"Well we'll cross that bridge when – *if* we come to it. Don't worry, Lorna and *please* stop crying. I hate to see you upset."

He tried to put his arm round her but she rolled away.

"I'd like you to go now, Will, please. I need to be alone for a while." She sniffed and reached for a handful of tissues.

"Yes of course. Lorna, I'm really sorry. I – I wouldn't have done anything to hurt you. You know that."

"Yes, Will, I know."

After he'd left, she cried again for her lost virginity and in deep repentance.

"Oh God, I never meant to do it," she cried. "Please forgive me and please don't let me be pregnant."

Supposing she was. However would her parents react? What would she do?

❖ ❖ ❖ ❖

Jenny stared closely at her breasts. Had they swollen slightly during the week after the transfer? She pressed them gently. Were they tender or was she imagining it? At least there had been no bleeding after the first day. She'd been in a real panic then and had phoned the clinic. But she had been assured that a little bleeding was normal after a transfer and it didn't signify a miscarriage. They had told her to live as normal a life as possible but that wasn't easy. She felt as though her body were a fragile glass vase containing the precious potential baby and if she moved too quickly or was too energetic, she might shatter it and her hopes. Peter, too, was treating her as though she were made of the most delicate china and this irritated her sometimes.

She turned from the mirror and picked up her bra. As she fastened it, she thought that it was tighter than usual. However, she'd washed it the night before and clean bras were always tighter at first. She stared distastefully at the pack of cyclogest pessaries on the bedside table. Apparently they contained the hormone progesterone which helped to maintain her pregnancy. She hated inserting one every day. It was different from using a tampon which was removed later. This *thing* dissolved and was absorbed into her body. But she would try anything to make sure she became pregnant.

Slowly she finished dressing and went to make herself some tea and toast before driving to school.

"I hope I'm eating for two now," she whispered as she buttered her second slice of toast.

She arrived early at school to find a pile of letters, notes and reports on her desk. She sighed as she sorted them into piles. She had just managed to complete her own reports but she would have to check the probationer's to see that he was following the guidelines she had given him. Thank goodness she didn't have to look at those of the rest of her staff. She trusted them. They were a good department, she reflected. They respected her and she liked them. The only slight fly in the ointment was the probationer who thought he knew it all and obviously disliked having a woman boss.

There was a note about a staff meeting after school the following day. Could she manage to keep her mind on her work during the next fortnight before she went to the clinic for the test to see whether the transfer had 'taken'?

By the time she'd answered her mail and dealt with some of the notes, the murmur outside had turned to a roar. The next generation was ready for its daily intake of education. She had a GCSE class first but was then free until lunch time so she would be able to get on with some of the administrative work she hadn't done over the half-term period.

Over the next few days Jenny was so busy she had little time to brood on her forthcoming test. She took books home to mark and tried not to think about what was happening inside her. But sometimes she allowed herself to dream happily about a positive outcome. At other times she had nightmares about the tiny creature inside her being hurled out in a flood of blood.

✥ ✥ ✥ ✥

"Can I have a word?"

Eleanor turned from the autoclave to find David behind her looking sheepish. She turned back to her work, ignoring him.

"Please, Eleanor, It's important."

"I really haven't got anything to say to you."

"But I have something to say to you."

"I'm very busy."

"You've just finished for the day."

"I've got a lot of clearing up to do."

"Let's have a cup of coffee."

"David, just say what you've got to say and then go. I don't want a cup of coffee."

Why on earth was she being so disagreeable when all she wanted was to throw herself into his arms? She busied herself at the autoclave with her back to him.

"Eleanor, I'm sorry I – I kissed you the other day. At least I'm not sorry. I enjoyed it but I'm sorry about the way I did it. But most of all I'm really sorry about walking out on you the other day. You really hurt me by not believing me and I was just lashing out and … Oh please say you forgive me and we can start again."

She sniffed. Of course she forgave him but she was going to burst into tears at any moment and she was furious with herself for being so emotional. She sobbed and then she felt his hand on her shoulder.

"Don't cry, Ellie. I can't bear to see you cry."

She gave another gulping sob and she felt a handkerchief thrust into her hand. "Thank you," she mumbled. She scrubbed her face and looked up at him.

He put his arm comfortingly around her. "I really don't do abortions, Ellie. You do believe me, don't you?"

"Of course I do. I'm sorry." She turned her face into his shoulder and sobbed again.

"Ellie, stop crying. It's all right. Look at me."

When she did so, he retrieved his handkerchief and gently wiped her cheeks with it before stuffing it into his pocket. Then he put his hands either side of her face and kissed her tenderly on the lips. It was as if a live electric wire was running right through her body from her lips to the tip of her toes. She put her arms round his neck and hugged him as his kisses became more demanding.

Eventually he gently disengaged himself but retained her hands in his. "I must go before I forget myself."

Gazing at him, she wondered how could she ever have thought she was in love with Chris? Carol was welcome to him. She wanted him to kiss her again and tried to pull her hands away so she could put her arms round his neck; but he held them tightly.

"Are we friends again?"

"Of course."

He took her hand and raised it to his lips. His gentle kiss, sent more tremors of electricity up her arm.

"How about dinner tomorrow night?" he asked, still holding her hand.

"I'd like that."

"I'll pick you up about seven."

"OK."

"Fancy a coffee now? Or a drink. We could go to the pub."

"Not a drink," she said, laughing. "Remember the first time we went out? We could hardly hear ourselves think. I'll make some coffee."

✤ ✤ ✤ ✤

The day before her pregnancy test passed in a blur for Jenny. She could think only of her appointment at the clinic. Would the test confirm she was pregnant or would she have to go through the whole procedure again?

On that evening she and Peter were watching a documentary when suddenly she gasped.

"Oh!"

"What's the matter? Are you in pain? Where does it hurt?" Peter leapt up and came to kneel in front of her.

"It's all right, I think. I've had a dull ache in my stomach all evening." Her eyes filled with tears. "Oh Peter, do you think it's my period? Perhaps I'm not pregnant." She sobbed.

He put his arms round her. "Now don't get upset. You're bound to have a bit of discomfort, aren't you? Perhaps it's starting to grow."

She managed to laugh. "Perhaps." She put her hand behind her. "My back aches too. Pregnant woman have backache, don't they? And it hurts – here." She put her hands over her left breast.

"You mustn't worry, dear. You'll know tomorrow. Perhaps you should go to bed now. It's nearly ten o'clock."

She made no objection but she had difficulty sleeping. Her mind was a jumble of everything that had happened over the past few weeks. Tomorrow she would know.

"Oh please Lord, let tomorrow come quickly," she prayed. "And please let me be pregnant."

She slept fitfully and was fully awake when Peter brought her a cup of tea. She drank it gratefully.

"How do you feel this morning?"

"Better. The pain's gone and there wasn't any bleeding."

"Good. You'll let me know as soon as possible, won't you? I'm sorry I can't come with you."

She nodded. As she showered and dressed, she felt as if her body didn't belong to her. She was dressing someone else. Was this how pregnant women felt? She touched her breasts again. Yes they definitely felt sore but fortunately the other pains had gone.

When she reached the clinic, she still felt rather like a robot and she was very tearful. She could have bought a pregnancy testing kit and done the test at home but she was a coward and she knew the clinic would still have to do another one. They wouldn't accept one she'd done herself. In the past she'd tested herself so often and it had always been negative.

"It's bound to upset you," Anne said kindly as she handed over a box of tissues. "You mustn't worry so much."

"But I had period pains and backache yesterday. My breasts were sore as well but there wasn't any bleeding. I can't be pregnant, can I?" She choked on a sob.

Anne sat down beside her. "That doesn't mean you're *not* pregnant. You can have those symptoms and still be pregnant."

"Can I? Really?" The sun shone again.

"We won't know until we've done the test. You've brought your sample, haven't you?" Jenny handed it over. "I'm afraid you'll have to wait for the result. Would you like to go home and ring us?"

Jenny shook her head. "No, I'd rather wait here." She nodded at the file beside her. "I brought some papers to mark."

"Very wise. I'll come and tell you when I know anything."

The time went so slowly Jenny thought her watch had stopped. It was over an hour before Anne came back. Jenny leapt up, scattering papers all over the floor.

"Well?" she asked excitedly.

Anne beamed. "I'm glad to tell you the test was positive, Mrs Adams. "You're definitely pregnant."

Jenny flopped back into the chair. "I'm pregnant," she whispered. Tears were beginning to seep out of her eyes and she didn't try to hold them back. "Oh how marvellous. Thank you." She stood up and started to scoop up the papers. "I must get home and phone Peter. Thank you. Thank you so much."

"You'll need to come back in two weeks' time for a pregnancy scan. Make an appointment at Reception before you go."

"Oh yes."

Having done so, she danced along the corridor, out of the hospital and rushed over to her car. As she drove, she was in such a hurry that she wasn't even aware that her speedometer was creeping up to fifty until she noticed a police car some distance behind her. She hurriedly dropped to a sedate thirty. Fortunately the other vehicle remained some way behind her.

Leaving the car in the driveway, she rushed into the house dropping books and bags as she went. She headed for the nearest phone and picked up the receiver.

"Jenny, how did you get on?"

Whirling round, she almost dropped the phone. "Peter, what are you doing at home? I was just going to ring you."

"I couldn't concentrate so I cancelled an appointment and came home, I didn't go to the clinic in case I missed you. Well? Don't keep me in suspense."

Now that the time had come, she wanted to savour the moment. "Go and sit down, Peter. I'll join you in a moment."

She saw his shoulders droop and turned away to hide a smile. But she wasn't going to torment him. Going into the kitchen, she took out the remains of the wine they had drunk the previous evening. She poured it into two glasses but only took a little for herself. Carrying it into the lounge, she handed one glass to him.

"Congratulations, Peter. You're going to be a daddy."

✣ ✣ ✣ ✣

Melanie was making a cup of tea when there was a frantic banging at her door. She glanced at the clock. It was after ten o'clock. Who on earth could be calling at this time? She had given up expecting Simon. He hadn't been to see her since he'd run after Joy when she'd seen them kissing.

Putting the kettle down, she went to the door. Simon stood there looking distraught. She stared.

"Mel. Please let me in. I don't know what to do."

Speechless, she stood back to let him in. He walked to the living room and collapsed onto the sofa which groaned under his weight. He put his face in his hands. Prickles of fear were already prodding her. Something was wrong and she was very apprehensive. Had she triggered something that she could not stop?

"I was just making a cup of tea. Would you like one?"

"Have you got anything stronger?"

"There might be some wine in the fridge. I'll have a look."

She found the remains of a bottle of white wine she'd opened a few days previously. She smelt it. It seemed to be all right still. There was only enough for one so she poured it out thoughtfully and then made herself a cup of tea. She didn't want to know what had upset Simon. Her imagination was overactive.

Carefully carrying the tea and the wine, she returned to the living room. Simon was still sitting slumped on the sofa staring at nothing. She handed him the glass, noting with fear how his hand shook. He took a gulp and she sat down and waited, sipping her tea. He would tell her when he was ready.

"Joy tried to commit suicide this evening."

Blood rushed to Melanie's head and there was a singing noise in her ears. She mustn't faint – she mustn't. She was going to be sick. The cup dropped from her hand. She tried to get up but her feet were nailed to the ground and her arms didn't belong to her any more. It was her fault. She knew it was. Joy had received her letter. How Simon must hate her. But perhaps he didn't know. Would he have come round if he knew what she had done? He seemed totally unaware of her. She took some deep breaths and the faintness receded. She tried to focus on what he was saying.

"I got home just after six this evening. The house was so quiet. I knew something was wrong. The kids weren't there, I went up to the bedroom. She'd taken nearly a whole bottle of paracetamol and she was just lying there. She looked dead, Mel. I'll never forget it."

"But she's all right?" The words came out in a croak.

"Of course she's not all right. The ambulance came and they rushed her to hospital and pumped out her stomach but it was touch and go. She's sleeping now but she wouldn't talk to me when she came round. Oh Mel, what am I going to do?"

To Melanie's horror he burst into tears. She'd never seen a man cry before and she hated it. She'd become so hard over the past few months. Now she wasn't even sure she loved him anymore. She felt confused. He continued to sob and eventually

Chapter Seven / 143

she went to sit beside him and put her arms round him. He turned and buried his face in her shoulder and her obsessive love came flooding back. Perhaps Joy would die after all and they could be married and live happily ever after. She relaxed her arms horrified at herself. How could she wish her rival dead? The devil must be laughing gleefully at having defeated so easily the good angel of her conscience.

She tightened her hold again. Certain now that her letter had triggered Joy's suicide attempt, she tried to rationalise it. She'd only "told the truth" and if Joy couldn't handle it, then Simon was better off without her.

"I don't want to go home. Can I stay tonight, Mel – please."

Over his shoulder, she couldn't prevent a small smile of triumph. "Of course you can." Then she remembered something. "What about the children? Where are they?"

"What?" He broke away from her. His face was blotched and he looked ten years older. "Joy took them to her parents. They don't know what's happened. She told me they were going to stay overnight with their grandparents. She must have planned this carefully. She was very odd yesterday, now that I come to think about it. Quiet and ..." He paused, frowning and Melanie felt the moment of truth must be approaching.

"What?" She had to know.

"Well, I think she had a letter that upset her but she wouldn't let me see it."

Mine, thought Melanie. She felt sick again. What had she expected to achieve by writing to Joy? She'd hoped Joy might be so angry she would take the children and leave the field clear for her. But she had never, *never* thought Joy would attempt to take her own life.

❖ ❖ ❖ ❖

"I feel so humiliated," Lorna told Eleanor. "He's a real bastard. I hate him."

"Lorna."

"Sorry." She had the grace to look ashamed and then muttered, "But he is. We were getting on so well and then ..."

"Then what?"

"Nothing." Lorna wouldn't look at her sister.

"Lorna, what is it?" Eleanor asked gently. "Why are you so upset?"

"He wrote me a note and said we should cool it for a while."

"Well what's wrong with that?"

"Why doesn't he want to see me again when we had such a great time? I suppose it's because …" She broke off.

"Because what? You'd better tell me, Lorna. If he's what you say he is, it's better to find out now. Things haven't gone too far, have they?" Lorna wouldn't look at her. "Oh Lorna, how could you?"

"I knew it was wrong but I … I didn't realise. We'd been to this party and I suppose I had too much to drink. I don't really remember much about it. I thought I was dreaming."

"Well I hope you've taken precautions," said her practical sister.

Lorna shook her head, tears welling up in her eyes. "I didn't think I'd need to. I never meant to …"

"When did it happen?"

"Last Saturday. We'd been out to this party and …"

"All right, spare me the details. That's a week ago. You can't take the "morning after" pill."

"What's that?"

"Oh Lorna, you are hopeless. There's a pill you can take for up to seventy-two hours after intercourse and it's supposed to prevent pregnancy. But it's too late for that now."

"I won't be pregnant. It was only once, Ellie."

Eleanor sighed. "Whatever difference does that make? We'll just have to wait and hope – and pray."

Lorna looked embarrassed. "Will you pray for me?"

"Of course I will."

"I've been very stupid, haven't I? And now he doesn't want anything to do with me." Her voice broke on a sob.

"He's probably embarrassed if it was your first time and he realised how upset you were."

Lorna clutched at the straw drifting towards her. "Yes it could be that, couldn't it? Perhaps I should write to him."

"Lorna, leave it for a bit. Please don't rush into anything. You're so impetuous. Why don't you ever think before you act?"

❖ ❖ ❖ ❖

Two weeks after having her pregnancy confirmed, Jenny was again back at the clinic, this time for another scan. Peter was with her.

"Now I'm just going to rub some jelly on your tummy," said Anne, "and then you'll be able to see your baby for the first time."

Jenny turned her head to smile at her husband. She was sure her grin reached almost to her ears and it was matched by his. He squeezed her hand.

"Look." Anne passed a probe over Jenny's stomach and pointed to the monitor. A large dark circle swirled in the middle of a moving pattern of black and grey. "That's your baby's head. Can you see it?"

Jenny squinted at the monitor and laughed. "Just about."

"And there are the legs – and the arms. He's perfect."

"It might be a 'she'."

"Of course it might. We can't tell at this stage. Would you like to take a picture with you?"

"Oh yes please."

"I'll just run it off while you dress."

❖ ❖ ❖ ❖

"I don't know what to do. I'm so confused. I – I didn't mean this to happen, Eleanor."

Eleanor looked steadily at Melanie. She was determined not to remind her, yet again, that she had been warned that the path she was on would lead to deep unhappiness.

"Why don't you go to see Joy?" she suggested gently.

"Oh I couldn't. She must hate me. It's all my fault." She grabbed another handful of tissues from the box thoughtfully provided by her sister.

Eleanor sighed. She had no idea how to help. All she could do was listen while Melanie poured out all her guilt and confusion. She felt the situation could only end in disaster. There was one solution but she didn't expect Melanie would listen to it. But she *could* suggest it.

"Perhaps you should move away from the area and find a job somewhere else."

Melanie stared at her as if she were a being from another planet. Her mouth opened and closed but only a croak emerged. Eleanor waited patiently. This had obviously never occurred to her sister. Finally Melanie found her voice – and used it to effect.

"I don't want to," she screamed. "I might have known you'd be all critical and ..." She dissolved into tears again and Eleanor thrust a new box of tissues at her.

"Do calm down. And don't shout. My neighbour's on night duty. She'll be sleeping."

"Sorry." Melanie sniffed.

"What are you going to do for Christmas? Will you come home? Mum and Dad miss you."

"You haven't told them about ... about me and Simon and everything, have you?"

"Of course I haven't. You know I don't gossip. It's *your* job to tell them – if you want to. But they do miss you. They know something's wrong."

"I phone them every week."

"But Mum can tell there's something wrong. Why don't you have a talk with her?"

"How can I?" snapped Melanie, exasperated. "She'd be horrified. Her nicely brought up 'Christian' daughter having an affair with a married man. She and Dad would disown me."

"Don't be so melodramatic," said Eleanor crossly. "Do give them some credit. Of course they won't approve of what you're doing but that doesn't mean they'll reject you. 'Hate the sin; love the sinner.' Remember?"

"It's easy to say," mumbled Melanie.

"Well I know they'll still love you but if you don't want to tell them, that's up to you."

Chapter Seven / 147

"I'll think about it. Thanks for listening, Ellie. I'm sorry I'm such a pain."

Eleanor gave her sister a hug. "No, you're not. I'm just sorry you fell for the wrong man."

Melanie gave a gulping sob. "I think I'm a one-man woman."

"Yes I'm afraid you are," returned Eleanor sadly.

✤ ✤ ✤ ✤

It was the Saturday before the Christmas weekend and Jenny and Peter had been working in their respective studies all Saturday morning. After a snack lunch in the kitchen, Jenny suggested they went in to the town together.

Peter looked up from his papers and made a face. "Today? You must be mad. It's the busiest day of the year. It'll be so crowded. Why do you want to go? I thought you'd done all your Christmas shopping ages ago."

"I have. I just thought we could buy some things for the baby."

"Surely that can wait till after Christmas. There'll be some sales then."

"But I want to go now. Do come with me, Peter. I'm fed up with working."

"Oh all right but don't drag me round too many baby shops will you?"

She laughed. "I promise. You can go and browse in the bookshop."

"We may not find anywhere to park."

"Don't be such a pessimist."

But he was right. They drove right to the top of the multi-storey car park and started to come down again before they were fortunate enough to find a car easing out from a space in front of them.

Peter's temper had become somewhat frayed. "You would pick today, wouldn't you? I told you it would be busy." He slammed the door and marched over to the ticket machine. He was back promptly. "The wretched thing's not working."

"There's one on the next floor."

"Thanks," he said sarcastically.

Jenny sighed. It was obviously going to be one of those afternoons. She knew Peter hated crowds. It had been selfish of her to persuade him to come. When he returned, his temper had not improved.

"None of the damn things are working. Have you got some paper and a pen? I'll stick a note on the windshield."

Jenny rummaged in her bag. It was a new one and the modern trend was for depth. Everything had accumulated at the bottom. She had to go into contortions to retrieve her small notebook which had wedged itself under the middle compartment. Her pen proved even more elusive and rolled away from her fingers every time they approached it.

"Hurry up for goodness' sake. What on earth are you doing?"

"I can't get hold of it," wailed Jenny. She was going to cry in a moment.

"Oh let's go home. I'm fed up with this."

"No. Here it is." She produced the pen triumphantly.

"Where's the paper?"

"I put it down. Oh it's slipped under the seat."

With an annoyed exclamation, he reached down. "It's full," he complained, turning the pages. "Can I tear off the cover?"

"I suppose you'll have to. Here let me do it."

By the time they'd written the note and left the car park, it was almost four o'clock. Jenny headed for Mothercare dragging her husband with her. She hoped looking at baby clothes might restore his good humour but she had her doubts.

"Oh look. Isn't this sweet?" She held up a tiny pink smocked dress.

"Very nice." Peter's temper had not improved. The shop was crowded with young mothers, prams, toddlers running around and harassed shop assistants trying to serve frustrated customers. "Let's go, Jenny. It's too crowded."

Jenny nodded. Suddenly she felt very tired. Her legs felt as though they might collapse under her. She took Peter's arm and hoped he wouldn't notice she was having trouble walking. He did. Suddenly his irritation disappeared.

Chapter Seven / 149

"Are you all right, darling?"

"Just tired. Perhaps we shouldn't have come after all. Sorry."

"Let's find a cup of tea."

But all the cafes had queues. Everyone had the same idea. The noise was drumming loudly in Jenny's head and the crowds were so dense it took them ages to walk anywhere. All she wanted to do was to go home

"Let's go home," she whispered. "I'm sorry, Peter."

"It's all right. Let's hope we don't have to wait too long for the lift."

But the end of the shopping day was nearing and everyone was heading home. There was nowhere to sit and suddenly Jenny felt a tell-tale trickle between her legs.

"Peter, I'm bleeding." Her voice was a gasp.

Chapter Eight

Lorna stared at the white plastic rectangle. The first blue line at the bottom of the pregnancy test kit had already appeared. Her heart was pounding and her hands were clammy with sweat as she waited to see if another line would accompany the first one. Gradually a hint of blue appeared and as it grew darker, she felt sick. Pregnancy tests didn't lie, did they? She was going to be sick again. She had already spent half an hour with her head over the toilet bowl. She had felt sick every morning for the past few days. She should have guessed.

She was pregnant. How could she have been so stupid? But it hadn't really been her fault, had it? She blamed Bob's dynamic brew. She'd been so thirsty she hadn't realised how much she was drinking. Neither had she realised how much alcohol had joined the fruit juices. It had been *so* deceptive, tasting like the most delicious fruit cocktail.

The memory of the one night she'd spent with Will filled her with shame and she was still angry at his desertion of her. She'd seen him around and it was obvious he was trying to avoid her. But Eleanor was probably right. He'd been embarrassed and he'd told her he wouldn't deliberately have hurt her. In her bemused state, she had obviously not repulsed him and the little she could remember had been extremely pleasant.

Well, he definitely had to know about the baby. She wasn't the only one responsible. Shocked though she was, she had almost been prepared for it. Suddenly she started to shake. She felt so alone. Tina had gone to her parents for the weekend but Lorna had chosen to stay in college although she'd intended to spend Sunday with her parents. Now she didn't think she could face them. Would they disown her? But she knew better than that. They would forgive her but they would be bitterly hurt. "Hate the sin; love the sinner" had always been their motto.

She must talk to someone. Ellie was the obvious choice. Would she be working? She had some weekends free, Lorna knew. Yes, she'd talk to Ellie. She'd know what to do. She dialled the number and then quickly replaced the receiver before she heard the ring. What a coward she was. Eleanor would certainly suggest she contacted Will. Would he marry her? She frowned. She thought she'd been in love with him but now she realised she didn't want to get married. She wanted to go on with her studies. She didn't want a baby cluttering up her life. Suddenly anger exploded out of her.

"Damn, damn, damn." She picked up the telephone directory and hurled it across the room. It struck the wall and knocked one of Tina's prized pictures askew but fortunately had no other effect. Her rage culminated in an unsightly bout of sobbing, wailing and screaming.

Having got that out of her system, she felt better but guilt was now buttering her conscience. "Please forgive me, Lord," she whispered. "And please help me."

But he hadn't prevented her from becoming pregnant. Her faltering faith had been shaken but not totally dislodged. Mopping up the damage to her face with a handful of tissues placed handily beside the telephone, she tried to compose herself. Taking some deep breaths, she dialled Will's number.

"Hullo, Will Baines speaking." He answered almost at once. She opened her mouth to speak but couldn't think what to say. Why hadn't she prepared her speech before she dialled. "Hullo. Is anyone there?"

"Will, it's me," she croaked. "Lorna."

"Hi, Lorna. What can I do for you?"

Blot out completely our last date, she thought. But that was impossible.

"I have to see you, Will. Could you come round now. Please."

She knew she sounded desperate but she was. Suppose he refused to see her.

"What's it about, Lorna?" He sounded wary.

"I can't tell you over the phone. Please come, Will."

"OK. I'll be with you in about half an hour."

Slowly she replaced the receiver and went to the kitchen to put on the kettle. At least she could give him a cup of coffee. He'd probably need several bagfuls of sugar to cushion the shock, she reflected. She had time to become even more nervous as she waited for him. When she opened the door, she realised he was as nervous as she was.

"Come into the kitchen. I'll make some coffee."

He followed her meekly and sat down at the kitchen table. She made the coffee and set it down in front of him. Then she sat facing him, summoning up the remnants of her courage.

"I'm pregnant, Will."

"Oh no." He buried his face in his hands. "Lorna, I'm *so* sorry. I thought you were on the pill. I'd never have …"

"Yes, yes, I know. But I thought you should know." Her lips trembled. "What are we going to do, Will?" She looked up at him with brimming eyes.

"I don't know. I'll have to think." He hesitated. "I think we're too young to get married and … and I don't really want that sort of commitment yet."

"I understand," she said in a small voice. Had she really expected him to do "the right thing"?

"You could have an abortion," he suggested, brightening.

"I don't think I could." She was horrified.

"Listen. I've got an uncle who's a gynaecologist. I'll talk to him. We'll sort something out. Don't cry any more, Lorna."

She sniffed. "All right. I'll try."

"Good girl. I'll talk to my uncle and I'll get back to you. Thanks for the coffee. Talk to you soon."

Chapter Eight / 153

And he was gone. He'd hardly drunk any coffee. He couldn't get out quickly enough, she thought sadly.

✤ ✤ ✤ ✤

"Lorna, don't cry any more. We'll support you." Eleanor gazed compassionately at her young sister whose face was blotched with tears. She had called to visit her sister soon after Will had left. "Something can be sorted out."

"I didn't want it to happen," wailed Lorna. "I'm so angry with myself – and with Will. He *knew* I didn't want to but he just went ahead."

Eleanor stiffened. "You mean he raped you? That's not what you said before."

"No, of course he didn't. But I'd already told him I didn't want to – to do anything before – well – before I was married. I said I was a Christian and it wasn't right. Oh Ellie, I didn't mean to. Do you think God will forgive me?"

Eleanor hugged her sister, "Of course he will, you silly girl."

"What am I going to do, Ellie? Will said he'd talk to his uncle who's a gynaecologist but I don't see how he can help – unless …"

"Unless what?"

"Oh nothing."

"Would you marry Will if he asked you, Lorna?"

"I don't know. Perhaps I would but I don't think he'd ask me. He doesn't want to commit himself. And he said we were too young."

"Perhaps he'll change his mind, although it wouldn't be a very sound basis for a marriage, would it?"

Lorna shook her head. "I feel so miserable, Ellie."

"You'd better tell Mum and Dad."

"Oh no," Lorna wailed. "They'll be so angry." She burst into tears.

"You'll have to tell them some time, Lorna."

"But not yet. Please, Ellie."

"All right. But you must tell them after Christmas. If you won't, I will."

✥ ✥ ✥ ✥

Jenny lay on the couch in the lounge, her eyes closed. She felt nothing and couldn't even cry because she was too depressed. What made it worse was the fact that she felt it was all her fault. If she hadn't forced Peter to go to the town on that fateful Saturday, she'd still have a baby inside her. She'd been told not to overdo it and she'd ignored all advice. Now they'd have to start all over again. She wasn't sure she could face it. Perhaps she would have to accept the fact that she and Peter would never have children of their own.

Could she try again to persuade him to adopt? He'd never given her a good reason for refusing this option. She was so tired. After the miscarriage, she'd stayed in hospital over the weekend and gone home on the Tuesday. Her department would have to cope without her for the rest of the term. It would only be a few days. It would be good practice for her deputy. She couldn't be bothered to organise anything. Rosa would just have to do it all.

✥ ✥ ✥ ✥

"Do you want some help, Mum?" Eleanor stuck her head round the kitchen door.

"Oh yes, dear, if you wouldn't mind." Dorothy stood up from where she had been peering into the oven. She looked flushed. "The turkey must be cooked by now. I put it in before we went to church. Could you check the brussel sprouts, please."

Eleanor retrieved a fork from the table and lifting a saucepan lid, poked at one of the floating blobs of green. "They're done I think."

"I've done a few carrots for Kate and some vegetarian sausages. At least she can still eat *some* of the things I cook."

"Smells good." Eleanor looked in the oven. "Mm, roast parsnips. My favourite."

"We always have them on Christmas Day."

"I know. Your Christmas dinners can't be beaten."

Chapter Eight / 155

Dorothy manoeuvred the turkey onto the working top beside the oven. "Every year I say it'll be the last one and we'll go to a restaurant."

"But no restaurant could compete with you."

"Flatterer. Here's the dish for the sprouts. I'll leave the turkey for the moment. Let's get all the vegetables on the table. Oh, the plates." She rescued them from the top oven. "Put these in front of your father's place, dear. Be careful. They're hot."

"Shall I tell everyone to take their places?"

"Yes please. And tell your father to open the wine."

It was another ten minutes before the entire Bradley family was sitting at the long table that was so familiar to the sisters. In the centre was the Christmas log that had been part of their Christmases for as long as they could remember. It took some time for everyone to cover his or her plate with all the delicious trimmings that Dorothy had provided. Edward carved the meat expertly and Peter, the only other male, officiated as the barman.

The murmur died down and for a while the only sound was the clatter of cutlery on crockery. Eleanor glanced round the table. Jenny was poking her food around the plate and eating hardly anything. Her mouth was turned down and she looked as if she were about to cry. Eleanor noticed that both Peter and her mother kept throwing anxious glances at the eldest daughter.

Lorna, Eleanor was glad to see, was attacking her food as if she hadn't eaten for a month. She was eating for two after all. Dorothy had already commented on her weight. It wouldn't be long before she made the obvious connection. Perhaps she could persuade Lorna to tell her mother. After Christmas she *must* decide what she was going to do about the baby. Plans must be made before it was too late. It was already two months.

Eleanor turned her attention to Melanie who looked in a dream world. What would happen to her young sister? She was obviously not happy but, like Jenny with her craving for a child, Melanie was obsessed with her employer. Eleanor wondered how much her parents had guessed about Melanie's situation. She had resolutely refused to take them into her confidence.

"A toast." Her father's voice broke into her reverie. "To the cook. A marvellous dinner as always, my dear."

"To the cook." They all raised their glasses to Dorothy who blushed and smiled. How pretty she looked, thought Eleanor. She really didn't look old enough to have five grown-up daughters.

After the turkey and its accompaniments had been cleared, the family indulged in the traditional Christmas pudding. Eleanor noticed with amusement that Kate had two large helpings. Obviously her vegetarian sausages had not been as satisfying as the roast turkey dinner the others had enjoyed.

The afternoon was traditionally given over to present opening. When the girls had been small, the presents had been opened one by one and each exclaimed over. Today by the time the last one had been opened, the lights on the small tree were glowing in the gathering dusk and Dorothy switched on the wall lights before disappearing to the kitchen to put on the kettle for the inevitable cup of tea and Christmas cake.

"Do you think anyone will have room for cake?" asked Eleanor as she followed her mother into the kitchen.

"Kate will," laughed Dorothy. "Did you see her tucking into the pudding. I don't know how she stays so slim."

"She was making up for missing out on the turkey, I expect."

"Lorna's putting on weight, isn't she? She was eating as if she hadn't had a decent meal for days. I'm sure she doesn't eat properly at college – probably too much junk food. She needs more exercise."

"You worry too much. I'm sure she's fine."

Eleanor turned away and clattered the cups. She didn't want to get into dangerous waters. Although they had always been a close family, the sisters had not often talked to their parents about any problems. It had been Eleanor who had always been their confidante. She probably always would be. At the moment she felt rather oppressed with her knowledge. Three of her sisters had problems that had to be resolved in some way and she could only advise. She couldn't wave a magic wand much as she would like to do so.

The following day was Sunday. Christmas was over for another year and Eleanor decided it was time for Lorna to face up to her responsibilities. She dressed early and made her way to her sister's room. Lorna was still humped under the pillows. Eleanor drew the curtains on a grey day and turned back to look at her sister who was rubbing her eyes and sitting up.

"Good morning, Lorna."

"Is it? Every time I wake up, I hope the baby's a bad dream. But it isn't, is it?"

"I'm afraid not. I really think you must tell Mum and Dad. Mum's already noticed you're putting on weight."

Lorna's lips trembled. "Must I? They'll be so angry."

"I think you must, Lorna. If you don't, Mum's bound to guess and you don't want that, do you? Shall I come with you? I'll tell Mum we want to talk to her. I know; I'll ask her not to go to church this morning and then we can talk to her first while the others are out. How's that?"

"If you say so."

Dorothy had already decided to miss church for once. "What did you want to talk to me about, dear?" she asked when Eleanor accosted her after the rest of the family had left.

"Come into the lounge and sit down, Mum."

Eleanor guided her mother from the kitchen into the lounge where she had left her young sister. Dorothy looked round.

"Where's Lorna? I thought she was in here."

"She was. I expect she's gone to the loo. She was here a moment ago."

Lorna erupted into the room looking rather pale. "Sorry. I've just been sick."

Dorothy looked hard at her. "Are you all right, dear? You look very pale. Would you like to lie down for a while?"

"Sit down, Mum." Eleanor gently pushed her mother on to the sofa and nodded to Lorna to sit opposite. She obeyed, casting an apprehensive glance at her sister.

"Well dear, what is it?"

Lorna's lips trembled. "Oh Mum, I'm pregnant. I didn't mean to be. I know it's wrong. I'm so sorry."

Dorothy's eyes widened. "Oh Lorna," she gasped.

"It was a mistake, Mum. Will wants me to have an abortion."

"Oh Lorna, you can't."

"I don't know. I wasn't going to tell you yet but Ellie said I should. Oh Mum, I really didn't want it to happen." She broke into sobs.

"I'm sure you didn't." Dorothy moved across to her daughter and put her arms round her. "Don't cry, Lorna. You know we'll support you whatever you decide to do. But I do hope you won't have an abortion. I don't think that would be right."

Lorna sniffed. "Will you tell Dad? Do you think he'll be very angry?"

"He'll be disappointed in you Lorna, as I am. But I'm sure he won't be angry." She thought for a moment. "You're welcome to move back here if you decide to have the baby. I think that would be the best thing. I'll talk to your father later. Don't worry, dear. We'll always be here for you. Now, would you both like some coffee?"

"Ugh!" Lorna fled the room.

✤ ✤ ✤ ✤

"You've got to pull yourself together, Jenny. You can't sit here for ever." Eleanor looked anxiously at her sister. The pretty plump girl she knew had disappeared and in her place was this wraith. There were dark smudges under her eyes and the skin on her cheek bones had sagged. She had lost weight and her usually thick fair hair hanging lankly round her thin face gave her a cadaverous appearance.

Jenny shrugged and turned her head away. "I can't be bothered."

"You're not eating properly, are you? We're all worried about you, Jenny. Have you eaten anything today?"

"Can't remember."

Eleanor gave an exasperated sigh. It was the Monday after Christmas and she'd had to work in the morning but she had the afternoon off so she'd decided to check up on her sister. She was hungry as she hadn't eaten anything since early morning. Should

Chapter Eight / 159

she offer to cook something or suggest they went out? She decided on the latter.

"Let's go out for lunch. My treat. You need cheering up."

"No!" The abrupt response startled her.

"Why not?"

Suddenly Jenny was sobbing and Eleanor went to put her arms round her rocking her gently as if *she* were the child her sister so desperately wanted.

"I can't go out, Ellie," Jenny gasped at last. "Every time I do, I see mothers pushing prams, babies in car seats, children playing. I just can't face seeing what they have and I can't have. Why is life so unfair? I don't even want to go back to school because they all talk about their kids." Her lips trembled.

"Oh Jen, I'm so sorry. But it will pass. It must. I wish I could think of something to help you."

"There's nothing you or anyone can do."

An idea was bouncing around at the back of Eleanor's mind. Should she catch it and toss it to her sister or would it make matters worse? She decided to take a chance.

"Jenny, have you ever thought of, well, commemorating in some way the baby you lost?"

Jenny's tears started to flow again but Eleanor had caught her attention. She wiped her eyes. "What do you mean?"

"I was talking to a mother who'd lost a tiny baby. She said it was important for her to grieve and she and her husband had planted a special rose bush in their garden in memory of the little one. As it grew, they remembered her and it was helping them to come to terms with their loss because they'd done something positive."

Jenny stared out at the garden. "Supposing it died. That would be a double loss."

"Well you could have something that wouldn't die. What about a garden ornament? You've got plenty of space."

"Yes." Eleanor held her breath. Jenny had stopped crying and her eyes had lost the glazed expression they had worn since the miscarriage. She even had a little colour in her cheeks. "Yes. That might help a little. Thank you."

"I'll get us some lunch," Eleanor offered.

"No." Jenny put out her hand to restrain her sister. "Let's go out as you suggested. We'll go to the restaurant in that garden centre in Wells Road. We could look for an ornament."

"Right," said Eleanor. She hadn't expected her suggestion to be taken up so promptly and she didn't like to suggest it might be diplomatic to talk to Peter first.

"Peter and I can't seem to communicate these days," sighed Jenny as they sat eating shepherds pie beside a window looking out on rows of trees and bushes. In the distance was a collection of stone ornaments. "We're both grieving but we can't talk about it."

"I'm sure that's fairly common after what's happened," comforted Eleanor.

"I *want* to talk to him but I can't find the words. Do you think he'll like the idea of something to commemorate our little embryo?"

"I'm sure he will. Do you want some coffee?"

Jenny shook her head. "I'm full. I haven't eaten so much for ages. I'm sorry I can't manage it all, Ellie. They did rather pile it on the plate."

"You've done very well. Do you want to go and look at the ornaments?"

"Yes please."

It was a grey day and Eleanor was glad she'd worn a scarf as it was quite chilly. She wrapped it more tightly round her neck as they made their way towards the garden ornaments.

"There are so many!" exclaimed Jenny looking round

"What sort of thing do you think you'd like?" queried Eleanor surveying a collection of draped ladies which she eventually identified as the three graces.

"I don't know yet. I need to see what there is."

"If you can't find anything, we can always go somewhere else or you could go with Peter."

"That's it." Jenny sounded excited. "Oh look, Eleanor. Isn't she sweet?"

Chapter Eight / 161

Eleanor looked at the ornament she indicated. Jenny was gazing at a cream statuette of a little girl dressed in a smocked dress with a Peter Pan collar. She was pushing a wheelbarrow and her head was tilted upwards as if towards the sun.

"She's beautiful," breathed Jenny. "And I can plant flowers in the wheelbarrow every year, can't I?"

"What a good idea. Where will you put her?"

Jenny considered the question. "I think I'd like her on the patio outside the French doors and then I can see her every morning when I draw the curtains."

✧ ✧ ✧ ✧

Lorna had returned to her lodgings because she wanted some time to herself. If she decided to have the baby, she'd probably move back home but she hadn't yet made up her mind. At the moment she was indulging in a Bank Holiday Monday treat, eating her way through a box of chocolates and watching a video of Laurence Olivier and Greer Garson in *Pride and Prejudice*. She'd behaved rather like Lydia, she reflected. But at least Lydia hadn't got pregnant and seemed to feel no shame at all at *her* behaviour. She'd married her lover but there was no indication that she'd lived happily ever after. When the doorbell rang, Lorna had to drag herself out of the eighteenth century.

"Can I come in for a moment?" Will stood on the doorstep.

"Of course." She led the way to the lounge and pressed the pause button on the remote control to halt the video.

"Uncle David says he'll arrange an abortion for you and he'll pay for it. It's the best thing, he says."

Lorna stared at him in horror. "But I can't have an abortion. I can't kill my baby. I'm a Christian and I believe that only God can take life."

"Well my uncle's a Christian too and *he* does abortions. He works at the Manor Hospital and he has a private clinic at the Queens Road Medical Centre."

Lorna burst into tears. "Oh don't, Will. I can't bear it. It's murder."

Will moved across to sit on the sofa beside her. He put his arm round her. "Lorna, listen to me. It really *is* the best thing, you know. It's not really a baby yet, is it? It's only a blob of tissue so it would only mean having a little clear out."

"You make it sound so clinical. When does it start being a baby then? It grows into a baby, doesn't it? I still think it's murder."

"Well if you had it, how would you cope? You don't want to give up your studies, do you? If you have an abortion, you can forget it ever happened."

As his words penetrated her soul, Lorna knew she had left behind her for ever the irresponsible teenager she had been. Now she was a mature woman with responsibilities. She stopped crying and turned her head to look at the young man beside her who had suddenly become a stranger.

"Do you really believe I'd forget, Will? I don't think I would."

He took her hand. "Lorna, believe me it would be for the best. Uncle David agrees with me and it can all be arranged very quickly. And it's all confidential. No one need ever know anything about it. You haven't told anyone, have you?"

"Only my sister, Ellie – and my parents."

"Well they won't say anything, will they? Promise me you'll at least think about it, Lorna – please. And you wouldn't have to worry about the money. That's all taken care of."

She felt so tired and now she was confused again. He was trying to be kind, she knew but she wished he'd go and leave her alone.

"I'll talk to Ellie again," she sighed.

"Don't take too long to decide. I'll come round again next week sometime."

"All right." She couldn't argue with him any more and this time it was *she* who couldn't wait to get rid of *him*.

What *was* she going to do? She must talk to Ellie. Was she working today? She couldn't remember. As Christmas Day had fallen on a Saturday at the end of the century, the following Monday and Tuesday were both Bank Holidays. But hospitals

Chapter Eight / 163

didn't close. She picked up the receiver. The answer phone was on.

"Ellie, it's Lorna. I must talk to you. Can you come round as soon as possible. Please."

She hung up and switched on the video. But she couldn't concentrate on Lizzie Bennett's problems. She had too many of her own. She felt as though her whirling thoughts were about to burst out of the top of her head and a headache was lurking behind her eyes. She stared disconsolately out of the window at the dripping rain. Tears from the heavens and tears in my heart, she thought, sadly.

It was dark before Eleanor came. Lorna opened the door and her sister came in, dripping water from her umbrella onto the carpet. "Ugh! It's pouring. What's all this about? What's so urgent?"

"I'm in such a muddle, Ellie."

"Let me get rid of my wet things and we'll talk." She disappeared and Lorna switched off the video and returned to her contemplation of the weeping skies. She turned back as Eleanor entered bearing two steaming mugs of coffee.

"You look as though you could do with this."

Lorna shook her head. "No thanks. I'm right off coffee."

"Sorry. I forgot."

"What am I going to do, Ellie? Will came to see me yesterday and offered to pay for an abortion."

"Oh Lorna, you didn't agree."

"No, of course not. But he persuaded me to think about it. He was very convincing. Said it was the best thing for me. It would be all confidential and I'd forget all about it. But I wouldn't, Ellie."

"No, I'm sure you wouldn't."

"He said he'd talked to his uncle who agreed with him. I told him I was a Christian and I didn't think abortion was right but he said his uncle was a Christian too but still did abortions. It's not really a baby at that stage he says. His uncle works at your hospital, Ellie. You probably know him."

Eleanor frowned. "I don't know any Christian gynaecologists who perform abortions. What's his name?"

"Will called him Uncle David. I don't know his last name. Oh it could be the same as Will's, I suppose. Baines. David Baines. Do you know him?"

Chapter Nine

Eleanor cradled her head in her arms and wept all over the table. She'd managed to control her tears until she'd reached her flat but she knew she'd been no help to her sister. She was *so tired* and in such a muddle. How could she consider a relationship with a man who was prepared to abort a perfectly normal foetus? How could he have lied to her? He'd been so convincing.

She had no idea how long she had sat there but she was getting cold. Struggling to her feet, she headed for her bedroom and went through the motions of getting ready for bed. She felt numb. All she wanted was the blessed oblivion of sleep. But sleep eluded her for a long time and when it finally came, it was interrupted by squealing foetuses pleading for mercy as they were dragged through a dark tunnel.

The next day brought no relief. She was not working till the afternoon and she had slept so badly that when she finally staggered into the kitchen to make a reviving cup of coffee, it was nearly eleven. When she had made it, she sat at the kitchen table staring straight ahead of her while her coffee cooled in the mug in front of her. She felt numb. So Chris had been right. David *did* perform abortions and he was prepared to do one on *her* sister. She felt sick. She never wanted to see him again. She would have to work with him but their blossoming relationship was definitely at an end. Somehow she would have to convey this to him in as few words as possible. She knew she wouldn't be able to bring herself to accuse him of lying on such an important issue. She'd tackled him once before and he'd denied it. Well this time there was no possibility that he could deny it. The facts were there. He'd told his nephew to recommend an abortion for Lorna. What had he said? "It would be the best thing."

How dare he! Her hands clenched on her lap. What sort of man could murder an unborn child? Her lips trembled. He was the man I was falling in love with, she thought sadly. She brought her hand to her mouth while tears rolled down her cheeks. Sobbing, she abandoned herself to her grief. She had never felt for anyone what she had felt for David and now her love was ripped apart as he would rip Lorna's unborn child if she agreed. She mustn't.

Eleanor stood up and carried her coffee mug into the kitchen. She must forget about David and concentrate on Lorna. She would bombard her with as much anti-abortion information as she could find and she would borrow the video, *The Silent Scream*, for her sister to watch. If *that* didn't convince her of the horror of abortion, nothing would.

The shrilling of the phone startled her and she let it ring. But the caller was persistent and eventually she picked it up.

"Hullo."

"Eleanor, it's Chris. How are you? I've been worried about you."

Her stomach knotted. "I'm all right."

"Are you sure? You don't sound it."

"I'm perfectly all right, Chris," she said crossly.

"What are you doing tomorrow?"

"Tomorrow?"

"It's New Year's Eve or had you forgotten? We're about to enter a new millennium."

"Oh that. Yes, I had forgotten."

"So you haven't any plans?"

"Not at the moment."

"There's going to be a service in the town square at eleven-thirty and we should be able to see the fireworks from there. I wondered if you'd like to come. You're not working in the evening, are you?"

"No. I finish at six. I've got the weekend free as well. The theatre's closed." Now why had she said that? She was certainly not hinting that she wanted to spend it with him.

"So will you come? It's a really special occasion, isn't it?"

"Jesus' two thousandth birthday," she said thoughtfully. "I wonder how many people think of that – or even know it."

"Sadly not many, I suspect. But perhaps there'll be a few more after tomorrow night. Actually it's his one thousand, nine hundred and ninety-ninth birthday. But everyone's been calling it the Millennium. You will come, won't you? It'll be a very special occasion."

"Thank you, Chris," she said formally. "I'd like to."

After all, she thought as she put the phone down, she might as well go out. There was no point in sitting at home brooding. She had to get on with the rest of her life and try to forget a certain blue-eyed, good-looking surgeon who'd lied to her.

✣ ✣ ✣ ✣

The last day of the twentieth century dawned grey and overcast. The heavens sprinkled a fine mist of rain on Eleanor's hair as she hurried across to the hospital. She was relieved David wouldn't be operating today. She couldn't face him at the moment. She felt dead inside and didn't even want to talk to anyone about her feelings.

The day was a busy one because of the weekend closure. Eleanor felt sorry for the nurses who worked in the accident and emergency department; it would have to stay open so some of them would be on duty. She hoped there wouldn't be too many accidents but New Year's Eve was always a busy night as drink flowed freely and fights broke out. The millennium eve would probably be even worse.

In spite of her depression, Eleanor enjoyed the evening and Chris proved a pleasant companion. She deliberately buttoned down any thoughts of Carol although she knew her friend was no longer dating Chris. She was relieved they had little time to talk and was determined to appreciate the unique occasion. Fairy lights glittered in the trees around the town square and it looked as though the whole of Hazleford had turned out to celebrate. All Saints' Church, known as the Town Church, was floodlit and a large red and blue poster on the wall proclaimed: JESUS 2000: IT'S HIS MILLENNIUM.

The local band had taken up its position in front of the central war memorial and was playing familiar hymn tunes. Eleanor slipped her hand into Chris's arm and squeezed it. "It's an exciting night, isn't it?"

"Certainly one to remember," he agreed. "Have a hymn sheet." He handed her one he'd been given by one of the many young people moving through the crowd and distributing their offerings.

The Vicar of All Saints Church, wearing his white surplice, decorated only with the black stole and followed by the choir, processed slowly from the church through the opening left by the crowd and joined the band in the centre. The crowd fell silent as he welcomed them all and announced the first hymn, *Oh God our help in ages past*. It seemed appropriate, Eleanor reflected.

As the band struck up, she felt a lump forming in her throat making it difficult to sing the first two lines. She lifted her head and gazed at the poster. All her life, references to Jesus' birth had been 'nearly two thousand years ago'. Now it really was two thousand years. She knew the original calculation was probably four years out but that didn't matter. Today it was the end of the twentieth century and God was still waiting patiently for his children on earth to recognise his Son. She wondered sadly how many of those singing so lustily did. She glanced around as the sound soared upward and blinked away emotional tears. Chris glanced at her and she smiled at him before looking down her hymn sheet and joining in the singing.

It was a moving service. The prayers encompassed the whole world and Eleanor wished she hadn't been working earlier. She could have watched the celebrations on television as the cameras moved around the world focusing on the celebrations of the New Year throughout the day as twelve midnight struck in different time zones.

The Vicar's address was thoughtful and relevant. He talked about the past and the Christian hope for the future; he reminded the crowd that the only reason they were there was because two thousand years ago a baby had been born in Bethlehem and thirty three years later he had died a dreadful death on a cross but had risen triumphant from the grave. Jesus Christ was still alive today, he reminded them. All were invited to visit the church after the fireworks display. On the walls inside the body of the church they would find blank paper lining the walls. The Vicar invited the crowd to write on the paper any hopes and prayers for the new millennium. Hot chocolate was also on offer, he added.

He finished his address by quoting the words of Minnie Louise Haskins which King George VI had used in his Christmas broadcast of 1939 when the Second World War had just started and the free world was facing its greatest challenge: *And I said to the man who stood at the gate of the year: "Give me a light that I may tread safely into the unknown. And he replied: Go out into the darkness and put your hand into the hand of God. That shall be to you better than light and safer than a known way."*

The hair prickled on Eleanor's neck. The King had certainly put *his* hand *into the hand of God* and he had called for days of prayer to combat the dreadful evil that faced his country. The evil had been defeated then – with God's help, she was sure. She, like many of those present, hadn't even been born then. To her it was history but the many stories of heroism and faith always stirred her. Sadly, since those dark days the country seemed to have turned its back on God. She wondered how many of the crowd ever gave thanks for their deliverance. Her grandfather had been a Battle of Britain pilot and she never tired of hearing stories about the time before she was born.

The service closed with the hymn *Abide with me*. As the last line died away, Eleanor glanced up at the church clock on the tower. The minute hand was creeping closer to twelve. Most of the crowd were also looking up. Then, as the first stroke of midnight boomed out to celebrate the start of the new millennium, the crowd cheered as they watched dramatic bursts of light silhouette the church. For the next thirty minutes fireworks crackled and sparkled in the dark sky above the church tower. It was a spectacular display. Eleanor gasped with the rest of the crowd. "It's beautiful!" she exclaimed. "Where are they setting them off? It's so effective watching from here."

"I think the display's organised from the roof of the multi-storey car park. The council's organised it."

"They've done brilliantly, haven't they? Oh look." She pointed as circles of light catapulted into the air and exploded in a burst of dazzling colour.

She was disappointed when it was over and still stared hopefully into the sky. Her hope was rewarded. Suddenly from behind the church, bright yellow balloons cascaded into the sky and floated into the distance. She could still see some when Chris said, "Shall we go and have some hot chocolate? I'm beginning to feel cold now and it's starting to rain."

"I'm so glad it didn't start until the fireworks were over."

"It's only spitting. It probably won't come to much."

They followed the crowd and squeezed into the church. The back of it was usually partitioned off and used as a coffee shop. Now the doors had been flung back providing easy access to the church itself. The tables at the back were covered with paper cups of steaming chocolate.

"Lovely," murmured Eleanor, taking a sip from the cup Chris had handed her. "What a great idea."

Chris wandered from the "coffee shop" into the church and she followed him. Some of the paper around the walls was no longer blank and Eleanor was touched by some of the things written there. "Please heal my wife of her illness." "I promise to try harder to be good in the New Year." "Please God, make my mummy well again." She assumed some of the pleas had been written before this evening.

"Are you going to write something?" asked Chris.

She shook her head. "I'd rather *talk* to God but I think it's a lovely idea." She yawned. "I'm sorry, Chris. I'm quite tired now. I've had a long day. Do you mind taking me home now?"

"Yes of course." He took her cup and deposited it on a nearby table before guiding her out of the church.

As they walked to the nearby car park, he asked tentatively, "Would you like to go out for dinner tomorrow?"

She hesitated but she had no other plans and they'd had a lovely evening. She wouldn't be hurting Carol as Chris was apparently no longer taking her out. She had no idea whether Carol know about her own outings with Chris. She made up her mind.

"All right. Thank you."

"I'll try to book somewhere."

"It may not be easy. It's New Year's Day."

"True. But I'll find somewhere. Don't worry."

He did find somewhere. It was a Chinese restaurant in the centre of Hazelford. "You do like Chinese food, don't you?" he queried as they drove off the next day.

"I haven't had it for ages but yes, I like it. I'm always hungry again fairly quickly though."

"We can always have a pizza afterwards," he laughed.

"I don't think I'll need that."

She sat back and relaxed. She'd enjoyed the previous evening and she felt comfortable with Chris, as long as he didn't ask any awkward questions. He found a parking space outside the restaurant and they went in. A Chinese waiter greeted them and bowed. "I take your coat, Madam."

"Thank you." She handed him her jacket after stuffing her gloves into the pockets; then they followed him to a table where he ceremoniously handed them each a huge menu.

"My goodness! What a selection!" There was such a variety of dishes she felt quite bewildered. Usually she'd gone with friends to a restaurant where meals for two, three or four would be indicated. She realised they'd not necessitated her making any decisions as the choice had usually been made for her.

"How about some seaweed to start? Do you like duck?"

She put the menu down. "I think you'd better order for me. I'm sure I'll like whatever you choose."

"Aromatic Crispy Duck is nice. You make your own pancakes. Shall we share that and I'll show you how to make them?"

"Sounds good."

"How about some dumplings to start and chicken satay. Do you like that?"

"What is it?"

"It comes on a skewer: pieces of chicken and vegetables in a spicy sauce. Shall we have one of each and we can share them?"

"All right."

"Red wine or white?"

"White please."

"Shall I order a bottle or shall we have glasses? I'm driving so I can't drink much."

"We'd better have glasses. I can't drink a whole bottle."

"You want use these?" The waiter picked up the wrapped chopsticks beside her plate. "Or I bring you spoon and fork?"

"Er – I think I'd like a spoon and fork but leave the chop sticks. I'll try to use them."

"Good girl." Chris grinned.

"I'm not very expert. I never got the hang of them."

"You'll have to practise."

He ordered and they sat back to enjoy their meal. There was not much time for talking as Eleanor was concentrating on manipulating her chopsticks. She was determined not be beaten and she was aware that Chris was watching her with an amused glint in his eye. She glanced up at him and quickly looked away again. She'd seen that look on his face before. She hoped he wouldn't spoil the evening by saying something she didn't want to hear.

She gave up any attempt to eat seaweed with her chopsticks. The crisp, green curled strings slipped off the slim cream sticks as soon as she attempted to pick them up. It was much easier with a spoon and she enjoyed the feeling of the crispness melting in her mouth.

The chicken satay was easier to eat, she discovered. She started by biting off the chunks from the wooden skewer but soon gave up and transferred them to her dish. She was delighted to find she could use her chopsticks to pick them up.

"You're doing very well," remarked Chris with a grin.

"I'm almost full up already. I don't think I can manage any of those dumplings although they look delicious."

"You must leave room for the duck. Here it is."

A brown dish appeared on the table containing a number of thin steaming pancakes. The remains of the seaweed, chicken satay and dumplings were replaced with a plate of slivered cucumber, courgettes and onions and a pot of aromatic brown sauce. A plate containing shredded pieces of duck completed their main dish. Eleanor eyed the delights apprehensively. Chris competently abstracted a single pancake and deposited it on her plate.

"Now cover it with sauce and add the vegetables and the duck." She spread a thin layer of sauce as directed and deposited a few vegetables on top. "You need more than that. Look." Using his chopsticks, he piled a generous portion onto his brown painted pancake. "Now you fold it up like this and eat it with your fingers. Delicious."

Eleanor copied him but her attempts were not so successful and pieces of vegetable dribbled down her chin. She laughed and mopped herself up with her napkin. "It's very tasty."

"Mm." Chris was on his second one. Eleanor glanced at him. She suddenly realised that the dull ache that had been with her since she'd heard about David, had subsided slightly. She was enjoying the evening. "That last pancake's yours. I've been greedy." Chris held it poised over her plate.

She shook her head. "No, you have it. I've had enough."

"Are you sure?"

"Quite sure."

He polished it off and sat back dipping his fingers in the finger bowl provided. "Would you like some dessert?"

She shook her head. "I've had enough."

"Coffee?"

She opened her eyes wide at him. "Coffee? In a Chinese restaurant. I'll have jasmine tea, please."

"Oh of course. My apologies." He gave her a mock bow and beckoned the waiter.

The tea, when it came, was fragrant and delicious and contentment seeped though her as she sipped the comforting brew. The feeling was not to last.

"Now you can tell me what's upset you." Chris looked sternly at her. "It's no good saying nothing because I know something has. Please tell me, Ellie." His voice was gentle.

She took a reviving sip of jasmine tea and looked at him over the rim of the cup. The desire to unburden herself to someone suddenly became unbearable. Although she was the confidante of her sisters, she didn't always find it easy to confide in others. Jenny had always been the closest to her but recently she'd been too bound up in her own troubles. Gently replacing the cup, she sighed. The wine had loosened her tongue. She *would* confide in Chris. He had, after all, raised the first doubts.

"You were right," she said. "David does perform abortions. In fact ..." She broke off. She could speak of her own unhappiness but had she any right to betray Lorna's confidence?

He gave her a quizzical look. "In fact what?"

"Nothing."

"How did you discover he was doing abortions?"

She was trying to esponge the private sections and produce a reasonably "clean" version for him. "He ... he encouraged my – someone I know to have an abortion. He said it was the best thing for her. "She – she was student and had ... made a mistake."

"Poor girl." His sympathetic tone triggered the lurking tears and he quickly put his hand over hers. "I'm so sorry. But I did warn you."

She snatched her hand away. "I might have known you'd take the opportunity to crow."

"Ellie, I'm sorry. I didn't mean to say that. Please forgive me." He sounded contrite and her tears dried as she considered him. She realised he was being truthful. He probably hadn't intended to sound so self-righteous.

She dabbed at her eyes with her capacious napkin. She'd probably smudged her mascara but she was past caring.

Chapter Nine / 175

"I loved him, Chris," she murmured, her lips trembling. "I still love him but – but I can't forget what he did. *And* he lied to me about it."

This time she didn't try to remove his hand and she felt him squeeze it. She glanced up at him and then looked quickly away again when she saw the tenderness in his eyes. For the first time she thought that perhaps he did love her – as much as he was capable of loving anyone. But she wasn't sure of her own feelings.

"More tea?" he asked. "I think this pot's stewed. It's very refreshing when it's first made but it's too strong now, I think."

"Yes, I'd like some more. Thank you."

They sat in companionable silence as the waiter swiftly removed the tea and replaced it with a fresh pot. Chris removed his hand as he poured some into her clean cup.

She was taking a sip when he said quietly, "I suppose you wouldn't like to carry on where we left off?"

Her cup jerked and she felt hot liquid on her chin. Mopping it up, she wondered if she'd heard aright. Was he again asking her to marry him?

"What?" She couldn't think of a politer response.

He possessed himself of both her hands holding them firmly as he gazed at her. "I love you, Ellie darling. I've loved you ever since I met you. I can't bear to see you unhappy. Please marry me."

Her thoughts churned around in her mind like a washing machine on its fast spin. Whatever she had expected from this evening, it was not this and she felt momentary anger that he'd taken advantage of her current vulnerability. Gently she removed her hands. "It's too soon, Chris. Don't press me."

"But I can hope."

"I don't know. Please take me home now."

✣ ✣ ✣ ✣

"What on earth's the matter, Simon?"

Melanie stared at her boss. He looked drained and he was slumped into his chair staring at nothing.

"Joy and I aren't getting on. I thought we'd got over our problems. We had a nice Christmas with her parents although they were a bit cool to me."

Melanie wondered if Joy had shown them the letter. She had obviously *not* let Simon see it because he'd said nothing about it. She was relieved, as she often wished she hadn't set in motion the train of events that had led to Joy's attempted suicide. She mustn't pressure him. Perhaps Joy would leave him. She would be patient and let things take their course. Looking at him slouched despondently in his chair, she knew she loved him as obsessively as ever. It was like a disease. Perhaps she was possessed. Her flesh cringed at the thought. Why on earth had that leapt into her mind?

She was in no doubt about the existence of evil and she had never denied that the devil held sway over the hearts of evil men – and women. But until now she hadn't seriously considered she was one of them. But she was. *You shall not commit adultery.* It was the seventh commandment and hadn't Jesus said that whoever "lusted after a woman in his heart" was just as bad as he who actually committed the act. Presumably "lusting" after a man was just as bad. She'd certainly been the partner in an adulterous relationship. She had rebelled against the Christian teaching that sex should be saved for the marriage bed.

That's out of date today, she thought angrily. Surely it was better to find out before marriage if you were suited sexually. Then if you weren't, you wouldn't have a lifetime of misery. But *that* wasn't relevant today either. If you weren't suited, you got a divorce and that had become easier over the past few years. What had happened to those marriage vows? *For better, for worse ... till death us do part.*

Those words were said so lightly today. Solemn vows were made before God and a number of witnesses – and then broken. She supposed people meant them when they said them. Would she mean them if she said them to Simon? Yes, she would but she had already helped him to break his vows to Joy. She looked lovingly at the man she had injured. If he patched it up with Joy, she would be devastated and although her conscience would have been salved, she would then develop into a bitter twisted woman.

She went over to the kettle and made them both a cup of coffee. It was all she could think of to do.

For the next few days they were distant with each other but gradually the atmosphere thawed and they worked almost normally although Melanie was beginning to realise it was unlikely that their relationship would be resumed as Simon seemed determined to make his marriage work. Her bitterness at the way things were working out gnawed at her and she was powerless to stop it.

❖ ❖ ❖ ❖

"Lorna, there's five hundred pounds in this envelope. That should cover the … the termination. I've booked you into the Queens Road Medical Centre for next Wednesday."

Lorna stared at the envelope in Will's hand. "I said I'd think about it. I haven't decided yet. You'd no right to go ahead and organise it without consulting me."

Will looked embarrassed. She deliberately hadn't invited him to sit down and she didn't want to be pressured into making a decision. It had to be right for *her*. She couldn't go ahead against her conscience just to please Will. But she was certainly tempted. The thought of returning to "normal" and getting on with her studies was starting to bulldoze her conscience onto the sidelines where it sat shaking its head at her.

She made no attempt to take the envelope and watched him place it on the table. "I'm sorry, Lorna. I didn't mean to pressure you but I had to sort it out now for my own peace of mind."

"Oh I see, conscience money," she sneered and then wished she'd held her tongue as she saw the stricken look on his face.

"It's not that. It's – I have to go away, Lorna. You know the French course I'm doing. I have to spend several months in France. I'm going to Bordeaux next week. I should have gone before but there were problems with some of the courses and it's only just been sorted out. I don't think I'll be coming back until July as I may have to work in the Easter vacation. I didn't want to leave you without arranging something."

Now it was her turn to be embarrassed. She was still not happy about his methods but she could understand his reasons and she was touched that he was showing so much concern for her.

"Thank you, Will. I know you're trying to do the best for me. I just wish it hadn't happened in the first place."

"So do I," he said fervently. "I never meant to upset you, Lorna. I honestly thought you wanted it as much as I did and I was sure you were on the pill. I thought all girls were."

"Well you thought wrong," she retorted tartly.

"I know that now. Will you ever forgive me?"

She hesitated and unbidden into her mind leapt Alexander Pope's famous line: *To err is human, to forgive divine.* Ellie had assured her that God had forgiven her because she'd repented, so surely she should forgive Will as she had been forgiven. What did the modern version of the Lord's Prayer say? *Forgive us our sins as we forgive those who sin against us.* What was the point of saying those words every Sunday if she didn't mean them? It hadn't *all* been Will's fault. It was wrong for her to lay the blame entirely at his door.

"It wasn't only you, Will. I was just as much to blame. After all it takes two to tango, doesn't it?"

"So you forgive me?"

"Of course. I hope you enjoy your time in France."

"Thanks."

He gave her a quick peck on the cheek and headed for the front door. "I hope everything works out, Lorna. I'll give you a call when I get back to see how you are."

✤ ✤ ✤ ✤

"I do want to try again, Peter. Part of me is frightened because I was so upset when I lost the baby. But I can't give up. I have to keep trying."

Peter came across to kneel in front of his wife's chair. "Are you really sure, dear? You know how upset you were. Suppose it happens again. Will you be able to cope with it?"

Jenny looked out of the window at the little girl with the wheelbarrow. The statue had been in residence now for over a

Chapter Nine / 179

month and she couldn't imagine the patio without her. As Eleanor had predicted, the "memorial" had helped to assuage her grief. She turned back to Peter. "I've tried to block out the last experience and think positively about starting again. There is one thing though, Peter. Do you think you could ring the clinic this time? I do want you to be involved and to feel it's *your* baby as well as mine."

"But I *do* think that. I really think it's better for you to phone them. After all it won't be necessary for me to go this time, will it?"

She frowned. "Why not?"

"Well they already have some embryos in the deep freeze, haven't they?"

"Oh yes. I'd forgotten that. So it won't take so long, will it? I just have to have them transferred. I'll ring now." She started to get up.

"It's Saturday lunch time, Jenny. Wait till Monday."

"All right. I'll ring from work, if you won't do it for me."

"I'd rather not."

This time Jenny knew what to expect. She felt more relaxed and after the embryo transfer, she tried to keep her life as calm as possible. It was not always easy but Rosa, her deputy, knew what was happening and unobtrusively tried to spare Jenny as much stress as she could. Jenny had had two more embryos taken from the deep freeze placed in her uterus.

Once again the frustration of waiting made her irritable and she couldn't concentrate. She knew Peter was trying to be sympathetic but sometimes she could sense his frustration.

At the end of two weeks she sat again in the clinic waiting for the result of her pregnancy test. This time she was determined nothing would go wrong.

"I'm so sorry, Jenny." Anne had come into the room and was sitting beside her. Jenny felt the blood rush to her head and then recede leaving her cold inside. She knew it was bad news. Anne had never called her *Jenny* before.

"It hasn't taken," she whispered.

"I'm afraid not. I'm so sorry."

"I had a little bleeding but last time you said I could still be pregnant."

"Yes, but this time I'm afraid the embryos haven't implanted."

"Neither of them?"

"No. I'm sorry."

"Can I try again?"

"I think you need to rest for a while. It's been a very stressful time for both you and your husband. Try to relax."

That was easy for her to say, Jenny reflected bitterly. She wasn't the one who was a complete failure. Could she face going through the whole procedure again? She felt so very tired. There were still two frozen embryos left. She'd been told they could be kept for five years. But she didn't want to wait too long. In any case the chances of her actually going full term were becoming increasingly remote. She'd have to think of something else. She was definitely not ready to give up totally the thought of having a baby one way or another.

❖ ❖ ❖ ❖

A loud banging startled Melanie who was dozing in front of the television. She was always so tired now when she arrived home from work and she had no interest in anything. Simon never came to see her and she now knew his feelings for her had never been as strong as hers for him. For a moment she thought the noise was coming from the screen or she was dreaming but as she swam towards full consciousness, she realised that the persistent drumming was at her door.

"All right, I'm coming," she muttered as she struggled to get out of her chair. Her legs felt like tree trunks reluctant to leave their roots and her brain seemed to have disintegrated into a pile of sawdust, some of which was floating in front of her face obscuring her sight. She'd taken her glasses off and she collided with the table as she fumbled her way to the door. The banging had increased. If she didn't open it soon, it would be smashed in. Her hand out to open it, she paused. She should check the identity of her caller. She had no idea what the time was but it felt like midnight. She peered at the door. She'd forgotten to put on the chain and without her glasses, she couldn't focus properly.

"Who is it?" she croaked.

"It's Simon. Hurry up and open the door, Mel. I've been banging for ages."

"Why didn't you ring the bell?" she demanded as she opened the door and he almost fell into the room. Shutting the door, her hands flew to her head. She must look awful and the room was in a mess. Her supper plate was still on the floor and she'd knocked over her glass of water when she'd struggled out of the chair. She located her glasses and put them on. She'd given up wearing contact lenses; there seemed no point any more. Peering through her glasses, she realised Simon looked even worse than she felt. He'd slumped into an arm chair and was staring sightlessly at the television which was blaring out an advertisement for a washing powder featuring a particularly precocious small child.

She turned it off and went over to kneel in front of him. "What's the matter, Simon?"

"Joy's left me. And she's taken the kids. I don't think I can bear it, Mel. I found a note when I got home. She said she was leaving the field clear for you."

Melanie dropped her eyes and lowered her head. She didn't want him to see the gleam of triumph in her eyes. Her heart started to beat fast. At last! Surely *this* time Simon would have to turn to her. She'd been so patient. She forced down the sympathy for Joy that was trying to take over and looked at him. Tears were cascading down his cheeks and his mouth was trembling.

"Oh Simon, I'm so sorry," she lied as she levered herself onto his knees and cradled his head on her shoulder. She could feel him shaking. He'll get over it, she told herself.

He stood up abruptly, depositing her on the floor. Glaring down at her, he snarled, "It's your fault. You told her, didn't you? Didn't you?" He grabbed her arm and, pulling her to her feet, he shook her until she thought her head would be jerked off her body.

"Simon, don't – don't – please, you're hurting me." He released her and she collapsed on the floor sobbing. "I'm sorry, Simon."

There was no answer and she looked up. He no longer looked angry, just bewildered. "It's all right. She'd have found out anyway. I must go. Goodbye, Melanie."

He left her on the floor and then she heard the front door slam. She wondered why he'd come. Her mind and body were numb and she felt herself sinking into the black mud of despair. She had lost him. Joy had won in spite of the fact that she had left him. What *was* she to do now? Her brain wouldn't function properly.

Eventually she struggled to her feet. Picking up her plate, she took it through to the kitchen and washed it mechanically. She felt like a robot. Her watch told her it was nearly two o' clock. In her bedroom she crawled under the duvet without undressing and waited for sleep to bring welcome oblivion. It was a long time coming. Over and over she replayed the scene with Simon until she felt dizzy with his violent shaking. She knew her arms were bruised. He'd never before touched her in anger. She shuddered. She even tried to pray but the thick fog of her wrongdoing swirled around her preventing her from reaching the God to whom she was crying out. She sobbed. She wanted to repent of what she had done but she couldn't. She knew she was still obsessed with Simon and would take him back on any terms.

It was late when she woke the next morning but it was still dark and she could hear rain clattering against the window. She lay still, remembering the previous evening. She couldn't go to work. Getting out of bed, she drew back the curtains and stared out, resting her hot forehead on the cool window pane. She felt dead. Would she ever feel alive again? She couldn't be bothered to get dressed – or eat. She should phone Simon to say she wasn't going in to work. But why should she? He'd been cruel to her last night. She rolled up the sleeves of her nightdress and gasped. Both arms had purple bruises above the elbows. She touched them gingerly; they were *very* painful. No, she wouldn't phone him. She'd go back to bed. She was too depressed even to cry.

For the rest of the day, she dozed and slept. The phone rang but she ignored it. She didn't want to talk to anyone or do anything. That night she had trouble sleeping again. As she had slept most of the day, it wasn't surprising. In the middle of the night she decided to have a bath. As she lay soaking in the hot water, she reflected that it would probably disturb her neighbours as the walls of her flat were so thin but she didn't care. She put on a clean nightdress and changed her sheets. Then she realised she was hungry so she went into the kitchen and made herself some tea and toast. She was beginning to feel a little better. She carried her tea into the living room and drew the curtains. A faint pink on the horizon heralded the approach of dawn. She contemplated her future. Bleak though it would be without Simon, she had to decide what she was going to do. She didn't want to see him again. It would be too painful. She couldn't subject herself to another humiliation. She must write a letter of resignation and then look for a temporary job to fill in the gap until she joined the new publishing firm in September.

She would write the letter now. It would be brief and to the point and she would go out to post it and then buy some papers at the local corner shop. The rest of the day she would look for jobs and write some letters of application. Purposefully, she returned the crockery to the kitchen and than sat down at her computer to compose her letter. She made several attempts before she was satisfied. Having written it, she couldn't wait to post it. She headed for the door, grabbing her anorak on the way. A blast of cold air attacked her as she opened the door and she hastily shut it again. Looking down at herself, she realised, to her horror, she was still wearing her nightclothes. She giggled.

Later, clad warmly in trousers and thick jumper, she posted her letter and bought a collection of both national and local papers. It had stopped raining but she had to battle her way home against a strong wind. It was still early and few people were about. Melanie had always liked the early morning and it was at this time she would often work on her novel. She hadn't done any writing for some time. Perhaps she'd do some today. She could forget her own troubles and immerse herself in those of her characters. She wondered how Simon was coping without her. But she mustn't think of him.

"Today is the first day of the rest of my life," she told herself firmly.

But she knew that her recovery was only superficial and that a small thing could plunge her back into despair.

It wasn't long before the "small thing" happened. The phone rang at about half-past nine. She was on her third cup of coffee and she wondered whether to pick it up. She did.

"Melanie. Are you all right? I've been so worried. I ..."

She put the phone down. Hearing his voice made her realise again what she had lost. Putting her head on her arms, she burst into tears. She'd been too depressed to cry before. Now she let it all out. She sobbed and screamed and drummed her heels on the floor. She ignored her neighbours but she knew they all went to work early so she hoped no one would hear her. Afterwards she felt slightly better and settled down to study the 'Situations Vacant' columns. The phone rang several times but she ignored it. She highlighted several possibilities and made some phone calls. Several posts had already been filled but one or two sounded hopeful and she was asked to send in an application. Meanwhile, she'd work on her novel and not think about the applications until the following day.

She was soon plunged deep into her characters' lives. She worked until she realised she was hungry and then made herself a sandwich. There was little food in the house so in the afternoon she went out and stocked up. She hadn't thought about money. Wasn't she supposed to work out her notice? She couldn't remember whether she had actually signed a contract for her present job but there was no point in worrying about it now.

By the evening, she felt she'd accomplished a lot and was preparing for an early night when the doorbell rang. Simon? It couldn't be. She started to shake. At least he wasn't banging the door down. Perhaps it was Eleanor. Should she ignore it?

She crept towards the hall as the bell rang again insistently. Opening the door with the chain still on, she peered out.

"Mel, It's me. Please let me in. I'm so sorry."

Hurriedly she shut the door. Seeing him again brought all her love burgeoning through her. She was still obsessed with him. She could never let him go. She shut her eyes. The bell rang again. Slowly she unhooked the chain and opened the door. Stepping swiftly in before she could shut it again, he took her in his arms and she cried into his shoulder. She thought he was crying too.

Chapter Nine / 185

"Mel, my love. I'm so sorry. I shouldn't have hurt you. I'll never leave you again."

She heard his words but wasn't sure whether she believed them. But it didn't matter. He was back and she wanted to believe they would be together for ever and ever. Suddenly her prayers of a few nights ago wriggled uncomfortably into her mind. She had prayed for help. It hadn't come because she had done wrong. Now she was going to do the same again. She knew it wasn't right but she couldn't help herself. She blotted from her mind her parents' teaching and the knowledge that she was breaking the seventh commandment.

"I'll make some coffee." She eased herself out of his arms and went into the kitchen. She needed time to think. Having almost come to terms with having lost everything she cared about, it was now being freely handed back to her. Did she want it? Yes, of course she did. She smiled to herself as she poured water on to the coffee in her *cafetière*. It would keep her awake but tonight that wouldn't matter. It was unlikely they'd sleep much!

She found some Garibaldi biscuits which she knew were his favourite and carried the tray into the lounge. He was sitting relaxed in 'his' armchair and certainly looked as though he was there to stay. Putting the tray on the table, she sat on his knee and he put his arms round her.

"Oh Mel. I've missed you." He was looking at her with such tenderness that she felt her insides melting as they always did when he looked at her like that. But she had to be sure.

"Do you really love me, Simon?"

He leapt out of his seat so swiftly that she leant back over the table. He grabbed her and she felt his mouth bruising her lips. She struggled briefly and then relaxed; her arms went round him. He released her mouth and his hand stroked her hair.

"You little fool. Of course I love you. Why do you think I've come back? I tried not to, Mel. Really I did. When I got your letter, I was devastated. Then I thought you were better off without me. I tried not to contact you but in the end I couldn't help it. I had to come back to you. You won't send me away, will you?"

"Of course I won't. You know I love you. But I didn't think you loved me any more. But you do, don't you?"

"How can you doubt it?"

She slipped out of his arms. "Let's have some coffee. I presume you're staying tonight."

"All night, if I may."

She nodded. This was what she had wanted, wasn't it? Then why did she feel cheated in some way? She poured two cups of coffee and handed him one. Sitting opposite him, she wondered how things would work out. Her flat was small and there was not really room for *two* people to live comfortably in it. It had worked well when he spent the occasional night with her. Perhaps she should suggest that. But he had other ideas. He sipped his coffee and there was silence for a while. then they both spoke at once. Embarrassment flared and died. She smiled.

"You first."

"No you."

"Oh go on, Simon. You're the boss."

"OK." He looked apprehensive. "How about moving in with me?"

She gasped. "Into Joy's house?"

"It's mine too."

"Yes but …"

"Look, Mel. This flat is far too small for us both. Presumably Joy will file for divorce eventually and the house will have to be sold. But in the meantime …"

"I'll think about it. It's a big step."

"I know, but it seems logical. What were you going to say?"

"What? Oh, I've forgotten. It wasn't important."

Their lovemaking that night was not the ecstatic experience for either of them that it should have been. After it, Simon fell asleep beside her quite quickly but Melanie lay awake, her thoughts becoming more and more tangled as she worried over the decision she had to make. Much as she wanted to be with Simon, she was not at all sure she wanted to move into the house where he had lived with Joy. On the other hand the flat was certainly too small for comfort.

By the morning she had made no decision. She got up early and made a cup of tea which she took up to him. He smiled sleepily at her and held out his hand.

"Sit beside me. Aren't you having a cup?"

"I thought I'd shower while you drink your tea and then you can get ready while I rustle up some breakfast."

"Are you coming in today?"

"You want me to, don't you?"

"I certainly do. It's been hopeless without you. I don't know what I'm going to do when you leave in September."

She made a face at him as she left the room.

He was right about the office. The post had piled up and a number of manuscripts were waiting to be proofread.

"Are you going to get another proofreader now Joy won't be doing it?"

"I suppose I'll have to."

She was so busy she didn't have time to worry about the future but towards the end of the day when Simon hadn't returned, she started to become anxious. She still wasn't happy about going to live in "Joy's house". She remembered having dinner there when she had first started working for Simon. Joy was an excellent housekeeper and a superb cook. Melanie knew she could never replace her in those departments. She hoped Simon wouldn't make comparisons. Shutting such thoughts firmly away, she glanced at her watch. It was nearly seven o'clock. She reflected that Simon would probably not return to the office. He would presumably go back to his house. If she went back to the flat, that would delay a little the time when she had to make a decision about moving in with him.

The rest of the week she was very busy catching up with the mound of work that had accumulated during her absence. She saw little of Simon as he had a number of appointments with authors. She wondered if he was having second thoughts about his invitation. She felt in limbo. She didn't belong anywhere. He had not come to the flat or phoned so presumably he was giving her time to make her decision. Part of her definitely didn't want to leave her cosy little flat.

However, on the Friday, Simon was already in the office when Melanie arrived soon after eight.

"My goodness, you're early," she exclaimed.

He brought his hand out from behind his back.

"Red roses! Where on earth did you find those at this time of year?"

"Aha! I decided you were worth a little expense."

"I thought you were avoiding me," she muttered as she took the flowers and buried her nose in them to cover her embarrassment. He'd never given her flowers before.

"Of course I wasn't. I've been busy. After Joy ... Well anyway, I couldn't concentrate so the work piled up and you weren't here to keep me organised." He gave her a hug. "How do you feel about moving in with me tomorrow?"

"Tomorrow? But I haven't even said I will."

"You will though, won't you?" She glanced up at him. He was looking apprehensive and suddenly tenderness flooded over her.

"Yes. Yes, of course I will. Can you pick me up about twelve? That'll give me time to pack up. I haven't had time to sort out the flat yet. I'll have to give a month's notice."

❖ ❖ ❖ ❖

Eleanor knew her family was worried about her but she couldn't reassure them. She felt as though everything was happening at a distance far beyond the invisible glass cage in which she was imprisoned. She had returned to work after Christmas but she no longer felt any enthusiasm. She went thought the motions mechanically and hardly spoke to the surgeons or the nurses on her team. She changed her shifts so she didn't have to work with David. She realised now what a fool she had been. She'd been attracted to him from the beginning and the more she came to know him, the more she liked him. She'd never felt the same about any other man. Certainly not Chris. But since Lorna had bombed her hopes by the casual announcement that David performed abortions, she'd avoided the surgeon whenever possible. They still worked together but she had refused his invitations to dinner. He must have understood her refusals by now for he hadn't invited her out recently. In fact, she reflected sadly, he had definitely reciprocated her own coolness. So she must forget about him. She could never marry a man who performed abortions.

It was now nearly the end of January and Chris had proposed on New Year's Day. She *must* give him an answer soon. It wasn't fair to keep him dangling. She was relieved he hadn't pressured her. They'd been out together a few times but he had told her he was happy to wait until she was ready to give him an answer. Could she settle for second best or should she wait for another man to make her pulses race? She didn't think she would ever feel about anyone the way she had felt about David.

It was Saturday morning and she was still in bed although it was half-past nine. The curtains were drawn and she could hear the rain pattering against the windows. It was so dark it felt like the middle of the night. There was no reason to get up, she decided. She would never see David again and her life was over.

She turned over and shut her eyes. When she opened them again and squinted at her alarm clock, it was nearly twelve o'clock. She really should get up. Suddenly she realised she was hungry. She hadn't eaten anything the previous evening. She'd been so tired when she reached home, she'd flopped straight into bed. She'd had a rotten night, waking up frequently and not being able to sleep again. As well as her own problems, she was desperately worried about Jenny who seemed to be living in a fantasy world. Then there was Lorna. Somehow she had to convince her young sister that abortion was wrong.

Sitting up, she groaned. She felt stiff all over and her neck hurt. She'd obviously been lying in an very awkward position. She still felt very tired. Easing her legs over the side of the bed, she felt for her slippers. One of them had disappeared under the bed and as she bent down to retrieve it, her head started to thump.

"I need something to eat," she muttered as she dragged on her red velvet dressing gown, a Christmas present from her parents. Tying the belt around her waist, she padded to the window and drew the curtains. Droplets of rain decorated the window with a changing kaleidoscope of dots. She watched two of them race each other to the bottom and disappear. A raucous wind was hurling more wet circles against the glass and chasing strangely-shaped clouds around a gloomy grey sky. The weather matched her mood.

    She sighed and headed for the kitchen to put on the kettle. She'd feel better after a cup of coffee and something to eat – if there *was* anything. She found a tin of baked beans and some stale bread which she dumped in the toaster. Beans were supposed to be nourishing she remembered. After she'd eaten, she felt she bore a little more resemblance to a human being. She must get dressed to complete the metamorphosis. Then she'd phone Chris. She'd thought a lot about his proposal and she must give him an answer soon. She still wasn't quite sure what it would be.

Chapter Ten

"I don't know what to do, Ellie. Will's given me this money for an abortion and he's even booked me into the clinic." Lorna was so bound up in her own affairs she didn't notice how tired and drained her sister looked. She had phoned Ellie to ask if she could talk to her and she'd waited outside the flat until her sister had finished work. She had hardly given her time to get in the front door before she started on her problems. "It would make life simpler if I did have the abortion, wouldn't it? No one need know anything about it and I could get back to a normal life without worrying. It would be best, wouldn't it?"

She followed Eleanor into the kitchen and watched her grab the kettle and fill it. She hadn't spoken a word since she came in and all her movements were angry. This was so unlike Eleanor that Lorna stopped talking and stared at her. "Ellie, what's the matter? Are you all right?"

"Of course I'm not all right. You do what you want. You've obviously made up your mind. Go ahead. Murder your baby. It'll only be one of millions to be hurled down the waste disposal unit, won't it?"

"Ellie, don't be so cruel. How can you say that?"

"Because it's true. I don't think there's ever a good reason to perform an abortion. There certainly aren't any proved *medical* reasons for it. *You* don't even have a good reason. You're just selfish. You get pregnant and think you can just throw the baby away like a ... a – like a piece of paper you've done your rough work on. Well it's not like that, Lorna."

"I know it's not."

"Sit down for goodness' sake and I'll make some coffee. Or would you rather have tea?"

"Tea please. I seem to have gone off coffee."

"Probably because you're pregnant."

"Oh do you think so? Yes I suppose it could be." She sat down at the kitchen table, while Eleanor continued to illustrate her irritation by dragging off her coat and throwing it and her scarf out into the hall. Lorna stood up and retrieved the garments from the floor and placed them carefully on the hook designed for the purpose. She'd never seen Ellie in such a bad temper. Surely it couldn't only be the thought of abortion.

"Here you are." Her sister banged a steaming mug in front of her and then buried her face in her own mug. Lorna was beginning to feel uncomfortable. She wished she hadn't come. Ellie was certainly not going to give the advice she wanted to hear. She was sure of that. For the first time she could think of nothing to say to her sister and it was obvious Ellie was not going to break the silence.

Finally she could bear it no longer. "So what do you think I should do, Ellie? Please help me."

"I thought you'd made up your mind."

"Well I had – sort of – but ... " Her voice trailed off and she looked pleadingly at her sister.

Eleanor was frowning down at the mug in her hand as if she'd suddenly discovered it contained poison. She didn't reply. Watching her, Lorna noticed for the first time how tired and unhappy she looked. There were dark circles under her eyes as if she hadn't slept and her face seemed thinner. Her usual serene expression was marred by the vertical lines between her eyebrows and her tightened lips made her mouth turn down at the corners. Why was her sister so unhappy? She wanted to ask her but Eleanor's forbidding expression prevented her. Worried about her own situation, she could sympathise with another's although she couldn't guess what had caused Eleanor to look so miserable.

At last Eleanor raised her head and looked straight at her sister. Lorna looked away hurriedly. She felt as though she had been intruding on a very private grief. But Eleanor gave no indication about what was causing her own unhappiness.

"I'm sorry I snapped at you, Lorna. It's been a long day and I'm tired."

"That's all right. Perhaps I shouldn't have come. It *is* late."

"No it's fine. I'm glad you did but you won't like what I'm going to say. I've thought and prayed about it and I think I should tell you how I feel. I'm a nurse and I probably know more about abortion and its effects than you do."

"I don't know much at all," admitted Lorna.

"No I don't suppose you do." She hesitated and then took a deep breath. "Since you told me, I've been doing some research and what I've discovered is quite horrific. I've got some books you can borrow and there's a video you can watch but I decided I should talk to you first. Is that all right?"

Little prickles of fear were creeping over Lorna. She didn't want to listen but she knew she had to. She nodded and waited.

"First of all, Lorna, you can't have an abortion just to please Will and make it comfortable for him and his conscience. It's *your* body and it has to be *your* decision."

"I know that. He gave me the money because he's got to go to France for several months and he wanted to make sure I was all right before he went. He even booked me into the clinic for next Wednesday."

"My goodness, he doesn't waste time, does he?"

"I think he meant it for the best."

"That's a matter of opinion. Now I don't suppose either of you has thought of the effect an abortion would have on you."

"No," Lorna muttered sulkily. She hadn't come here for a lecture but she was obviously going to get one.

Eleanor continued. "There's a possibility that it could affect your having children in future. You do want to get married and have children some time, don't you, Lorna?"

"Of course I do."

"Sometimes an infection can damage the fallopian tubes and that can affect your chances of becoming pregnant again."

Lorna put her hand on her stomach. It still felt very flat. Was there really something growing inside her? But a doctor had confirmed her own diagnosis. She hadn't gone to Dr Reynolds. She'd gone to a clinic where she'd hoped no one would recognise her.

"When does it become a baby, Ellie?" she asked shyly.

"Once it's conceived, the cells start to multiply and form the nucleus of a human being."

"Will said his uncle said it was just a 'blob of tissue' and … What on earth's the matter, Ellie?"

Eleanor had leapt to her feet and rushed out of the room. Lorna stared after her, bewildered. She reflected that Ellie must feel very strongly about abortion because she was behaving so oddly.

"Sorry!" Eleanor swept back into the room blowing her nose. "I needed a tissue."

"There are some over there."

"Are there? Oh, so there are." She grabbed a handful and blew her nose again. "Lorna, have you thought about what actually happens? That tiny human being which you call a 'blob of tissue' will be broken into pieces and pulled out of you."

"Oh don't, Ellie. I can't bear it." Lorna covered her face with her hands. How much more of her sister's battering words could she take?

But Eleanor hadn't finished. "You *must* think about this carefully because, believe me, if you go ahead with it, you'll suffer for the rest of your life. You'll carry the guilt of having murdered your baby with you all the time. You won't ever forget. And even if you *do* have other children, you will always remember the day you killed your firstborn."

Lorna was beginning to feel sick. She wanted to leave the room but her sister's words were like a straitjacket around her. She had to listen. She couldn't move.

Her tormentor continued. "And suppose all your friends have babies and you can't. How will you feel then?" Eleanor tightened the bands around her sister. "Believe me, Lorna, you'll find the mental anguish you suffer will be worse than any physical illness. But you might have that too. Recent research shows that women who have abortions are more likely to develop breast cancer."

"Do you really believe that?" For the first time Lorna felt Eleanor might be giving her imagination too much freedom.

"I didn't make it up if that's what you think," snapped Eleanor. "Think about it. If you have a termination, you're upsetting your normal cycle and your breasts are bound to be affected, aren't they?"

"I suppose so."

"Lorna, every case study I've read shows how deeply affected women always are by abortion. They might think it's a good idea at the time and perhaps they return to their previous lifestyle for a while. But sooner or later post abortion trauma catches up with them. Termination is a tremendous shock to the system. It's not just another operation. You've agreed to the murder of another human being that was growing inside you and it's bound to prey on your mind. You were brought up by Christian parents and you know how sacred life is. It is given by God and only God has the right to take it away."

"I know all that but I don't want to think of it as a baby. It's just a few cells I want to get rid of."

"Oh Lorna, haven't you listened to anything I've said? Abortion won't solve anything for you; it will just create a whole new set of problems."

By now Lorna felt that her brain must be black and blue from the verbal battering she had received. It was difficult to absorb everything Eleanor had thrown at her. She had to go away, think about it and perhaps read for herself some of the books about women who'd had abortions. Fragments of information were swirling around her mind waiting to be slotted in to form a completed jigsaw puzzle.

"Just one mistake," she cried, "and it's already causing such problems."

"What you did was wrong, Lorna. But perhaps after all it was meant to be. St Paul said, 'All things work together for good for those who love God.'"

"I can't see any good coming out of this. I'll either have an abortion or an illegitimate baby that I can't cope with. What's good about that?"

❖ ❖ ❖ ❖

Eleanor stared, open-mouthed, at her eldest sister. "Jenny, you can't be serious."

"Why not?"

"You want to have a baby by a surrogate mother."

"Yes."

"Jenny, I really don't know what to say. The whole idea revolts me. Oh Jenny, don't cry. You didn't really think I'd agree with the idea, did you?"

"I don't see why not. I sent for some information from that place that does it and …"

"You mean it's done on a commercial basis," gasped Eleanor.

"Oh no. That's illegal in this country. The surrogate mother only gets paid expenses. There's been a series of programmes on television. I didn't know anything about it before. It's all done very carefully. They make sure the surrogate gets on with the family."

"Television has a lot to answer for," muttered Eleanor. "I can't think of anything worse than carrying a child for nine months and then giving it up."

"But the mother would know she was going to give it up from the start."

"That wouldn't make it any better."

"It's quite straightforward." Jenny had stopped sobbing and had obviously decided to ignore her sister's response. "You can have either *straight* surrogacy or *host* surrogacy. Apparently straight surrogacy is the most common. It's where the surrogate mother is artificially inseminated with the father's sperm or she could be a host surrogate and have one of our embryos implanted in her. There are still some in the deep freeze."

Eleanor stood up and stalked over to the window. It was almost dusk but the little memorial statuette still gleamed white on the patio. What *had* got into her sister? This obsession to have a child had obviously softened her brain.

"Surrogacy's not new, you know." Jenny was not retreating. "It's been around for centuries. Look at Sarah and Abraham?"

"What?"

"Listen." Jenny bounded over to the bookcase and removed the Bible. "I looked this up yesterday. Genesis chapter sixteen." She opened the book and turned the pages. "Here it is. *Now Sarai, Abram's wife, had born him no children. But she had an Egyptian maidservant named Hagar; so she said to Abram, 'The Lord has kept me from having children. Go, sleep with my maidservant; perhaps I can build a family through her.'* ." She looked up. "At least I'm not asking anyone to *sleep* with Peter."

"I should hope not."

"And then it says, *Sarai ... took ...Hagar and gave her to her husband to be his wife. He slept with Hagar, and she conceived.*"

She shut the book and regarded her sister triumphantly. "So you see, Abraham did it."

Eleanor tightened her lips. "I think if you read on, you'll find that things didn't quite work out the way they were planned. Anyway Sarah had Isaac afterwards, didn't she?"

"Well perhaps I'll conceive afterwards too."

Eleanor went to sit beside her sister. "You've obviously been thinking a lot about this but I really don't like the idea. To me surrogacy just doesn't fit with Christian morals. Have you talked this over with Peter?"

"Not yet."

"But you must. I'm sure he won't agree."

"Then I'll do it without him."

"Don't be so silly, Jenny. Of course you can't do it without him." Jenny turned her head away. "Goodness, you're not thinking of using a donor sperm, are you? Are you?"

Jenny still didn't reply and Eleanor felt a strong urge to shake some sense into her sister. But she knew that wouldn't help. Nor would becoming angry. Jenny needed a cooling off period and perhaps when she'd thought about it again, she would realise it wasn't right. Meanwhile she could give her sister something else to think about. She'd just made up her mind.

"By the way, I'm going to marry Chris."

Jenny looked startled. "Chris?"

"He works at the Health Club. I met him some months ago and we've been out a few times." She'd forgotten she hadn't told Jenny about him. There had been a very good reason for that. She hoped Jenny's preoccupation with getting pregnant had affected her memory. It hadn't.

Her sister frowned. "I thought he was going out with Carol. Isn't he the chap she brought to the anniversary party?"

"Oh that was over ages ago." She turned away so that Jenny wouldn't see the guilty colour.

"It's not a repeat performance, is it, Ellie?"

"What do you mean?"

"I seem to remember that once before you commandeered one of Carol's boyfriends."

"I told you she'd finished with him."

"Why don't I believe you? And what about that nice surgeon? I thought you were going out with him. Or are you stringing two men along?"

"Jenny, don't be so cruel. Of course I'm not. David and I are finished. We had a difference of opinion."

"Oh? Are you going to tell me about it?"

"I found out he did abortions and he lied to me about it."

"Oh, how awful. How can anyone have an abortion when there are people like me who are desperate to have a baby. It's not fair."

"I'm sorry, Jenny. I didn't mean to upset you. I must go. Do talk to Peter." She hesitated at the door. "Jenny, have you thought ...perhaps God doesn't want you to have children. Maybe he's got something else for you to do."

Jenny's lips turned down and she started to cry again. "Can't you stay for supper, Ellie? You could talk to Peter."

"No, I have some work to do and I have to start early tomorrow."

Jenny had obviously totally ignored her last comment. Eleanor sighed in exasperation as she left the room.

✣ ✣ ✣ ✣

Lorna turned off the video and stared at the blank screen. She was shaking. Eleanor's words and the case studies she had read had not prepared her for the horror of actually watching an abortion from the victim's point of view. She was horrified. The half-hour video, *The Silent Scream,* showed in graphic detail exactly what would happen to the tiny creature she carried inside her. It was unbearable. Tears poured down her face.

Putting her hands on her stomach, she sobbed, "I couldn't let that happen to you."

That night she slept better than she had for some time. She had made her decision and felt a surprising calm about the future. She knew it was in God's hands and he would care for both her and her baby.

✣ ✣ ✣ ✣

Saturday was bright and clear and Melanie was up early to pack up and organise everything. She still wasn't sure about giving up the flat as she felt that if she did, she was burning her bridges. Suppose it didn't work out. Seeing Simon occasionally and knowing that he was always going back to Joy was one thing. Actually living with him was quite another and she wasn't sure she was ready for it. But the die was cast. She couldn't back out now.

There was a knock at the door and she took a deep breath before opening it with a smile.

"Ready?" He looked excited.

"Yes. Can you take these cases down to the car and I'll bring the rest of the stuff."

"Right."

It took about half an hour to load up and Melanie was becoming more apprehensive. She wasn't sure why she felt so strange. This was want she had wanted, wasn't it? But now her dream was within reach, it had somehow turned a little sour. She climbed into the car beside Simon.

"All right?" He put his hand over hers. "You're not having second thoughts, are you?"

"Of course not." She squeezed his hand.

She wished the journey could have been longer to allow her to adjust but soon Simon turned into the drive and the car crunched over the gravel and stopped in front of the white garage door. She opened the passenger door and stepped out, staring up at the house that was to be her new home. There was a small porch by the front door and big bay windows jutted out over the side of the house. She felt a shiver of apprehension. What was she doing here? She felt an interloper in Joy's home.

"Welcome home, Mel." Simon was looking at her apprehensively and she summoned up a smile.

"Thank you."

She followed him into the house. It was clean and tidy so he'd obviously made an effort to make it welcoming for her. There was a huge vase of flowers in the centre of the table beside the front door.

"I thought we'd go out for a meal tonight. You won't want to be cooking when you've just moved in."

So he expected her to cook for him. He should know by now that cooking wasn't one of her skills. What *was* the matter with her? She now had everything she had wanted. Joy had vanished taking her children with her and she had Simon all to herself. But she was beginning to think she didn't want him. Her conscience was working overtime and she recalled Eleanor's words about wrecking four lives. She'd done a thorough job.

"Melanie," Simon called from upstairs and, mentally shaking herself, she moved to the stairs and started to ascend. She felt as though she were watching herself on a screen.

He was standing in the doorway of the master bedroom which she knew he had shared with Joy. She stopped.

"I can't go in there."

"What?"

"Simon, I can't possibly sleep with you in the same bed you shared with Joy."

He looked puzzled. "We'll get a new bed."

"You don't understand. I can't go in that room. It's – it's *full* of Joy."

He looked hurt. "But I've bought a new duvet cover and pillow slips. Do come and look."

She shook her head. "I can't. It doesn't feel right. In fact …"

"Yes?"

"Nothing." She moved across the landing and opened the door. "I could sleep here."

"But it's only a single bed."

"I know." She hesitated. "Simon, you don't seem to understand what an upheaval this is for me. It's *your* house, the one you shared with Joy. I feel like an intruder."

He moved swiftly across to take her in his arms. "Oh Mel, my love, you mustn't feel like that. Think of *us*. *We* have a future together now."

"Do we?"

"Of course we do. Come on. Get changed and we'll go out and celebrate the start of our life together."

"Can you bring up the clothes that were on the back seat of the car, please. I'll find something to wear for tonight."

"Good girl." He bounded down the stairs convinced that everything was fine.

But it wasn't. Melanie sat on the edge of the bed and stared around her. She knew this had been the guest room but she'd never slept in it before. She hoped she could persuade Simon to sleep in one of the other rooms tonight. She couldn't face him sharing her bed at the moment.

When he returned, she hung up her garments in the small wardrobe and selected a grey wool dress for the evening.

"That's nice." He grinned as he sat on the bed, watching her.

"Why don't you go and make us a sandwich and some coffee? I'd like to sort out my things and perhaps rest a little this afternoon. It's been a busy week." She sounded like an old lady, she thought resentfully. Why on earth would *she* need a rest in the afternoon? Even her mother hadn't reached the senior citizen stage yet.

Simon looked disappointed but disappeared, saying he'd see what was left in the fridge. "We need to do some shopping. I'll make a list; we could go this afternoon."

No doubt most of the essentials would be missing, she thought sourly. The dinner that evening was not a success. Melanie was tired and the future was weighing heavily upon her. She was beginning to feel she'd made a big mistake. The thought of Joy kept wriggling its way into her mind.

"What's the matter?" Simon put his hand on hers across the table. She let it lie but made no response to it.

"Nothing," she lied.

"Oh come on, Mel. I know you too well. I know something's bothering you."

"I don't want to talk about it now. I'm too tired." She hesitated. "Simon, would you mind if I slept alone tonight?"

He looked hurt. "If that's what you want."

"I need to sort my head out. My mind feels as though it's just come out of the washing machine and needs a good airing. Everything's happened so quickly."

"I understand." He squeezed her hand and released it. She felt awkward during the rest of the dinner but when they returned to the house, Simon kissed her gently and left her at the door of the guest room.

"Sleep well my love," he whispered. For a moment she regretted her decision but she had to iron out her thoughts before she saw him again.

✣ ✣ ✣ ✣

Eleanor was exhausted as she left the theatre complex and headed for her flat. It had been a busy Thursday morning but she was free for the rest of the day. She screwed up her eyes against the brilliant sun. There had been one of the first frosts of the season and the path still glittered from its effects. She walked carefully in case any black ice remained. By the time she reached her flat, some of her exhaustion had evaporated and she no longer felt like flopping into bed as she had intended.

She'd go to the Health Club. She hadn't been for a while and she was getting out of condition. Yes. She'd change and have a work out. Glancing at her watch, she saw it was after one. Was she hungry? Should she have something before she left or indulge herself at the club? A cursory inspection of her kitchen cupboard decided her. Like that of Old Mother Hubbard, her cupboard was virtually bare. She must do some shopping. She hadn't bought any food on Saturday.

It was nearly an hour before she was ready. Her new trainers were hidden under a pile of sandals she'd flung in the bottom of the wardrobe; the only clean tee-shirt she could find needed ironing and her leotards had disappeared entirely. She eventually found them coyly peeping out from under a skirt she rarely wore.

She'd recently bought a small second-hand car so she decided to drive to the Health Club. It was within walking distance but she didn't think she'd feel like walking home after an energetic hour in the gym.

The car park was crowded and, as she drove in, she noted that beads of frost still sparkled on the board; it looked as though glitter had been thrown over it in preparation for Christmas. She took a deep breath as she walked past the colourful flower border to the entrance and swiped her card. The gym was not as crowded as she had expected and she collected her card from the filing cabinet and reminded herself of her programme. Perhaps some energetic work would keep the thoughts of David at bay.

She struggled to adjust the saddle on the airdyne before straddling it and setting the clock for five minutes. It was hard work and she made a resolution to attend more frequently. She was badly out of condition. The humming of the huge circular fans and the rhythmic movement of the machines mingled with the constant beat of the loud music that jarred into Eleanor's already discordant thoughts.

As she cycled, her mind gradually moved into overdrive and raced in competition with her legs. Had she made the right decision in accepting Chris' proposal? He'd been so delighted but she wasn't in love with him in the same way as she had been with

David. And how could she help Jenny? Her elder sister seemed to have parted company with reality. She only hoped Peter would talk some sense into her. Lorna, she tried not to think about. She'd done her best to persuade her against abortion but the final decision had to be made by her sister.

Moving over to the treadmill, she glanced at one of the overhead television screens to discover one of the tennis tournaments was being shown. As it was live and Agassi and Sampras were playing the final set, she was riveted to the screen until she realised she had been walking for ten minutes and her legs were becoming tired. She walked the length of the gym to the recumbent cycle area and found one directly below another television screen that was also showing the match. Agassi was winning and her legs pumped more and more slowly as the tension built up. At last he won his serve and the match. Eleanor let out a sigh of relief and slowed down. She liked Agassi. Glancing at the screen on her "bicycle" she realised the pacer had had no difficulty in defeating her but she was beginning to feel more relaxed and for a brief space of time she had forgotten her problems.

Her arms needed some work and the problems returned as she pressed forward on the Compound Row and pushed her arms back and forward on the Chest Press. Before she climbed on it, it had been occupied by a very large man who had thoughtfully wiped his sweat from the seat and arm rests before she used it.

Adjusting the weight, she started work on her arms. Back and forward, back and forward. It was soothing in a way but her arms were soon aching. She had been pumping them faster and faster to keep up with her racing thoughts. Now she slowed down and replaced the arm supports, dropping her hands into her lap.

Easing herself off the machine, she picked up her towel and flicked it over the seat before rubbing her bare arms. She replaced her card in the tray so that her attendance could be noted and went to the changing-room to shower. Then she hurriedly dressed and made her way through the bar.

"Eleanor, can I get you a drink? You look as though you could do with one. And I hear congratulations are in order."

Chapter Ten / 205

She turned back. "Oh, hullo, Peter. Thanks. I'd love a drink. I've just had a work out in the gym. What have you been doing?"

"Playing squash. Only for an hour though. I've got to get back to the office this afternoon. What would you like to drink?"

"Something long and cool please. A St Clements would be nice. Do you think you could get me a ham sandwich too, please. I haven't had any lunch."

"Right."

Eleanor wriggled her toes. The trainer on her right foot was pressing on her big toe. She grimaced. She should have broken them in. It was the first time she'd worn them.

"Here you are." He placed the glass in front of her. "When's the happy day?"

"What? Oh we haven't decided yet."

"Chris is a lucky man. I hope you'll be as happy as Jenny and I ... have been."

"Thank you." She didn't want to discuss her marital arrangements and she had noticed his slight hesitation. She drank thirstily and then put the glass down and rummaged in her pocket for a tissue to wipe her mouth. She changed the subject. "Has Jenny talked to you?"

He was silent for a moment. "About anything in particular?"

"Yes." She didn't elaborate.

He nodded. "This surrogacy idea you mean. It's a non starter, Ellie. You must know that."

She was annoyed. "Of course I do. I told her so but she wouldn't listen. She's so stubborn. Did she listen to you?"

"Eventually. But now she's in a sulk and not talking to me."

"Oh Peter, I'm sorry."

"She'll come round. I think she knew it was a silly idea."

"It seems to work for some people though." Eleanor tried to be fair. "I watched the programme last Wednesday. It was quite interesting but I'm afraid I still can't understand how any woman can carry a child for someone else. It must be awful having to give it up."

"I hope she realises now it's not an option. She'll just have to come to terms with being childless."

"Would you really not consider adoption, Peter?"

"No." The reply was abrupt and then he softened. "In any case there are very few babies available for adoption now." He hesitated. "I've just booked her into Moorlands Court for her half term. Do you think that's a good idea?"

"The health farm? Lucky Jenny. It's a brilliant idea, Peter. She needs a break."

"That's what I thought. Perhaps it will give her time to think things out."

"I do hope so."

✧ ✧ ✧ ✧ ✧

"What's this?" Jenny looked at the envelope Peter had given her.

"Open it and see."

She did so. "Oh Peter, you shouldn't have."

"Why not? I thought you needed a break after what you've been through recently."

"You're too good to me." She hugged him. "I've always wanted to stay at a health farm."

"Well this is one of the best."

"Can we afford it?"

"Certainly we can. I hope the dates are all right. It is your half-term, isn't it?"

She looked at the card. "Monday 20 February to Friday 25 February. Yes. That's fine. Thank you. I'm sorry I've been such a pain recently."

"The break should help you come to terms with things."

✧ ✧ ✧ ✧ ✧

"I gather you're going to marry Chris."

It was the voice Eleanor had not wanted to hear until she had decided how to approach her friend. She felt like a lobster trapped in a pan of boiling water; the sweat was breaking out under her armpits and her face was burning. She knew she would have to turn to face the girl she had wronged and she wished she could either leap out of the window or sink into the floor. Neither was an option and there was only one door out of the staff kitchen. Slowly she put some instruments in the autoclave before turning to find Carol leaning against the door with her arms folded. She looked like a crumpled uniform that had just come out of the washing machine. Eleanor's voice deserted her.

"Well?" There was bitterness in her friend's voice.

"Yes." It was only a whisper and then because she couldn't think of anything else to say, she said, "Will you be a bridesmaid?"

Carol stared at her. "You've really got a nerve, Eleanor. You go out with my boyfriend behind my back – oh yes, I knew it was you – eventually – and then you pretend to fall in love with David and when he deserts you and swans off to Uganda, you take up with Chris again. What sort of a woman are you, Eleanor? You certainly don't behave like a Christian one."

Eleanor only heard the middle part of Carol's speech. "David's gone to *Uganda?* I didn't know."

"Perhaps he didn't like being deceived any more than I did. He obviously wanted to get as far away from you as he could."

"It wasn't like that. We had a disagreement."

"I bet you did. Well I hope you're satisfied now. And I hope you'll be very happy with that two-timing creep. You deserve each other." Bursting into tears, she rushed out of the room leaving Eleanor feeling like a broken jigsaw puzzle with missing pieces that would prevent her from ever being made whole again. Her legs collapsed and she sank down on the floor.

✤ ✤ ✤ ✤

She didn't want to go to lunch with her parents the following Sunday. Her feelings felt as raw as if they'd been systematically scraped with a cheese grater. Would she ever be able to live with herself again? Somehow she must redeem herself. It was some time since she'd seen her parents and she knew her mother missed her. She must put her own feelings aside and think of others. She was glad she'd made the effort when she saw that

Lorna was also present and looking better than she had done for weeks.

They were laying the table together and there was no one else in the room. Eleanor glanced at the door and lowered her voice. "Have you made a decision?"

Lorna nodded. "Yes, I'm not going to have an abortion. I watched that video yesterday. And I'll move back here until I've had the baby. It seems sensible."

Eleanor dropped the knives she was holding and hugged her sister. "Oh, Lorna, I'm so glad. I did so hope and pray you'd do the right thing."

"It's not going to be easy though, is it?"

"Are you all right, girls?" Dorothy put her head round the door. "What was that crash?"

"Sorry, Mum, I dropped the knives. I'd better wash them."

"Give them to me. Ellie, are you all right, dear? You look a bit peaky."

"I haven't been sleeping very well."

"You must take care of yourself. You work too hard."

"I can't help that."

"Why don't you two go for a little walk? Lunch won't be ready yet and it'll put some colour in your cheeks. You've got to take care of yourself, Lorna. Some exercise will do you good. Off you go."

"Yes, Mum." Lorna cast an amused glance at her sister.

"Come on, Lorna. It's a lovely day."

They walked for a while in companionable silence before Eleanor said, "Lorna, I've been thinking about you a lot recently and I've got an idea. You don't have to give me an answer now but please think about it."

"Is it about the baby?"

"Yes. You know Jenny's been trying for ages to have a baby."

"Has she? No, I didn't realise. I know they've been married for a while but they both work and I thought perhaps they didn't want to start a family yet."

Chapter Ten / 209

"No, it's not like that. Jenny's absolutely obsessed with the idea of having a baby. But they haven't been able to have one. She's even tried IVF treatment."

"What's that?"

"Intra Vitra Fertilisation. It's where they take out her eggs and put them with Peter's sperm and when they fertilise, they pop the embryo back inside her and hope it will grow into a baby."

"Oh." Lorna thought about it. She found it rather distasteful. "It sounds so … so artificial."

"Well, it hasn't worked anyway. She's had two treatment cycles. She's very unhappy. She's even thought about surrogacy."

"Surrogacy?"

"When a mother has a baby for someone else."

"Oh."

Eleanor glanced at her sister. Lorna was chewing her lip and looking thoughtful. They walked in silence for a while and then Eleanor decided to see if the stone she had tossed had found its first mark. Would it kill two birds? "Jenny's desperate, Lorna and I just wondered …"

Lorna stopped and turned to face her sister. She could feel a smile spreading over her whole body and even reaching to the new life within her. "You want me to give her my baby. It's a wonderful idea, Ellie. You *are* clever. I don't want the baby. I certainly couldn't look after it and there's no question of Will marrying me. It's the perfect solution. But will Jenny agree? And what about Peter?"

"Peter's the problem, I'm afraid. For some reason he's always been dead set against adoption. Jenny tried to persuade him to adopt soon after they were married but he refused even to discuss it. But if he knows whose baby it is, perhaps he'll think differently. I'm sure Jenny would be thrilled."

"I'd no idea they were having such problems. I haven't seen them for ages. Isn't life unfair? There's Jenny desperate for a baby and can't have one. And I make one mistake and get pregnant."

"Well all things work together for those who love God, don't they?"

"I suppose so. I don't think I've got as much faith as you, Ellie. But I think I've grown up quite quickly in the last few weeks." Lorna linked her arm in her sister's and gave her a squeeze. "Will you talk to Jenny, Ellie? You've always been closer to her than I have."

"Of course I will."

Lorna's mind was starting to whirl with the implications of what she had decided. "Will there be any problem, Ellie? I mean, can I give my baby to Jenny? What would we have to do? It has to be legal, doesn't it?"

"Don't worry about that at the moment. I'll find out about it. But I'm sure there won't be a problem. It's the perfect solution."

"You always like everything to be tidied up neatly, don't you, Ellie?"

"It doesn't always work though," said her sister sadly. Lorna glanced quickly at her. Why did Eleanor look so unhappy? But she couldn't ask her now. They had walked in a circle and were back at their parents' house. She must find a better time.

Chapter Eleven

"Goodness, what *have* you got in this case, Jenny? It weighs a ton."

"I didn't know what to take. I've never been to a health farm before. I know you don't have to dress up but it says I need a dressing-gown, a track suit and a swimming costume. And I need exercise kit. I have to have several outfits, don't I? And shoes are heavy. I've had to pack trainers *and* walking shoes. And I'll need something to wear in the evening."

"All right. All right. You've convinced me," Peter laughed.

"How far is it?" asked Jenny, as she settled herself in the passenger seat.

"About twenty miles. It should only take about half an hour. I've got a map. It shouldn't be hard to find. They'll give you some lunch when you get there."

"It looks beautiful on the card. The grounds are lovely."

"I'm sorry you're not going in the summer."

"Oh that doesn't matter. I'm really looking forward to it. It's been a ghastly term so far. It'll be so nice to relax."

"I probably won't recognise you when I collect you," he teased.

The reception area at Moorland Court reminded Jenny of a five star hotel and nothing during her stay changed her view.

After Peter had left, she was escorted to her room by a young man who forbore to comment on the weight of her suitcase. As he swept along the corridor, he flung out his spare hand to indicate the various rooms.

"I shall never remember," gasped Jenny almost sprinting to keep up with him.

"Don't worry. There's always someone around to ask."

He flung open the door and humped her suitcase onto the stand provided.

Pulling open a door, he indicated a safe. "Just key in your number. It's quite simple and there's a hair dryer in this drawer."

"Thank you," said Jenny wondering if she should tip him. She'd brought very little money and Peter would settle up for any extra treatments when he picked her up.

Left alone, she studied the appointment card she'd been given. She had half an hour to organise herself and change into appropriate clothing for the standard medical appointment that all guests were given. Details of meal times were also shown. It was only twelve and her appointment was for twelve-thirty. As lunch was served in the "Light Diet Room" until two-thirty, she'd have it afterwards. She saw, with pleasure, that she had an aromatherapy massage at four.

The consultation was with a sister. Jenny had been asked so many questions about her medical history over the past few months, she could almost answer them in her sleep. Unfortunately the question, "What do you hope to gain from your time here?" triggered the tears. The sister handed her a box of tissues and Jenny snuffled into them.

"I'm sorry. It – it was a gift from my husband. He thought it might help me. We've been trying for years to have a baby," she wailed.

"Oh my dear, I *do* sympathise. My husband and I haven't been blessed with children either."

Jenny's eyes flew up. "Really?"

"It takes a long while to come to terms with it, I'm afraid. But you will. You'll find something to replace the family you haven't had. Do you have a job?"

Chapter Eleven / 213

"I'm a teacher."

"Then you have a number of children to mother."

Jenny managed a watery giggle. "I don't think I'd want to mother some of them."

By the time she left the nurse, she was beginning to feel a little better. Perhaps the healing process had begun. Lunch, she was pleased to see, did not consist solely of rabbit food. In fact lettuce was conspicuous by its absence. The chef carved her a generous portion of cold turkey and she helped herself to a selection of salads. A note underneath each indicated the number of calories. She wasn't concerned about her weight so was determined to enjoy the healthy diet on offer without counting too carefully. For so long she'd been merely picking at her food.

It was the first time she'd had an aromatherapy massage and she thoroughly enjoyed the soothing music, the scent of a variety of oils and the relaxing massage all over her body. Why, she wondered, hadn't she had this before? It would be just the thing to ease away the stress of being a Head of Department.

"Do you mind if I massage your head?" enquired the aromatherapist. "It helps to alleviate tension but it will make your hair greasy."

"It doesn't matter," murmured Jenny sleepily.

The hour went too quickly and she wriggled herself off the couch and felt for her slippers.

"Take your time," she was told. "It's a good idea to leave the oils on overnight so if you can avoid having a shower this evening, it would be more beneficial."

Jenny nodded as she shrugged herself into her dressing-gown. At the moment she was too tired even to think of showering. She returned to her room and collapsed on the bed and slept. When she surfaced, it was dark and she struggled up and reached out for her bedside light. As she switched it on, she caught sight of a witch in the large gilt-framed mirror facing her. She blinked. Was that strange creature really her? Her hair was sticking up in spikes all over her head. She looked like Medusa with her head of snakes. Her hair was saturated in oils.

"Oh my goodness!" she exclaimed, heading for her handbag. She unearthed her comb and dragged it through her hair. It made no difference. She dropped the comb and smoothed her hair down all over her head. That was a little better. She longed to wash her hair but she'd been told not to do so until the morning and she wanted to benefit fully from all her treatments. Must she really go into dinner looking like a scarecrow. If she went early, perhaps no one would notice her. It was nearly dinner time so she changed back into the blouse and skirt she'd worn earlier. Apparently dressing-gowns were acceptable in the dining room at lunch time but not for dinner.

The dining room was quite full when she went down but she was escorted to a table for one in a corner where she hoped too many people wouldn't notice her greasy hairstyle. The dinner menu was impressive. There was a wide choice for each of the three courses. Jenny chose breast of pigeon on a bed of watercress as a starter and chicken tarragon as a main course. Each was marked with the number of calories as were the mixed fresh vegetables – only forty calories – and *boulangère* potatoes – 123 calories!

The food, as at lunch, was delicious and Jenny rounded off her meal with a mango sorbet. She missed her glass of wine but enjoyed the fruit cocktail, an interesting mixture of banana and orange which added 70 calories to her daily allowance of 1,200 calories. There was, of course, no alcohol served at Moorland Court.

She slept better than she had done for some time and organised a wake up call so she wouldn't be late for her appointment in the steam cabinet which sounded horrendous. She hadn't time to wash her hair before she went to the spa area so she apologised to the attendant who laughed and said, "If ladies' hair looks perfect, we wonder if they've been having any treatments."

Having removed her dressing-gown which was all she was wearing, and draped a towel round her shoulders, Jenny was inserted into a circular steel drum. The door was shut and she felt steam oozing into all her pores and before long sweat was streaming down her body. She shut her eyes; it was a pleasant sensation and she felt her tension easing away. Fortunately her

Chapter Eleven / 215

head poked out from the top and when another occupant was placed in the next cabinet, Jenny thought they must look like Tweedledum and Tweedledee. By the time she was released, she was dripping with sweat and was promptly bundled into a shower where she was relieved to be able to wash her hair. She'd have to dry it when she returned to her room. The attendant produced a refreshing glass of lime water and tucked her up on a bed with pads over her eyes to wait for her massage. Her mind, like her body, was becoming sluggish and her problems seemed to be receding as she drifted off to sleep.

"Mrs Adams." The voice of the masseuse startled her and she sat up too quickly finding the room go round. Apart from an early morning cup of tea, she'd had nothing since the previous night.

"Take your time."

Jenny removed the eye pads and smiled at the fair-haired girl in a white overall. She looked no older than one of her sixth formers. By the time she'd been pummelled and moisturised, Jenny was ready for another rest. She couldn't remember when she'd last slept so much and it was lovely to be pampered. Perhaps while she was here she could try to come to terms with the fact that she and Peter wouldn't have a family. She had explored every possibility.

By the end of the week she felt as though she'd been there for weeks rather than days and she felt more relaxed. Peter was picking her up after lunch so she was determined to make the most of the morning. After her daily dose of the steam cabinet followed by a massage, she took a book to the lounge and read for a while before deciding she'd finish her week in the sauna. Lying on her back with a towel loosely wrapped around her, she imagined she was sunbathing on a beach in the south of France. She was quite disappointed when the attendant opened the door and suggested she'd been "cooked" for long enough and offered her a shower which she gratefully accepted.

Back in her room, she finished packing and dressed for the return home. She'd worn no make-up all week and had decided not to take advantage of the beauty session recommended for the last day. Peter had spent quite enough on her and she was quite capable of putting on her own make-up. Picking up her bottle of liquid tinted foundation, she took it into the bathroom and tipped a little into her hand. Suddenly the bottle slipped from her hand and shattered into the washbasin. It had been almost full so the pristine white of the bathroom was now decorated with splodges of a delicate shade of rose brown. The stuff had splattered everywhere; the shower curtain was streaked with it, the tiled floor bore a resemblance to an Art Deco carpet and the walls and ceiling looked like the latest candidates for the soon-to-be opened Tate Modern Art Gallery.

Jenny stared in horror. *She* had not escaped either. Her blouse was no longer blue but blue and brown and her skirt had acquired an extra pattern. With an exclamation of annoyance, she grabbed some toilet paper only to discover that too had been a target. There was no way she could clear up the mess. What a horrible end to her pleasant week! Almost in tears she left the room in search of a maid. But there was not one to be seen so she headed for the receptionist; he was on the phone so she had to wait.

"I'm terribly sorry," she said when she at last had his attention, "but I've had an accident in my room. I've broken a bottle of make-up and I'm afraid it's gone all over the bathroom."

"Don't worry, madam. We'll sort it out. What's your room number?"

"Sixty-two. I'm leaving today. Could you please send a porter to take my case to the Day Room."

"Certainly, madam."

"Thank you." She returned to her room and by the time she'd finished packing and found something else to wear, the porter was knocking at the door. She picked up her coat and followed him to the Day Room. She hoped Peter would be prompt. Now she wanted to get home but she felt she had benefited from her few days away. It had been a good idea of his.

❖ ❖ ❖ ❖

Melanie had got over her apprehension and her feelings for Simon had burgeoned again. They had compromised over the sleeping arrangements. Melanie had continued to refuse to sleep in Joy's bedroom in spite of the offer of a brand new bed. Eventually a new double bed was installed in the guest room

Chapter Eleven / 217

which was redecorated in a pale aquamarine, Melanie's favourite colour. She chose matching curtains and bed linen. For a while she felt it was hers and there were now no reminders of Joy in the room.

The rest of the house was different. Simon had promised he would gradually have it all redecorated but it would be expensive and he procrastinated. However, he had acquiesced when Melanie relegated the collection of family photographs to a cardboard box at the bottom of the broom cupboard. There were enough reminders of Joy without her face making Melanie feel guilty every day. She firmly thrust the thought of Simon's wife into the cellar of her mind and locked it. But the lock was not very secure especially when Simon made tactless unflattering comparisons between his wife and his mistress.

"Can't you try to be a better housewife, Mel? There's dust an inch thick on the sideboard. Joy was always so fussy about dust."

"Joy didn't work full-time," Melanie hissed between clenched teeth. "Do you realise how often you compare me with her? I'm fed up with it. If you miss her so much, I'll move out and you can ask her to come back."

He looked shocked. "Oh no, Mel. I didn't mean that. I'm sorry. I didn't realise I was always talking about her."

"Well you are. It's not easy for me, you know."

"I'm sorry. I promise not to mention her again. Am I forgiven?"

"All right. I'll forgive you this time but don't do it again."

"That's my girl. Come here."

It was a cold March evening and although the days were lengthening, it had been a gloomy day and Melanie had been glad to draw the curtains and turn on the wall lights. Simon was sitting one side of the fireplace which contained a huge vase of multicoloured silk roses. She moved from her own chair and sat on his knee putting her arms round his neck. Harmony had been restored.

After an enjoyable interlude, she raised her head. "Have you ever lit a fire in here?"

"Yes, we used to at Christmas. Joy liked to see ... Oops! Sorry!"

"Let's have one tomorrow."

"I'll have to get some logs. I don't think we have any. Shall I go and see?"

She slipped off his lap. "I'll come with you."

Hand in hand they went though the kitchen and out of the back door to the shed that had once stored coal. Simon opened it.

"Can't see a thing. Hang on. I'll get a torch. There's one hanging up by the back door."

He disappeared and Melanie shivered. She should have put on a coat. The centrally heated house was many degrees warmer than where she now stood. The garden would be covered with hoar frost in the morning. A glimmer of white caught her eye and she tried to focus on it. As she became accustomed to the dark, she realised it was material of some kind. Stooping, she picked it up. Through the gloom she could just identify a silk scarf.

"Here we are." The torch shone directly onto Melanie's find. His voice sharpened. "What's that?"

"It was on the ground. I think it's a scarf."

He snatched it from her and in the shaft of light she could see it was delicately patterned and obviously very expensive. "It's Joy's. I gave it to her one Christmas. I remember she wore it when we went out for lunch on Boxing Day. It suited her. We were so happy then. What went wrong?"

He seemed to have forgotten Melanie and she crept back to the house leaving him with his memories. Now it wasn't only physical cold she felt. She shivered again. What a fool she'd been. She was sure now that he still loved Joy. She'd been deluding herself for months. Crouching in front of the silk flowers, she shut her eyes and tried to pray. God was the only one who could help her now. But he seemed to have gone away from her. She could sense an invisible barrier between her and her Maker. She wanted to say sorry for what she had done, for breaking the seventh commandment: *you shall not commit adultery.*

Bowing her head, she rocked herself back and forth in agony; when Simon returned and laid his hand on her head, she looked

Chapter Eleven / 219

up at him and only then realised that tears were flooding her cheeks and dripping into her open mouth.

"I'm sorry. I'm so sorry," she whispered.

He looked puzzled. "For what? What on earth's the matter, Mel? Look I've brought the logs. Shall we light a fire now?"

She looked at him with glazed eyes. She'd forgotten about the fire and couldn't focus on anything except her grief and regret. She shook her head. Still sobbing, she stood up and shook off his restraining hand.

"I'm going to bed."

She fumbled her way up the stairs to the bedroom they shared. Locking the door, she flung off her clothes, pulled on her nightdress and hurled herself below the duvet, hugging it round her as she sobbed and sobbed and sobbed.

"Oh God, what have I done?" she moaned. "Oh God, help me, forgive me."

❖ ❖ ❖ ❖

"Melanie, what on earth's the matter? You look awful."

"I must talk to you. I don't know what to do. You've got to help me."

"Come in here." Eleanor pulled her sister into the small kitchen. "I'm supposed to be working. Sit here for a moment and I'll see if I can sort something out."

She rushed out of the room. They had a full list of operations and she wasn't sure anyone could cover her. One of the student nurses was wheeling a trolley into the theatre.

"Sarah, will you tell staff nurse I've been held up. I'll be there as soon as I can. You can start to help, can't you?"

The girl looked up with wide frightened eyes. "I don't know, Sister. What do I do?"

"Staff Nurse will tell you," said Eleanor reassuringly. "I won't be long – I hope," she added under her breath. What had possessed Melanie to come to the hospital? Something serious must have happened.

Melanie was standing staring out of the window. Eleanor looked at her with a flash of irritation. No doubt there were more problems with Simon but she'd brought them all on herself. Mentally, she chastised herself for her unchristian feelings; while she was flattered her sisters confided their problems to her, she did find it wearing at times – and she had problems of her own.

"Sit down, Mel," she said gently, suppressing her annoyance. Melanie didn't move and Eleanor moved across to her and guided her to the nearest chair. Suddenly she was extremely worried about her younger sister. Melanie's eyes looked blank and sunken deep in their sockets. Jenny had worn a similar look when she had lost her baby. Melanie had obviously been crying and the whites of her eyes were bloodshot. Her hair hung lank around her pale face and she looked as if she had slept in her clothes. She looked much older than her twenty years. To the nurse's eyes Melanie looked as though she were on the edge of a mental breakdown. She must be handled carefully if she wasn't to be tipped over the precipice. There was a long silence which Eleanor didn't want to break. At last her sister spoke in a voice hoarse with tears and sorrow.

"I'm sorry. I'm sorry. I'm sorry." The dam burst again and tears rained down. Eleanor went over and put her arms round her sister until the storm had subsided a little. What was she to do? She had to go to the theatre. She spoke quietly.

"Melanie. I have to go to work, but I'll come in when I have a break. I finish at lunch time and you can come back to my flat. Do you understand?"

Melanie nodded and Eleanor left. The morning's work was busier than she had anticipated and she wasn't able to get away from the theatre until nearly two o'clock. She did her work automatically, worried about the little waif in the kitchen.

When she returned, Melanie was till sitting where she had left her, staring blindly into space.

"Sorry I couldn't get away before. Let's go and get something to eat. Can you manage to walk to my flat?"

"Of course I can." Melanie briefly snapped back to reality. "I'm not an invalid."

"I know you're not," said Eleanor soothingly.

"Sorry."

Chapter Eleven / 221

Back at the flat, Eleanor made a cup of tea laced with some brandy, which she kept "for medicinal purposes" as she told her friends! She watched Melanie drink it all and then made some scrambled eggs on toast. To her surprise her sister ate as if she'd been starving for days. Eleanor made no comment but was relieved to see a little colour return to her sister's cheeks.

When the meal was finished and she had washed up, she returned to face Melanie; "Now, are you going to tell me all about it?"

She nodded. The glazed look was disappearing from her eyes and she focused them on her sister as if to draw strength from Eleanor's calm demeanour.

"I've been such a fool, Ellie. When Simon asked me to move in with him, I knew it wasn't right. It didn't *feel* right – although I thought it was what I wanted. At least I thought it was. Oh God, I'm so mixed up."

"Take your time."

"Well, it all seemed to get better and I thought it was what I wanted. But then I began to realise that I wasn't really what Simon wanted. He kept comparing me with Joy. There were reminders of her all over the house although he kept promising he'd redecorate. But I knew he wouldn't. He never mentioned marriage and there didn't seem to be a question of divorce. But we seemed to be getting on OK until – until …" Her voice faltered and she stopped. Eleanor waited patiently. "I wanted a log fire and we'd gone out to see if there were any logs and – and Joy's scarf was on the ground. I picked it up and Simon snatched it from me saying he'd given it to her and they'd been so happy; then I knew he still loved her. He tried to pretend he didn't but I knew. So I went to bed and locked the bedroom door. I wouldn't open it or talk to him and I haven't seen him since."

"When was this?"

"Two days ago. I went back to my flat. I was glad I hadn't given in my notice."

"And you haven't been to work."

"Of course I haven't. I couldn't face him." She stared down at the shredded tissue in her hand. "I did love him you know, Ellie."

"I know you did, dear. But you'll find someone else."

Melanie gave a bitter laugh. "Who'd want soiled goods?"

"Melanie!"

"Well I am, aren't I? I've spoiled myself – and for what?"

"But you're sorry – aren't you?"

Again there was a pause before Melanie nodded. "Yes. You were right. I've ruined several people's lives. I should say sorry, shouldn't I? I've said sorry to God although that was hard. I couldn't get through to him at first."

"But you have now."

"Oh yes."

"Well he's forgiven you, hasn't he?"

"Mm. I suppose so."

"Steve preached a sermon about temptation last Sunday. It was quite helpful. He said we become stronger through temptation."

"But I gave in to it."

"I know but you've repented of what you did. Now what verse did he use? I made a note of it somewhere." She burrowed into her handbag. "Here it is. Hebrews chapter two verse eighteen." She picked up her well-worn Bible from the table and flicked through it. *Because he himself* (that's Jesus of course) *suffered when he was tempted, he is able to help those who are being tempted.*"

"But it doesn't mean those who've given into temptation, does it?"

"But Jesus *understands*. He was tempted, remember, and he must have wanted to change the stones into bread because he was so hungry. He'll *understand* that you weren't able to withstand temptation. *He* was divine. You're only human. And look at Eve."

"Eve?"

"She was tempted by the serpent and disobeyed God by eating the apple. Because of that, she and Adam were thrown out of the Garden of Eden and sin entered the world. But because God loves us, he sent his Son to die and break the power of sin by dying on the cross and defeating the devil by rising from the dead."

Chapter Eleven / 223

"All right, Eleanor, you don't need to preach at me. I've heard it all before, remember?"

"Sorry. I got carried away." She was annoyed with herself. Melanie didn't need any reminders. She'd obviously worked it out for herself. There was an uncomfortable pause and Eleanor wondered if she'd forfeited Melanie's trust.

But her sister was thinking and presently she asked quietly, "You really think God's forgiven me, Ellie?"

"Of course he has because you're really sorry."

The silence lengthened again and then Melanie said, "Do you think I should say sorry to Joy?"

Eleanor hid her surprise. "I think it's the least you could do!"

"She'd probably slam the door in my face."

"But you will have tried."

"Yes. I will. Sometime. Can I stay here for a few days, until I sort myself out?"

"Why not go home? It would be more comfortable."

"I can't face the parents yet. Do you think they know about me and Simon? You haven't told them, have you?"

"Of course I haven't. But I think they've probably guessed. Mum was only saying on Sunday that she hadn't heard from you recently."

"I'll go and see them soon. But I need some space."

"You know you've welcome to stay if that's what you really want. But you'll have to sleep on the sofa. I don't have a spare room."

"I don't mind. It won't be for long."

✢ ✢ ✢ ✢

"I've got something to tell you."

"You'd better come in." Jenny shut the door behind her sister.

Eleanor was shocked at the sight of her sister. She looked drawn and thin. When she'd returned from the health farm, she'd looked better and seemed to have come to terms with her situation. But now she'd apparently slipped back into depression. In spite of her own recent unhappiness, Eleanor was desperately sorry for Jenny. But she also had to curb feelings of irritation. Why couldn't Jenny rise above her troubles instead of giving into them? She couldn't go through life with this huge plank of wood on her shoulder wearing her down and making her old before her time. After all *she*, Eleanor, had been badly let down by the man she thought she'd loved but she had to make the most of what she had and she was sure Chris would make her a good husband. He'd been trying to persuade her to marry him for months so he must care for her.

Jenny lay on the sofa with her eyes closed. She looked ten years older than her age, Eleanor reflected. What she had to say should bring a sparkle back to her eldest sister. At least she hoped it would, but she wouldn't tell her yet.

"How's school?" She asked.

"Depressing. Rosa's doing more and more of my work at the moment. I just can't seem to cope, Ellie."

"Didn't the health farm help?"

"It did for a while but it seems so long ago now. Another life."

"You can't go on like this, Jenny. It's not fair on Rosa – or Peter. You've got to pull yourself together."

"It's easy for you to say," snapped Jenny.

Eleanor wondered why she hadn't told Jenny about Lorna immediately. Something seemed to be holding her back. Was it such a good idea after all? Would Jenny make a good mother or would she be so possessive and protective she'd smother the poor child? Outside, the curtain of darkness was moving towards the patio doors and she could barely see the white outline of Jenny's little "Memorial girl".

She pressed a switch and soft lighting shadowed the pale walls; she drew the curtains. "I hope spring comes quickly. It's been a depressing winter. Perhaps spring will cheer us all up."

"You should be all right. You've got Chris and I expect you'll have lots of babies."

She really has got a one-track mind, reflected Eleanor. For the first time, she wondered whether her sister would be allowed to adopt. Would the "powers that were" decide she was too

Chapter Eleven / 225

obsessive? But she must tell Jenny about Lorna. She'd promised. She sighed. Perhaps it was time she put her own life in order instead of interfering in everyone else's. But she'd always been her sisters' confidante. Ever since she could remember they'd always told her their troubles.

She took a deep breath and opened her mouth but before she could speak, Jenny said, "You said you'd got something to tell me. What is it? Have you changed your mind about surrogacy?"

Eleanor shut her mouth. Jenny was looking so eager. When she heard about Lorna, perhaps she'd be able to put her craving for a baby into perspective.

"Well what is it? Why are you looking so cross?"

"Sorry. I didn't realise I was frowning." She pushed her eyebrows up to remove the frown lines and forced a smile at her sister. "Lorna's pregnant."

"What!" Jenny sat up and stared at her sister. Then her face crumpled and she started to cry great heaving sobs that shook her entire body. Eleanor moved across to sit beside her.

"Jenny, don't cry. Please. You'll make yourself ill."

"It's not fair," Jenny screamed. "I've been trying and trying to have a baby and Lorna – Lorna … She's not even married and I suppose she just got carried away. It's not fair."

"I know it's not. She's very upset and she contemplated getting rid of it."

"What! That's murder. Oh Ellie she didn't, she hasn't …" Eleanor winced as Jenny gripped her arm.

"No. I persuaded her against it."

Jenny's sobs subsided and only the occasional shudder remained. Eleanor continued to hold her. The solution had obviously not yet occurred to her sister. Was now the right time to tell her? Eleanor decided it was.

"Lorna couldn't cope with a baby, Jenny and she wondered – er – whether you'd like to adopt it."

Jenny became so still that Eleanor wasn't sure she'd understood. It seemed an eternity before she moved and when she finally drew away from her sister's encircling arm, Eleanor felt as though she'd been frozen in time. She flexed her fingers and shrugged her shoulder which had become stiff. Still Jenny didn't speak. She moved over to the window and, drawing back the curtain, stared out into the blackness.

"I can still see her if I look carefully. My little wheelbarrow girl did help me for a time, Ellie, but then everything went black again." She turned back to face her sister and her eyes were large pools of water overflowing her cheeks. But Ellie knew they were not, this time, tears of sadness but of some other emotion. "I would love to adopt Lorna's baby; it would have the same blood as me, wouldn't it?"

"It might not," returned nurse Eleanor, "but I know what you mean. Do you think you'll be able to persuade Peter?"

Jenny sat down again and twisted her wedding ring round and round on her finger. "I do hope so but he's been so odd about adoption. He's always refused to discuss it and he's never given me a proper reason."

"You're going to have to sit down and have a serious talk with him. As it's Lorna's baby and he'll know its origins, perhaps he'll agree."

"He must!" Jenny had ignored the water trickling down her cheeks but now she left the room, and returned with a green toilet roll. "I've run out of tissues. We've run out of everything. I must shop soon. I'd ask you to say for supper but I don't know what there is."

"Jenny, you must eat. And what about Peter?"

"He's been very good. He usually has a meal at lunch time and he does a snack for us both in the evening."

"Do you eat at lunch time too?"

"Sometimes."

"Oh Jenny."

"I'll improve now. I promise. I've got something to live for again. I'm sure Lorna didn't want to get pregnant but perhaps God arranged it so that we could have a baby."

"Yes. I said something like that to her. But don't say anything to her, Jenny, until you've talked to Peter. You don't want to get her hopes up for nothing."

"Did she think it was a good idea?"

Chapter Eleven / 227

"She was over the moon."

"I do hope it works out. Oh there's Peter now. Do you want to say and share our snack?"

"No I don't think so. I think you should talk. But for goodness' sake let him relax a bit first. Don't start as soon as he comes in." She stood up as her brother-in-law came into the room. "Hullo, Peter."

"Aren't you staying?"

"No, I must go. Remember what I said, Jenny."

"Yes, Miss."

"I'll let myself out. 'Bye."

After Eleanor had gone, Peter looked at his wife. "What was that all about?"

"I'll tell you later. Would like a cup of tea? Or a drink?"

"I'll have a shower first and then a drink. You look a bit more cheerful. Has something happened?"

"Yes. Yes. I think it has. But it'll keep."

"I bought some steaks on the way home and some vegetables. I didn't have time to eat at lunch time. Do you feel like cooking tonight? Or shall I do it? Or we could go out."

"No. I'll cook." Jenny headed for the kitchen. She hummed as she unwrapped the steaks and peeled potatoes and parsnips. If only she could persuade Peter. But it might be an uphill task. She worked automatically, her thoughts elsewhere.

"That smells good." Peter drifted into the kitchen.

"The steaks are nearly done. Can you open the wine please."

"Certainly, madam. Do you want a glass now?"

"Thanks. Shall we eat out here?"

"It's more cosy. I'll lay the table."

Jenny deliberately kept the conversation light until they'd finished their steaks. She couldn't offer dessert but they both liked to have coffee after their meal.

"I'll make it and bring it into the lounge." Jenny collected the plates and stacked them in the dishwasher. "You go in and sit down. I won't be long."

Now the moment had come she was nervous. It was all very well for Eleanor to tell her to talk to Peter but where adoption was concerned he had always been adamant. Why did she think she could persuade him to change his mind now? He'd never even given her a reason for refusing to adopt. Perhaps if she prised *that* out of him, she could demolish it and start from there!

When she carried the tray into the lounge, he was fast asleep in the armchair. She knew he'd been worried about a case in which he was involved but she hadn't realised how tired he was. Perhaps she'd better postpone their *tête à tête*. She put the tray down on the coffee table and he stirred.

"I didn't mean to wake you. You must be tired," she said gently.

"It's been a hard few weeks." He stretched out his long legs and yawned.

Handing him his coffee, she decided that she couldn't delay their talk. She *must* try to get him to agree.

"Peter."

"Mm." He sounded half asleep.

"I want to ask you something."

"It's not about a baby again, is it?"

"Well – sort of."

He sighed. "All right. What is it this time?"

"Peter, please tell me why you're so set against adoption. I'd like to understand but you've never given me a good reason for refusing to adopt."

"There aren't many babies to adopt now, are there? And we wouldn't want an older child, would we?"

At least he was talking but he still hadn't answered her question.

"Suppose there was one." She was reluctant to mention Lorna until she'd done some more probing.

"Jenny, I don't want to adopt."

"But why not? Please tell me."

He stared morosely into his coffee cup. He was silent for several minutes but this time Jenny was sure he was going to give her an answer. Patiently she sipped her coffee and waited for him to speak.

"I was adopted."

Whatever she had expected it was not that. Had the signs always been there and she hadn't noticed them? His "parents" had been middle class, affluent and very proud of their barrister son. She had never had reason to suspect they were not his natural parents. She waited for him to continue.

"I didn't discover until I was thirteen. For some reason I had to produce my birth certificate at my new school. My parents were reluctant to give it to me but the school was adamant that I had to take it with me on my first day to show to my house master. Of course I looked at it."

He was having difficulty in continuing. To Jenny's horror, she noticed that his lips were trembling and she almost wished she hadn't reopened a wound which had obviously not healed. Moving to sit on the arm of his chair, she put her arms round his neck and hoped he would continue. She needed to know what had upset him so much.

Trying to keep his voice under control, Peter said, "The name under *mother* was one I'd never heard of. It certainly wasn't the name of the woman I'd always known as 'mother' and under father it said, *Unknown*. So you see, Jenny, I don't know who I am and I certainly don't want to adopt a child who doesn't know who it is. I finally persuaded my ... *parents* to tell me about my adoption. Apparently they found me under a blackberry bush." His lips tightened and Jenny dropped her arms to stare at him. She hardly knew whether to laugh or cry. The account seemed to be descending into farce. "They told me I was about eight months old and was wearing a blue jumper suit – perhaps to indicate I was a boy. The birth certificate had been put inside the suit. They took me to the nearest hospital and the authorities tried to trace my mother but she'd either given a false name or vanished without trace."

Jenny slipped down to sit on the floor and look up at her troubled husband. "Poor Peter," she said gently. "Did you try to find her later?"

He nodded. "It was hopeless. Every lead I had led to a blind alley and in the end I gave up. But I still wonder." He put his hand on her head and gently stroked her hair. "So you can understand why I don't want to adopt, can't you, Jenny?"

Chapter Twelve

"Lorna. The midwife's come to see you."

Lorna heard her mother and emerged from the bathroom where she felt she had had her head over the toilet bowl for hours. The annoying thing was that she hadn't been sick. She'd just been retching continuously and now she felt her legs wouldn't support her. Staggering over to the bed, she collapsed on it.

"Lorna. Are you all right?" Her mother appeared at the door. "Oh you poor dear, you look awful. Have one of your digestive biscuits. They should help a bit. Did you have one when you first woke up as I suggested?"

"Yes I've been doing that but it doesn't seem to help." She took some deep breaths. "I feel better now. I'll come down and see the midwife. But please stay with me, Mum. I'm scared."

"There's nothing to be scared of. She's nice."

The midwife was young with a round face and short fair hair. She greeted Lorna with a big grin. "Hi Lorna. I'm Sue. How are you feeling?"

"I've just been sick but I feel a bit better now."

Sue cast a critical eye over Lorna. "How many weeks are you now? I doubt if you'll have morning sickness for much longer. It usually stops after about fourteen weeks. When was your last period?"

Lorna frowned. "I can't remember but I know when I got pregnant." She blushed. "It was only once. I can give you the exact date. It was Saturday November 13."

"Well that's certainly helpful. So you're about fourteen weeks and your baby should be due in the middle of August. Now I'd like to ask you a few questions."

Lorna was relieved her mother was with her as she wouldn't have known the answers to some of the questions about her family's medical history. And she certainly couldn't answer anything about Will's.

"Are you allergic to anything, Lorna?" Sue was ready to take a few notes.

"I don't think so."

"Good. But you should be aware that an allergy to nuts, especially peanuts, is on the increase so I advise you to avoid those."

"I don't like nuts anyway."

"That's all right then. Now I'd also advise you to avoid soft cheese and pâté and if you eat eggs, they should always be well-cooked. You'll find other foods to avoid in this leaflet." She handed it to Lorna who glanced at it and wondered if there was anything she *was* allowed to eat. "Do you take much exercise?"

"I go swimming sometimes."

"Excellent. Keep that up but don't overdo it. Now about feeding. 'Breast is best' remember. It's important to put your newborn baby to the breast as soon as possible – preferably within the first hour."

"My goodness," said Lorna taking the leaflet Sue handed her. 'Breast is Best' was in large letters on the front. "I don't know whether you plan to breast-feed but you'd better take these leaflets which tell you about feeding." She pulled a handful of leaflets out of her briefcase and handed some to Lorna. "There's also one which will tell you what benefits you are entitled to. You're a student, aren't you?"

"Yes but I think I might take the rest of the year off and start again next year."

Chapter Twelve / 233

"That's a good idea. It would give you a wonderful opportunity to get to know your baby."

"Actually my sister's going to adopt it. She can't have children of her own, you see, so it seemed a sensible idea as I wouldn't really be able to look after a baby."

"I see," said Sue thoughtfully. "But once the baby is born, you many find it difficult to give him or her up."

"I suppose so. I hadn't thought of that."

"But that's some time off. There are a few more things to sort out. What about alcohol? Do you drink much?"

Lorna blushed. "No. No, I don't; hardly at all."

"And the father?"

"He doesn't drink much either."

"What about drugs?"

"Drugs?"

"Are either of you taking any drugs of any sort. Or have you any history of drugs?"

"No. Definitely not."

"That's good."

"Do you smoke?"

"No, definitely not."

"Good. Now I'll just take your blood pressure and a sample of blood and then we've almost finished."

Lorna turned her head away as the black material was tightened round her arm. She hated having her blood pressure taken. Sue unwound the armband. "That's fine." She positioned Lorna's arm. "Now just a little scratch."

She took the blood sample and then handed Lorna a small pot. "Do you think you could manage a sample of urine? I need to check it."

Embarrassed, Lorna took the pot and left the room as she heard her mother offering the midwife a cup of coffee. The thought of it made her retch again and she clung on to the wash basin. She'd gone completely off coffee. Fortunately the nausea passed quickly and she was able, with some difficulty, to produce the required sample in the receptacle provided. She called Sue who dunked a dipstick in the yellow liquid. Removing it, she inspected it and nodded. "All's well. You can dispose of this now." She tossed the dipstick into the bin. "Keep the pot because you'll have to take a sample to your antenatal appointments."

"Thanks for coming. I was really scared until I met you."

"There's no need to be. I'll be looking after you. Give me a ring if you're worried about anything and I'll pop in to see you every month."

✣ ✣ ✣ ✣

Eleanor stared at the letter in her hand. On the left side of the white envelope was a blue airmail sticker. The stamps on the right were colourful and on each was printed Uganda. Her heart started to pound. Blindly she made her way to the kitchen and sat down at the table. Her hands were shaking as she grabbed a knife and slid the blade under the flap. Somewhere she had a paper knife but her memory had gone on strike and she couldn't remember where it was. Trembling she drew out two sheets of blue airmail paper.

Dear Eleanor,

First of all I must apologise for not saying goodbye to you before I left. I'm working at a hospital in the south of Uganda. It's very different from Manor Park! They were desperate for medical staff and I've always been attracted to the mission field so I'm employed for a short time by Mid Africa Ministries who send missionaries to East Africa.

Life here is very basic. It's not unusual for the electricity generator to fail and the tap water to be reduced to a mere trickle. I have a supply of boiled water for drinking which is kept in the fridge but when there's no electricity, it becomes rather warm! I never appreciated all the mod. cons. when I had them. I just took them for granted. Facilities here are also minimal and yesterday I had to do an operation on a kitchen table by candlelight. I shall never complain about the NHS again!

I am so sorry that our friendship didn't blossom. I'm not quite sure what went wrong as I thought we were getting on well but I hope you'll be very happy with Chris. Carol told me you were going to marry him. I want you to know that it was a privilege knowing you and I shall always treasure the time we had together. You are an excellent nurse and I hope my successor appreciates you as much as I did.

As I doubt if we'll meet again, I just wanted to say goodbye and wish you well for the future.

God bless you
David Baines

Eleanor's hands were shaking as she finished reading. She felt numb. She couldn't bear the thought of never seeing him again. That was the only thing she could think of. He's gone. I'll never see him again. Laying the letter carefully on the table she re-read it. It was so very final. He had made a new life for himself and there was no room in it for her. Why should there be? She had rejected him but she still loved him. The numbness that had paralysed her as she read, gradually receded and was replaced by a grief the depth of which startled her. She drew a shuddering breath before the tears came and she sobbed uncontrollably. There was no one to hear her, no one to comfort her and she abandoned herself to the luxury of sobbing and screaming her despair. Why had God let her meet the man of her dreams and then snatched him away again? It was cruel. God! God! He was still there but she had ignored him for the past few weeks. She had been so unhappy that she had not even been able to pray.

Underneath are the everlasting arms. Why had that verse from the Bible insinuated itself into her mind? She remembered a seriously ill patient once saying to her during her training, "I've been too ill to pray for myself but I know other people have been praying for me and that reminds me of the verse, *Underneath are the everlasting arms.*"

Her face was saturated with tears and her nose was dripping. Holding her hand up to her face, she moved to the sink and tore off some kitchen towel to mop herself up. Of course God hadn't deserted her even if she'd left him for a while. Hadn't Jesus told his friends, "I will never leave you or forsake you"? And she was still one of his "friends", wasn't she?

Standing in the middle of the kitchen floor, she frowned. There was something she had been about to do. What was it? She looked down. Why was she still in her night clothes in the middle of the day? Of course. She had been about to dress and then she had seen the post. Thank goodness it was Saturday and she didn't have to go to work. She had tried so hard to forget David but it seemed she couldn't. She was engaged to one man but loved another. What *was* she to do? She couldn't marry Chris feeling as she did. It wouldn't be fair.

✥ ✥ ✥ ✥

"Have you told Peter yet?"

Eleanor had been worried that she had not heard from Jenny for some time and had decided to visit her when she knew Peter was working. It was late afternoon on a grey March day and she found her sister submerged under a pile of GCSE coursework which she was attempting to mark and assess. She was obviously relieved to abandon it for a visitor.

"I still haven't found the right moment," she replied to her sister. "But I did ask him why he was so set against adoption and I can understand it now. That's why it's so difficult."

"So what did he tell you?"

"He was adopted."

"Good gracious. I'd no idea."

"Nor had he till he was thirteen and found out by accident. Apparently he – he ..." she stopped and to her amazement Eleanor saw that she was struggling to control her giggles.

"What on earth's the matter?" Was Jenny becoming hysterical?

"He was found ... under a blackberry bush when he was a baby," wailed Jenny succumbing to her feelings and covering her face with her hands while her shoulders shook.

Chapter Twelve / 237

"What?" Eleanor suddenly had a vision of a minute Peter peering up through a cluster of blackberries. It was so vivid that she too collapsed into gales of merriment.

For several moments the two women squealed with mirth as they collapsed on to the floor and rolled around trying to control themselves. At last Jenny sat up and reached for a handful of tissues to wipe her streaming eyes.

"Oh dear!" Eleanor also grabbed some. "It's not really funny, is it? But oh …" She was off again.

"Oh stop it," implored Jenny. "We're behaving like a couple of hysterical females. Peter will be in soon. He mustn't find us like this."

Eleanor wiped her eyes. "It must have been an awful shock to him." She stifled a giggle.

"Yes, it was." Jenny became serious. "He says he doesn't know who he is and he doesn't want to adopt a child who doesn't know his origins."

"But if you took Lorna's baby, he *would* know, wouldn't he?"

"I'm afraid to tell him in case he says 'no' again. Oh what am I going to do? It seems the perfect solution."

"Shall I try to talk to him? Would that help?"

"Oh would you? He's listened to you before. He thinks I'm obsessed but if you could explain about Lorna and how it would be such a good thing for her *and* the baby, perhaps he'd listen."

"I can try."

"Why don't you stay to dinner tonight and you can talk to him while I'm in the kitchen."

Eleanor hesitated. She would have preferred to have had more time to prepare her case but at least it would briefly keep her mind off her own unhappiness. She realised Jenny was still waiting anxiously for her answer. She sighed.

"All right. I'll talk to him."

"Oh thank you. What a kind sister you are." Jenny leapt up and hugged her.

"I can't promise that I'll be successful. Did he try to find his parents?"

"Yes, but he never got anywhere so he gave up in the end."

"Poor Peter."

"He'll be in soon. Do you want to look at the paper while I rummage in the freezer for some food?"

"No thanks. I think I'd better think about what I'm going to say to Peter."

Jenny nodded, and sweeping up the papers she'd abandoned, took them out of the room leaving her sister to wonder why she was always the one who volunteered to iron out other people's problems when she couldn't sort out her own.

Her conversation with her brother-in-law went more smoothly than she expected. He seemed delighted to see her and even raised the subject of Jenny's obsession himself. The opening was there and Eleanor seized it gratefully.

"Adoption seems to be the only option left to you, doesn't it?" she remarked thoughtfully. "You know Jenny will never be really happy unless she has a baby."

Peter's lips tightened. "I don't want to adopt a stranger. How would we know how he – or she – would turn out? We'd know nothing about the background. It's too much of a risk."

"I think you would be told something of the baby's origins," objected Eleanor.

"We're unlikely to find a *baby* though, aren't we? Most children up for adoption now are much older. I certainly don't want an older child coming into my home."

Was there a slight crack into which she could insert the splinter of an idea? She must word her next remark very carefully.

"Suppose you knew exactly who the baby was. Would that make a difference?"

He hesitated and Eleanor held her breath. "I suppose it might."

She exhaled. It was now or never. "Lorna's expecting a baby."

"Lorna?" He looked bewildered at her apparent change of subject. "She's not married, is she?"

"No. She's at college."

"Of course she is. You took me by surprise. Is she going to marry the father?"

"I don't think so." Eleanor waited. Was it possible that he might find the solution himself? She wondered what thoughts were tangling in his mind. Would he be able to straighten them out and reach the conclusion she wanted?

"Poor Lorna," he said at last. "What happened?"

"I'm afraid she had too much to drink at a party. She's very upset about it. Will wanted her to have an abortion."

"She's not going to, is she?" His voice was shocked.

For a moment Eleanor was tempted to use a prospective abortion to persuade him into adoption. But that would be blackmail, she decided and not at all a Christian thing to do. The situation was so fragile that one wrong word could shatter Jenny's hopes.

"No, she won't have an abortion," she said gently, "but she is very worried about it. She doesn't want to give up her studies and she's in no position to bring up a baby."

"She'd have plenty of support though, wouldn't she?" he said thoughtfully. "Do your parents know?"

"Yes."

"Does Jenny?"

"Yes." She clasped her hands tightly in her lap. He *must* agree. She was sure the idea was waiting to be planted. If only she could find the right words. The clatter of crockery in the kitchen broke the silence and she prayed that Jenny would not return until she had her answer.

"Would you consider adopting Lorna's baby, Peter?" She would add nothing else. The decision was his.

It seemed an eternity before he said slowly, "I suppose it seems the perfect solution, doesn't it?"

"I think so."

Suddenly he smiled and stood up. She watched as the burden that had weighed him down was suddenly shrugged off and years seemed to roll away from him.

"I'll find some champagne. This calls for a celebration."

✣ ✣ ✣ ✣

Melanie cautiously pushed open the door. Her heart was pounding so loudly she was sure it must be audible to anyone in the office. At first she thought Simon wasn't there and then she saw him standing by the window staring out. She watched him. Did she still love him? She wasn't sure. She only knew that since she had talked to Eleanor and, more importantly, to God, she was experiencing a calm inside her she had never felt before. She had the comfort of knowing she had been forgiven but she still had to make her peace with those she had injured.

"Simon." He turned slowly and looked at her. There was sorrow in his eyes and he seemed to be looking at her across a wide gulf. She held out her hands to him. "Simon, I'm so sorry. I've hurt you and Joy and your children. Can you forgive me?"

He gave a wry smile and the gap was bridged. "It takes two to tango. I was just as much to blame."

"Have you seen Joy?"

"No. I don't think she'll forgive me."

"Why don't you ask her?"

"Because I'm a coward. I can't face being rejected again."

Tears trembled beneath her eyelids. "I'm going to see her."

"I don't think that's a very good idea."

"Why not?"

"Well, she – er – won't be too keen to see you, will she?"

"I shall pray about it," announced this changed Melanie. He gaped at her. "What?"

"I said I shall pray."

"I didn't know you were into all that stuff."

"Well I wasn't – I mean I went away and – oh I don't know. It's difficult to explain. All I know is God has forgiven me for my sin and so have you and now I have to ask Joy's forgiveness."

She waited for him to scoff but all he said was, "Sin is a very old-fashioned word."

"There's no real synonym for it, though is there?"

He considered this. "Evil, 'wrongdoing', 'wickedness'. No they don't mean quite the same, do they?"

Chapter Twelve / 241

"The dictionary calls it 'transgression against divine law or principles of morality'. I looked it up."

He grinned. "Is that the wordsmith in you popping out?"

"I guess so. It certainly fits what I did."

"I did it too."

She hesitated before asking shyly, "Do you regret what we did?"

He frowned. "I enjoyed it but I don't think I ever really saw it as long term – as you did. I didn't want Joy to find out and I certainly didn't want her to leave me and take the children. I feel I've lost everything." His voice broke.

She went to him and put her arms round him but there was no passion any more. She stroked his hair as he wept for what he had lost. At last it was over and she moved away.

"Can you give me the address of Joy's parents. They'll know where she is. I'm going to see her. I'm sure she's as unhappy as you are."

He rubbed his face with a handful of the tissues she had handed him before rummaging in the drawer of his desk and eventually unearthing a tatty address book.

"I'm sure it's here somewhere. Yes here it is. 32 Queens Road, Hazelford."

"Not far away. I'll go there this afternoon."

"How will you get there?"

"I'll walk of course."

"I'll drive you."

"But …"

"No I will. Then if you've talked her round, I can – er – go and see her and – er …"

She shook her head. "No Simon. Let me go alone. She will need time to adjust and think about what I've said to her."

"All right – but you'll come straight back and tell me, won't you?"

"I promise."

The ordeal was not as bad as she had expected. Joy and the children were staying with her parents and Joy herself opened the door. Her first words were not welcoming.

"What do *you* want?"

"Can I talk to you? I've come to apologise and to ask you to go back to Simon. He's devastated without you."

Joy looked suspiciously at Melanie. There was a long pause before she at last said grudgingly, "You'd better come in."

After that things went well. From her new found strength, Melanie found the courage to apologise for the hurt she had caused and to emphasise that Simon had never stopped loving his wife.

"I wanted him to divorce you and marry me but I know now that was never on the cards. He accepted me as his – er – 'bit on the side' but I'd have been a disastrous wife. I'm no cook and my housewifely skills leave a lot to be desired."

Joy managed a watery smile. "There's more to marriage than that."

"I'm sure there is. Perhaps I'll find out one day. So you'll go back to him?"

Joy's lips tightened. "I'll think about it."

"Please don't think too long. He really is desperate."

"I believe you. He's pretty hopeless without someone to organise him, isn't he?"

"He certainly is." Melanie stood up. "The office is in a mess. I don't know how he'll cope when I leave in September."

"Nor do I." Joy escorted her visitor to the front door. "Tell him to ring me."

"I will."

Skipping down the path, Melanie felt as though the final weight had just slipped from her shoulders. She said a quick prayer of thanks and returned to the office as quickly as she could to give her employer the good news.

❖ ❖ ❖ ❖

"Lorna, do hurry up. We don't want to be late for your first appointment at the clinic."

Chapter Twelve / 243

"You'll have to wait. I'm still trying to provide the sample. I hate having to pee to order." Lorna's voice was sulky and Jenny grimaced at the bathroom door. She still could hardly believe that her dreams were about to come true and she would be able to hold "her" baby in her arms.

"I'm ready." Lorna appeared holding her pot as far away from her as possible.

"I'll get you a plastic bag. You don't want it to leak!"

Lorna giggled. "At least *I* won't 'leak' on the way there. I might coming home though. Don't be surprised if I disappear to find a loo."

At the clinic Jenny looked round. The waiting room was full of women of all ages in various stages of pregnancy. Some of them were still little more than children themselves. She sighed. It was very hard that teenagers who "made a mistake" should get pregnant so easily while she hadn't been able to conceive. But Lorna's "mistake" was to prove a blessing for her. She looked anxiously at her sister. At five months Lorna's 'bump' was becoming obvious and she was fidgeting as she tried to get comfortable. Jenny wished she'd brought a cushion for her to sit on.

"Lorna Bradley." A midwife, clutching a sheaf of papers appeared and Lorna struggled to her feet. Jenny stood too and followed the midwife into the cubicle.

"Are you a relative?" the midwife enquired.

"I'm her sister. I'm hoping to adopt her baby."

The midwife nodded. She showed no surprise and Jenny wondered if she should have kept quiet. The precious pot was removed without any accidents and Lorna was instructed to lie on the couch while Jenny sat on a nearby chair. She watched intently as the midwife took Lorna's blood pressure and then put a listening device on to Lorna's tummy.

"That sounds strong and regular, just as we like it." They could both hear the heartbeat.

"It's so loud," said Lorna in amazement. Jenny shut her eyes trying to imagine that the baby was in *her* tummy and not Lorna's.

"Everything seems fine. I'll see you in a couple of weeks to check everything again." The midwife picked up her diary and suggested a date.

Lorna nodded. "That should be all right. I'm not doing much at the moment."

Jenny helped her sister off the couch and they left.

"I'm so thrilled you're going to give me your baby, Lorna. You won't change your mind, will you?"

"I don't see how I can. I couldn't give it much of a home, could I? And at least I'll see it."

"Do you have to say 'it'? It sounds so impersonal."

"Well I don't know what it – sorry – is, do I?"

"Do you want to know? I think they can tell now."

"Do you?"

Jenny shook her head. "I think I'd rather wait."

As they drove off, Lorna remarked, "Sue said I wouldn't want to give the baby up once he or she was born." She sounded sad.

"Oh Lorna, I'm sure you'll feel like that but you can see her as much as you like and – and – you could be her godmother, couldn't you?"

"Oh that would be nice. I hadn't thought of that. You think it will be a girl then."

Jenny laughed. "Well there's a fifty per cent chance."

It had long been a tradition that the Bradleys, as a family, went to Hazelford Cathedral for the Maundy Thursday Service in the evening. Even after Jenny married, she and Peter continued to attend the service with the rest of the family.

The first Easter of the new millennium was later than usual; it was nearly the end of April and the earlier sunshine had lined the roads with frothy pink and white marshmallow blossom. It rained heavily during the day but the evening was clear and the starred sky glittered down on the floodlit golden angel on top of the cathedral that could be seen for miles around. The family joined the stream of cars heading up the hill to the capacious car park.

Kate and Melanie rode with their parents, Lorna had been driven by Peter and Jenny while Chris had picked up Eleanor. She would have preferred to go with Jenny and Peter but she could hardly object to her fiancé joining in the service with her. She hoped he wouldn't notice her unhappiness and vowed to keep her false mask of happiness in place until she had decided how to tell him she couldn't marry him. She'd been putting it off for weeks and she had refused invitations saying she was busy. He must be getting suspicious but he hadn't tackled her about it.

Lorna was almost beginning to regret agreeing to Jenny adopting her baby; her sister was so terrified of something going wrong, she'd smothered Lorna with such tender loving care that the younger girl felt she would scream if she wasn't given some space of her own.

"Are you sure you're all right, Lorna?" she asked for the hundredth time as they bumped over the ramps. "I've brought a pillow for you to sit on. I thought you'd be more comfortable."

"Thanks," said Lorna through gritted teeth. "I'm perfectly OK, Jenny. For goodness' sake don't keep fussing. You're driving me mad."

"Sorry." Jenny sounded hurt. "I only want everything to go well."

"It will. I'm perfectly healthy."

"Leave the poor girl alone," interjected Peter. "She'll wish she hadn't agreed to give up her baby if you keep nagging her." He stopped the car and switched off the ignition.

"Oh Lorna, you wouldn't change you mind."

"No. Of course I wouldn't but *please* give me some space."

"I will. I promise."

Lorna sighed as she followed her sister up the steps of the cathedral. She wasn't at all comfortable. In fact she felt extremely *un*comfortable. She looked like a rhinoceros, she thought crossly, fat and ugly. Would she ever retrieve her slim figure afterwards or would she remain fat?

"Oh!" She suddenly sneezed. Blow it! Now she'd have to go to the loo.

"What's the matter?" Jenny turned back anxiously.

"I've got to go to the loo. It's one of the hazards of being pregnant."

"I'll come with you." Jenny took her sister's arm and marched her down the steps and across to the refectory where the toilets were situated. "Will you be all right?"

"Of course I will. I don't need you to come in with me. I've been going to the toilet for a long time by myself. Do stop fussing, Jenny."

"Sorry. Oh dear. I forgot your cushion. I'll go and get it. See you outside the cathedral. Can you walk across by yourself?"

Lorna didn't reply. She went into a cubicle slamming the door to vent her irritation. At least when the baby was born Jenny would no doubt transfer her mothering to *it*. Lorna was beginning to feel quite sorry for her unborn child. She made herself comfortable and waddled back to the cathedral where she leant against the wall to wait for Jenny. It was uncomfortable to stand for a long time.

"Sorry." Jenny rushed up clutching the precious cushion. "I hadn't got a key and had to get it from Peter."

"I could have managed without it," sighed Lorna.

"Nonsense. You'll be much more comfortable with it."

They walked up the long aisle and Lorna looked at the cream walls which rose into an arch high above her head. The huge wooden cross below the rose window stood out against the blue velvet background. The candles on the altar had already been lit and the sanctuary glowed with a golden light. The rest of the family had arrived and were sitting near the front. Taking her cushion Lorna slipped in beside Melanie. The organ was playing softly and she felt the music gently stroking and smoothing the ragged edges of her soul.

It was a communion service and she was not sure whether she should take communion. She had talked to the vicar who had said he was happy to allow her to receive it as she had repented of her "sin". If she knelt at the altar, she reflected, she'd probably not be able to stand up again and she didn't want Jenny fussing around her any more. No. She wouldn't go up. She glanced at Melanie beside her.

Her sister's eyes were closed and her head bowed. She too was thinking of communion. Like Lorna, she had "sinned" but also

Chapter Twelve / 247

repented. Since she had seen Joy and apologised, she had felt happier about the situation and was trying to put it behind her and concentrate on her novel. She'd nearly finished it. Her thoughts skittered around her head like so many juggler's balls. Why could she never concentrate when she was praying? She meant to pray for her family. She was only just beginning to realise that she had not been the only one with problems over the past few months. She finished her prayer with thanks to God for his care of her and for the supportive love always shown by her family. Peace seeped through her as the procession entered and the choir led the singing of the first hymn and the packed congregation rose to its feet.

As the voices swelled upwards, Jenny found it difficult to sing for the growing lump in her throat. It was true that "all things work together for those who love God" she thought. She couldn't wait to hold Lorna's baby in her arms. Even if she and Peter couldn't adopt it immediately, she was sure that eventually she would be able to do so. Meanwhile she would look after it as if it were *her* baby. Of course Lorna could visit whenever she liked and the child would be told about the background later. Peter had insisted on that. She pushed to the back of her mind those who had said that perhaps God didn't wish her to have a baby. Hadn't he provided one for her? And hadn't that solved Lorna's problems? She glanced at her sister who had struggled to her feet at the beginning of the hymn but was now sitting down again.

"Are you all right?" she hissed.

"I'm fine. I'd prefer to sit. That's all."

Eleanor leaned forward raising her eyebrows at Lorna who nodded. Eleanor sat back satisfied. It was a moving service but, as it progressed, she found concentration difficult. Then as the voices of the choir drifted heavenwards, she felt herself gradually uncurl at the edges and start to relax. This was a recreation of the Last Supper and the last communion before Christians commemorated the Resurrection of the Lord Jesus Christ on the first Easter Sunday. As she knelt and the chalice bearer tipped the wine down her throat, she shut her eyes remembering those dramatic events of two thousand years ago.

Back in her seat, she bowed her head and asked God for help. By the time the last communicant had returned to her seat and the choir was singing *O Sacrum Convivium* by Thomas Tallis, she knew she couldn't any longer put off breaking her engagement. She might never see David again and she would never forget that he performed abortions and had lied to her about it but, feeling as she did, she knew she could never marry Chris. It wouldn't be fair to him. And it certainly wasn't fair on Carol who was still in love with him. Somehow she must try to sort things out.

The lights were now going out all round the vast cathedral and the only remaining light shone on the plain wooden cross behind the altar. The congregation made no sound as quietly and reverently shadowy figures moved around the sanctuary stripping the altar of its candles and coverings while the choir sang softly from the back of the cathedral. Eleanor felt choked with emotion. She always found this part of the service almost unbearably moving. As the purple cloth covering the altar was finally removed and the last notes died away, the congregation remained still for several moments. Eleanor gazed tearfully at the bare table above which hung the plain wooden cross. There was a slight rustle and gradually the congregation left the darkened building in silence.

Chapter Thirteen

Eleanor was very quiet as Chris drove her back to the hospital after the service. Having made up her mind to break the engagement, she wanted to tell him straight away. It might be some time before she had another opportunity as she was on call over the Easter period and preferred not to go out in case she was needed.

"Will you come in for a coffee?" she said, as he drove into the hospital car park.

"Thanks."

Once in the flat, she ushered him into the living room and busied herself in the kitchen, her mind racing. There was no easy way to tell him. He was browsing through her bookshelves when she returned. "Have you read all these?" he queried.

"Most of them. Would you like a biscuit?" She offered him a plate of custard creams.

He took one. "Thanks. My favourite." Accepting a cup of coffee, he placed it on the coffee table and sat down on the sofa obviously expecting her to sit next to him.

She poured her coffee and sat opposite him absent-mindedly stirring it.

"What's the matter, Ellie? Something's bothering you."

She looked up at him. How she hated to hurt him. "Chris, I'm so sorry but I can't marry you. I should never have agreed and I ... ". Bother! She was going to cry and as usual she had no tissues handy.

"Here." He passed her a large white handkerchief and she blew loudly into it.

"I'm sorry, Chris," she mumbled into the white material.

He didn't reply and she glanced up at him. For a moment she felt frightened as his eyes met hers. He looked furious and his lips had started to tighten. Hurriedly she looked away, her heart thumping.

"I'm sorry," she repeated.

"So am I. I don't like being messed around, Ellie. You only got engaged to me on the rebound, didn't you? I warned you about Mr High and Mighty Baines but you wouldn't listen."

"I know. You were right but I still love him, Chris, whatever he's done. It wouldn't be fair to marry you."

"No. You're right. It wouldn't. I'll let myself out. Keep the handkerchief as a souvenir." There was bitterness in his voice.

"Chris, wait." He turned expectantly but she had remembered something. "Your ring."

She held it out. He stared at the solitaire diamond as it flashed, red, blue, yellow and green. Then he took it from her, shrugged and put it in his pocket.

"Goodbye, Eleanor." He left, slamming the door behind him. Would he go back to Carol? She hoped so but she hadn't had the opportunity to remind him of her friend.

She sighed. She knew now she must apologise to Carol. Jenny had reminded her that it wasn't the first time she'd detached one of Carol's boyfriends from her. Well, it would never happen again. She had at last learnt her lesson and she had no intention of marrying anyone; the only man she'd ever really loved was several hundreds of miles away – not only physically.

Going into her bedroom, she knelt by her bed and prayed for forgiveness for what she had done. She knew God would forgive her but would Carol?

Chapter Thirteen / 251

Carol was off duty the next day. Eleanor knew that her friend had been avoiding her ever since their recent skirmish and she was feeling very apprehensive about apologising; she had no idea how Carol would react. They had been friends for so long and had shared so much although there had been friction in their teens over that other incident. Carol had forgiven her then but Eleanor knew that her feelings had not been so deeply involved.

She found it hard to concentrate on her work as she had decided that she could no longer live comfortably with herself until she had talked to Carol. Her friend's flat was on the floor above hers and, at the end of her shift, she climbed the stairs of the Nurses' Residence.

Taking a deep breath, she rang the bell and waited. Perhaps Carol wasn't at home. Part of her hoped this was so but, having reached this point, she was eager to take her dose of humble pie while the adrenaline was still pumping. At last the door opened. Carol was wearing a dressing-gown; she was pale and her eyes were rimmed with a red that matched the tip of her nose. She was clutching a handful of crumpled tissues and Eleanor's sympathy immediately swamped any other feelings.

"Oh, Carol, aren't you well? I'm so sorry. Why didn't you ring me?"

"I'm all right. There just didn't seem any point in getting up. What do you want?"

"I want to talk to you."

"I haven't got anything to say to you."

"But I've got something to say to you. Can I come in?"

She suddenly realised it was probably constant tears that had caused the red eyes and nose. Carol moved away from the door; she didn't shut it so Eleanor followed her into the living room where she stood awkwardly in the middle of the room. Carol had sat down on the sofa and was snuffling into her tissues. She scowled at Eleanor,

"Well? What do you want to say?"

"I'm sorry." Eleanor sat down opposite her friend.

"Is that all?"

"No. Carol, I really am very, very sorry for going out with Chris when I knew how much you liked him." A sob interrupted her. "Do you still love him, Carol?"

"Of course I do. I don't know why! I don't even like him after the way treated me but I still love him. I know he's the only man for me and I shall never love anyone else like this. But I can't have him, can I? He's going to marry you?"

"No, he isn't."

"What?"

"Carol, I'm not going to marry him. I should never have got engaged to him. In fact I should never have gone out with him in the first place. I don't know why I did now. I suppose I was infatuated with him and ... and I tried not to think of you."

"History repeated itself, didn't it?" said Carol bitterly.

"Yes, I'm afraid so. Jenny reminded me about John. But that was years ago and it wasn't the same, was it?"

Carol shook her head. "I wasn't in love with John. In fact I was quite glad to be rid of him. It was my pride that was hurt then but Chris is different. I think he's selfish and thoughtless – but I still love him."

"I'm sure he cares for you too, Carol."

"Not in the way I love him but I'd settle for less."

"Would you?"

"I think so."

"Do you think you could possibly forgive me, Carol? Believe me, I do know how you feel. I feel the same way about David. He does abortions and he lied to me but I still love him in spite of that. Please say you forgive me."

There was a long pause before Carol looked at her friend. "We're a couple of idiots falling for men who couldn't care less about us, aren't we?"

"I'm sure that's not true in your case," objected Eleanor.

Carol shrugged. "I have missed you, Ellie. We've been friends for so long. It's very hard to forget what you did to me but I think I understand and yes, I do forgive you."

"Oh Carol." Eleanor felt as though the backpack that had been weighing her down had suddenly fallen off. She got up and sat

Chapter Thirteen / 253

down on the sofa beside her friend, putting her arm around her. "Thank you. I was so afraid you wouldn't be able to forgive me. Why don't you get dressed and we'll go out and have a meal to celebrate."

"Do we have anything to celebrate?"

"Of course we do. Chris is free again so I'm sure he'll come back to you." She paused, frowning. "In fact he never seemed very keen to let you go even when he was going out with me. He'd probably have liked to have had both of us."

❖ ❖ ❖ ❖

Melanie dropped her pen on the garden table beside her. She flexed her fingers and lay back on the lounger, shutting her eyes and letting peace flow over her. The only sound was the twittering of the birds and the occasional drone of a plane overhead. She breathed in the delicate scent of the climbing roses over the trellis at the end of the lawn that her father tended so carefully. They were already in full bloom although it was only the end of May. After the debacle with Simon, she had abandoned her flat and moved back to her parents' house. The first May of the new millennium had started off with a heat wave.

She opened her eyes and looked round appreciatively. The lawn had recently been cut and the earlier rain had heightened the vivid green. Edward Bradley was justifiably proud of his garden. The pristine lawn was bordered on either side with colourful pansies, petunias and geraniums. An arched trellis at the end led on to a patioed area where pots of geraniums and busy lizzies were scattered haphazardly around. From the patio where she was sitting she could appreciate fully the large bed in the centre of the lawn where roses of every imaginable colour bloomed. She was sure they were smiling at her and could not resist smiling back. She was so happy; a smug dot of achievement inside her was expanding all over her body. She stretched luxuriously. She had finished her novel and she was sure it was good. She had read enough manuscripts to know what was acceptable and her recent experiences had given depth to her work.

Picking up the A4 pad that lay on her lap, she reread her ending, correcting the occasional error and altering one or two words. She deleted an adverb and replaced the adjacent verb with a more appropriate one. That was definitely an improvement, she decided. Now all she had to do was type it up, print it and hope that a publisher would be interested.

Chewing the end of her pen, she reflected on the last few months. It had been a strange time but she felt that she had come to terms with what had happened and her future beckoned enticingly.

"God's in his heaven; all's right with the world," she whispered.

Lying back against the padded cushions, she regarded the wispy clouds gliding across the blue background. What should she do with her novel? Should she send it to Simon? She knew he published the type of novel she'd written and if she used a pseudonym, he wouldn't know it was hers. She'd never told him the plot so he wouldn't recognise it. However, if he accepted it, he would, of course, discover her identity. There were several other possible publishers she could try. She'd write a synopsis and a covering letter and send that with three opening chapters to several publishers but not Simon.

❖ ❖ ❖ ❖

Lorna picked up the phone and dialled. "I wondered if you wanted to come with me to the Parentcraft classes, Jenny. They start on Monday."

"What time?"

"Eleven."

"Yes that would be fine. I have two lessons first thing on a Monday and then I'm free till lunch time. Shall I pick you up?"

"Thanks." Lorna replaced the receiver and eased herself out of the chair. She felt as though she was exploding. She seemed to get larger and larger. Sleeping was difficult as she couldn't get comfortable. Her "bump" got in the way whichever way she tried to lie. Her mother had given her a small cushion to put under the "bump" when she lay on her side and that had helped a little.

She enjoyed the Parentcraft classes. At the first one she was delighted to discover that the midwife she had been seeing for check ups was running the course. It was explained that a physiotherapist and health visitor would also be in attendance and at later courses there would be guest speakers talking on a variety of related subjects. Watched by Jenny, she sat on a chair to do some exercises which she found quite difficult.

"Squeeze your back passage muscles and lift to the front. Feel it lift off the chair," instructed the physiotherapist.

Lorna tried and collapsed back into the chair in giggles. Others around her, just as embarrassed, were having the same problems, but gradually it became easier. Jenny sat on a spare chair and tried, not very successfully, to do the same exercises."We can practise together at home," she whispered.

"Mm. Help me up. I feel as though I need a hoist like Henry VIII used to get on his horse."

Jenny and the midwife heaved her to her feet. Other exercises followed and Lorna felt bemused by all the information she'd been given. Once again she was showered with leaflets.

❖ ❖ ❖ ❖

Melanie carefully slit open the envelope. Her heart was thumping against her ribs as she drew out the single sheet of paper.

> Dear Miss Bradley
> Thank you very much for allowing us to see your manuscript but I am sorry to say that it is not suitable for our list at present.
> Yours sincerely
> James Cartright
> (Editor – Carstairs and Carstairs)

Melanie sighed as she tossed the letter into the waste bin. Surely one of the other publishers she'd contacted would be more receptive.

❖ ❖ ❖ ❖

"Jenny, do calm down. You'll send up my blood pressure if you keep bouncing around."

"I'm sorry, Lorna. I just can't help it. I'm so excited. Do you think they'll really give us a picture of the baby?"

"The midwife said so but I expect it's just squiggles."

"I don't care. It'll be lovely to see it."

"I suppose so." Lorna was starting to feel weepy but the midwife assured her this was usual and she'd be thrilled when she saw her baby for the first time. Lorna doubted it. She just wanted to get back to normal. She was beginning to feel tight and uncomfortable. Soon she would have to wear maternity clothes. She sighed as Jenny drove into the hospital car park. She wished she could go to sleep until it was all over.

But she changed her mind as the midwife pointed to the screen beside the couch on which she lay.

"Look, Lorna. Can you see the head there?"

Jenny craned forward to see. "I can see its little arms and legs, too." She pointed.

"Yes, it's got the right number of limbs," smiled the midwife.

Jenny squinted at the screen. "I'm sure it's going to be a boy."

The midwife laughed. "It's very difficult to tell! Would you like a picture of the wee one?"

"Yes please," they both said enthusiastically.

On the way home as Lorna, her earlier depression forgotten, was gloating over the picture, she suddenly gasped and put her hand on her stomach.

"Are you all right?" queried Jenny anxiously.

"I felt it kick. It usually waits till I'm in bed."

" He, " corrected Jenny.

"All right. 'He' then. Perhaps he'll be a footballer."

"That would please Peter. Are you very tired, Lorna, or shall we go to Mothercare to buy you some maternity clothes? I'd like to treat you to a really nice dress."

"OK. Thanks."

"You really are starting to look blooming you know. Pregnancy suits you."

"My hair and skin certainly feel good but I hadn't connected it with being pregnant."

"Lorna, I've had an idea. Would you like to move in with me and Peter until the baby's born? Please say yes. As you know we've got four bedrooms. One we'd started to do up as a nursery when – when I was pregnant." Her voice trembled.

"Oh Jenny, I'm so sorry. I never realised the problems you were having. I guess I was too wrapped up in my own."

"Don't worry. I didn't want anyone to know until I was sure it was all right. It wasn't, so I didn't tell anyone – except Ellie, of course. So what do you say about moving in?"

Lorna contemplated the idea. She had no "partner" to support her through the pregnancy and birth. As Jenny was going to adopt her baby, it would be pleasant to have someone with her.

"I think it's a good idea," she said at last. "But on one condition."

"What's that?"

"You don't fuss over me all the time. You're like a mother hen, Jenny."

Jenny laughed. "Sorry. I won't promise, but I'll try. Will that do?"

"It's a deal. When shall I move in?"

"The sooner the better."

✤ ✤ ✤ ✤

Dear Miss Bradley

Thank you for your letter of 10 May enclosing a synopsis and three chapters of your novel *Thicker Than Water*. It is very well written but I am afraid that we are unable to make you an offer. I wish you every success with another publisher.

Yours sincerely
Susan Ash
(Editor – Chester Press)

Melanie screwed up the letter. It was the tenth rejection she'd received and she was getting very depressed. Perhaps her novel wasn't as good as she thought it was. But she was determined to keep trying.

❖ ❖ ❖ ❖

"You really have definitely finished with Chris, haven't you, Ellie?" Carol was frowning as she stirred her coffee during their short morning break.

Eleanor looked at her in surprise. "Of course I have. I told you. I thought we'd agreed to put all that behind us. You said you'd forgiven me."

"I just had to make sure. You won't realise you've made a mistake and take up with him again, will you?"

"Of course I won't. Carol, how can you think that of me?" Colour flamed in Eleanor's cheeks. She was bitterly hurt that her friend could think so little of her. But she had to admit she'd given Carol cause to distrust her.

Carol resumed her contemplation of her coffee but to Eleanor's consternation, her friend's usually fair skin was becoming dusted with a rosy red. Unlike Eleanor, she rarely blushed. The silence lengthened but it was not a comfortable one. While Eleanor didn't expect an answer to her rhetorical question, she would have liked some sign that Carol had really forgiven her even if she couldn't forget what had happened.

At last Carol put down her coffee cup. Her blush had receded and Eleanor was relieved to see that she looked happier than she had done for some time. She looked straight at Eleanor. "Chris rang last night. He apologised for the way he'd treated me and asked me out again."

"And you'll go?" Eleanor held her breath. She'd prayed so hard that God would put right the wrong she'd done her friend.

Carol nodded. "I can't help myself. I'm sure he'll let me down again but I really love him, Ellie. I'll always love him whatever he does."

"I do hope it works out for you, Carol." Eleanor's tension was expelled in a sigh of relief. "I'm so very sorry for what I did. There certainly won't be a repeat performance. I've learnt my lesson. I've been as selfish as Chris but I hope I can change. I know God has forgiven me and I hope in time, you'll not only forgive me but forget what I did."

✤ ✤ ✤ ✤

"I've had a letter." Melanie burst into the dining room where her parents were having breakfast. It was the middle Saturday in June and the sun blazed through the window.

Her father looked up from *The Times*. "Good news?" he asked.

"I think so. Masterman Books are interested in my novel and suggest I send them the rest."

"That's wonderful, Melanie. I'm so glad." Her mother smiled warmly at her. "Are you going to read the letter to us?"

"Of course. It says, *I was very interested to read your novel* Thicker than Water. *It is the type of book we are currently looking for but we would like to see the rest of it before we commit ourselves to offering you a contract. Please send the rest of the chapters as soon as possible and include a brief CV.* It's signed Fiona Rivers (Fiction Editor)"

"It certainly sounds hopeful," agreed her father.

"I'll get it ready to post on Monday. Do you think I should send return postage or does that suggest I expect them to return it?"

"You should know more about that sort of thing than we do," said Dorothy.

"I could always ask for it to be returned if they reject it, couldn't I?" remarked Melanie, thoughtfully. "I think I'll just enclose a stamped addressed envelope and hope she says she wants to meet me. Oh I *do* hope she takes it. It's been *so* depressing to keep getting rejections. I must go and get it ready." She headed for the door.

✤ ✤ ✤ ✤

"Which do you want first, the good news or the bad news?" Eleanor had just spent the morning on the phone to the Adoption Agencies, the Social Services and even the Registrar.

"The good news." Jenny looked at her expectantly.

"Well, legally you can adopt Lorna's baby and you don't have to go through an adoption agency."

"That's all right then, isn't it?"

"Not quite. Nothing can be done until some time after the baby is born and I'm afraid it's quite a long process. You have to notify the Social Services in writing that you want to apply for an adoption order. It'll be quite a gruelling process, Jenny. The Social Services have to support the adoption before it can go to court and they have to submit a report. They'll go into your medical history, check with the police ..."

"The police!" exclaimed Jenny, outraged.

"They have to make sure you don't have a criminal record." She broke off and started to giggle. "Oh, Jenny, your face."

Jenny's horror also turned to amusement. "Peter's a barrister," she spluttered. "I don't think he'll take kindly to the police vetting him. Actually he said it might be a long process. How long does it take?"

"It might be months."

"So what happens in the meantime?"

"Oh apparently there's no reason why Lorna can't hand the baby over to you when it's born. You can look after it just as if it's yours. But the legal process of actual adoption takes longer. They have to make sure the mother doesn't want it back and the father has rights too. In fact she said there's a new Human Rights Bill coming out in October and it will give even more rights to the father."

"Oh dear. It does sound complicated."

"I shouldn't worry, Jenny. I'm sure it will be all right. Lorna knows she wouldn't be able to cope and her – her boyfriend seems to have disappeared."

"I thought you said he'd gone to France."

"Oh yes. Well I'm sure you'll give him access if he wants it."

"Have you told Lorna all this?"

"Not yet. It seemed more applicable to you. She's made it quite clear she wants you to adopt her baby."

Chapter Thirteen / 261

"I hope she doesn't change her mind. Apparently mothers don't want to give up their new-born babies. I can understand that. I could never give my baby away."

"But your situation is different, Jenny. And it's not as though Lorna will never see her baby. She can visit as often as she likes, can't she?"

"Of course."

✢ ✢ ✢ ✢

"Jenny!" Lorna screamed. "Ooh ..." She clutched her stomach and rolled out of bed, doubling up in pain. "Jenny, I think the baby's coming."

Jenny erupted into the room. "Are you sure? It's not due for another month. Quick, where's your bag?"

"In the corner," gasped Lorna. "Oh it hurts."

"Take some deep breaths like you were told. That's right. I'll tell Peter to get the car out. Keep breathing deeply and doing everything you were told."

"I can't remember any of it," groaned Lorna. The pain had eased for a while and she wondered if she should dress. But she couldn't be bothered. The hospital would have to accept her in her nightdress.

Jenny flew back. "How far apart are your contractions? I forgot to ask."

"Goodness I don't know. I've got too much else on my mind at the moment. Oh." She screamed again. "Sorry."

"Can you walk to the car? I'll time your contractions. The hospital will want to know."

Lorna struggled to her feet and wriggled her toes into the sandals she had kicked under the bed. It was a warm night but Jenny draped a cardigan round her shoulders.

"Peter will drive and I'll sit in the back with you."

"Thanks."

Peter was looking anxious as they eased themselves into the back of the car. "All right, Lorna?" he queried. "You're not going to have it in the car, are you?"

"Don't say things like that," scolded Jenny. "Just drive – fast."

There was little traffic in the middle of the night and it only took about fifteen minutes. Jenny hauled Lorna out of the car and hurried her in.

"My sister's in labour," she announced almost before she reached the reception desk.

The receptionist eyed Lorna critically. "Just take a seat," she said cheerfully. "I'll send someone to you."

"Oh." Lorna doubled up again and she squeezed her sister's hand.

"Come along, Lorna." It was Sue, her own midwife.

"Oh Sue. It's coming."

"Let's have a look, shall we?" She led Lorna to the labour room and hoisted her onto the couch. "How far apart are your contractions?"

"They seem quite irregular." Jenny answered for her. "She had two close together – about ten minutes and then there was a long gap."

Sue examined her patient. "I'm sorry, Lorna; it's a false alarm. You'll have to go home."

"But it felt as though it was coming."

"I know, dear, but you won't produce for a long time yet. Go home and rest."

"I wanted it to come," sobbed Lorna. "I'm so fed up with looking like a fat cow."

She felt like a very large elephant and couldn't wait to get rid of her "intruder".

"Come along, Lorna," soothed Jenny. "Are you sure you're right?" she asked Sue anxiously.

"I'm right. I've been doing this job for ages."

❖ ❖ ❖ ❖

"Do I look right for a visit to my publisher?" Melanie pirouetted in front of her parents. She was wearing a lemon two piece, the skirt of which was about four inches above her knees, and a cream blouse. The recent heatwave had tanned her skin to a healthy bronze and the lemon accentuated this.

"You look very nice, dear," said her mother.

"I expect the editor will be wearing jeans and tee-shirt but I thought I'd better dress up."

"I'll give you a lift to the station on the way to work."

"Thanks Dad. I'm ready when you are."

She managed to catch one of the numerous fast trains to Waterloo but as it was early it was crammed with commuters and she had to stand. It was uncomfortable standing in the aisle envying all those sitting down reading the *Financial Times* or the *Mirror*. She shifted her weight from one foot to the other and leaned back as someone squeezed past her. A mobile phone went off followed by a loud conversation about someone called Julius who wasn't pulling his weight and would have to be "spoken to". She wondered if she should remove her jacket but, although she was hot, she'd have to hold it and it would then get creased. The overhead racks were full of briefcases and raincoats.

It wasn't quite as hot as the previous day and rain had been forecast but London was very warm and sticky. She took the underground to Oxford Street and turned right down Regent Street until she came to Margaret Street. Standing at the crossroads, she pulled out the editor's letter with the directions. Unfortunately, there was no number on the address but, unless she was holding the map upside down, she had to turn right. Masterman Books had their offices in Dominion House which was near a large building which specialised in photographing the famous and not so famous. She scanned the street but Dominion House remained well hidden. On the corner she came to one of the many internet cafes that were springing up all over the country. She was early so she had time for a coffee. It was cool inside and she ordered a cappuccino.

"Can you tell me where Dominion House is?" she asked as she waited for the sizzling of the coffee machine to die down.

The girl nodded. "It's just across the road."

"Oh thanks. I thought it was on this side."

She took her drink to a seat by the window and looked across the road. There it was. **Dominium House** was blazoned across a tall, brick building with "blind" windows. She could just see the list of offices it housed but it was too far away for her to read them. She glanced at her watch. It was nearly ten-thirty and her appointment was for eleven. She'd go across at a quarter to eleven. She didn't want to be late.

Taking out the precious letter from Fiona Rivers, she read it again:

Dear Melanie

Thank you for sending the rest of your novel. I have sent it to two readers and have now received their comments on it. On the whole they were favourably impressed. There are some areas that I feel need more work but I consider it a promising first novel. Although we cannot, at the moment, make you an offer to publish, I would like to talk to you about it. I shall be in London until September. Perhaps you could ring me and we could arrange a time for you to come to the office.

Yours sincerely
Fiona Rivers

Melanie had wasted no time in making the phone call and in a few minutes she would meet Fiona. Her heart was pounding as she crossed the street and pressed the bell beside Masterman Books.

"Yes?" A disembodied voice floated down. She opened her mouth but no sound came. "Who is it?" demanded the voice impatiently.

"It's Melanie Bradley. I have an appointment with Fiona Rivers."

"Come in. We're on the third floor." There was a click and she opened the door. Steps led up to a huge reception hall where several girls were manning phones behind a long counter. Business men in suits and girls wearing smart trousers and matching shirts were moving purposefully about their work. On the left were two lifts designed to look like panelled wooden doors. Melanie moved over to them and pushed the "up" button. She was becoming more nervous every moment.

Chapter Thirteen / 265

The lift doors opened silently and, as they closed behind her, she glided upwards to the third floor and stepped out onto a plush green carpet. Looking around, she saw a number of doors leading off from the spacious central area. She walked round them until she found one with the name she wanted. Taking a deep breath, she knocked timidly and a voice bade her "enter". Opening the door, she found herself faced with a busy office humming with working computers.

"Can I help you?" A girl who had obviously made the most of the recent sun, pushed back the glass panel.

"I have an appointment with Fiona Rivers."

"Just a moment. I'll see if she's free." She returned to her desk and Melanie waited patiently until the girl returned. "Take a seat. She'll be out in a minute." She waved to a couple of armchairs beside the lift doors and Melanie perched on the edge of one. If she sat back, she'd have difficulty getting up again.

"Melanie, it's nice to meet you at last." A girl came towards Melanie with her hand outstretched. She had certainly kept her distance from the sun. Clear grey eyes smiled out of a flawless complexion that was so beautifully made-up that it looked completely natural. Her short-sleeved white blouse and pleated polka dot navy skirt suggested a model rather than an editor. Beside this dainty doll, Melanie felt clumsy and huge.

But appearances were deceptive. There was nothing dainty about Fiona's brain. She opened Melanie's masterpiece and proceeded to carve it up until the would-be author wondered why she'd come.

"Now," said Fiona, waving her hands over the desecrated manuscript, "we can get down to business. In spite of what I've said, this has definite possibilities but a lot of it needs to be rewritten. Are you happy with that?"

"Oh yes – yes of course."

"Good. You'd be amazed at the number of authors who consider their every word sacred and refuse to change anything." I wouldn't, Melanie reflected; I've met them too. Fiona hurtled on. "I thought we'd go through it carefully and I can explain where changes need to be made. Would you like a cup of coffee while we work?"

"Yes please." The shock of Fiona's onslaught had dried her mouth but after her first bewilderment, she thought she was going to enjoy the challenge of working with this editor who obviously knew exactly what she wanted. Melanie wondered how long it would be before she moved on to one of the larger, more prestigious publishing houses.

✥ ✥ ✥ ✥

"Jenny." Lorna was standing in the doorway of her sister's bedroom. "Jenny, wake up. The baby really *is* coming this time although it's still a bit early."

"What? Peter. Peter wake up."

"Don't panic. The contractions are about twenty minutes apart but I think we should go."

"Yes. Go and get ready while we dress. Peter, do hurry."

Lorna wandered back to her room. She felt strangely calm. She knew the baby wouldn't come until the contractions were closer together and she hoped her waters wouldn't break until they reached the hospital.

They didn't. She had hardly been hoisted onto the bed when water poured out.

"That's good." A midwife she didn't know, smiled encouragingly.

During the next couple of hours Lorna suffered the most excruciating pain she'd ever known. An oxygen mask was placed over her face but she kept pushing it away. She could hear someone screaming but didn't recognise her own voice. She was vaguely aware of Jenny beside her, letting her squeeze her hand and mop the sweat that was pouring down her face.

"Push," the midwife kept saying. "Push."

What did they think she was doing for goodness sake? She couldn't push any harder. She was *so* exhausted.

"Just one more hard push. You're doing very well. Good girl. Push. I can see the baby's head. Push Lorna. Push."

"Aaah!" Lorna gave one last almighty shove as she screamed and then her scream was suddenly joined by the welcome sound of a lusty pair of lungs objecting strongly to being forced out of their warm cocoon into a cold world.

"You have a lovely little boy." A red muffled bundle was placed in her arms and Lorna forget the pain and indignity as she gazed into the blue eyes of her little son.

Jenny was sobbing uncontrollably beside her. "Oh Lorna, he's beautiful."

"Yes, he is," said Lorna softly. "And he's all mine."

She was oblivious to Jenny's horrified gasp as she tightened her hold on her precious bundle. Sue had been right. She didn't want to let him go. But she wasn't losing him. She could see him every day and Jenny would care for him better than she could.

"Jenny," she whispered. "Jenny, please don't cry. He *is* mine but you are going to look after him so he's yours too. Do you want to hold him?"

"Oh yes," Jenny breathed. Lorna watched her take the tiny mite and gaze down at him with such love that tears filled Lorna's eyes. She was *so* tired and she ached all over. She shut her eyes. Her throat was very sore too. It must have been the result of all her screaming.

"Lorna," Jenny whispered. "Can we call him Sam?"

Chapter Fourteen

"No, Jenny. This is something I want to do by myself."

"But if I'm going to adopt little Sam, why can't I register his birth with you? I don't understand." Jenny was near tears and Lorna put her arms round her.

"Jenny, you're going to have Sam for the rest of your life. I won't change my mind but at the moment he's mine. I'm his mother and it will be *my* name on his birth certificate. Please let me do this one thing as his mother."

"Can't we wait and talk about it with Peter. Perhaps we needn't register him until we've got the adoption papers."

Lorna sighed and sat down by the hall telephone table. She'd been on her way out when Jenny had waylaid her. For an intelligent woman, Jenny could be very dense sometimes.

"Jenny, the birth has to be registered within fourteen days. Sam was born on 30 July and it's now 11 August. If I leave it till Monday, it'll be too late and I don't suppose they're open at the weekend. I must do it today and I want to go alone."

Jenny sniffed. "All right. I'm sorry, Lorna. I know I'm being selfish. I'm just terrified something might go wrong."

"Nothing will go wrong and anyway I think you'll get an adoption certificate when you adopt. I'd better go." She stood up.

"Are you sure you're all right to go out alone, Lorna? I could come with you and wait outside."

"No, Jenny. I feel fine. A walk will do me good."

"Could you get some more pampers on your way home, please. We've run out again."

"Can't you wash them?"

"Oh, Lorna. They're disposable."

"OK. OK. Do you need anything else?"

"I don't think so."

Lorna closed the door behind her and took a deep breath. The tussle with Jenny had been going on for several days and she had found it very tiring. But she knew she was right. This was one thing *she* must do for her baby son. The sun was laughing down at her out of a blue sky and she smiled back. She felt content. She loved little Sam but she was very happy for her sister to care for him. Jenny would make a better mother than she would although she did hope her sister wouldn't become too possessive.

Now that the baby was safely born, she could think about her future. Fortunately the college had been sympathetic and she would be starting her course again at the end of September. That would give her several weeks to get her figure back and readjust.

It was early on Friday morning, so the town centre was not yet flooded with school refugees making the most of the start of their long vacation. She was gazing longingly at an evening dress in one of the many boutiques in the High Street when she heard her name called and footsteps behind her. She stopped.

"I thought it was you. I – I didn't know whether to speak or not. I thought you might not want to see me."

She turned to face him. "Hullo, Will. What are you doing in this part of the world?"

"Staying with Ben. Do you remember him?" She shook her head. "How are you?"

"Fine. And you? How was France."

"Still there. Have you got time for a coffee? For old times' sake."

She hesitated but realised she should talk to him. She must tell him he had a son; and she still had the five hundred pounds he had given her. He looked anxious as he waited for her reply.

"All right," she said at last.

Hazelford still retained a typical English tea room called The Copper Kettle and they made their way to it.

"Coffee?" he asked as they sat down.

She nodded. At least she was drinking coffee again since she was no longer pregnant. In fact she liked it better than she had before. There was an awkward pause. Lorna couldn't think of how to broach the subject and she thought he was having the same trouble. The waitress brought their coffee.

"Anything to eat?" he enquired.

She shook her head. "No thanks."

The waitress departed and Will said quickly, "Was the abortion OK? No after effects?"

Lorna stirred her coffee. She took her time to answer. "I didn't have it."

He blenched. Then he asked hopefully. "Did you have a miscarriage?"

"No." The pause lengthened as he waited for her to elaborate. "I had the baby."

"Oh."

"I'm sorry, Will. I just couldn't go along with an abortion. Ellie told me such awful things and – and then I watched a video, *The Silent Scream*. It was awful, Will. It showed how the baby must feel."

"It's hardly a baby at that stage," he objected.

"Well it can still feel pain. No, I couldn't do it."

"When was it born?"

"The end of July. It was early."

"Can I see it?"

"Him."

"Oh, it's a boy."

"Yes, he's really cute. Of course you can see him. He's called Sam."

Chapter Fourteen / 271

"Why did you call him that?"

"I didn't. My sister, Jenny did."

"Oh."

"She and her husband are hoping to adopt him. It seems the perfect solution. She can't have kids you see and I couldn't cope with a baby on my own, could I?"

"I suppose not." He looked quickly at her. "I would have helped, you know."

"I'm sure you would but it wouldn't have been easy for either of us."

He was building castles with the sugar. She looked at him, frowning. "What's the matter, Will? Are you annoyed I didn't have the abortion? I've still got the money you gave me. I'll give it back to you."

"No," he said quickly. "Please don't. Keep it for – Sam. It must be expensive looking after a baby."

"Yes it is but Peter's a barrister and Jenny's a Head of Department so they're not exactly short of money."

"I'd like them to have it for him though. Do you think they'd accept it?"

"I don't know. I'll ask them."

He was still fiddling with the spoon. "I'd like to see him."

"I'll try to arrange something."

"Would you like another cup of coffee?"

"No thanks. I must go. I was on my way to register the birth. It was nice seeing you again, Will." She stood up.

"Wait while I pay the bill and I'll walk with you."

As they walked down the high street towards the Registry Office, Lorna was concentrating on the forthcoming interview. She felt a little apprehensive.

"Lorna."

"Yes?"

"Could I come in with you?"

She stopped and faced him. "Do you really want to?"

"Yes I do. Please. And – and can we put my name on the birth certificate as the father?"

She stared at him. "You've changed your tune since you wanted me to have an abortion."

He looked embarrassed. "I know. I suppose I always felt guilty about it. I'm so glad you didn't have it. And I can't wait to see little Sam. Can we put my name on the certificate?"

She hesitated. Would it cause problems later for Jenny? But Eleanor had said that fathers had rights anyway and whether his name was there or not, she knew he was the father. But she had to make sure he understood the position.

"You're quite happy about Jenny and Peter adopting Sam, aren't you? You won't make any difficulties later."

He looked shocked. "Of course I won't. I'm so glad he'll be looked after well. It wouldn't have worked out with you and me, would it?"

She shook her head. "We're too young. I'm going to start college again in October."

"I'm glad. Shall we go then? Can my name go down as the father?"

"I think it will be much nicer for Sam to have a named father. 'Father unknown' sounds horrible doesn't it?"

❖ ❖ ❖ ❖

Melanie tore open the envelope bearing the logo of Masterman Books. The post had come while she was still in bed and she'd rushed downstairs as she'd done every day since she'd sent off the first three chapters of her revised novel. Her parents had both left for work early and she was alone in the house on this Friday at the beginning of August.

She squinted at the letter and then rushed upstairs. She couldn't read it without her glasses. She hadn't time to put in her contact lenses. She groped for her glasses and sat down on the bed to read it.

Dear Melanie

Thank you for the new chapters of your novel. I am delighted with them. I am sure you will be able to work on the rest of the novel in the same way. In view of this, I will be sending you a contract for the novel in the near future. Do you think you'd be able to let me have the completed manuscript by 31 December or is that too early? If I don't hear from you, I will assume that is acceptable and will draw up the contract accordingly. You will be sent two copies to sign and one will be returned to you. Please read it carefully before you sign and let me know if you have any queries.

I look forward to seeing the final work.

Yours sincerely
Fiona Rivers

Melanie read it again slowly. Then she jumped up and did a dance round the room.

"Hurrah!" she yelled. "I've done it!" She was glad she was alone and she sat down on the bed and hugged herself. She'd keep her secret until Sunday when most of the family would be at Sunday lunch. She'd make an announcement.

She stared out of the window. She could hear the wind chimes tinkling in the gentle breeze and the grey-white canvas of the sky was slowly being painted bird's-egg blue. What a beautiful world it was, she thought. She frowned. Something was wriggling its way into her brain. There was something she had to do. What was it?

Of course. She must thank God for Fiona's letter. She had prayed so frequently that her novel would be accepted and up to now the request had been refused. Now the answer was "yes" and she must certainly say, "Thank you." Why was it, she wondered, that humans always turned to God when they needed help but when he supplied it, they forgot to say, "Thank you"? This time she would remember.

✤ ✤ ✤ ✤

Will and Lorna were both smiling broadly as they left the Registry Office. Lorna was clutching the piece of paper that identified Sam Bradley as the son of Lorna Bradley and William Baines.

Will glanced at his watch. "It's lunch time. Have you got time to have some lunch to celebrate or do you have to get back?"

"Jenny will be expecting me. In fact she's probably produced a whole litter of kittens by now. But I'd like to have lunch with you. I'll find a phone and ring her."

"Use my mobile." He fished it out of his pocket and handed it to her.

"Oh thanks." She dialled hurriedly. "Jenny? I – I've met a friend so I'm having lunch in town. I'll see you later." She threw her eyes up at Will. "Yes, I'm still fine. No I'm not tired. I must go. 'Bye." She handed the phone back. "She's been treating me like a piece of very fragile glass ever since we talked about adoption."

"It's nice to have a caring family."

"I suppose so. But I do feel rather suffocated sometimes. I'll be glad when I go away to college again. Where shall we go for lunch?"

"Is a pub OK?"

"Yes. I'll even have a glass of wine. I couldn't drink alcohol while I was pregnant."

They headed up the road to the Fox and Geese and Lorna studied the menu while Will bought some drinks.

"Thanks. Cheers." She lifted her glass of white wine to him.

He responded. "Here's to Sam Bradley. May he have a long and happy life." They clicked their glasses together. "Now what are you going to eat?"

"Scampi and chips please. Jenny doesn't approve of chips and I love them."

She watched him go to give the order. She sensed something was on his mind and felt there was an ulterior motive for the lunch invitation. She was right. When he came back, he stared down at his beer, frowning.

"What's the matter, Will? You look as if you've got the cares of the world on your shoulders."

Chapter Fourteen / 275

He looked at her with pain in his eyes. "Lorna. I've got a confession to make."

He looked so miserable that she felt herself go cold. Please God, he wasn't going to tell her he had AIDS or something equally ghastly.

"What is it? Please tell me, Will. You're scaring me."

"You know the money I gave you. I said it was from my uncle. Well it wasn't. It was mine. I was saving up for a car."

She almost laughed with relief. "Well I don't see what's so bad about that."

"It's not that. I – I lied about my uncle. I told you he performs abortions and that he said it was the best thing for you to have one. He didn't. He told me I'd no right to take advantage of you and I should do the decent thing and marry you. If I didn't do that, I should at least support you and the baby. He went absolutely wild when I suggested an abortion. He said it was murder but I wouldn't listen to him."

"That's what Eleanor said. I'm glad I listened to her."

"So am I, now. You didn't tell her about – about Uncle David, did you?"

Lorna frowned. "I can't remember. I think I mentioned it but she said she didn't know of any Christian obstetricians who performed abortions."

"Did you tell her his name?"

"I wasn't sure of it. I may have said he probably had the same surname as yours."

Will was beginning to look very uncomfortable. "I think she did know him, Lorna. I think she worked with him. You'd better put the record straight and tell her what I've told you. Not that it matters too much now. He's gone to work as a missionary in Uganda."

Lorna was silent. Her brain was working furiously. Finally she said slowly, "She behaved very oddly after I told her you wanted me to have an abortion. She got really mad at me. I thought it was because she felt so strongly about abortion but perhaps ... Oh, Will, *why* didn't you tell me the truth?"

276 / Whiter than White

"I suppose I thought you'd take more notice of a surgeon and I wanted you to have an abortion. But I'm glad you didn't now." He was looking as worried as she felt. "Do you think that's why he went to Uganda? She wouldn't have anything to do with him if he performed abortions, would she?"

"Oh, Will, what *are* we going to do?"

✢ ✢ ✢ ✢

"So that's it. Will was lying and his Uncle David thinks the same about abortion as you do. I thought I ought to tell you."

"Thank you." Eleanor's voice came out in a croak. She felt stunned. Why had she made no attempt to tackle him after Lorna had come to her? Why had she believed Lorna and given him no chance to speak for himself? She knew why. She'd asked him once how he felt about abortions and he'd denied performing them so when Lorna dropped her bombshell, she'd decided he had to be lying. What a fool she'd been. She had no one to blame but herself.

"Ellie, are you all right? Shall I get you a drink?"

"No thank you. I think you'd better go now, Lorna. I need to think. Thank you for coming round."

✢ ✢ ✢ ✢

"I've got something to tell you all."

Lorna looked up at Melanie's excited voice. It was the first time for several weeks that all the Bradley family had met together for Sunday lunch. They'd all been to church in the morning – even little Sam who'd been as good as gold in his carrycot beside Jenny. Lorna had noticed that even Peter was casting the occasional fond glance at her son.

"Well, what is it?" demanded Kate. "Come on, Mel. You've been looking like a cat that's swallowed the cream all weekend."

"My novel's been accepted by Masterman Books and they're going to send me a contract."

"Oh brill."

"Congratulations."

"Well done."

Chapter Fourteen / 277

A chorus of voices greeted the announcement. "When will it be published, Mel?" asked Kate. "Can I have a signed copy?"

"I haven't finished it yet."

"I thought you finished it ages ago."

"I did but I've had to rewrite it. I've got to send it off by the end of the year. Then I think it takes about nine months before it's finally published. Like a baby." She giggled.

"That reminds me," Lorna broke in and they all turned to her expectantly. "I want Sam to be baptised soon. Peter and Jenny have agreed but I'm still his mum at the moment."

"Have you spoken to Steve yet?" asked her father.

"No not yet. I wanted to tell you all first."

"Steve usually slots the baptism into the Sunday morning service," said Edward. "Are you happy with that or do you want a private service?"

Lorna hesitated and glanced at her older sister. "What do you think, Jenny?"

Jenny passed the buck to her husband. "Peter?"

"It's up to you."

"It's not exactly straightforward, is it?" said Edward thoughtfully.

"What do you mean?"

"Well, Sam is Lorna's baby but Jenny and Peter are hoping to adopt him. And what about Will? His name's on the birth certificate and he *is* the father. You can't have two sets of parents."

"Can't we wait until we've properly adopted him, Lorna?" asked Jenny.

"That could take months. I want him done while he's still a baby."

"Jenny and Peter could be godparents," suggested Kate.

"We can't be godparents if we're going to adopt him."

"There's a service of Thanksgiving after adoption," remarked Edward. "You could have that after everything's finalised, Jenny."

"Oh what a brilliant idea. I'd like that, wouldn't you, Peter?"

"Yes, I would."

"So what are we going to do now? Haven't you any ideas, Ellie?" Lorna asked. Eleanor had hardly said anything all morning. Lorna felt very guilty because she was now sure she knew why her sister was so unhappy. But she hoped that she and Will might somehow be able to make things right for her. "You always come up with the answer, Ellie."

"Not always. It seems to me it would be better if Sam is baptised as Lorna's baby. After all it's *his* baptism that's important, isn't it? Can't Jenny and Peter go up with the baptism party as 'supporters', Dad?"

"Yes I'm sure they could and there's no reason why they shouldn't make the responses as well. Who are you going to ask to be godparents, Lorna?"

Lorna glanced quickly at Eleanor. "I haven't decided yet."

"Can I be one?" demanded Kate. "I think Sam's sweet. I'd love to be his godmother. Please let me."

"I'll see. Does it matter how many godparents there are, Dad?"

"I don't think so."

"Well, I'll let you all know when I've decided. But I think it would be nice to have it in the morning service." She returned to attack her roast beef which was growing cold. She had a lot to think about. The germ of an idea was growing in her mind but she must talk to Will first.

✣ ✣ ✣ ✣

"Have you come up with any ideas, Will?" Lorna settled herself at a table in The Copper Kettle and gazed hopefully at Will who was obviously about to burst with his news.

"Something's happened. Have you seen the news recently?"

"Sometimes. It's usually doom and gloom. Were you referring to anything specific?"

"Uganda."

"Uganda?"

"Yes," he said impatiently. "There's been trouble in the area where Uncle David was working and he's had to come home."

Chapter Fourteen / 279

"Oh."

"Is that all you can say? It's good news, isn't it?"

"It certainly is. I was wondering how we could get him back to England. Well that's certainly an answer to prayer."

"You still believe in all that then."

"All what?"

"Prayer, Christianity, you know …"

"Of course I do. You know I do. I'm going to have Sam baptised soon."

"That's nice."

"Will you come to the service and be part of the baptism party? You *are* his father."

He looked horrified. "I don't go to church much. Don't you have to make promises or something?"

"Yes, you do but …"

He shook his head. "I'm not a hypocrite, Lorna. I'm not a Christian and I don't think it would be right for me to make all the vows if I don't believe in what I'm saying. It would be perjury, " he said warming to his theme.

She was silent. "I suppose it would," she said at last. "I never thought of it like that. It's very honest of you. But you'll come to the service won't you? There'll be a buffet lunch in the church hall afterwards. Carol, one of Ellie's friends is making a cake for us."

"Who are you going to have as godparents?"

"My sisters will be godmothers. Eleanor, Melanie and Kate."

"I didn't realise you had three sisters. What about godfathers?"

"That's why I said it was an answer to prayer that your uncle was home. Do you think he'd agree to be one?"

"Uncle David?" He looked startled and then laughed. "Lorna, you're brilliant."

She grinned. "I am, aren't I? The idea suddenly came to me while we were discussing the baptism at Sunday lunch. The whole family was there and Kate, my youngest sister, was badgering me to let her be one of the godmothers. I wouldn't say who I was going to ask although I'd already decided on Ellie and then I thought – if your Uncle David could be persuaded … well they might get together, mightn't they?"

He looked concerned. "Suppose we've made a mistake."

"I'm sure we haven't. She was shattered when I told her what you said and she hardly said a word at lunch. She looks really miserable."

"I'm only guessing about him though."

"Mel said Ellie was going out with one of the surgeons and then it suddenly stopped so I'm sure we're right. She ditched him because she couldn't face him doing abortions and he was broken-hearted and went to Uganda."

"You've been reading too many Mills and Boon romances. Why didn't she ask him if it was true?"

"*I* don't know. But she can't have done or he wouldn't have gone to Uganda, would he?"

"I've no idea." He thought for a moment. "He's never mentioned missionary work before. It was rather sudden. Well, if we're wrong, nothing will come of it, will it? But at least we've tried."

"Have you told him you lied to me?"

He shook his head. "I haven't seen him since he came back."

"He doesn't know Ellie's my sister, does he?"

"There's no reason why he should."

"Good. Don't tell him. But tell him I've had the baby and we both want him to be godfather."

"Suppose he doesn't agree."

"Oh for goodness' sake, Will, stop making difficulties. You'll just have to use your powers of persuasion. I should think he'd be delighted you want the baby baptised. He's a Christian, isn't he?"

He nodded. "Are you going to tell Ellie?"

"Certainly not. It will come as a nice surprise when she sees him again and they can sort everything out."

"I only hope you're right. I'd forgotten how bossy you were, Lorna."

"Sorry. Now we'd better arrange for him to meet me and Sam before the big day, hadn't we? On the day you can bring him to the service at the last minute so he won't have time to get cold feet. The baptism party always sits at the front so I'll save you both seats at the end of the row by the wall so you won't have to walk up the centre aisle. That way, Ellie won't see him until he goes up to the front."

"Got it all planned, haven't you?"

"Well someone has to. Oh I'm going to have another godfather."

"Who?"

"He works at the Health Club. His name's Chris. Ellie was engaged to him but she broke it off. I wondered why at the time but I can guess now. And Carol, who's making the cake, will be the other godmother. I know she's always been keen on Chris so I'm hoping they'll get together too."

"Proper little matchmaker, aren't you?" he said with a grin.

✢ ✢ ✢ ✢

Eleanor glanced at little Sam sleeping peacefully in Jenny's arms and the sisters exchanged smiles above the sleeping child. The baptism party was hovering in the church porch when Steve appeared wearing his surplice and black stole.

"You can go in now if you like. The front two pews have been reserved for you. Are you all here?"

"I think so." Lorna looked round. "Oh Carol and Chris aren't here."

"Here they are now." Eleanor had glimpsed the couple walking though the lych-gate talking animatedly together. Did she feel a tiny twinge of jealousy? But she was glad Chris looked more cheerful. She hoped things were progressing well. Carol would make him a good wife even if he hadn't yet realised it.

Lorna reclaimed her son who had opened his eyes and Eleanor followed her into the church and up the aisle. The new mother had already stipulated that only Jenny, Peter, Eleanor and she were to sit in the front row. The rest of the Bradley family and Chris and Carol were to occupy the second row. Eleanor had been very impressed with the way Lorna had organised this very special occasion. She settled her wide brimmed hat more firmly on her head. She and Carol were the only ones wearing hats. Carol always wore one to church and she had persuaded Eleanor to keep her company on this occasion.

The organist was playing *Sheep may safely graze* and Eleanor shut her eyes letting the music wash over her. The baptism would be in the middle of the service. The buzz of conversation from the congregation died away as the organist played the last note and Steve entered and stood at the front.

"I welcome you all to the Lord's house on this beautiful morning. I'd like to give a special welcome to Sam Bradley who is to be baptised this morning and of course to his family who have been members of this church for many years."

How very tactfully put, thought Eleanor. Good for Steve. It was going to be a lovely service and she was glad everything had worked out. In fact, it seemed that everyone was happy except her but she must put her unhappiness behind her now and move on. Her aborted friendship with David she must chalk up to experience. She knew she'd never see him again.

She scrambled to her feet to join in the first hymn and, as the singing swelled up, Eleanor sneaked a glance behind her. The church was full and many of the congregation would be joining them for the buffet lunch in the church hall. The hymn ended, the service started and soon it was time for the baptism. Steve invited the family to take their places at the front. Eleanor stood up, vaguely aware that the front row was now full. She frowned and glanced back as she followed Lorna out of the pew. William, Sam's father, was sitting there. She smiled at him, remembering that Lorna had said he would feel a hypocrite if he said such solemn vows lightly.

She followed Lorna up to the front where the family and godparents turned to face the congregation. Lorna handed the baby to the vicar.

> Children who are too young to profess the Christian faith are baptised on the understanding that they are brought up as Christians within the family of the Church.

Chapter Fourteen / 283

Eleanor had heard the words so many times but she always found the baptism service moving. Having agreed that they all turned to Christ, repented of their sins and renounced evil, Steve made the sign of the cross on Sam's forehead and invited them to follow him to the font at the back of the church. As they moved down, Eleanor felt there was something wrong. There were too many people. Her hat had prevented her from seeing anything at the side of her but as she moved towards the aisle, she was aware of a tall figure beside her who shouldn't have been there. She looked up at him and stifled a gasp. David looked as startled as she felt and she almost missed the step down from the sanctuary. She felt his hand steady her and tried to restore her face and her hat to normality. It wasn't easy! *What* was he doing here? He was supposed to be in Uganda and why on earth was he part of the baptism party? Her young sister would have some explaining to do. As they reached the font, Lorna caught her eye and grinned at her. Eleanor stared stonily back.

She found it hard to concentrate on the rest of the service and was only vaguely aware of Steve tipping water over the baby's head from a scallop shell and then carrying him up the aisle so that the congregation could greet him with murmured approval. When she returned to her seat, David took his place at the end of the pew next to Will and she was on Will's other side.

After the baptism, the service dragged for her and she desperately wanted to find out *why* David was sitting so near her. Her insides were already performing acrobatics at the thought of his proximity. Had Will confessed to his perfidy? Would she have a chance to tell him how she had misjudged him or would she then betray his nephew? She was sure now that Lorna and Will had engineered the meeting. She was puzzled because she'd given Lorna no indication she'd known the surgeon who was Will's uncle. Or had she?

Eventually the last hymn was sung, the blessing given and the baptism party made its slow progress down the aisle while baby Sam basked in the adulation being paid him.

"Wasn't he good?"

"Isn't he cute?"

"You must be so proud of him."

As Eleanor followed Lorna and her baby down the aisle, she felt a glow of happiness at the Christian love that was being shown. No one had ostracised Lorna or even criticised her for her "mistake" and she noticed with pleasure that one or two people greeted Will and David who were obviously visitors to the church although David had been once before with Eleanor. They all made their way to the church hall where long tables, groaning with delicacies, lined one wall and opposite was another long table for the baptism party. Other small tables with chairs were scattered around the middle of the hall.

"Eleanor." She turned and gazed up at the man she had never stopped loving. "It's so nice to see you again. I'd forgotten this was your church when Will asked me to be godfather. I hope you don't mind."

Something was wrong with her vocal chords. He was behaving so normally. Perhaps she'd been mistaken in his feelings towards her. She eventually managed to mutter something but he didn't hear.

"What did you say?" He bent his head towards her and she had difficulty in breathing.

"It's nice to see you again, too," she whispered. "I thought I'd never see you again. Why have you come back?"

"There was trouble in the area and we were all recalled."

"Oh." Was she disappointed he hadn't said he'd come home to see her?

"When are you getting married? Have you fixed the date?"

"What?" She was bewildered.

"Aren't you engaged to Chris?" He glanced across to where Chris was laughing at something Carol had said. She followed his gaze, with her thoughts doing a juggling act.

"I – I broke it off. I didn't love him and it wouldn't have been fair."

"I see." She could feel his eyes pleading for her attention but she was embarrassed and wouldn't look at him. She could feel the inevitable red seeping up her neck into her cheeks.

"Hullo, Uncle David." Lorna bounced up to them. "I'm so glad you could come."

"So am I? What have you done with your offspring?"

"He's sleeping peacefully in the church office. One of the Pathfinders has promised to keep an eye on him. Help yourself to food and then come and sit down. I've put place names on the table so no changing them." She wagged her finger at them.

"I'd no idea you were so organised, Lorna," said Eleanor, surprised.

"Bossy, too," grinned David.

"That's what Will said. I must go and talk to Steve. Enjoy yourselves." She rushed off.

"She's full of life," said David as they moved to the food table. The next few moments were absorbed by selecting a plateful of goodies but Eleanor's mind was not on food and when she reached her place, she realised she'd helped herself to a whole quiche and nothing else. Lorna had placed David beside her and he laughed at her confusion.

"Have some of mine," he offered. "Or shall I change it for you?"

"No it's fine. I'm not hungry."

"Why not?" he asked softly and her stomach did another somersault as she glanced swiftly up at him.

She must put the record straight. "I'm so sorry," she whispered. "I thought you did abortions. I know now you don't."

He looked puzzled. "I told you I didn't."

Oh help! Will hadn't confessed. Now what was she to do? He was still looking at her.

"I know that now. I *did* believe you but then something happened and I got confused."

His brow cleared. "Are you unconfused now?" he queried softly.

"Oh yes."

"Good."

The rest of the party had now taken their seats. Lorna was in the centre with Jenny and Peter on her right and Will on her left. Melanie and Kate were next to David and Carol and Chris were at the other end of the table.

Lorna leant across Will and Eleanor to speak to David. "Will's got a confession to make, haven't you, Will?" She jabbed him with her elbow and he cast an agonised glance at Eleanor.

"It's all right," she said quickly. "You don't need to say it."

"Yes I do." Will took a deep breath and leaned across to his uncle.

"I'm really sorry, Uncle David. I told Lorna you'd do an abortion for her and that you'd said it would be the best thing."

"But I never said anything of the sort." He appeared justifiably angry.

"I know but I thought she'd listen to what *you* said. And it seemed the best thing at the time. Neither of us wanted the baby, did we, Lorna?" She didn't answer and he blundered on. "I – I didn't know you knew Lorna's sister, Uncle David. I'm so sorry. But I'm glad Lorna didn't listen to me."

"So am I." David's anger seemed to have died Eleanor was glad to see. She felt sorry for the boy but at least he'd confessed – in public too.

She looked at David and felt his hand on hers under the table. He was gazing deep into her eyes until she thought she would melt from the heat of his touch. The pause lengthened to a silent pool of realisation amid the babble of conversation around them.

He broke the silence at last. "I missed you – so much. I was so relieved when I had to come back. I hoped to see you but I didn't think you'd want to see me. But *this* was certainly a surprise. I think we have a couple of very devious relatives, don't you?"

She laughed. "Yes, but I'm glad we do." A bubble of happiness burst inside her as she squeezed his hand. She was sure they would have a lifetime together to sort out any misunderstandings.